PROLOGUE

BADAKHSHAN PROVINCE, AFGHANISTAN
12 YEARS AGO.

It was just before dawn when Second Lieutenant Andrew Sterling and Corporal Frank Malone crept up the final incline towards the top of the ridge. Since their helicopter insertion a couple of hours earlier near the village of Tergaran close to the border with Tajikistan, the two special forces operators had been making their way laboriously up through the dry and arid ravine towards the ridge above them. If their intel was correct, they should soon be able to look down into the valley on the other side where the Taliban opium compound was supposed to be located.

The mountain air was cold and crisp, and small puffs of condensation formed in front of their mouths whenever they exhaled. The peaks in this region of northern Afghanistan are 2,500 metres above sea level, so as they proceeded up through the ravine, they could feel how much thinner the air was up here. Despite both of them being extremely fit, they nevertheless had to make short stops on a regular basis to catch their breaths.

They were carrying suppressed variants of the MP5 submachine gun in order to suppress firing noise and also eliminate muzzle flashes, and they were wearing the mottled-looking pale yellow and grey desert camouflage of the UK's special forces in Afghanistan. On the shoulders of their jackets were the easily-recognisable badges with the SAS logo. Two light blue flames on either side of a white sword pointing down. Often mistaken for a dagger, the sword was originally conceived as being Excalibur, the legendary sword of King Arthur. On a scroll underneath the logo was the famous motto: *'Who Dares Wins'*.

The two highly trained special forces soldiers felt right at home here in the mountains and the high deserts of Afghanistan, and so they should. The SAS, or Special Air Service, had its origins in the deserts of North Africa during the beginning of the Second World War. This covert unit was originally envisaged as a deep-penetration commando force specialising in parachute insertion behind enemy lines and was initially tasked with intelligence gathering and sabotage of enemy military assets, particularly aircraft. Its first combat mission during November of 1941 was to attack two German airfields about 100 kilometres west of Tobruk in Libya, and it ended up as an unmitigated disaster. Adverse weather conditions and bad intelligence resulted in the death or capture of 22 men, which was about one-third of the entire force. Having learned from this bitter experience, the Regiment's second mission turned out to be a major success.

Delivered to their objectives by jeeps operated by the Long Range Desert Group, which was a reconnaissance and raiding unit of the British Army, the SAS attacked three German airfields and managed to destroy 60 aircraft while suffering minimal losses.

Having now proven itself to be an effective covert fighting force, the SAS was then deployed numerous times throughout the rest of the war in Tunisia, Egypt, Greece, Sicily and mainland Italy. Eventually, the SAS also took part in the allied invasion of France and Germany, conducting covert raids behind enemy lines deep inside Germany.

In the decades following the Second World War, the Regiment played a role in virtually every military operation the UK was engaged in, from Malaya to Borneo and Oman, through to 'the Troubles' in Northern Ireland.

Following the 1972 massacre at the Munich Olympics, the British government ordered the formation of a dedicated counter-terrorist unit to be formed inside the SAS, with the aim of being able to respond rapidly and effectively to any terrorist threat in the UK or abroad. The most notable and high-profile such incident was the 1980 Iranian Embassy siege, where six armed Iranian revolutionaries captured the Iranian embassy in South Kensington in London, holding 26 people hostage. After six days, the kidnappers killed one of the hostages, after which it was decided that the SAS should be sent in. Designated *Operation Nimrod*, the effort involved two teams of SAS soldiers entering from the roof and the rear of the building. The whole raid lasted only 11 minutes and resulted in the death of five of the six kidnappers. One hostage was also killed.

There had also been SAS deployments to Korea, The Gambia, Colombia and several other countries, and the regiment saw extensive action during the Falklands War in 1982. From 1990 onwards, the SAS took part in numerous deep reconnaissance and sabotage missions in Iraq to attempt to deny Saddam Hussain the ability to launch SCUD missiles at Israel and allied forces in neighbouring countries. At the time, this was feared to have the potential to bring Israel into the war, possibly triggering a wider regional conflict and even World War Three. From October 2001, and for the next two decades, the SAS would be heavily involved in counter-terrorism and counter-insurgency operations in Afghanistan, assisting in the efforts to defeat the al-Qaeda terrorist network and suppress the Taliban across that enormous country.

Often portrayed as ragtag bands of simpletons with ancient Russian-made equipment, al-Qaeda and even more so the Taliban were in fact sophisticated organisations consisting of many thousands of men with considerable resources, and these organisations were not cheap to run. They needed to be funded, and relying on money from wealthy Middle Eastern donors with radical tendencies was not nearly enough to sustain them. They needed their own revenue. This was where the drugs trade came in, and that was why Sterling and Malone were now making their way up the mountain.

The faces of the two SAS men were painted with deliberately messy streaks of light brown and dark grey. Combined with their camouflage clothing, it allowed them to blend in with their surroundings as long as they moved slowly or lay still. The public image of the SAS and other special forces groups like the SBS, Delta Force or the U.S. Navy SEALs, was often one of huge muscle-bound Rambo-type soldiers crashing through an enemy camp with all guns blazing, but the reality was that special forces operators often spent the vast majority of their time concealed and observing the enemy from a distance, sometimes for days on end. Most often vastly outnumbered, remaining hidden was almost always the best way to achieve their mission, and today was no different.

On the face of it, Sterling and Malone couldn't have been more different. One of them was from a well-heeled middle-class family in the south of England, the other was from a broken family in a deprived part of the North. While one of them had spent afternoons with private tutors during his childhood, the other had spent his time with the types of children that most parents would give anything for their offspring *not* to associate with. One of them had kept on the straight and narrow all his life, developing friendships among like-minded people from a similar background. The other had already had more than one brush with the law and had ended up with friends in low places, before eventually joining the army and leaving that life behind. But out here in the barren mountains of Afghanistan, none of that was important. The only thing that mattered was their skill and training, and the fact that they knew each other as well as any two brothers.

This was not the first time the two of them had been sent out on a recon mission together. Since they had first been paired up during their training at SAS Hereford, Sterling and Malone had exhibited an uncanny ability to understand each other and work effectively as a unit, both of them seemingly always knowing exactly what the other was thinking. This gave them the ability to move unseen and to outwit the enemy on covert missions even when the two of them were unable to communicate. They both instinctively knew what the other person was about to do.

By now, the two SAS men had acquired a reputation among UK forces in Afghanistan for reliably being able to get in, do the job and then get out, often without the Taliban being any the wiser. Sometimes all they had to do was observe, but sometimes they were tasked with taking out a Taliban commander or destroying a weapons cache.

Before their deployment, they had both undergone intensive training in Pashto, originally an eastern Iranian language. It is the native language of a large proportion of the Afghan population, mainly the Pashtuns, and is spoken primarily in the southeastern part of Afghanistan. They had also received lessons in the Dari language, which is essentially Persian, and equally important but spoken mainly in other regions of the country. Being able to communicate with the local Afghans was often a prerequisite for being able to operate here. Even though the Taliban had taken power in the country and tightened their grip in the run-up to September 11th 2001, most people in Afghanistan had in fact not been affiliated with the

Taliban at all during those decades. They were mostly farmers living simple lives in the mountainous country, and just like most people in the world, they just wanted to till the earth, feed their families and get on with their lives.

Being able to talk to the locals was particularly essential for special forces soldiers since they would often be able to provide information on Taliban movements and recent events in a particular area. Out of the two of them, Malone was the gifted one when it came to languages, despite his less privileged background and education. He just seemed to have a natural gift for it, on top of being an extremely proficient soldier. Sterling's forte was mainly weapons handling and the ability to keep a cool head and make strong tactical decisions under extreme pressure. Both were expert operators, but Sterling had always been at the top of his class when it came to kicking in doors and shooting things.

On this particular mission, the two of them had been flown out from the American-led Forward Operating Base Kunduz and inserted by helicopter onto the valley floor near Tergaran village. Having watched the chopper disappear over the ridges towards the south, they had then quickly begun making their way north. Their task was to approach and reconnoitre a small valley on the other side of the mountain range where satellite imagery had uncovered a large compound with newly erected buildings and a handful of large vehicles, many of them heavy transport trucks.

Following the success of Operation Diesel, during which UK and US forces had raided and shut down a major drug manufacturing and distribution plant in Helmand earlier that year, the joint forces command at Bagram Airbase north of Kabul had decided to attempt similar strikes against suspected drugs factories in other parts of the country. These factories, often hidden away in remote valleys, were the main source of income for the Taliban and they thus represented a clear threat to security in the country as well as the ability of the Afghan government to retain control. However, the first step of any such operation was always to try to get eyes on the area and observe what was actually happening, and this required a small team of special forces soldiers to get close.

The two men arrived at the top of the ridge and used several large boulders and rocks to move unseen to a position that afforded them a full view of the valley below. The valley itself was small, perhaps a kilometre across, and it was shaped vaguely like a bowl with several single-storey buildings at its centre. Radiating out from the compound were several small dirt roads that extended out through what looked like fields. At the far end of the valley was a road, which seemed to snake its way over the lip of the bowl and down into a larger valley beyond where a river flowed several kilometres away.

Andrew used his binoculars to examine the sprawling compound below them. There was a large factory structure, something that looked like a couple of barracks, and what might have been some sort of administration building. The sun was now just peeking over the mountains to the east and lighting up the rooftops of the buildings down in the valley.

'Bingo,' said Andrew in a hushed voice, lowering his binoculars. 'That's an opium factory all right. Poppy fields, processing facilities, logistics, accommodation for workers. It is all there.'

'And a big one too, mucker,' replied Malone, shuffling slowly into a comfortable position on the ground, placing his rifle in front of himself and looking through the scope. 'Perfect little spot they found here. Decent size. Seems completely hidden from view. If you were driving along that road by the river down in the valley, you would never know it was here.'

'Exactly,' said Andrew. 'I wonder how long the Taliban have been running this place?'

'Who knows,' said Malone rhetorically and shrugged, his northern accent thick as always. 'Could be years. The real question is. How much money did this place make for them?'

'Millions,' replied Andrew. 'In fact, hundreds of millions. Enough to buy plenty of weapons to continue the insurgency more or less indefinitely.'

'Bloody hell,' said Malone slowly, scanning the compound with his scope.

'Well, we're going to shut this place down,' said Andrew, studying the various buildings inside the compound. 'But first, we need to get closer. We'll keep observing from here for a bit longer, but then we should get inside and verify what is actually happening in there. Camp Bastion is not going to risk a handful of choppers and a hundred coalition soldiers without absolute proof that this place is what we think it is.'

Malone shook his head slowly, still gazing down at the compound. 'I can't believe how much money these goat-herders are able to make from a couple of fields of poppy flowers. And then they live in rickety shacks with no toilets and no running water. It seems mad.'

'I know,' replied Andrew. 'The opium itself isn't worth much here, but once it has been processed, refined and smuggled into Europe, its street value becomes astronomical. Most people down there never see much of the profits. It's the middlemen who are making millions, and they probably don't even live in this country.'

'When I was a young lad growing up in Grimsby,' said Malone pensively. 'A million pounds seemed like all the money in the world. Now I realise that it is just pocket change for some people.'

'There is a lot of money in the drugs trade, that's true,' said Andrew, 'but consider the damage it does.'

'Yeah, I've seen plenty of junkies,' replied Malone. 'Growing up, we had our share of people who had fallen into that trap. And once you're in it, it's hard to get out. I might even have ended up like that myself if it wasn't for the army. Spent a bit too much time with the wrong crowd for a while as a teenager, if you know what I mean. Some of those lads had suspicious amounts of cash, and it was pretty obvious where it all came from.'

'Drugs are everywhere these days,' said Andrew. 'Not just in hard-up places like where you grew up. A lot of supposedly respectable people in London are snorting mile-long lines of coke every year. So, if we can help shut down places like this, it will be good for Afghanistan and good for the UK.'

'I know,' replied Malone. 'We're also wrecking the local economy, but I suppose that is a small price to pay.'

'There are other things they can grow here,' said Andrew. 'They won't be nearly as profitable as poppy, but at least it won't do any harm to anyone else.'

Malone shifted his rifle slightly to the left and looked through it for a few seconds.

'Couple of guys coming out,' he said calmly. 'They are walking towards the white truck.'

Andrew shifted his binoculars to the location Malone was looking at. Two bearded men in typical dark brown Afghan garb were walking lazily toward a pickup truck that was parked next to the factory building. They were smoking and talking, and both had an AK-47 slung casually over their shoulder.

The two SAS soldiers watched as the men got into the truck and began driving slowly out of the compound and along the dirt road towards the point where it wound its way down into the larger valley several kilometres away.

'Two less Taliban to worry about,' said Andrew. 'I don't think there are that many people here right now. We're still several weeks out from peak harvesting season, so they are probably just running a skeleton crew. We should get moving.'

'All right,' said Malone and backed up slowly until he was out of view of the compound.

The two men knelt behind a couple of large sand-coloured boulders and checked their weapons and magazines to make sure that everything was ready. Malone reached inside his shirt and pulled out a large silver coin on a leather strap. It was a £5 Millennium

Crown struck by the Royal Mint in London in 1999 to commemorate the turn of the millennium. A gift from his now-deceased father. The coin, which was almost four centimetres in diameter and weighed about five times as much as a standard £1 coin, was slightly deformed and had an irregular-shaped hole near its edge where the strap went through. The hole had been made exactly where a 9mm bullet had once impacted during a hostage rescue mission in Mali. During that raid, Malone had been carrying the commemorative coin along with the usual number of gold sovereigns that SAS operatives always brought along on missions. The gold coins, which were usually taped to the inside of their body armour, were meant to allow the operatives to bribe their way out of a sticky situation, and Malone always had the £5 Millennium Crown mixed in with the sovereigns for good luck. Sweeping into a room with two other SAS operatives, one of the hostage takers had opened fire, and a bullet had gone through a weak point in his body armour and struck the coin, lodging itself into it. The impact had knocked the wind out of Malone and given him a large circular purple bruise on his chest. But through sheer luck, the coin had stopped the bullet and he had lived to tell the tale. The hostage taker and his two comrades had not been so lucky.

Andrew looked over at him at gave a sly smile.

'Are you going to keep carrying that thing around for the rest of your life?' he asked.

'Affirmative,' said Malone matter-of-factly. 'This coin has saved my life once already. I am not about to go jinx it by leaving it at home, am I?'

Holding the coin between his fingertips, Malone kissed the coin, took it in his big hand and squeezed it tight. Then he slotted it back inside his shirt.

'Whatever works, mate' shrugged Andrew and smiled. 'Let's get out of here.'

The two soldiers began making their way slowly down into the valley towards the compound, which was around three hundred metres away. As they descended carefully across the rocky ground, they made sure to use boulders and vegetation to stay hidden from view of anyone inside the suspected drug compound. The small valley was completely quiet, except for a cockerel that seemed intent on making everyone there aware of his presence. As far as anyone inside the compound was concerned, this was a morning just like any other.

The initial stages of heroin production in the dry climate of the mountains of Afghanistan are relatively simple. The poppy seeds are planted in the soil, and after about three months they bloom into colourful poppy flowers. As the petals fall away, they expose a large egg-shaped seed pod which contains a milky sap. This sap contains opium in its crudest form. Poppy farmers then use a small curved knife to cut vertical slits around the sides of the pods, through which the sap then seeps out and turns into a brown gum. This is then scraped off and packed into small bricks of opium which can be sold off or processed further. In the case of further processing, the opium is mixed with lime and boiling water, after which foamy morphine forms on top of the solution. This can be ladled off into separate containers, mixed with ammonia, and then boiled and left to dry to create a thick morphine paste which can be smoked. However, continuing the processing, the morphine paste is mixed with acetic anhydride, which is an acidic chemical reagent, and then heated to about 85 degrees Celsius for several hours. Then a series of filtering and purifying steps are carried out using chloroform, water, charcoal and alcohol, finally yielding purified heroin.

For each step along the way, the output becomes orders of magnitude more valuable. The more steps that can be carried out in close proximity to the poppy fields, the more profitable the entire enterprise. The compound that Sterling and Malone were approaching appeared large enough to be able to carry out a completely integrated process from opium paste to refined heroin, which would make it an extremely valuable asset to the Taliban. This also meant that it was worth protecting, but ideally without drawing too much attention to itself.

The two SAS soldiers arrived on the edge of the compound next to a derelict outhouse that seemed to have been a part of the original farmstead before the Taliban had converted the entire site into a heroin production facility. Crouching down next to a stone wall and peeking over its edge towards the compound, they both checked their weapons and equipment one last time.

'Let's move up next to that building,' said Andrew, 'and then we'll try to gain access to the main factory building through that door at the end. Body cams on.'

'Roger,' nodded Malone and reached up to flick a switch on the small camera that was mounted on his tactical vest. 'Let's go.'

Andrew switched on his own camera, and then the two of them moved swiftly but quietly in a crouched position through the bushes towards the small wooden door at one end of the main building. Once they had reached it, they stopped to listen for movement or voices inside, but they could hear nothing. The only audible sound was that of some sort of machine, possibly an air conditioning unit, whirring somewhere nearby. The main building was about fifty metres long and fifteen metres wide. Large enough for a decent-sized drug factory complete with chemical processing and storage.

Andrew placed his hand on the door handle and pressed down on it. He then pushed gently against the door and opened it a sliver. Peering inside, he could see a large factory floor with rows of polished metal vats. This was where the morphine that had been extracted from the opium in the poppy plants, was converted into heroin through a series of chemical processes. There were aluminium ventilation ducts running above the entire floor, and a couple of workers with face masks were walking calmly among the vats, inspecting the progress of the chemical processes.

The door that Andrew had just opened led immediately into what appeared to be a messy storage area. There were several tall shelving units containing lots of different tools, as well as a section with a number of large metal barrels that looked like they might contain the chemicals used in heroin production. The air was humid and carried an odd and slightly pungent and acidic smell, and there was a low hum coming from various pumps and ventilation systems mounted throughout the building. Beyond the storage area, the rest of the factory building looked significantly more organised, but the mess near the door should allow Sterling and Malone to enter and observe without being spotted.

They quickly slipped inside, closed the door behind them, and then made their way silently to the barrels while making sure to stay out of sight. Andrew unclipped the camera from his tactical vest and held it out past the barrel he was hiding behind. Panning it slowly from left to right, he allowed the camera to record the entire layout of the drug factory's interior.

'I am itching to blow this whole fucking place sky-high,' whispered Malone with a mischievous grin.

'We'll let the top brass decide on that,' replied Andrew quietly.

Just then a set of wide double doors opened at the far end of the building, flooding the gloomy interior with bright morning sunlight from the low morning sun in the east. A small group of men walked inside. Leading the group was a tall bearded man who was flanked by several burly-looking Talibs carrying Kalashnikov assault rifles. Sterling and Malone watched as the men entered and began inspecting some of the vats and a wooden pallet full of small plastic-wrapped packages stacked neatly in a large cube shape. The group were silhouetted by the bright light beyond them, so neither the two SAS soldiers nor their cameras were able to pick out enough detail for a possible ID later on.

'That's got to be the chief of this operation,' whispered Malone. 'He looks important.'

'Yeah,' replied Andrew. 'Probably the local Taliban commander.'

The tall bearded man proceeded to inspect the pallet while the workers stood by, looking nervous. A few times the commander asked one of the workers a question, and seemingly satisfied with the answer he received, he then nodded and stroked his beard. Then he turned around and headed for the door followed by his entourage of heavily armed fighters.

'We need to find out where this guy goes,' whispered Sterling. 'If we are going to shut this place down, we will need to remove him from circulation as well.'

'All right, mucker,' said Malone. 'Let's exit and see if we can get some pictures of him and his vehicle.'

The two of them slipped back out of the small door to the rear of the factory and began making their way towards the corner of the building. When they reached it, Sterling knelt down and peeked around it to see if he could spot anyone. There was no one there, so he signalled for Malone to follow him. Just as they were moving around the corner, there was a sudden shout from nearby. Their heads whipped around to where the sound had come from, and both of them instinctively brought up their suppressed MP5s.

Standing about twenty metres away was a young man staring back at them through the bushes. He was barely out of his teens with a thin shaggy beard, a Taliban headdress and a Kalashnikov slung over his right shoulder. He looked at them wide-eyed and wavering. Then he suddenly reached for his automatic rifle and began bringing it up to aim at the two intruders. He never got even close to being able to fire. Both Sterling and Malone released a three-round burst, their weapons producing only muffled clicking sounds, and all six bullets slammed into the young man's chest. Still gripping the assault rifle, he staggered backwards a single step and then fell on his back onto the rocky ground. As he hit the dirt, his finger must have tightened around the trigger, because the rifle suddenly fired off a rapid salvo, producing the characteristic dry staccato cough of the AK-47. The loud noise from the weapon reverberated around the valley, and Sterling and Malone instantly knew that it was time to leave. For all they knew, there might be dozens of Taliban fighters inside the two barracks buildings near the far edge of the compound, but they did not have time to hang around and find out.

As it turned out, they did not have to wait long. After less than twenty seconds, the doors to the barracks buildings burst open and about ten fighters came running outside, holding Kalashnikovs and looking like they were spoiling for a fight. As soon as they spotted the two SAS soldiers, they opened fire. Sterling and Malone bolted for a smaller warehouse building just a few metres away and barged through the flimsy wooden door as the bullets whizzed past them and smacked into the surrounding walls sending fragments of wood flying everywhere. They crashed onto the dusty floor of the small virtually empty warehouse, but then quickly got back onto their feet.

'Are you hit?' shouted Sterling.

'Negative,' replied Malone as he got to his feet. 'You?'

'No,' panted Sterling. 'How the fuck did they manage to miss all of those shots?'

Amid the sound of multiple voices shouting outside, they both frantically began to look around the warehouse for another exit. There seemed to be no other doors, and the warehouse was empty except for a handful of steel barrels at the far end.

'Shit. I don't see a way out,' panted Malone.

'I think we're about to have company,' said Sterling. 'Take cover behind those barrels. That'll buy us some time.'

They both began moving towards the barrels.

'And then what?' asked Malone. 'We're outnumbered. We need to get out of here.'

'I know!' replied Sterling tensely as he took cover behind one of the barrels. 'But before we do that, we need to not die. Get ready.'

They had barely taken cover behind the barrels before two Taliban fighters burst through the doorway. They immediately opened fire and bullets began peppering the steel barrels creating a cacophony of loud metallic clangs. Without a word, Sterling and Malone remained in cover until the firing abated, and then, moving in perfect unison, they swung their MP5s up and over the barrels and returned fire, hitting the first fighter who dropped to the floor dead, and sending the other scrambling for cover behind a large wooden support beam. At that moment, two more fighters entered. The two SAS soldiers ducked back down behind the barrels and began changing magazines.

'Rinse and repeat,' shouted Malone, looking over at Andrew with a grin.

'Ready. Go!' shouted Sterling, and then the two of them re-emerged from cover and opened up on the two new arrivals. This time both fighters dropped dead.

Apparently, this made the remaining fighters still outside the warehouse think twice about barging in to join their dead comrades. Instead, they shouted something in Pashto to the fighter who was still inside taking cover behind the wooden beam. The fighter shouted back at them, and after a brief exchange, everything fell quiet.

'What the hell are they up to?' asked Malone, looking around the warehouse.

'I don't know,' replied Sterling, 'but I am not sure we can afford to wait around and find out. Get ready to leave.'

No sooner had he finished his sentence than a dull metallic clonk could be heard on the other side of the barrels as if something had been thrown inside the warehouse and had landed close by. Sterling and Malone barely had time to look at each other, an immediately unspoken realisation forming between them about what was about to happen, before the grenade exploded with a deafening crack inside the confined space of the warehouse. The explosion was powerful enough to produce a big cloud of dust, and it knocked over a couple of the barrels.

'Bloody hell!' yelled Sterling as they scrambled for cover, dust and dirt raining down on them. 'We need to leave now! Ready grenade.'

'Roger,' shouted Malone, and then the two men got to their knees and extracted a grenade each from their tactical vests.

'Ready?' asked Sterling.

'Ready,' replied Malone.

'Go!' said Sterling, and then they both pulled the pin and hurled their grenades across the warehouse and out through the doorway to the exterior.

Instantly, there was panicked shouting coming from outside, and a couple of seconds later the grenades detonated in quick succession with two muffled crumps. Before the reverberations of the explosions had died down, Sterling and Malone were back on their feet and sprinting towards the door. Their only chance was to try to exploit the panic and confusion created by their grenades, and to get as far away as they could as quickly as possible.

As they ran, they trained their MP5s at the Taliban fighter still hiding behind the wooden beam, and once he came into view, they both fired several rounds to make sure he wouldn't shoot them in the back as they left the warehouse. They burst out through the doorway and immediately opened fire on the few Taliban fighters they could still see, and then they bolted for the corner of the factory building. Several shots rang out and a couple of bullets smacked into the factory building next to them, but it seemed that most of the remaining fighters had been so stunned by the grenades and the sudden appearance of the two SAS soldiers that they had been more concerned with taking cover than returning fire.

Sterling and Malone sprinted around the corner of the building and continued back towards the edge of the compound where they had entered less than half an hour earlier. They were now partially obscured by vegetation as they ran through the poppy fields.

Behind them, they could hear renewed shouting and a couple of shots ringing out, but none of them seemed to be aimed directly at them.

After a couple of minutes, they reached the edge of the small bowl-shaped valley and began scrambling back up the rocky incline towards the boulders from where they had observed the compound during daybreak. It seemed they had gotten away.

'Fuck me!' panted Malone. 'That was close.'

'Too close,' replied Sterling.

'We got out, didn't we?' grinned Malone. 'Let's call for extraction. Get back to the base for tea and medals.'

He seemed to be genuinely enjoying himself, despite having just been under intense enemy fire.

'We're not out yet,' said Andrew and reached for his radio. 'I am going to call in the chopper.'

'RPG!' shouted Malone suddenly, and Sterling just had time to see the smoky trail of the rocket-propelled grenade out of the corner of his eye as it approached them from the compound before Malone crashed into him in an attempt to get them both out of harm's way.

The RPG slammed into the rocks less than five metres away and the explosion flung them both violently through the air to crash onto the rocky ground. The last thing Sterling registered was a bright flash and the first brief moment of the deafening explosion. Then everything went dark.

When he came to, his eyes felt puffy and squeezed shut, and his ears were ringing. There was an unpleasant smell of scorched flesh in his nostrils, and he could taste the dust in the air as he breathed. Feeling disorientated and strangely disconnected from reality, he then sensed muffled voices and movement nearby. His sensory system was overloaded, and it was as if he was inside a thick fog where he could neither see, hear or feel much of anything. He suddenly felt several sets of strong hands grabbing him and hauling him to his knees. Agitated voices were shouting in Pashto, and someone slapped his face several times. He tried to open his eyes, but they seemed caked in something wet and sticky. Was it his own blood? Had he been blinded?

'Malone?' he managed to shout out, but he was immediately rewarded with the butt of a Kalashnikov rammed into his chest, making him cough and struggle for breath.

There was no reply. Was Malone dead?

'Malone!' he repeated, more urgently this time. 'Are you there, mate?'

An instant later the butt of the rifle connected with the back of his head, and then he passed out again.

⋆ ⋆ ⋆

The next time he came to, Sterling was sitting tied to a chair with a grimy linen hood over his head. He could feel the dry dirt and blood caked to his face, and the inside of the humid hood stank of sweat and dirt and something else. Had he vomited? His arms had been bent behind his back, ropes were cutting into his wrists, and his feet were bound firmly together and tied to the legs of a creaky wooden chair. His whole body ached and he immediately tried to wriggle slightly to determine if any part of his body had been seriously injured. It did not seem that way.

Through the tiny holes in the hood, he could tell that he was inside a small building. There was bright sunlight spilling in through a small window somewhere on his left, and he sensed at least one other person moving around next to him. From somewhere outside the building, he could hear voices and then the sound of a car arriving, pulling up and stopping. Then he heard the sound of several people getting out and walking across the gravel. They were speaking to each other in Pashto. After a few seconds, a door opened, allowing more sunlight into the room, but then it closed again and he immediately sensed the presence of several more people.

He could hear someone approaching him, soft footsteps coming nearer. Then he sensed the outline of a dark shape looming over him. The man barked a command at someone, and then another person moved up behind him and violently yanked his hood off. Sterling blinked a couple of times, squinted and looked up at the imposing figure standing in front of him. He was still disorientated. His vision was blurry and his face was smeared with blood and dirt, so he was struggling to see the tall man's face clearly. But he had a large black beard and looked like he might have been in his mid-fifties, although it was notoriously difficult to tell with native Afghans. From the way he stood there, barely moving and looking down at his prisoner, Sterling sensed a coldness and natural authority which made him think that this was almost certainly the local Taliban commander. The same man they had seen earlier inside the opium factory. His face was expressionless as he looked at Sterling.

'American?' he said in a gruff voice with a heavy accent.

Sterling shook his head.

'British,' he whispered dryly, his voice sounding hoarse, and his split lower lip stinging as he spoke.

'Hm,' responded the commander. 'Him British?' he continued and stepped aside.

Behind the commander was Malone, strapped to another chair opposite Sterling's, and seemingly unconscious. He was also tied up, and slumped forward looking dirty and badly roughed up. However, Sterling was unable to tell whether that was the result of the RPG or if he had been beaten. His breathing was shallow, his grimy hair was hanging down in front of his face, and his talisman, the £5 Millennium Crown, had popped out of his shirt and was now dangling languidly back and forth in front of his chest as he breathed.

Sterling took a closer look at him and winced. Malone's lower left leg was bent at an unnatural and disturbing angle. Open fracture. His trouser leg was ripped and burnt. His left boot was soaked in blood and there was a dark red pool on the floor under his feet.

'Frank!' said Sterling hoarsely. 'Mate, are you with me?'

There was no reaction from Malone, but the commander took a quick step towards Sterling and slapped him hard across the face, making his left ear ring once again. Sterling slowly brought his head up to look straight at the commander, anger flashing in his eyes.

'He's got an open fracture,' he said. 'He needs a doctor right now or he could die.'

The commander scoffed and smiled.

'Doctor expensive,' he said dispassionately. 'Bullet cheap.'

Then he pulled out a large pistol, pointed it at Malone and pulled the trigger. The dry crack from the gun was deafening inside the small space, and the large calibre bullet slammed into Malone's upper body causing his torso to twist away to one side and his chair to topple over.

'No!' shouted Sterling, his whole body tensing and straining against the ropes.

Malone's body thudded heavily onto the dusty floor where he lay completely still, a pool of blood slowly spreading out from his chest.

'You fucking bastard!' spat Sterling, writhing furiously in his chair, eyes burning with hatred as he stared down the Taliban commander. 'I'll fucking kill you for this!'

The commander looked impassively at Sterling with a strangely detached look on his face.

'Business,' he said evenly and shrugged. 'You, we sell. Good money.'

Then he barked another order at the man standing behind Sterling, and an instant later the hood was pulled back down over his face. He felt the ropes around his legs being loosened and then he was yanked to his feet. Only then did he fully appreciate how roughed up his whole body was after the RPG explosion. Every joint and muscle ached, and he felt a sharp stinging inside his right knee as he was made to walk outside and then hobble along towards a vehicle.

He was bundled into the back, and two large fighters sat down in the seats on either side of him. Then a driver got in and started the engine.

A couple of minutes later the car was making its way along what he assumed was the dirt road leading towards the north and out of the valley. His suspicion was soon proven correct as he sensed the vehicle beginning to make its way down an incline and perform several tight turns as the driver navigated the series of hairpin bends down towards the river on the valley floor. Once down, the car turned onto what felt and sounded like a slightly bumpy but paved road, and then it sped up. Sterling sat passively between the two Taliban fighters, the tight restraints around his wrists cutting into his skin. He realised that any attempt to struggle or escape now would not end well for him. But at least he was alive, and it seemed as if that might continue if the Taliban commander had been telling the truth about selling him off.

The heat was stifling inside the car, sweat was pouring off him, and even though he sensed that at least one window was open, the car stank of body odours, most of them probably his. Neither the two fighters nor the driver spoke a single word for the duration of the journey, and the only sounds he could hear were the car's engine and the noise from its tyres as they traversed various surfaces like asphalt and gravel. The car barely changed direction, and it seemed to remain on the same road most of the time. Once in a while, they would pass what sounded like other cars or trucks, and it required a large effort to resist the urge to attempt to escape the car and start shouting, even though he knew it would be futile. His entire being was in fight-or-flight mode, but there was nothing he could do but sit and wait.

Around half an hour later, much of it spent driving along what Sterling guessed was a main road, the truck slowed down. Then it pulled off the road. The driver had a brief exchange with someone, and then Sterling heard the sound of metal gates being opened. The car moved forward a bit further, after which it stopped and the driver turned off the engine. The metal gates creaked and then clanged shut behind them.

Immediately, the vehicle's doors were opened and Sterling was pulled out and dragged along, half walking and half stumbling as he went. He was manhandled inside a building and down a set of stairs to what smelled like a damp basement. Suddenly his hood was yanked off and he was shoved violently into a small dimly lit room with only a tiny window high up on the wall. Due to the force of the push, he tripped over his own feet and crashed to the floor, earthy and damp-smelling dust entering his nostril. The heavy metal door to the room was slammed shut, and he heard the rustling of keys and the sound of the door being locked. Then there was the sound of slow footsteps receding, and another door closing and being locked. Then there was silence, except for the sound of his own pounding heart, and the faint but persistent ringing in his ears.

Sterling slumped down onto the floor next to the wall. Within just a few hours, things had gone from routine and under control, to chaotic and tragic. Frank was dead. Was it his fault? Could he somehow have prevented this? Should he have left him on overwatch up on the ridge while he went inside the drug factory by himself? Had the whole thing been a mistake from the very beginning? And how was anything they could have achieved in that compound worth Frank's life?

Sterling grimaced and slammed his bound fists down onto the dusty ground.

'Damn it!' he hissed.

He reached down to his right ankle and was surprised to find that the small switchblade he always kept strapped to his leg was still there. The Taliban had taken his MP5 and his Glock 17, but they had done a poor job of searching him properly. He pulled out the knife and flicked it open. The blade was only about three inches long, but in the right hands, it was both a versatile tool and a lethal weapon. He cut through the restraints around his wrists and then he did the same with the rope tied to his ankles. The rope had left purple bruises around his wrists, and his fingertips were tingling from a lack of blood flow. He rubbed them in an effort to try to reinvigorate them.

He then spent the next several hours going over everything that had happened that day several times, but he eventually concluded that there was very little he could have done to prevent Malone's death. If the young man with the Kalashnikov had not happened to be at that exact spot just as he and Malone had been making their way around the corner of the factory building, then everything might have turned out differently. For some reason, neither he nor Malone had spotted the young lad, and when the Talib had reached for his rifle, there was only one thing they could have done. They simply had to take him out, and if his Kalashnikov had fallen onto the ground slightly differently it might not have fired and given them away. But it was done now, and there was nothing Sterling could do about it.

As darkness fell, he gingerly began taking off his clothes to inspect his body for injuries. Miraculously, he had sustained only cuts and bruises from the explosion and the shrapnel from the RPG. Malone's body had clearly absorbed most of the force of the blast as he threw himself into Sterling and barged him out of the way of the explosion. Malone had saved his life. It was as simple as that. But he had ultimately paid with his own. It was an impossible trade, but he had done it without hesitation, and Sterling knew that he would have done the same for him. In these sorts of situations, you don't have time to think. You simply act on instinct, the most basic of which is to keep yourself and your comrades safe.

Sterling shook his head despondently. The training grounds back at Hereford suddenly seemed a million miles away. He looked up and out of the small narrow window under the ceiling, and he suddenly realised that even though it was closed there was a very faint sound of cars coming through it. Straining his ears, he thought he was able to hear the occasional scooter horn and even a murmur of voices from time to time. It sounded like he was in a built-up area, possibly inside a small town. This meant that if he was able to get out of his makeshift cell, then he might be able to find a vehicle or some other means of transportation back to Camp Bastion under cover of darkness. He no longer had his radio, but if he could acquire some wheels, he might have a decent shot at being able to make his way south during the night and out of

Taliban-controlled area before dawn. First, however, he had to get out of this improvised prison cell.

There was no guarantee that he would actually end up being traded back to the British Army as the Taliban commander had hinted. If there was a higher bidder, such as the Iranians or the Russians, then he might well disappear into a prison cell for the rest of his life as they interrogated him about the tactics, capabilities and equipment of the SAS. And once they were done with him, he was likely to end up in a shallow grave.

As it turned out, he did not have to wait long for an opportunity to make his escape. A couple of hours after darkness had fallen, he heard the sound of the outer door being unlocked and opened, and then the sound of voices. Two, perhaps three men. Keys rustled against the metal door to his cell, and then the door opened noisily. The only light in the room was a small sliver cutting into the space from the outside through the narrow window under the ceiling. He guessed that it came from a street light, which meant that he was definitely in some sort of urban area.

Andrew had placed himself on the floor leaning against the wall opposite the door, arms resting on his knees with his head down, giving the impression of a man broken and physically exhausted. He did not move when the door opened, keen to convey that he now considered himself under their control. Like a man simply awaiting his fate.

Holding his switchblade inside the closed fist of his right hand, he sat immovable as he waited for an opportunity to strike. With his head down, he could only see the boots of the three men entering his cell, but he could hear the soft clacking of their rifles as they entered. No Talib ever went anywhere without his Kalashnikov, so Sterling would need to take all three of them out before any of them could use their weapon.

He swayed his head slowly from one side to another and produced a weak drawn-out groan as if he was in pain and semi-delirious. It seemed to be convincing, because the three fighters exchanged a couple of derisive-sounding words in Pashto, and one of them chuckled dryly.

While one of the fighters placed himself directly in front of Sterling about a metre away, the other two walked up to stand on either side of him. Here they reached down, grabbed him under his arms and began hauling him to his feet. Whilst producing a pained groan, he deliberately made himself limb and heavy, forcing the two men to grab him tightly and pull hard to attempt to bring him up.

When he was almost upright, Sterling suddenly brought his arms in tight to his body, fixing the two men at his sides, and then he used their grips to leap up and kick the man in front of him hard in the chest. His boot connected forcefully with the fighter's chest, and taken completely by surprise he fell back and smacked into the wall behind him, knocking the back of his head into the concrete and dropping to the floor along with his Kalashnikov, which then clattered away from him. Before he had even hit the ground, Sterling was already back on the floor and spinning to his left side with his switchblade gripped tightly in his right hand. He slammed the short blade into the side of the head of the fighter standing there. Before the man could even register what was happening, the blade broke through his skull and stabbed three inches into his brain. His legs immediately gave way and he dropped to the floor in a heap.

Scrambling frantically for his rifle, the man on Sterling's right attempted to bring his weapon to bear, but before he could aim and pull the trigger, Sterling had closed the distance and punched him three times square in the chest with the blade still gripped firmly in his right hand. Blood squirted out every time he extracted the knife, and then he brought the blade up and forcefully cut across and in front of himself, slicing open the fighter's throat and then instantly grabbing his Kalashnikov and yanking it towards himself.

As the fighter staggered backwards with a look of shock and panic in his eyes, whilst also desperately trying to stem the gushing flow of blood from his throat, Sterling flicked the fire selector to automatic and spun around to aim at the third fighter who by now was scrabbling around on the floor trying to reach his own rifle. Without hesitating, Sterling fired, sending a short but loud burst of bullets into the fighter's body. The impact of the projectiles knocked him onto his side against the wall where he lay still with a vacant look on his face. One of the bullets had gone straight through his head and had splattered parts of his brain across the wall behind him. Sterling could hear the sound of the second fighter sliding down the opposite wall amid disturbing gurgling and choking noises.

He turned slowly and looked at the man who was now sitting on the floor and leaning back against the wall, his lips moving but no words coming out. His hands, still clutching his throat, were drenched in blood that was streaming down his chest, and his eyes had a frightened and pleading look. For a fleeting moment, Sterling felt sorry for him, but then his demeanour hardened. He brought up the Kalashnikov and aimed it at the man's forehead.

'This is for Frank, you piece of shit,' he snarled.

Then he pulled the trigger.

ONE

DAMASCUS, SYRIA – PRESENT DAY.

The storage facility was located on a large plot the size of half a football field on the southwestern outskirts of the capital city, just on the other side of a busy highway that connected Damascus to the west of the country and the border with Lebanon. In the centre of the fenced-off and barbed-wired plot, which was surrounded by open fields on three sides, was a concrete bunker of which only the top was visible. The facility itself was underground and only accessible via an entrance that led to a series of secure doors, each one requiring a separate and unique passcode.

From the outside, it was impossible to guess what the facility's purpose was, but that something important was stored there was evident from the fact that it was guarded 24 hours a day by a team of roughly twenty Syrian Army soldiers. The soldiers were based in barracks at a nearby military base, and they worked in eight-hour shifts to man the single-gated access point, patrol the perimeter fence and stand guard at the end of the long and wide concrete ramp that led down to the entrance to the bunker itself.

The sun had just slipped beneath the mountainous horizon to the west, and the twilight was becoming dimmer with every passing minute. Inside the guardhouse by the main entrance sat two soldiers watching a Lebanese TV show. They were talking and smoking cigarettes, occasionally glancing outside to where two more soldiers were standing on either side of the entrance. Just inside the closed chain link gate was a row of retractable steel bollards protruding from the road, which made it impossible for any vehicle to enter the compound even if they were to smash through the tall gate.

As dusk slowly closed in and the sky gradually turned from light yellow to pale orange, the muffled traffic noise from the nearby Highway 1 gradually subsided. It was a pleasant and balmy evening, and there was no wind.

Suddenly the quiet was disturbed by the sound of vehicles revving up. It sounded like diesel engines, and it was coming from the end of the long access road that ran parallel to the highway at a distance of around one hundred metres and connected to a flyover roughly half a kilometre away. The two soldiers by the gate heard it first and turned to look. After a few seconds, one of them turned his head slightly and yelled something over his shoulder in the direction of the guardhouse. A moment later, the two men that had been watching TV emerged and joined their colleagues. Mystified words were exchanged as the men stood there and watched what was approaching.

It was a convoy of four vehicles. At the front was an army jeep, but it did not have the usual Syrian Army insignia on it. Behind it was a black Mercedes limousine with tinted windows. It carried number plates indicating that it belonged to the Syrian Army's senior officer corps and was used to ferry military VIPs in style to where they needed to go. Then followed a large bulky-looking truck, and then another jeep. The vehicles in the convoy all had their lights on, and they were accelerating along the access road towards the storage facility's gate, reaching speeds that somehow seemed unnecessary on this otherwise calm and quiet evening. There was an aggressiveness about the whole thing that immediately put the soldiers on edge, and the most senior of them took a step back and glanced briefly over his shoulder towards the guardhouse, as if uncertain about what to do.

After less than a minute, the convoy arrived at the gate where it stopped. A man jumped out from the passenger seat of the lead vehicle. He was a stocky character and looked to be in his late forties, and he was wearing a uniform that the soldiers immediately recognised as not being Syrian Army. It was a dark green Russian camouflage uniform with the top buttons on the chest undone, revealing his *telnyashka*, which is the characteristic light blue and white striped undershirt worn by the VDV, Russia's airborne forces. On his head was a blue beret with black trim, but the man was wearing no flags or insignia of any kind that would indicate which country he represented, or even his rank or unit affiliation.

He marched confidently up to the gate, quickly identifying the most senior of the Syrian Army soldiers by his uniform, and called out to him in Russian. The soldier, looking uncertain and glancing briefly at his colleagues, walked hesitantly towards the Russian but stopped about a metre away from the closed gate. The Russian stepped forward and extracted an envelope from inside his uniform jacket and handed it through the chain link fence. The Syrian Army soldier quickly opened it and studied it for a moment. He looked up at the Russian, then back down at the document, and then he shook his head and muttered something that sounded somewhat less than confident. The two men had a quick exchange in an awkward mix of Russian and Arabic, but then the soldier shook his head again. The Russian raised his voice and remonstrated, but the soldier stood his ground.

The Russian then marched off in a huff, walked past his jeep and stopped next to the passenger door on the right-hand side of the black Mercedes. The window rolled down slowly and a small puff of cigar smoke wafted out through the opening and up into the night air. There was a quick exchange of words, and then the door opened. A man wearing the light brown uniform of a senior Syrian Army officer stepped out. He was of average height and a slightly portly build, and he had black hair and a thick and neatly trimmed moustache. His immaculate uniform was perfectly pressed, razor-sharp folds extending down the front of his trouser legs to his black polished and mirror-like shoes, and he wore an impressive collection of medals and commendations on the left side of his chest. His demeanour was that of someone who was used to getting things exactly the way he wanted them, and who did not tolerate people who caused him trouble or inconvenience.

As he strode quickly and resolutely towards the guard post with an angry look on his face, the senior Syrian Army soldier behind the gate silently cursed his luck. He now recognised the officer, and he knew that he was about to get his ear chewed off.

The senior officer walked up to stand next to the gate facing the soldier, and he immediately began shouting at him and gesticulating. The soldier seemed to visibly shrink under the barrage of angry words and obscenities being hurled at him. Then he nodded, snapped to attention and saluted. Immediately after that, he turned around and barked an order at one of the other soldiers who quickly ran inside the guardhouse and pressed the button to open the gate and lower the steel bollards. He then pressed another button that engaged a shrill muster alarm. A few seconds later, all of the army personnel in the storage facility began converging on the guardhouse as quickly as they could. They lined up in an impromptu formation of two rows, and the senior officer then stood in front of them, appearing to deliver a well-rehearsed message. It lasted less than a minute, after which they all returned to their posts.

The senior officer and the Russian got back into their respective vehicles and the convoy drove through the open gate and proceeded to the concrete ramp leading down to the underground complex.

Here, the truck turned around and began reversing down the ramp until it was directly in front of the large reinforced double doors to the complex. The Syrian Army officer remained in the black Mercedes which had stopped at the top of the ramp, but the jeep carrying the Russian drove down next to the truck. Here he exited his vehicle again and walked over to the truck. He slapped his hand twice on the back of it, and after a few seconds it opened up and a team of four soldiers wearing camouflage uniforms similar to his own climbed down onto the concrete. They then extracted something large and bulky from the truck. It was a solid-looking dark grey case constructed from moulded carbon fibre, and it had been built to be fire and impact-resistant up to and including being able to survive a high-speed plane crash and the subsequent inferno of burning jet fuel. The case had four rubber-coated metal handles, two on each side, and the four soldiers manoeuvred it out of the back of the truck and carried it swiftly towards the door to the compound where the Russian wearing the telnyashka was waiting.

He turned to face the reinforced double doors and then opened up a panel on the wall next to him. Behind the panel was a keypad, and he swiftly punched in a six-digit passcode. The keypad beeped and the double doors unlocked with a hard metallic-sounding snap. Then they opened inward to reveal a brightly lit corridor about ten metres long. The Russian entered and walked to the end where the corridor opened up into a space that was about six metres wide and ten metres long.

In the middle of a glass wall opposite the corridor was an airlock that protruded around four metres into the room. It was made from steel and glass, and it had an outer door and an inner door, each controlled separately from a console mounted on the outside. Beyond the airlock and the glass walls was a sterile-looking metal-lined compartment that was roughly five by five meters in size and bathed in an eerie red light. On the back wall of the compartment were eight sturdy-looking polished steel cabinets.

The Russian stepped up to the outer door of the airlock and entered a code on its keypad and then pressed a button to disengage the locks and open the door. There was a hiss of air as the door opened, and then he waved through the four-man team carrying the dark grey case. As soon as they were inside, he pressed another button to close the outer door. After a couple of seconds, the airlock had cycled and then the inner door opened. The four men walked swiftly and purposefully into the metal-lined compartment and placed the case on the floor in front of one of the steel cabinets.

One of the men placed himself directly in front of the cabinet where he disengaged its lock. He then pulled on the handle and opened the door to reveal three metal racks, all mounted on rails that allowed them to be pulled out. Each rack had 16 glass spheres the size of baseballs, all placed in rubber cradles and arranged in a grid. The glass spheres contained a slightly luminescent blue liquid. The soldier turned his head and nodded at the three others, who quickly turned the grey case so that it opened towards the cabinet. They then unlocked it and opened the lid.

The case had a hard foam interior with circular cut-outs precisely matching the dimensions of the glass spheres. There were 24 cut-outs in total.

The soldier who had opened the cabinet carefully picked up one of the glass spheres and held it in his hand, looking at it for a few seconds. The slightly gooey blue liquid was mesmerising as it moved slowly inside the sphere. He then nodded at one of the other soldiers who stepped up to the other side of the rack, and the two of them then began transferring the spheres to the case, using both hands to hold each sphere and placing them gently inside the cut-outs. When they had transferred the first 16 spheres, they pushed the empty rack back in and pulled out the one below it to reveal another 16 spheres. They transferred an additional 8 spheres from there, thus filling up all the slots in the grey case. Two of the soldiers then closed and locked it, and spun it around on the floor so that it would be easier to walk it back out and into the airlock.

The soldier by the cabinet pressed on the rack that now held the remaining 8 spheres, in order to slide it back in and close the cabinet. Halfway in, one of the rails suddenly caught on something, jolting the entire rack to an abrupt stop and causing one of the spheres to jump out of its rubber cradle. He barely had time to register what was happening before the sphere rolled along the side of the rack and off the edge. Time seemed to slow down as the blue sphere fell impossibly slowly towards the concrete floor. The soldier stared at it helplessly, and he only just managed to turn his head and yell a warning to his comrades before the sphere smacked onto the floor and cracked open.

The two soldiers nearest the airlock saw it happen and immediately sprinted across to the inner door and threw themselves inside the airlock. The soldier who had been attempting to slide the rack back into the cabinet just stood there as if petrified, frozen to the spot as he stared down at the blue liquid that was now slowly oozing out of the broken glass sphere. A faint wisp of vapour began to rise as the contents of the sphere began to evaporate. He knew what was coming, but found himself unable to move, paralysed by terror and the realisation of what was happening. Deep down, he already knew it was too late for him to run. He was already a dead man.

The soldier who had been helping load the spheres into the case had been about to bend down and grab a handle on the case when the accident had happened, and so he had his back turned when the sphere cracked open. He heard the sound of the glass breaking, but seeing his two colleagues running for the airlock, he instinctively turned around to look behind him. As soon as he saw the blue liquid escaping from the sphere at his feet, he too bolted for the airlock but immediately tripped over the case, falling face-first onto the concrete floor.

Inside the airlock, the two soldiers scrambled to their feet and threw themselves at the outer door. They were shouting at the Russian, who was still standing at the control panel to let them out. He quickly tapped a button on the panel and then the inner door closed, sealing the two men inside the airlock and trapping the two others inside the storage compartment.

By now, the two men by the cabinet were lying on the floor in agony, clawing at their throats, their eyes bulging, their mouths foaming and convulsions beginning to ripple through their bodies. They were dying an agonising death, and no one in the world would be able to stop it from happening. After just a few seconds, blisters began to form on their hands and faces, and soon after, it was as if their skin was beginning to melt and liquefy. All the Russian and the two men inside the airlock could do was watch as the gruesome scene unfolded. Within less than a minute, the two men inside the compartment were dead.

Suddenly one of the two men inside the airlock began to cough uncontrollably. He and his colleague had managed to get away from the blue sphere and its deadly vapour, but some of it had made it inside the airlock with them. The other man instinctively scrabbled away from his colleague, as if afraid that whatever he had been afflicted with might be contagious. But then he himself started coughing violently, a panicked look instantly spreading across his face. He looked pleadingly up at the Russian through the glass door. His eyes began to water, and then he banged his fists angrily against the glass. The Russian watched impassively as the two men inside the airlock fell to their knees and then onto the floor, heaving and struggling for breath. One of them soon began to spasm and foam at the mouth, and small blisters then began to form across both of their faces. They were now both screaming in agony, and, spitting blood and saliva, they cursed the Russian who looked at them with a vague hint of regret and disgust on his face. Eventually, the two men passed out, but they were still breathing.

The Russian stood there alone for a while, looking at the two dead soldiers inside the compartment, now barely recognisable as human, as the deadly vapour ate into them and dissolved their skin. The two unconscious soldiers lying inside the airlock would live, and that was going to be a problem. He would have to run the decontamination cycle and then solve that problem in a permanent way. Letting them live would complicate things. It would just be too messy.

He reached inside a pocket in his jacket and extracted a mobile phone. He would need to call in another team to clean this place up, and then transport the spheres to the warehouse a few kilometres to the north. There was no way in hell he was walking away from this now. He had committed to acquiring and delivering 24 of the spheres to his client, so that was what he was going to do. He didn't much care where they ended up after that. As long as he got paid.

Two

CLEETHORPES CEMETERY, GRIMSBY – OCTOBER.

The two figures stood silently over the gravesite near one of the neat tree-lined avenues that ran through the cemetery. One was a tall dark-haired man wearing a long black coat and black leather gloves. He was holding a large black umbrella, easily big enough for him and his companion. His head was bowed slightly as he looked down on the grave at his feet, his muscular physique discernible under his coat, and his usually cheerful and handsome features marred by a quiet pained expression. The other figure was a short, slender and attractive woman wearing jeans, a white knitted jumper and a light grey raincoat to protect her from the downpour that seemed to have gone on all day and if anything appeared to have gotten worse since their arrival from London about an hour earlier.

Raindrops were falling on the lawns, the few remaining leaves on the trees and the concrete footpath, creating a gentle cacophony of pitter-patter sounds as the two of them stood there in silence. Overhead, the ominous dark grey clouds hung low and moved slowly from the west to the east. Far away could be heard the occasional rumble of distant thunder.

'Are you all right?' asked Fiona.

'Sure,' replied Andrew in a husky baritone voice, but sounding less than convincing. 'I've been coming here for more than ten years now, but I never really got used to it. Every time I do, I think of everything Frank and I would have been able to achieve if I hadn't got him killed that day.'

'Andrew, you can't think like that,' said Fiona placatingly. 'You said it yourself. It was no one's fault. Just bad luck.'

Andrew pressed his lips together and gave a brief sigh. She was right. But it didn't feel right.

'I know,' he finally conceded. 'It just never quite ends up feeling that way. We were like brothers, Frank and I. I think about him most days, and I've never managed to let myself off the hook. There is always a part of me that thinks I should have done something different that day. But I suppose we were young then. We knew the risks, yet somehow we were still convinced that we were bulletproof. You always think it will happen to someone else. Turns out, that was a mistake. I barely made it out myself. That drive back down to Fayzabad is not something I would like to do again in a hurry. At least they had an old Soviet airstrip that was under coalition control, so I managed to hitch a ride on an American chopper back to Bagram from there.'

'What happened to Frank's body?' asked Fiona.

'It was never recovered,' replied Andrew glumly. 'The compound was raided by coalition forces just four days later, but they found no trace of him except for his blood on the ground inside that shed. Those Taliban savages could have fed him to the dogs for all I know. I wouldn't put it past them.'

Fiona produced a sharp intake of breath. 'That's awful,' she said. 'I really hope someone did the right thing and buried him properly.'

'Unlikely,' said Andrew bitterly and looked down at the tombstone. 'I guess we'll never know. The only thing I know for certain is that they buried an empty coffin in the ground right here.'

Fiona took Andrew's hand and squeezed gently.

'Do you want to leave?' she asked.

'Yes,' he replied hesitantly. 'I come here to pay my respects every year, but I can't say I enjoy it.'

'Come on then,' she said, tugging gently at him. 'Let's go. We'll find a pub and I'll buy you a pint.'

Andrew turned his head and glanced at her with a weak smile.

'Fiona Keane in a pub?' he asked. 'Well, I never…'

'What?' smiled Fiona. 'I do visit pubs, you know. Just not very often.'

'All right then,' shrugged Andrew. 'Let's go.'

Ten minutes later they were sitting in a booth in a local pub, Fiona sipping a glass of Coke and Andrew having a pint of Doombar. Off to one side, a man was preparing a small raised stage for a live music performance later that evening, and up at the bar, a group of regulars were guffawing and arguing good-naturedly but loudly about football. There was a faint smell of stale beer having been spilt on the floor the night before, and near the doors to the street was an electronic slot machine whose lights were flickering unnaturally.

'Charming place,' smiled Fiona.

'Well,' shrugged Andrew, and looked around. 'It's not exactly The Ritz, but it's not too bad either. If you were expecting a swanky bar, then you're in the wrong town.'

'Oh, I am sure it gets lively here on a Saturday night,' she said. 'I might even enjoy it.'

'Hmm,' said Andrew, looking dubious. 'Anyway, thanks for coming along today. I usually do this alone, but it is nice to have some company for a change.'

'Can I ask you a question about the sort of work you and Frank used to do together?' asked Fiona.

'Sure,' said Andrew, taking a swig of ale.

'After you get back,' said Fiona with a quizzical look on her face. 'How do you process the things that happen out there? I mean, seeing people get shot and blown up. Watching your squad mates get killed. How do you stay sane, especially after you come home and they are no longer here anymore?'

Andrew sighed and thought for a few moments.

'This is where I am supposed to say something about king and country,' said Andrew, 'but the simple answer is that you go on because you have to. The alternative is to abandon everything you've invested your entire adult life in, and then go and sit in a corner rocking back and forth. That's just not something I would ever do, and I know Frank wouldn't want me to end up like that either. It would feel like I was somehow disrespecting his memory if I didn't press forward and go on the next mission and the next one after that. It's just who we are.'

'I couldn't do that,' observed Fiona. 'Sounds really tough. I think I would go mad.'

'Not really,' replied Andrew. 'I realise that a lot of guys come home and have various psychological issues. They struggle to get past what they have experienced. But for whatever reason, I have been able to compartmentalise things. I have seen some things that most people would consider quite traumatic, but I feel like I am able to put it all into perspective and realise that those things are part of being a soldier, and that ultimately we were all there to do an important job and make a real difference in the world. I think Frank was the same.'

'You two were very different, weren't you?' asked Fiona. 'Just in terms of your backgrounds.'

'Oh absolutely,' replied Andrew. 'Frank was from a council estate here in Grimsby, and he told me about how he hung out with the wrong sorts of people growing up. The military pretty much saved his arse and got him onto the straight and narrow. If he had kept hanging around drug dealers, he might have ended up like one of them, or maybe even dead at a young age. I was practically born with a silver spoon in my mouth. Well-off parents. Private schools in London. But I wanted to see the world and not have to work in an office all day, which paradoxically is what I do most days now. But Frank and I became close. We somehow connected across that great gulf of the class system. In fact, one of the things that we all noticed about the SAS was that in many ways it was a classless society within a very classist society. Everyone in the Regiment has a say. Everyone is valued equally and no one calls the officers 'Sir'. It was only ever 'Boss'. We were all on the same page and we all wanted the same thing. Frank and I both took it very seriously and we trained hard. And we were both very good at what we did, especially when we were on missions together.'

Andrew hesitated for a couple of seconds, staring into his ale. 'When he died, it wasn't just a painful experience for me, but it was a real loss for the Regiment.'

'Well, for what it's worth, I am glad you're still around,' said Fiona quietly, reaching across the table and squeezing his hand. 'The world needs people like you, even if you don't get credit for putting your lives on the line.'

'Thank you,' said Andrew and gave her a subdued smile. 'That means a lot, coming from you. Somewhere, Frank is looking down at you with a smile on his face. He would have liked you.'

Just then, an email pinged in on Andrew's phone. He opened up the app and tapped on it.

'It's from Colonel Strickland,' he said. 'Wants me back in London as soon as possible.'

'All right,' nodded Fiona. 'Does he say what it's about?'

'No,' replied Andrew. 'And even if he did, I couldn't tell you. Well, I mean. I could, but…'

'But then you'd have to kill me?' teased Fiona.

'Technically speaking, yes,' replied Andrew with a wry smile. 'But Strickland trusts you by now, so I don't think we would have a problem.'

'Would you like me to drive?' she asked.

'No thanks,' said Andrew and finished his pint. 'I like driving on the motorway, and I am pretty sure I am under the limit. Let's get out of here.'

* * *

Later that afternoon, having driven the roughly 150 miles back to London in near silence and then dropped Fiona off at his house in Hampstead, Andrew made his way to SAS headquarters at Sheldrake Place and walked into Colonel Strickland's office, knocking gently on the doorframe of the open door as he entered. The office, with its dark wood flooring covered with Persian rugs, and its wall decorated with wood panel mouldings, exuded a colonial elegance and calm that fitted the colonel's character. As usual, he was sitting at his desk with his pipe in the side of his mouth, wearing his neatly pressed and ironed uniform and studying a document.

'Afternoon, Sir,' said Andrew.

'Ah. Good afternoon, Andrew,' said Strickland, getting up from his desk. 'Thanks for coming by. I've got something I need to discuss with you. Please, do sit down.'

The two of them made themselves comfortable on Strickland's antique Chesterfield leather sofas.

'Thank you,' said Andrew and leaned forward, hands clasped together. 'What can I do for you?'

'Well, we've got a bit of a situation in Syria which I would like you to look into,' said Strickland. 'A couple of days ago, a number of men were admitted to a hospital in Damascus showings signs of exposure to a chemical agent. We are not yet sure precisely what type of weapon it was, but we are working on that. However, what really got our attention was that it turns out that those men were Russians, but not part of the regular Russian army deployment in Syria.'

'Mercenaries?' asked Andrew.

'Almost certainly, yes,' replied Strickland. 'There is a good chance that they belonged to the infamous Wagner Group. As you know, Russia has been using them in various hotspots across the Middle East and Africa for years. They are essentially the private army of the Kremlin. They go in and do the dirty work that Russia doesn't officially want to be associated with.'

'Yes, they are a lovely bunch,' said Andrew sarcastically. 'But what does that have to do with us? We have no jurisdiction there, and I think it is fair to say that the Syrian authorities are less than friendly towards the UK.'

'Oh, absolutely,' replied Strickland. 'The reason we're looking into this is that Syria has no independent chemical weapons production capability, so whatever chemical weapons are in the country have been supplied by the Russian military. We already know that the Syrian regime has used chemical weapons against its own civilian population in areas that they deem to be controlled by rebels. However, this has only ever happened with the direct involvement of the Russian Air Force. Up until now at least, the Russians have tightly controlled the storage, handling and delivery of those weapons, so the fact that a group of mercenaries ended up becoming exposed leaves some unsettling questions about why they were even in close proximity to those weapons. Not to mention what they might have been planning to do with them.'

Andrew nodded. 'I see what you mean.'

'More concerning,' continued Strickland, 'is the fact that, as far as we have been able to ascertain, the symptoms shown by the mercenaries do not match any chemical agents previously known to be in Russia's possession. In other words, there is a high likelihood that we are dealing with an entirely new type of weapon that Russia was potentially preparing to field test in Syria. And our intelligence people assess that there is a real risk that this weapon was somehow removed from Russian control. As far as we know, weapons like these on Syrian territory would have been stored either at the Russian airbase in Latakia or at their naval station in Tartus on the Mediterranean coast, although it is also possible that they could have been guarded by the Syrian Army in other locations. Either way, they somehow seem to have ended up in the hands of Russian mercenaries.'

'That is worrisome indeed,' said Andrew. 'What symptoms did those mercs exhibit?'

'All the classic nerve agent symptoms,' said Strickland ruefully. 'Profuse mucous production, breathing difficulties, vomiting, muscle seizures, paralysis, coma and ultimately death. But on top of that, they also suffered heavy blistering all over their bodies, which is something that is normally associated with vesicating agents such as mustard gas. In short, it was an unholy combination of the worst symptoms known to be caused by several different types of chemical agents, all at once.'

'Some type of new multi-spectrum weapon?' asked Andrew, looking concerned.

'Possibly,' replied Strickland.

'How many mercenaries were exposed?' asked Andrew.

'Our source tells us there were four of them,' replied Strickland. 'There were no survivors.'

Andrew nodded slowly, carefully considering the implications of what Strickland had relayed.

'Do we know anything about how or where they were exposed?' asked Andrew.

'We are working on that,' replied Strickland. 'We are still trying to glean as much information as we can from the hospital, but it seems to have happened at a civilian warehouse inside an industrial estate on the outskirts of Damascus.'

'Really?' said Andrew surprised. 'So, whatever was in that warehouse was controlled by Wagner, and it was outside of the control of the Russian military or the Syrian government?'

'Precisely,' replied Strickland. 'Somehow, what must have been a significant amount of this particular Russian chemical agent ended up in a civilian facility. This obviously has the potential to become quite ugly, especially if those weapons were ever to end up in the wrong hands.'

'Not that Wagner could ever be called the right hands,' interjected Andrew.

'Well, yes,' said Strickland. 'But there are plenty of well-funded terrorist groups inside Syria who would love nothing better than to get their hands on high-grade Russian chemical weapons. The bottom line is that we need to find out precisely what was in that warehouse, where it came from and where it has gone. If it has ended up with a terrorist group, we are potentially looking at a very serious threat. As you know, many of these chemical weapons are relatively easy to transport, and you only need a tiny amount to kill dozens or even hundreds of people. And if we are dealing with an entirely new type of weapon, we could be looking at a grave situation in short order, especially if that weapon were to somehow make it out of Syria.'

'Do we have any assets on the ground there?' asked Andrew.

'No, unfortunately not,' replied Strickland and gave a slight shake of the head. 'All of our information so far has come out of our Syria Monitoring Group which operates from inside the British Consulate in Istanbul. The SMG is effectively a whole desk from MI6 that has been transplanted into the consulate under diplomatic cover, and they have developed a decent network of technical and human assets inside the Syrian regime. That's how we learned about this whole thing. Apparently, the hospital in Damascus that the mercenaries were brought to, like all other hospitals in the country, was obligated to report any instances of suspected WMDs to the intelligence services. It would appear that Syrian intelligence is aware that the Syrian Army is less than reliable when it comes to the handling and safekeeping of these sorts of weapons, so their intel-gathering apparatus is keen to keep track of events like this. Anyway, we have someone on the inside there. A low-level clerk who has access to a lot of the paperwork related to these sorts of incidents. He flagged it to us, and I think we need to look into it.'

'Can't we send in someone from the MI6 group in Istanbul?' asked Andrew. 'They seem to have a decent handle on things, and you mentioned that they have human assets on the ground.'

'It is not quite as simple as that,' said Strickland, rubbing his chin. 'Each one of them has had very elaborate covers constructed in order to allow them to operate inside Turkey, and any deviation from their regular activities, such as suddenly travelling into Syria, would arouse a lot of suspicion amongst Turkish intelligence services. The UK and Turkey are obviously allied NATO countries, but it is no secret that there is a distinct lack of trust between our two governments, and that extends to our intelligence agencies as well. We can safely assume that Turkish intelligence is doing whatever they can to eavesdrop on us and covertly monitor everyone working at the consulate in Istanbul as well as at the embassy in Ankara.'

'I see,' said Andrew. 'So, you'd like me to go instead?'

'Yes,' nodded Strickland with a serious look on his face. 'This needs to be done under the radar, so I would like you to fly to Istanbul and have a chat with our people there. And then we might need you to travel into Syria to see what you can find.'

'All right,' said Andrew calmly. 'When do I leave?'

'Tomorrow morning,' replied Strickland. "I have already arranged it, and I have had our chaps at

GCHQ produce a false identity for you. As of this afternoon, you are Dr John Elliot of Northwind Engineering Plc, which is a company in the business of designing and manufacturing the next generation of turbines for windmills.'

'*Doctor* Elliot?' said Andrew, looking dubious.

'PhD in engineering,' said Strickland. 'Titles like that carry a lot of weight in that part of the world, so we thought we would leverage that.'

'There is no such thing as Northwind Engineering Plc, is there?' asked Andrew.

'Correct,' replied Strickland. 'But GCHQ have constructed a completely believable façade for the business, including a website, subsidiaries, filings at Companies House and financial reporting going back over a decade. For anyone looking at it from the outside, it will appear entirely legitimate. And so will your doctorate degree from Cambridge.'

Strickland slid a small pile of documents across the coffee table to Andrew, including his new passport and travel documents.

'Here is everything you'll need,' he said. 'You'll be staying at the Sheraton Istanbul, which is just a ten-minute walk from the consulate. The consulate has its own accommodation and we could easily have put you up inside there, but that would immediately have flagged you to Turkish intelligence as a UK government agent.'

'All right,' said Andrew. 'Who is my contact there?'

'A chap named David Jenkins,' replied Strickland. 'Officially, he serves as one of the UK's trade representatives, but he has been heading up the Syria Monitoring Group for the past six years. He's a good egg. Produced some valuable intelligence both on the Syrian government and on the various Islamist groups that have been operating in that country for several decades now.'

'Very good,' said Andrew. 'Anything else I need to know?'

'I don't think so,' replied Strickland. 'Just keep your wits about you. It is a complicated part of the world, as you well know, and both the Turkish and the Syrian governments would be incensed to discover a covert UK operative in their country. Anyway, I am always here if you need anything, either in terms of intelligence or practical support.'

'Thank you, Sir,' said Andrew and rose. 'I will go home and pack a small suitcase. Hopefully, this shouldn't take more than a couple of days.'

'Excellent,' said Strickland. 'Please keep me updated.'

'Will do, Sir.'

THREE

The next morning, rather than going to RAF Northolt and boarding one of the small VIP jets that he had become accustomed to using, Andrew hailed a cab on Kensington Park Road and asked the driver to take him to Heathrow Airport's Terminal 5. Once there, he walked to the British Airways desk and checked in using his fake passport and travel documents. If he was going to enter Turkey under a false identity, he would need to look the part all the way from the UK.

The flight to Istanbul took two hours and forty minutes, and Andrew spent most of that time reading the short preliminary report on the incident in Syria and then going over the most recent write-up from MI6 about Russia's chemical weapons capabilities and recent weapons development programs. According to the latest intelligence assessment, around eighty percent of Russia's chemical weapons were nerve agents such as Sarin, Soman and VX gas, all of which are volatile liquids that evaporate relatively quickly. The most volatile is Sarin, which evaporates at roughly the same rate as water. The least volatile is VX, which has the consistency of motor oil and persists for much longer, which in turn means that it is about 150 times more toxic than Sarin if victims are exposed on their skin or through breathing in the VX vapour.

Nerve agents all work by disrupting the body's nervous system, causing nerve impulses to continually be transmitted where they would normally only be fired once and then stop, for example when contracting a muscle. For this reason, some of the many effects of exposure to nerve agents are muscle spasms, seizures and abnormal heart rhythm. The Soviet Union initially developed the so-called R-VX gas, which was very similar to western VX gas, except that it was more prone to decomposition and thus had a much shorter shelf life. Since then, Russia has developed several new weapons including *Novichok*, which means 'New Boy', and which can be delivered as either a solid or a liquid, depending on the use case. The intelligence assessment from MI6 also stated that Russian scientists had publicly claimed to have developed versions of Novichok that are five to eight times more potent than VX. Both US and UK intelligence indicated that these claims were accurate and that the most recent iteration was already weaponised.

Andrew switched off his tablet and placed it on his fold-down tray table, a concerned expression spreading across his face. If it was actually true that Russia had somehow managed to combine a more potent form of VX with a blistering agent similar to mustard gas, then it would appear that they had leap-frogged anything the West had developed. And the prospect of this type of weapon falling into the hands of terrorists, and potentially being used on civilian populations in Europe filled him with dread. He could only hope that the Syria Monitoring Group in Istanbul would have something more than what Colonel Strickland had conveyed so far. He needed something tangible. Something that would allow him to get into Syria and then try to unravel what had actually happened and whether a real threat to national security was developing.

As he walked through customs and exited into the arrivals area at Istanbul Ataturk Airport wearing a light grey suit, a pair of glasses and carrying a briefcase, Andrew felt decidedly out of place. He was used to working covertly, but this type of James Bond cloak-and-dagger operation, using a false identity and a disguise, was new territory for him. He felt decidedly silly, as if everyone would look at him and realise that he was playing dress-up.

Up ahead, standing at the front of a small crowd on the other side of a barrier, was a man in his mid-fifties wearing light brown linen trousers and a dark blazer over a white shirt. He was sporting a dark and neatly trimmed beard, and in his hands was a sign reading 'Dr. Elliot'. His dark hair was slicked back and he was glancing impatiently at his watch.

Here goes, thought Andrew and approached him.

'Jenkins?' said Andrew, and offered his hand.

'Ah. Dr Elliot,' said the man politely and smiled. 'Yes, I am David Jenkins. Pleased to meet you, and welcome to Istanbul.'

'Thank you. Likewise,' replied Andrew.

'Please come with me,' said Jenkins, and gestured towards the exit. 'Your car is waiting.'

The two men walked to a black Mercedes with tinted windows and diplomatic plates that was waiting outside. From there it was a 25-minute drive along the main traffic artery northeast through western Istanbul, across the Haliç Köprüsü, or Golden Horn Bridge, named after the ancient estuary by the same name, and then south to the upmarket and cultured Kamer Hatun neighbourhood where the British Consulate was located. Along the way, Andrew watched the city roll by and reflected on how this city had been one of the major political and cultural centres of the world for millennia. It was now home to almost twenty million people, and it had once been the capital of both the Byzantine and Ottoman Empires straddling the Bosporus Strait, which connects the Black Sea to the north with the Sea of Marmara to the south, Istanbul had found itself at the centre of many struggles between Europe to the west and Asia to the east, both militarily and culturally. Despite this, it had also been a melting pot for thousands of years, and the push and pull of more liberal and secular western values versus more conservative Muslim values was as pertinent today as it had been for centuries.

The British Consulate was inside a large three-storey rectangular colonial building sitting on a large plot overlooking the Golden Horn waterway. It was surrounded by tall stone-block walls with barbed wire running along the top, and as the black Mercedes swung off the busy three-lane thoroughfare called Refik Saydam Cadessi that wrapped around the plot on two sides, an armed uniformed guard came out to greet them. He quickly checked the driver's ID and had a brief look inside the back where he recognised Jenkins. Then he nodded and waved them through. The car parked up, and the two men, who had only engaged in small talk on the way through the city, got out and walked up the steps to the building. They proceeded through the large oak double doors leading into an extravagant foyer that practically oozed past colonial glory. Then Jenkins asked Andrew to follow him down two flights of stairs to the building's basement level. Here they continued for about twenty metres along a wide and dimly lit corridor until they arrived at another set of double doors. However, these were modern sturdy-looking things, and next to them on the wall was a keycard reader.

Jenkins swiped his ID card across the reader in a manner suggesting he had done this thousands of times before. The reader produced a cheerful two-tone bleep, and the locks on the doors disengaged with a muffled clack.

'Welcome to the SMG,' said Jenkins as they entered and walked down three steps to the floor of the large open-plan office space.

The room was windowless and dark, and the floor was covered with a navy-blue carpet which muffled much of the ambient noise, leaving only a soft murmur of voices mixed with the occasional sound of a phone ringing. Spaced out across the room were tables arranged in small squares with four or five people sitting at their computers around each group. Clearly, these were different teams focusing on different tasks. It all seemed relatively quiet and calm, but Andrew could sense the intensity and seriousness with which these people were carrying out their responsibilities.

'Looks like you guys are keeping busy,' observed Andrew, surveying the room.

'Well, there's never a shortage of things to look at inside Syria,' said Jenkins. 'That place is in constant flux, even if it doesn't look that way from the outside.'

'How do you source your intelligence inside Syria?' asked Andrew, as the two men began making their way along the centre aisle that ran from the double doors to the far end of the large space. 'It is pretty closed-off, especially to countries like ours.'

'We have a decent network of sources, both technical and human,' replied Jenkins. 'Syria is a chaotic place. It might look like the regime has got a firm hold on power, but the country is fractured along ethnic and religious lines, like most places in the Middle East, and there is never a shortage of people who would like to affect a change in leadership. This creates opportunities for people like us to cultivate intelligence sources in and around the government or even inside the military. We've got people inside the ruling party, the army, the air force, and the government bureaucracy. Most of them are not particularly high profile, but they are close enough to the decision-makers to provide us with a relatively detailed picture of what is going on in the corridors of power. Putting the human intelligence from all of these different sources together, and combining it with our signals intelligence, we think we've got a pretty good handle on things.'

'And those desks here?' asked Andrew, jerking his head gently towards the groups of MI6 staff in the open-plan office. 'They collect and coordinate everything?'

'Yup,' said Jenkins. 'We're a tight-knit group. Most of us have been here for several years. It's an interesting job if you can stand never looking out of the window.'

Andrew smiled. He knew that he would have lasted about two hours in this place before resigning and running for the hills – quite literally.

'See those people over at that desk over there?' said Jenkins. 'They spend all day tracking the movements and politics of the various Islamist groups in the country.'

'I bet they are never short of things to do,' said Andrew dryly.

'Not for a long time now,' said Jenkins.

'Who is currently in the ascendancy?' asked Andrew. 'I imagine it changes from year to year.'

'Sometimes from month to month,' replied Jenkins. 'But for a while now it has been a group called Tahrir al-Sham, which is a merged entity consisting of many of the smaller groups. The main player is the Jabhat Fatah al-Sham, previously known as the al-Nusra Front, a.k.a. al-Qaeda in Syria. They pretend to be a completely different group now, but it essentially consists of all the same individuals, especially at the top where all the old al-Qaeda commanders are still running the show.'

'There's has been a lot of infighting between them over the years, right?' said Andrew. 'But it seems like they all buried the hatchet for a while to fight Assad and the Syrian government forces.'

'More or less,' replied Jenkins. 'At least for a time. But it is very obvious that if the Syrian government was ever to fall, much of the country would descend into civil war, similar to what happened in Libya. So, rather depressingly, the Russian presence there is actually somewhat of a stabilising force, even if that also means they bring in mercenaries with questionable skills and discipline.'

'How many Russian regulars are currently in the country?' asked Andrew as they continued along the wide aisle between the different groups of desks.

'We estimate around eight thousand at the moment,' replied Jenkins. 'That includes both army, navy and air force personnel. And then on top of that, of course, are the mercenaries like Wagner.'

The two men arrived at a large glass-walled office located at the far end of the room. Jenkins gestured for Andrew to enter.

'I suppose that brings us neatly to the situation at hand,' said Andrew, as they entered and Jenkins closed the door behind them. 'Dead Russian mercenaries in a Damascus hospital.'

'Yes, replied Jenkins, motioning to a couple of sofas placed on opposite sides of a small coffee table. 'I take it Strickland gave you a brief overview already?'

'He did,' nodded Andrew, sitting down on one of the sofas. 'Just the headlines though. I was hoping you could flesh things out a bit more and help me with a place to start.'

'I certainly can,' nodded Jenkins amiably, making himself comfortable and flipping open a laptop that had been sitting on the table.

He powered it up, logged into the computer network and brought up a satellite image on the screen.

'This is Damascus,' he said, turning the laptop so that Andrew could see, and pointing to an image that showed the Syrian capital as well as a large part of southwestern Syria.

'This here is the Al Mazzeh municipality, southwest of central Damascus,' said Jenkins, pointing to an area on the left side of the screen. 'It is near the edge of the capital and has one of the main highways into the city running through it. Down here you can see the Mazzeh Military Airport.'

'Mainly used by the Syrian Air Force, I guess?' asked Andrew.

'Yes,' replied Jenkins. 'The Russians rarely operate out of there. They practically own the Khmeimim Air Base near Latakia on the coast, so they don't need to use this one. We do see flights coming in and out of there from Russia, so there is definitely some sort of Russian activity, but we think it is mainly advisors and government representatives going to meet the Syrian government and the military top brass in Damascus.'

'So where did the chemical weapons incident happen?' asked Andrew.

Jenkins pointed to a set of four large curving offramps near the highway quite close to the military airport.

'Right here,' he said. 'The warehouse is a couple of hundred metres from the highway, inside a small industrial estate. It is only about a kilometre from Mazzeh Military Airport, and less than four kilometres from the presidential palace, which sits up here on top of an elevated rock plateau overlooking the whole of Damascus.'

'I need to get into that warehouse,' said Andrew without hesitating.

Jenkins smiled and nodded. 'Strickland told me you'd say that.'

'Which hospital were the soldiers taken to?' asked Andrew.

'According to our source, they were taken to a military hospital somewhere in the Shikh Saad neighbourhood over here,' replied Jenkins, pointing at a location closer to the centre of the city. 'It is supposedly just a few kilometres from the warehouse. Strickland is going to send the exact location through as soon as it is confirmed.'

'I need to pay that place a visit too,' said Andrew. 'Oh, and one more thing. Do we have any idea which Russian storage facilities the Syria-bound chemical weapons tend to come from? That might give us an idea as to their exact nature.'

'We do,' replied Jenkins and zoomed out on the map, shifted the view several thousand kilometres north and zoomed in again. 'There is a Russian Airforce research and storage facility at a site in Russia called Leonidovka. It is an old Soviet facility that exclusively stores VX weapons, and there have been regular flights from there to Syria for several years now. That obviously doesn't mean that they are hauling chemical weapons into Syria all the time, but it does strongly suggest that Russia has been using Syria as a testing ground for these types of weapons and then letting the Syrian government take the blame.'

'Makes sense, I guess,' said Andrew and shrugged. 'It's not like Syria could become much more of an international pariah than it already is. The same could be said for Russia, but Russia clearly has the Syrian regime by the balls, so they might as well force them to take the hit.'

'Yes, Russia is very much running the show at the moment,' replied Jenkins. 'If Russia were to leave, there is every chance that the various Islamist insurgency groups would reconstitute themselves and threaten the central government in Damascus in short order. Add to that the likelihood of the Kurds then trying to carve out a piece of eastern Syria for themselves, and possibly even Israel and Turkey getting involved, and it is suddenly not too difficult to see why the Syrian government is prepared to put up with pretty much anything to make sure the Russians don't go anywhere.'

Andrew studied the map for a few moments, looking pensive and rubbing his chin.

'What, if anything, do we know about the warehouse itself?' he asked. 'And do we have any leads on where that chemical agent came from and how it ended up in that warehouse?'

Jenkins shifted in his seat and pressed his lips together.

'To be honest,' he said. 'Most of what we have is speculation. Or as we like to think of it - educated guesses. But we do have a few solid hints that our sources on the ground have been able to provide for us. We are still working on who actually owns the warehouse, but in terms of who might have been involved, we already have a candidate who seems to fit the bill pretty nicely. And there is at least anecdotal evidence that he was involved somehow.'

'All right,' said Andrew and moved forward to sit on the edge of the sofa. 'Who?'

'A former Wagner Group mercenary called Mikhail Tokarev,' replied Jenkins, showing Andrew a grainy black-and-white photo of a stocky, rough-looking short-haired man in a Russian military uniform. 'A real character. He was in the regular Russian army for a number of years. Then he joined the elite 45th Guards Spetsnaz Brigade in Russia's Airborne Forces the VDV, where he took part in military action in Chechnya, South Ossetia and the initial stages of Russia's involvement in Syria. At this point he must have decided that the grass was greener on the other side, so he swapped over to join Wagner where he made a name for himself as a brutal but very effective field commander. Seems he liked it so much in Syria that he decided to stay when most of his comrades rotated home.'

'So, he's gone freelance?' said Andrew.

'Very much so,' replied Jenkins. 'And you could say he's gone native too. He runs a nightclub in Damascus, which as you can imagine is somewhat of an achievement in itself, given that Syria is ostensibly a relatively conservative Muslim country.'

'How did he manage to swing that?' asked Andrew.

'He's connected,' said Jenkins. 'It appears that he has spent several years cultivating relationships with senior figures in both the government, the military and the local police, many of whom frequent his nightclub. There is also a regular contingent of local Russians there, especially Wagner Group mercenaries, and all of these people rub elbows at the club. It's called *Porok*, by the way. It literally means *Vice*, in Russian.'

'Cute,' said Andrew sarcastically. 'So that's where he entertains all of the bigwigs?'

'He does a lot more than that,' said Jenkins. 'He wheels and deals in all kinds of illegal stuff. Business is good, and the nightclub is busy. From what we understand, Porok has everything a morally frayed Syrian army officer or government official could wish for. Booze. Women. The works. By all accounts, the vodka flows freely in that place, and there is a veritable conveyor belt of young Eastern European women working there, providing various services to these high-ranking people.'

'I can well imagine,' said Andrew and raised his eyebrows. 'I see why he named the club the way he did.'

'One of his patrons is a major in the Syrian Army by the name of Zahir Obaid,' continued Jenkins. 'Just about as corrupt as they come. He has personal connections to the Syrian president's extended family, and he is not shy about leveraging that in any way he can. Most recently, Major Obaid has been investigated for selling huge volumes of stolen Russian-supplied Syrian Army fuel and then attempting to launder the money through a private wealth management firm based in Basel, Switzerland. Let me show you a photo of him.'

Jenkins opened an image file showing a picture of a military parade. At the centre was the Syrian president watching formations of Syrian Army soldiers march past, and he was flanked by a handful of seemingly high-ranking military officers, most of whom looked overweight and shoddy in their uniforms. However, one of them stood out. Jenkins tapped his finger on a man with a moustache wearing and sharply dressed in a crisp uniform. Judging from his insignia, he was not as senior as the other officers in the photo, but unlike most of the others, he had the confident look of someone who was at ease in the company of the head of state.

'This is him,' said Jenkins.

'Charming character,' said Andrew evenly. 'High profile for someone of his rank. But why is he important?'

'Because,' replied Jenkins, 'we suspect that Tokarev and Obaid were working together to lift the chemical weapons from an army-controlled warehouse. It is possible that these Russian weapons were housed in a Syrian Army storage facility, and that Obaid somehow managed to provide Tokarev with access to them, or perhaps Obaid even used Syrian Army personnel to move the weapons off the base where they were stored, and then on to the warehouse where the mercenaries were ultimately exposed to it. The details are quite vague so far, but hopefully, you will be able to help throw some light on this. Anyway, the fear now is that Tokarev and Obaid are working together to sell the weapons on to the highest bidder.'

Andrew sighed, then winced slightly.

'That is pretty much our worst-case scenario, isn't it?' he said.

'Very much so,' replied Jenkins. 'The risk to the public, both in the UK and elsewhere, would be significant if what appears to be a highly concentrated multi-spectrum chemical agent were to fall into the hands of terrorists. We don't even know how much of this stuff was in that warehouse, but given how only tiny amounts are required in order to have a lethal effect, the potential for mass civilian casualties is significant. The prospect of this type of weapon being released in the middle of a large European city is frankly terrifying.'

'What else do we know about this Tokarev character?' asked Andrew. 'You can't be in the business of stealing chemical weapons for a living. That seems like an opportunistic one-off. And the nightclub is clearly just a tool to insert himself into Syrian power circles and obtain leverage. So, what's his main line of business?'

'Guns and drugs,' replied Jenkins. 'He has connections in the Russian Army, which can give the Syrian Army a run for its money in the corruption stakes. Tokarev pays off high-ranking Russian officers to supply him with weapons pilfered from Russian Army storage facilities, mainly small arms but also explosives and anti-tank weapons. These weapons are transported to Afghanistan where they are sold to local warlords and the Taliban for serious money. Tokarev then uses the proceeds to buy Afghan heroin, which he ships out on the transport aircraft that brought in the weapons. The transports fly to Syria where we believe the drugs are loaded onto civilian cargo ships in the port city of Tartus where we believe Tokarev has bribed the local port officials, and then they are smuggled on to a host of European countries including the UK. We are not sure precisely what Tokarev's source is, but we think he gets his supply of opium and heroin from an Afghan warlord.'

'Do we know who?' asked Andrew.

'We're not sure,' said Jenkins, shaking his head. 'The only thing we know is that he has been around for a long time and that he has a reputation for being absolutely brutal and completely ruthless in asserting his position in the heroin market in that country. We think he operates out of Pakistan, but our intel on him is sketchy, to say the least. Anyway, as you know, drugs are big business in Afghanistan. The latest estimates indicate that the drug trade in Afghanistan is worth around 3 billion dollars per year, and that about one-hundred-thousand people make their living from it. Somewhere in the region of sixty percent of the Taliban's income is from the opium and heroin trade.'

'I know,' nodded Andrew. 'That's something we never managed to stamp out, and I doubt anyone ever will.'

'There is one more string to Tokarev's bow,' said Jenkins. 'He has been involved in the looting of valuable artefacts from ancient Syrian archaeological sites. These sorts of items can fetch hundreds of thousands on the black market, and Tokarev is in the business of smuggling artefacts out of Syria and into Europe. We believe Major Obaid is also involved in this, using army personnel to provide access and security at the dig sites while Tokarev's so-called archaeologists go in and loot anything valuable.'

'Quite the entrepreneur, this Tokarev chap,' said Andrew caustically.

'Indeed,' replied Jenkins. 'Anyway, according to our sources on the ground, Tokarev is at his nightclub most evenings, and Major Obaid is often there on Thursday evenings, so you might want to try to get in there.'

'That might be risky,' said Andrew. 'But it is probably worth a shot. If I am going to get anywhere with this thing, then I will need to get close to Tokarev and Obaid.'

'It is probably the only way,' nodded Jenkins. 'Our sources are extremely useful, but there is only so much that they can provide. You have to remember that none of them are ever close to Tokarev or Obaid or anyone else in a position of power inside the regime. Everything they provide to us has been gleaned indirectly, and every time they put out feelers, ask questions or pull information from the Syrian bureaucracy, they are risking their lives.'

'So how do I get into the country?' asked Andrew.

'Via Lebanon,' replied Jenkins. 'You could conceivably enter Syria directly from Istanbul, but even if they won't be able to prove that you are a British agent, they might suspect, and then you would either have an army of Syrian intelligence operatives shadowing you everywhere you go, or they could just detain you and lock you up indefinitely. The Syrian authorities are paranoid about western spies. So, for those reasons, you will fly to Beirut from here. You'll keep using your cover as Dr Elliot. From there you hire a car and make your way to the border with Syria where we will have one of our local assets waiting for you. All you have to do is cross the border without getting caught.'

'Simple and low-risk then?' smiled Andrew wryly.

'Well,' said Jenkins, returning his smile. 'I have no doubt that I would get myself killed within the first five minutes if I had to do it, but I was told you would be able to swing it.'

Andrew nodded pensively. 'As long as we find a decent spot to do it. And if your guy on the Syrian side is reliable, then we should be all right.'

'Our man is solid,' said Jenkins. 'His name is Faisal, and he will take you to Damascus and give you the keys to a safe house in the suburbs. You don't need to know anything else about him. He has taken quite a risk in helping us, so the less you know the better for him.'

'Fine by me,' said Andrew. 'As long as he can get me into Damascus unnoticed, then I'll be fine from there.'

'Very good,' said Jenkins. 'The main reason for going in via Lebanon is that the Syria-Lebanon border is extremely porous. Yes, there are official border crossings where people have to show their passports and so on, but away from the border crossings, there are often no barriers, no fences, and no indication at all that you are even crossing an international border. There are dozens of smaller roads that crisscross the border area going in and out of both countries. This is especially true southeast of the Masnaa border crossing.'

Jenkins brought up a map of the area on his laptop.

'You need to proceed through the village of Mazraat Deir al-Ashayer, which is only about three kilometres from the border. Then up over the hills to the southeast and down the other side to a small road that runs parallel to the border. Follow that towards the east, and you will find Faisal in an old white Toyota Land Cruiser at a petrol station at the end of the road. From there, Highway 1, also known as Dimashq Beirut, will take you to the outskirts of Damascus. It is only about 15 kilometres. I will give you a GPS tracker and the coordinates you'll need. The only thing you have to watch out for is Syrian Army patrols. Precisely because the border with Lebanon is so porous, the Syrian Army has committed a good number of troops to patrol it and stop and search vehicles crossing over. The Syrian regime likes to think of the Lebanese as their younger brothers, but that doesn't mean they trust them.'

Andrew nodded and thought for a few seconds. 'I will need weapons and equipment.'

'Already planned for,' said Jenkins. 'The British Embassy in Beirut has a very well-stocked armoury in the basement, so you should swing by there after you land. I have arranged for you to meet their quartermaster there. A chap by the name of Jones. I am sure he will be able to provide you with everything you need.'

'Good,' Andrew said and nodded. 'I have a feeling this is going to get interesting.'

FOUR

Fiona was sitting on the sofa in the living room of her and Andrew's house in Hampstead in London. Andrew had inherited the large Georgian property after his parents died in a car accident, and he had lived there happily as a bachelor by himself for over a decade before he met Fiona. However, after their relationship had developed, he had decided to invite her to join him there. She had initially felt reluctant to give up her independence, but in the end, her desire to settle down somewhere with the man she loved had won out over her more selfish impulses. Or perhaps it was simply a deep-seated compulsion to build a nest. Either way, she was happy with the choice she had made, and the two of them were a strong team, both privately and professionally.

Originally from Dublin, Fiona had moved to London in her late teens to study archaeology at Kings College more than fifteen years ago now. She had then completed a PhD and had worked at the

British Museum ever since. She had just put down her teacup and picked up a book when her mobile phone rang.

'Hello?'

'Hey Fiona, it's me,' said Andrew, sounding slightly distracted.

'Oh. Hi Andrew,' she said. 'You sound like you're in the middle of something. Are you all right?'

'Yeah,' he replied. 'Sorry, I am just packing up my stuff. I am still in Istanbul, but I wanted to touch base before I go on a little excursion.'

'I don't suppose you can tell me where you're off to?' said Fiona, already knowing the answer to her question.

'I am afraid not,' replied Andrew.

'That's all right,' she smiled. 'My international man of mystery.'

'I suppose,' said Andrew. 'Anyway, Fiona. The reason I am calling is that I wanted to ask you if you are familiar with the names Mikhail Tokarev or Zahir Obaid. Tokarev is Russian, and Obaid is Syrian.'

Fiona thought for a moment.

'They don't ring a bell,' she said haltingly, trying to scour her memory for any references to the two men that she might have come across. 'Should they? And why do you ask?'

'Well,' replied Andrew. 'I am looking into something that might involve smuggling of ancient artefacts from Middle Eastern countries to buyers in Europe and the US. These two names came up, and I was wondering if you could look into them for me. The more information we can get on these characters the easier it will be to dig out what else they might be up to. They seem to be involved in something a lot more sinister than art smuggling, but again, I can't really tell you much more than that. National security and all that.'

'I understand,' said Fiona. 'Well, I am certainly familiar with the trade in stolen artefacts, especially from the Middle East. It is something we increasingly have to deal with at the British Museum. We are forced to spend more and more of our time verifying the provenance of items that are put up for sale in London's auction houses, especially if we are considering whether to acquire them or not. There is a big market for ancient sculptures, vases, and even entire mosaic floors looted from former Roman colonies around the Mediterranean. And there is so much money in it that it is attracting a huge number of very entrepreneurial criminals. Every year there are more items being funnelled through London, and every year they get better at forging their provenance to make them look legitimate. And as I am sure you already know, several of the Islamist movements have used the art trade to fund their operations. So, it has become a bit of a minefield for us.'

'Yes, I am aware of organisations like ISIS generating revenue this way,' said Andrew. 'This is slightly different, though. Sorry, I can't be more specific.'

'No problem,' said Fiona. 'Anyway, I am pretty sure that I have never heard of either Tokarev or Obaid, but that doesn't mean they aren't players. I am far from an expert, but I can certainly look into it.'

'Thanks, Fiona,' he said. 'I appreciate that. It might really help push this thing along. The more we know about them, the more we will be able to find out.'

'I will do what I can,' said Fiona. 'Give me a day or two.'

'Great,' said Andrew. 'Anyway, I will probably be off the grid for the next couple of days, so don't worry if you don't hear from me.'

'Ok. I won't,' lied Fiona. 'Just be careful, ok?'

'I am always careful,' said Andrew attempting to sound cheerful, although he knew that things were likely to get dicey and that there was no way Fiona didn't also realise that.

'All right,' said Fiona with a small sigh. 'That will have to do, I guess. I'll start looking into this thing for you right away. I might send you an email if I find anything. You can read it whenever you're back online.'

'Sounds good,' said Andrew. 'And Fiona?'

'Yes?' she asked.

'I love you,' he said softly.

'I know,' she replied playfully, and Andrew could hear that she was producing that gorgeous smile of hers as she did so.

'Bye, Fiona,' he said.

'Bye.'

Fiona pressed the 'End Call' button, put her mobile phone back down on the coffee table and sat back for a moment, staring into space with a slightly anxious look on her face. Andrew was off on one of his missions again. Of that, she was sure. But she did not have the faintest idea exactly where he was going, what he was facing, how dangerous it might become and how long it might end up taking. She liked to think that she had gotten used to this by now, but the truth was that she probably never would. All she could do now was keep herself busy and remember that on every previous occasion where he had gone away like this, he had always come back in one piece. At least, so far.

She got up and walked to her studio office, which used to be one of Andrew's spare bedrooms. She sat down at her PC and switched it on, rubbing her eyes and trying to focus her mind.

She already had a good understanding of how this smuggling and art laundering game worked. And she had been closely following how it had developed from small beginnings several decades ago to now industrial-scale looting by various organised crime syndicates, as well as other even less savoury organisations such as ISIS. Unlike the fanatical Taliban who destroyed ancient art in Afghanistan for religious reasons, the much more pragmatic ISIS instead looted dozens of sites across Iraq and Syria to fund their military operations. When the Syrian and Russian armies eventually kicked ISIS out of Syria, and following the NATO-led effort to destroy ISIS in Iraq there were rumours that high-ranking Syrian officials had cottoned on to just how much money ISIS had been making from the trade and that they had effectively taken it over themselves. There had already been several instances of high-profile London auction houses being caught selling stolen artefacts from Syria, and she was sure those would not be the last.

Fiona began combing the internet for references to Tokarev and Obaid but found nothing conclusive. There were several people by those names in Russia and in several Middle Eastern countries, many of them with professional or social media profiles that were publicly available, but none of them even remotely matched what Andrew had hinted at. She decided to look closer to home and visited the Companies House website which has a public and searchable database of all directors and affiliates of all registered businesses in the UK. If they were involved in smuggling and selling stolen Syrian art in London, then they would need a legitimate business to do it through, which meant that such a business would have to be registered. Because of the nature of their alleged business dealings, she decided that the two men were unlikely to be registered anywhere other than in the Greater London area, and so she began her search there.

After about half an hour, all she had come up with under the name Zahir Obaid, was a plumber from Ealing, a taxi driver from Croydon and a doctor from Primrose Hill. There was no evidence at all of anyone by the name Mikhail Tokarev in the database, and she could find no other references to a man by that name anywhere else.

Fiona leaned back in her chair, staring blankly at the screen. Then she had an idea. If Obaid was a Syrian national, he would almost certainly have been educated in Syria, and if he was somehow connected with archaeology then she might be able to find references to him on Syrian academic websites. She quickly found the website of the University of

Damascus and was vaguely surprised to find an extensive English-language section. She clicked on the link to the Faculty of Fine Arts, which among other things focuses on the arts of Syria's ancient past. Within a couple of minutes, she found a list of the faculty's alumni arranged by year. Painstakingly going through them all, she eventually found two people with the surname Obaid. She went back to the Companies House database to cross-reference the names, and a few seconds later she had what was almost certainly a match. A man by the name of Nadeem Yassin Obaid had studied archaeology at the University of Damascus more than a decade ago. Intriguingly, the Companies House database had a listing of a London arts business called Malakbel Gallery & Auctions, clearly named after the sun god of ancient Syria. It was based on Ludgate Hill just opposite St Paul's Cathedral, and the sole owner and director was listed as Nadeem Yassin.

Bingo, thought Fiona. *This has to be the same guy.*

Fiona felt sure that the London gallery owner was also the same Nadeem Yassin Obaid who had studied archaeology in Damascus, and that he had to be related to Zahir Obaid somehow. It was too much of a coincidence that they were both Syrian, shared the same surname, and that one was connected to archaeological looting in Syria, and the other involved in the sale of ancient Syrian artefacts right here in London.

The question now was - what was she going to do about it? She sighed as a hint of a smile spread across her face, knowing herself well enough to realise that the answer would not end up being 'Nothing'.

Andrew was not going to like this, but there was no way she was just going to sit here idly, now that she had developed this lead.

The next morning, she got up early and had a quick shower and a change of clothes. She then spent about twenty minutes on makeup and jewellery to make sure she would look the part. Then she went down into the basement where Andrew had arranged for an enormous bulky safe to be installed. It held no cash or other valuables, but it was stocked with items that might come in handy if he had to leave on an assignment in a hurry. Many of them were also useful for self-defence. Both he and Fiona had made more than a few enemies over the past few years in their efforts to thwart acts of terrorism and prevent the looting of priceless artefacts, so Andrew had decided to keep a small stash of weapons and other equipment in the house, just in case. The safe also contained various advanced gadgets such as listening devices and other hardware for covert operations. What she was after was a small device that plugged into the micro-USB port on her phone. It was only about the size of a small matchbox, and it snapped onto the phone seamlessly. However, its small size belied its potential for intelligence gathering. Andrew had shown her how to use it, thinking that a day might come when they would need it. Today was just such a day.

Fiona closed the safe, locked it, and went back upstairs. Then she left the house and walked to the nearest underground station to head for the City of London.

Time to pay Nadeem Yassin a visit, she thought

* * *

The next morning, Andrew woke up at the Sheraton Istanbul, had a quick breakfast in the restaurant and then got into a taxi that had been booked for him by the British Consulate staff. The driver took him south and then west across the Ataturk Köprüsü bridge. As they crossed over the Golden Horn estuary, he could see the imposing Hagia Sophia mosque towering over the rest of the Fatih district of Istanbul ahead of him and to the left. It was a sprawling building with a huge spiked dome at its centre and four tall minarets surrounding it. Andrew had been unable to see it on the way to the consulate the day before, but now, as it sat there in the golden morning sunlight, he could hardly imagine a better view of it. Built in 537 BCE as the patriarchal cathedral of Roman Constantinople, it was later converted into a mosque in 1453 when the city fell to the Ottoman Empire. Andrew had read somewhere that a strange inscription had been found on a parapet on the top floor of one of its galleries in 1964. It had turned out to be Viking runes, spelling out the old Nordic name 'Halfdan', and it was thought to have been made by a bored Norseman member of the Varangian Guard, which was an elite bodyguard unit in Constantinople that had been tasked with protecting the Byzantine emperors. Vikings, prized as they were for their massive size and handiness with an axe, as well as their loyalty, were known to have been part of the Varangian Guard around the 9th century. They had no doubt been able to dissuade any would-be attackers from an attempt on the emperor's life, simply through their strange and fearsome appearance. A useful ability, since more often than not, the emperor's enemies were to be found inside his own court, as opposed to beyond the walls of Constantinople.

Andrew couldn't help smiling at the notion of a military man standing in that very building a thousand years ago, idly using his knife to etch his name into the marble parapet. Boredom was a fact of life in the military, especially so for special forces like the SAS, and that seemed to have remained unchanged for a thousand years and probably much longer than that. He would have liked to have met Halfdan, and talked to him about how he ended up working for an emperor in these exotic lands thousands of miles from his home in Scandinavia. Perhaps they could have swapped war stories. Perhaps they would have a lot in common. Perhaps Halfdan had also once been to the British Isles. It was an intriguing thought, and Andrew couldn't help but feel a certain kinship with this sword-for-hire, even if he himself had never considered becoming a mercenary.

The taxi eventually reached the other end of the bridge after which the mosque was obscured from view. Twenty minutes later the driver pulled up at the drop-off point outside Ataturk International Airport. Andrew paid the fare and stepped out. He joined the throngs of other passengers and made his way past the security check where he presented his boarding pass and passport in the name of John Elliot, and then strolled casually out to the gate where the aircraft had just begun boarding.

He had been booked a seat in business class, and as he walked onto the plane and made his way towards his seat, he looked back at the regular travellers in 'coach' and produced a sly smile and a gentle shake of the head. The so-called *business class* was increasingly a scam, as far as he was concerned. There was essentially no difference in the experience, except for sub-standard food and a barely noticeable increase in legroom. And whoever had come up with the word 'class' to denote different service levels on planes? He decided that it was almost certainly a British invention.

As he got into his seat, another passenger brushed past him and accidentally bumped into his hip.

'Sorry,' said the man and gave him a friendly apologetic smile.

He was a tall olive-skinned man with a full but short beard, neatly trimmed hair with a side parting and thin-rimmed glasses. He was wearing a grey suit, and looked to Andrew like a local Istanbul banker, probably off to Beirut to see a wealthy private client. The man carried no briefcase or any other carry-on luggage. As he moved past, Andrew picked up a faint scent of citrus and something else from the man's aftershave. Sandalwood?

'No problem,' Andrew said, returning the man's smile with the expression of an experienced traveller having done that exact thing plenty of times himself.

It was a relatively short one hour and fifty minutes flight from Istanbul to Beirut, and as the wheels of the Turkish Airlines A320 touched down on the black searing-hot runway, the local time was just after 11 a.m. The aircraft taxied towards the gate, and as

Andrew looked out of the window, he could see the heat shimmering off ground vehicles and other aircraft. It was already a hot day here.

He walked through the terminal at Beirut-Rafic Hariri International Airport, and it somehow had a noticeably more Middle-Eastern feel to it than Ataturk International Airport. Perhaps it was the sound of Arabic being spoken all around him.

As he walked from the gate towards passport control and baggage claims, he was able to look out towards the east through a set of large floor-to-ceiling windows. Stretching away from him was the noisy bustling city of Beirut. On the horizon, some 20 kilometres away, he could see the Mount Lebanon mountain range, beyond which lay the Beqaa Valley and the border with Syria. Damascus was only about 80 kilometres from Beirut as the crow flies, but he knew that getting there might take some effort. First, however, he needed to get out of the airport. And then on to the British Embassy to stock up on the kit that he knew he would need over the next couple of days.

When he arrived at passport control, there was an air of officiousness about the resident staff. They were wearing crisp dark blue short-sleeved military uniforms, and their faces were seemingly locked in a permanent half-bored, half-suspicious expression. Andrew wondered if the ability to pull off that combination for a full working day might be a prerequisite to being hired for the job.

As a heavily overweight and moustached border control officer inspected his passport with a slightly annoyed look on his face, Andrew caught a faint scent of citrus and sandalwood. He turned his head casually to his left to glance behind him, and a few metres away in the queue he spotted the bearded banker who had bumped into him on the plane. Or perhaps he was no banker at all.

'Purpose of visit, Mr Elliot?' asked the border control officer in heavily accented English, somehow managing to look as if he was supremely disinterested in the reply.

'Business,' said Andrew with an accommodating smile. 'Windmills.' He felt like a terrible actor.

The border control officer looked up briefly at Andrew's face, and then down again at his passport. He then once more looked up, seeming to inspect his suit for a moment, as if it might somehow provide him with more insights into the character of this particular traveller. He appeared to waver for a moment, but then seemed to decide that he was in no mood to investigate further.

'Welcome to Lebanon,' he said flatly, handing Andrew his passport and sounding anything but welcoming.

'Thanks very much,' replied Andrew cheerfully, putting his passport back into the inside pocket of his suit jacket.

Andrew exited the terminal building and walked to a taxi stand and got into the taxi at the front, asking the driver to take him to the British Embassy. The driver looked uncertain, so Andrew showed him the address on his phone. The driver then nodded vigorously and made agreeable-sounding noises, pointing out of the windscreen and repeating the address.

'British Embassy, yes,' he said, sounding as if he now knew exactly where to go. 'Ten minutes.'

'Excellent,' said Andrew and sat back as he looked out of the window and the taxi exited the airport.

Soon they were driving along the busy Hafez al-Assad Road, named after a former president of Syria who, amongst other things, was known for saying that the Syrians and the Lebanese were "one people in two countries". The road was a four-lane main traffic artery that stretched due north from the airport and through the city. It ran parallel to the Mediterranean coast towards the commercial container port near the northern part of the city centre where the British Embassy is located. On either side, it was lined with tall boxy-looking buildings that had clearly been built with little consideration for aesthetics.

Andrew glanced casually over his shoulder through the rear window of the taxi. Directly behind them, he saw a black Audi at a distance of around twenty metres. He only had a brief look and was unable to make out any details, except that there was a man sitting in the passenger seat next to the driver.

Andrew got out his phone, selected the camera and held it up in front of himself and slightly to one side. Then he took a picture over his shoulder and out of the rear window, opened it in a viewer and zoomed in on the passenger. He produced a vague smile and gave a slight shake of the head. It was the bearded man from the plane. Clearly, the Turkish intelligence services were keen to see what he was doing in Lebanon, which meant that they strongly suspected that he was working for British intelligence.

*Keep your friends close, but your enemies close*r, thought Andrew, silently quoting Sun Tzu, the Chinese military strategist and author of The Art of War.

The taxi driver turned out to be true to his word, and just under ten minutes later the vehicle pulled up outside the embassy complex on Serail Hill in Beirut's Central District. Here, the British Embassy shares a large building with the embassies of several other nations, including Australia, Denmark and Japan. The building is located next to an enormous Ottoman quadrangle with an open courtyard called the Grand Serail, which is also known as the Lebanese Government Palace and serves as the office of the Lebanese prime minister

Andrew paid the driver, got out and began walking towards the glass and steel entrance to the embassy which had a Union Jack placed above it. It was moving lazily in the warm breeze. As he walked, he briefly glanced to his left, noting that the taxi with the Turkish intelligence operative was parking up by the side of the road about fifty metres away under a couple of trees.

Andrew entered the cool interior of the embassy lobby and walked to the front desk where he gave his name and asked for Matt Jones. The receptionist asked him to take a seat in the waiting area, and one of the staff members soon brought him a paper cup with cold water, which he quickly drank. His suit was much too hot and heavy for this climate, and he couldn't wait to change out of it and into something more casual. After a few minutes, he heard footsteps approaching from behind and to his right.

'Mr Sterling?' said a deep voice.

Andrew rose to his feet and turned to see a stocky and fit-looking man in his late forties approaching him. The way he carried himself left Andrew with no doubt that he was a former service member. He had the demeanour and physique of a man at least ten years younger. He was wearing dark blue trousers and a light khaki long-sleeved shirt, and he had short dark hair. His face was somewhat leathery, and he had a friendly and calm air about him.

'I am Matt Jones,' he continued, a slight hint of a Welsh accent as he spoke. 'I'm in charge of security. And I'm also the quartermaster around here. Nice to meet you.'

The two men gave each other a firm handshake.

'Call me Andy,' said Andrew, keen to cut out the formalities.

'All right then,' smiled Jones. 'This way, please. The armoury is in the basement. You'll need to pass through the scanner.'

Jones led him towards the corner of the lobby, where a set of open stairs extended up through the building. There was a small cordoned-off area in front of it with two guards standing next to a security scanner.

'Please walk through here, sir,' said the guard in a friendly tone of voice.

Andrew took off his belt, placed it in a plastic tray along with his phone and wallet, and put his small suitcase in a separate tray. Then he walked through the small portal. The scanner immediately chirped twice, so one of the guards checked his pockets and asked him to take off his suit jacket. Andrew walked through again, and the guard then followed after him holding the jacket. The scanner chirped again. Andrew looked puzzled.

The guard walked to a desk and ran a handheld scanner over the jacket, and it instantly squealed and flashed a red light. The guard searched the pockets and extracted a small black circular object, roughly the size of a 5-pence coin but slightly thicker. He held it up in front of his face and studied it for a few seconds, turning it over as he did so.

'Looks like you've been bugged, sir,' said the guard and looked at Andrew. 'Any idea who or when?'

'I've got a pretty good idea, yes,' nodded Andrew and smiled wryly. 'A chap on the plane. Bumped into me. He must have slipped it into my pocket. Is it a tracking device?'

'Looks like it, sir,' replied the guard and slipped the device into a small sealable plastic bag. 'I'll have it sent to the lab. They'll have a look at it. They should be able to work out who it belongs to.'

'I'd be happy to wager that it says 'Made in Turkey' in tiny letters on the back,' said Andrew. 'Does this sort of thing happen a lot around here?'

The guard shrugged, looking unfazed. 'It happens.'

'Right,' said Jones, seemingly unperturbed. 'Let's get going. I was told you're on a schedule.'

'Sort of,' said Andrew as the guard handed him back his jacket. 'I am keen to see what you've got here.'

'Oh, I think you'll be pleasantly surprised,' said Jones. 'We have a pretty decent amount of kit. Can't be too careful in this part of the world.'

FIVE

Andrew and Jones descended two levels to a small area in front of a large metal door that looked more like the entrance to a bank vault than anything else. The door was painted a matt black and was operated by a keypad on the wall next to it. Jones punched in the correct code and the door's locking mechanisms snapped loudly inside their housings, after which the door swung open amid the sound of small hydraulic motors whirring.

'Jenkins in Istanbul told me you were in Iraq too?' said Andrew.

Jones nodded.

'I was,' he said. '42 Royal Marine Commandos. We were some of the first guys to go into southern Iraq after the Americans began their shock and awe campaign up in Baghdad.'

'Operation Telic,' said Andrew and nodded, referring to the codename for the overt British military operation during the Iraq War. 'You guys were tasked with taking Basra, weren't you?'

'That's right,' replied Jones. 'But before we could do that, we first had to secure the port of Umm Qasr and a large chunk of the Al-Faw peninsula. It was us, the US Marines and the Polish GROM special operations guys.'

'I've heard a lot of good things about GROM,' said Andrew. 'Never worked with them myself.'

Jones nodded. 'Top lads. Highly trained. Very professional. The Iraqi army put up more of a fight than the intel had suggested they would. Lots of sniper fire. The Marines lost one guy, and it took us two days to clear the old town just west of the port. I think we ended up taking something like 200 prisoners.'

'I guess that was before the Iraqis realised what they were actually up against,' said Andrew.

'Most likely. How about you?' asked Jones. 'Did you see any action?'

'You could say that,' said Andrew. 'I can't really give you the details, but we were in there for weeks looking for SCUDs and WMDs.'

'Didn't find many WMDs, I guess,' said Jones, knowingly.

'Yeah,' nodded Andrew ruefully and pressing his lips together. 'The less said about that the better.'

'Gotcha,' replied Jones, and then he smiled as if he had just thought of something funny. 'By the way,' he said. 'About Operation Telic. Apparently, it is a Greek word that means something like *purposeful action*, but someone came up with the idea that it really meant 'Tell Everyone Leave Is Cancelled'.'

Andrew chuckled.

'Clever,' he said. 'So, were you also part of the brigade that came up against the Fedayeen in Basra?' he asked, referring to a well-equipped Iraqi paramilitary group that was fiercely loyal to Saddam Hussein, and which had originally been established to quell internal unrest in the country. 'I've heard stories about that.'

'I was,' said Jones darkly. 'Crazy bastards. They gave us a tough time for a while. We took our first casualties there. It wasn't even that they had much better kit than the regulars, although I am sure they might have had slightly superior equipment. It was more about their mentality. Those guys were like the brownshirts of 1930s Germany. They were basically a bunch of political zealots. And they had absolute loyalty, not to the country but to Saddam himself. I remember one episode when my squad were on a flat roof of a house inside the old town, firing down at a street corner where a handful of Fedayeen were hiding. They knew we were there, and they could see we had a machine gun, an L7A2 if I remember correctly, and that thing is no joke. 750 rounds of 7.62 ammunition per minute. Anyway, they kept popping out to take potshots at us even though they had virtually no chance of hitting us behind our cover on that roof. Then suddenly, one of them stepped out with an RPG. He was fully exposed, but he still took the time to aim and fire. I don't know if he thought he was bulletproof or if he didn't care, but our machine gunner dumped something like twenty rounds into him. He still managed to get the RPG off, and the damn thing smacked into the wall of the house beneath us and exploded. It rained dust and dirt for a good while and we decided to pull back and reposition. If the enemy doesn't mind dying, then you suddenly have to think a bit differently about how you conduct yourself.'

'Sounds familiar to a lot of things I saw in Afghanistan,' said Andrew as they entered the armoury. 'Maybe we'll grab a beer some other time and swap stories.'

'Sounds good,' said Jones and hit the light switch. 'Anyway, here we are. Let's see what we've got for you.'

They entered a small room that was packed with gun racks and various weapons hanging on the walls. Andrew was taken aback by just how well-stocked the embassy was, but as Jones had correctly observed, one could never be too careful.

'I already know you'll probably want one of these,' said Jones and took down a Heckler & Koch MP5SD from a rack on the wall. 'Small. Quiet. Incredibly reliable. But I guess you're more than familiar with it.'

The MP5SD is the integrally suppressed version of what many in the special forces community consider to be the best submachine gun ever made. It is only 66 centimetres long and weighs 3,4 kilos, and it can fire approximately 800 rounds per minute.

'Very nice,' said Andrew and nodded, taking the submachine gun into his hands, feeling the familiar weight. 'I wouldn't go on a mission without this.'

He had fired tens of thousands of rounds with this weapon over the years, mainly on the firing range back at Hereford, and it instantly felt comfortable as he gripped it. It occurred to him that this model had been in service with the SAS for a lot longer than he had, although it had been further developed and improved several times over the years, unlike him.

The initial variant of the MP5SD was developed in the 1970s when the special forces of what at the time was West Germany asked the H&K manufacturer in Oberndorf in the far south of the country to develop a suppressed version of the standard MP5. In order to fully suppress the submachine gun and eliminate the loud dry crack from the report as the bullet leaves the muzzle, the Heckler & Kock engineers had to slow down the bullets from supersonic to subsonic. This was done by using a perforated barrel that bleeds gas when the gun is fired, and then by making the bullet pass through a series of metal gates inside the integrated suppressor. This innovative suppressor design is a large part of the reason why it is a favoured machine gun by special forces the world over. Because the suppressor is integrated into the weapon, the MP5SD is only marginally longer than the standard MP5, which allows it to remain useful in tight quarters during breaches and room clearing, or if covert operators are required to move through tight spaces to get to their objective. An added advantage to the suppressor is the fact that the already low recoil is reduced further due to the slower bullet velocity. Equally important is the fact that the suppressor eliminates muzzle flash, which in turn allows for the submachine gun to be fired at night without giving away the operator's position.

Andrew picked up one of the slightly curved steel magazines that have a capacity of 30 rounds of 9x19mm ammunition and slotted it into the main body of the gun where it locked into place with a satisfying click. He then pulled out the retractable stock and locked it in place. In a single continuous movement that hinted at the thousands of times he had done this over the past many years, he then yanked back the cocking handle, brought the weapon up in front of himself, pressed the stock into his right shoulder and tilted his head slightly to the right to look down the iron sight, his finger resting on the trigger. He quickly cycled the fire selector from safe to single fire, to two-round burst, to fully automatic and then back again, satisfied with how the weapon felt in his hands.

'All right,' he said, placing the submachine gun on a table in front of them. 'What have you got in terms of handguns? Do you happen to have a Glock 19?'

'I wouldn't call this a proper armoury without a few of those,' said Jones and pulled out a drawer in front of them that was packed with different handguns laid out neatly alongside small ammo boxes.

Andrew stepped forward and picked up the matte-black 9mm semi-automatic pistol. The dull finish made it look like it was made of metal, but it was in fact a polymer gun. It was equipped with an under-mounted laser and sported a 15-round magazine. Being a smaller version of the Glock 17, which was standard issue for many armies and police forces, the Glock 19 was lightweight and more compact. This made it ideal for being carried concealed, and it had been used extensively by different special forces operators around the world since its introduction in 2010. With a muzzle velocity of 375 metres per second, it had an effective firing range of around 50 metres. The Olight Baldr combined light and laser designator was mounted at the front of the barrel just under the muzzle, and it would provide Andrew with a powerful torch as well as a laser to allow him to see where his bullets would hit before he squeezed the trigger.

'You should take one of these as well,' said Jones and brought a cardboard box down from a shelf above his head.'

He placed it on the table and took the lid off to reveal something that would give Andrew a serious advantage in a pinch during the night. It was a set of Steiner AN PVS-21 night vision goggles. Unlike first-generation goggles that had long thin tubes placed in front of the user's eyes, thereby giving them only a very limited tunnel of vision in front of them, the Steiner goggles were effectively small augmented reality screens placed about an inch away from each eye, allowing the user to have full peripheral vision whilst still being able to look through the goggles with near perfect night vision.

Andrew made his way around the room, picking out additional things that he thought he might need. A tactical vest to hold gadgets and mags. A handheld military-grade GPS unit. Three hand grenades and a couple of flashbangs. He also picked out a thin full-body disposable hazmat suit that was packed into a pouch the size of a small handbag. It was not as durable as the real thing, but it was designed to be 100% effective against nerve agents and would do if the real thing was not available. He also grabbed a full-face gasmask, which, along with the hazmat suit should allow him to remain safe, at least for a time, even if he became exposed to a chemical agent aerosol. He also took a book-sized LCAD unit from a shelf and placed it in his bag. The Lightweight Chemical Agent Detector uses ion spectrometry to detect chemical warfare agents and would serve as an early warning system. Finally, he picked up two jet injector systems with atropine, just in case. This tropane alkaloid chemical is able to partially counteract the effects of nerve agents. It does this by blocking the receptors in the brain that would normally be sent into overdrive by nerve agents, thereby causing extreme salivation, lung secretions and convulsions if left untreated within just a few minutes of exposure.

He placed all of the kit inside a large black backpack, which he tied shut and slung over his shoulder.

'That'll do nicely,' he said and turned to Jones. 'Thanks, mate.'

'My pleasure,' said Jones with a sincere look on his face. 'Happy to help. Oh, and one more thing.'

He turned to one side and picked up a cardboard box which he opened. He then extracted a mobile phone which he gave to Andrew who studied it for a few seconds. It looked like some Chinese make that he had never heard of, and he could tell that it was definitely not new. In fact, it looked decidedly battered and third-hand.

'What's this?' he asked perplexed, looking up at Jones.

'That,' said Jones, 'is a knackered old phone with a prepaid SIM. One of our assets in Damascus bought it from a local shop there and had it transported here.

Once you're inside Syria, it will connect to the local network. It means you don't have to use any military communications equipment. You simply piggyback off the country's own mobile network. It only has one pre-programmed number, and that is Colonel Strickland's. The whole thing was his idea. If you need to make contact, then you use the encrypted messaging app already installed. It'll go straight to him, and Syrian intelligence will have no idea who is using it or what is being sent. Just don't use it too often, and obviously try not to send any sensitive information, just in case. The Russians are probably helping the Syrians sift through electronic communications, but Strickland's boffins were confident you would be out of there before they would have a chance to track you down, even if they were able to intercept and decrypt your messages.'

'Clever,' nodded Andrew. 'Hopefully I won't need it, but I suppose it is a good backup.'

'When do you want to leave?' asked Jones.

'The sooner the better,' said Andrew. 'I'd like to get close to the border just after sundown, so I should get a move on before too long.'

'All right,' said Jones. 'You should probably keep an eye out for Lebanese military intelligence, as well as the Russians and the Turks. There's a lot of spook cat-and-mouse shenanigans going on in this city.'

'Funny you should say that,' said Andrew with a wry smile. 'I seem to have made a new friend from Turkish intelligence. He followed me from Istanbul and is probably still sitting in a black Audi just down the street.'

'I see,' said Jones and nodded slowly. 'The chap from the plane?'

'That's the one,' replied Andrew.

'Well,' said Jones. 'Turkey tends to see itself as the main regional player, and they probably wouldn't think twice about shadowing a UK covert operation, or even intervening if they didn't like what they were seeing. They take quite an active interest here in Lebanon and in Syria too, which I think they consider to be part of their backyard. It was obviously all part of the Ottoman Empire once upon a time. It's a sphere-of-influence thing. Not unlike the way the Kremlin views Belarus and Ukraine. I think they call them White Russians and Little Russians respectively. That's more or less how the Turks treat other smaller countries in the Middle East. With Lebanon in particular, they can't seem to shake the idea that it is really theirs. And the Syrians feel exactly the same way about Lebanon too, so things can get quite complicated around here.'

'Could the Turks get the Lebanese to help them out and shadow someone like me?' asked Andrew.

'I am not sure,' replied Jones. 'Even if relations between the two countries would allow for this type of joint surveillance, I think it is unlikely that there would have been enough time for them to arrange it. But that's just my guess. I am no counter-intelligence expert.'

'You are probably right, though,' said Andrew. 'Anything else you think I should know?'

Jones thought for a moment. 'The only thing I would say is that your trip across the border might seem simple enough since the border is so porous.

But don't be complacent. Precisely because there are so many small roads crossing over, both countries patrol the border quite a bit. I am talking about well-armed military patrols, not just police and border force. So, you need to keep your wits about you. You'll have the benefit of crossing at night, but I wouldn't assume it is going to be easy.'

'All right. Thanks,' said Andrew. 'First, though, I need some wheels. I was going to rent a car, but since I am already being followed, I don't want to do it in either Doctor Elliot's name or in my own.'

Jones nodded and gave a quick thumbs up.

'All right, mate. I can go down to the airport at rent one for you and bring it back up here?'

'That would be great,' said Andrew. 'I would really appreciate that.'

'Consider it done,' said Jones. 'I can be back here in about an hour, so feel free to rest up in our cafeteria while I am gone. The local coffee is a huge step up from back in Old Blighty.'

'Thanks. And one last thing,' said Andrew. 'I was wondering if you could do me a favour and make sure that chap from Turkish intelligence doesn't follow me?'

'Sure,' said Jones without hesitation. 'What do you need?'

* * *

Just over an hour later, Matt Jones walked back into the cafeteria and found Andrew reclining in a chair with a cup of coffee.

'All set,' he said. 'The car is out the front. White Honda Corolla. Very ordinary-looking, just like you asked for. Here are the keys. Say, five minutes?'

'Yep. That sounds great,' said Andrew. Thanks. I really appreciate this.'

'No problem at all,' replied Jones with a wink and a grin. 'I am not the one who will have to deal with the insurance claim.'

Andrew nodded and finished the rest of his coffee in a large gulp.

'Take care, mate,' he said, wiping his mouth with the back of his hand.

'You too. See you in five.'

Jones disappeared out of the cafeteria towards the building's back entrance and the staff car park. Once there, he got into one of the small vehicles used by embassy staff to courier physical documents to different parts of the city when needed.

Andrew finished his coffee, picked up his backpack, rose from his seat and walked back into the lobby and out of the building. As soon as he exited, the heat hit him like a sledgehammer. Unlike most days here in this eastern Mediterranean city, there was barely any wind today, and he could practically feel his pores open up and begin sweating profusely. As he walked towards the white Honda, he pressed the button on the key and the car dutifully chirped once, its orange indicator lights flashing.

That thing had better have air conditioning, he thought. But then it occurred to him that it was probably impossible to sell a car in this city unless it had top-of-the-range air con.

He got in, closed the door and put the key in the ignition. Turning it, the engine and then the air con sprang to life, soon blasting him with cold air. He glanced casually up into the rear-view mirror and spotted the black Audi with the Turkish intel operative parked about thirty metres behind him further down the street. After less than a minute, the Honda was nice and cool, and he looked at his wristwatch.

Any second now, he thought.

The large sliding metal gates to the embassy's staff parking lot, which were almost directly across the street from the parked Audi, began to open noisily. That was Andrew's cue, so he placed his hand on the gear lever and put it into first, holding down the clutch. As soon as he saw the front of the embassy courier vehicle slowly emerging through the gate, he released the clutch and turned out into the road towards the west. Almost immediately, the Audi began moving out as well. As soon as it did so, however, Jones' courier vehicle accelerated out of the embassy gate and swerved in a wide arc onto and across the street where it slammed into the back left corner of the Audi. Even inside his own car, Andrew could hear the sound of metal crashing into metal, and of glass from headlights shattering and falling onto the road. The courier vehicle was smaller and lighter than the Audi, but it had picked up enough speed and kinetic energy to shunt the rear of the Audi to the right and up onto the pavement where it ended up jammed between the courier vehicle and a large cedar tree.

Steam rose from the deformed front of the courier vehicle and a tall bearded man jumped out of the

Audi, waving his arms and looking agitated. Andrew watched as Jones got out of the courier vehicle unsteadily and put his hands on his head, gawping at the damage he had caused and feigning distress. He was clearly embracing his role. The bearded man turned and looked in exasperation in the direction of Andrew's Honda as it drove away. Then he reached inside his suit for a phone.

Sorry mate, Andrew smiled, looking at the man in the rear-view mirror. *All is fair in love and war.*

SIX

Nadeem Yassin arrived at his gallery in the City of London just after 8:30 a.m. and unlocked the sturdy metal-framed glass front door. The gallery was on the corner of Ludgate Hill and Dean's Court, directly opposite the enormous St Paul's Cathedral and the square in front of it called St Paul's Churchyard. This location ensured a steady flow of tourists coming into the gallery every single day of the week. Of course, the vast majority of them were nowhere near wealthy enough to buy anything, even if they were cultured enough to understand what they were looking at, and they usually weren't. But every once in a while, prospective customers would enter the gallery, usually couples, and typically a man in his fifties or sixties with a significantly younger female companion.

Yassin liked to think that he could spot prospects as soon as they entered his gallery. By now, he had a pretty good sense of who might end up purchasing something or bidding on a piece of ancient art at an auction. What usually gave it away was the way in which the men would perform their man-of-the-world routine, holding forth about the items on display while the young ladies fawned dutifully over their knowledge and wisdom, as well as their ability to simply buy anything they fancied. Business had been good over the time he had owned the gallery, and he had made huge profits from the imported items from his homeland.

Yassin had grown up in a wealthy suburb of Damascus. His father was a bureaucrat in the Ministry of Finance and his mother was a homemaker, and Nadeem was an only child with a normal and happy upbringing. His interest in archaeology had been kindled by his father who had taken him on outings to Palmyra and other ancient sites when he was around ten years old. His father had told him about the ancient civilisations in that part of the world, which predated European civilisations by millennia. And he had explained how the hunter-gatherers had settled in this land and become the first people on Earth to domesticate, breed and enhance crops and livestock over countless generations. His father's passion for the ancient past, and his pride in his native Syria, which in many ways was the cradle of civilisation, rubbed off on the young Nadeem. When he was old enough, he enrolled as a history student at Damascus University in the centre of the capital just opposite Damascus National Museum.

After his studies, his uncle, who was a very well-connected officer in the Syrian Army, had arranged for him to be offered a job at the museum. Nadeem had jumped at the chance but had quickly become disillusioned by the bureaucracy and the lack of imagination exhibited by that institution. The employees and so-called researchers there seemed more concerned with internal power struggles and prestige than with organising new archaeological digs and recovering more of Syria's magnificent ancient past.

After almost a decade, Nadeem had been on the verge of quitting, when one day he had an unannounced visit from his uncle who had presented him with a simple proposition. Nadeem would be given a team of young archaeologists and a free hand to find and remove whatever he wanted from Syria's many cultural heritage sites. His uncle would arrange for military protection of the sites while they worked, and he would also ensure that the artefacts were spirited away to serious buyers, mainly abroad. The plan was for Nadeem and his uncle to split the profits evenly. Nadeem did not have to think about the proposition for long before he agreed, and not just because his uncle was a force of nature who never took 'No' for an answer. He knew that some might say that he was assisting foreigners in robbing Syria of her historical treasures, but that was not how he had come to view it. From his perspective, these treasures were indeed valuable cultural artefacts, but the sad truth was that they were safer in well-guarded museums or with zealous private collectors in European capitals than they would ever be in an unstable country like Syria. The experience of ISIS and the way they had ravaged cultural heritage sites across the country was ample proof of that. So, all he was really doing was making sure that the necessary excavations took place and that the artefacts ended up in a safe place. If he then found himself making lots of cash in the process, then he saw nothing wrong with that. As far as he was concerned, this way, everyone was a winner.

Three years ago, Yassin's uncle had helped him secure funding for a more prominent location for his gallery in London. The money for the purchase was not ultimately his uncle's, but he had never revealed who had fronted the not-inconsiderable sum required for buying a location like this outright and with cash. The new gallery was not any bigger than the old one, and it did not serve its purpose any better, but its location was unbeatable. Only later did his uncle tell him its true purpose.

He now knew that he was on the clock, in a manner of speaking. He needed to shift as many artefacts as he could through the gallery and the auction house before the second weekend of November, after which his gallery would be unusable and he would have to give up his life in the UK and disappear. But he had had a good run of it by any standard, and he wasn't bitter. And at any rate, coming across as bitter or ungrateful was not something his uncle would react well to. Especially since he had single-handedly enabled Yassin's entire career in London and the good life he had led there. Without his uncle, Nadeem Yassin would still be in Damascus earning peanuts and being bossed around by two-legged fossils with no idea what was possible if they would just think outside the box once in a while. Of course, all of that was irrelevant now. This chapter of his life was coming to an end, and he had accepted that fact. But he was going to make sure that he made the most of it during the time he had left.

Yassin stepped inside the gallery, disabled the alarm system and engaged the electric motors that retracted the protective metal grille that was lowered just behind the gallery's large windows every evening at closing time.

The interior was roughly fifteen metres wide and thirty metres long, and it sported large floor-to-ceiling windows out to the street. Placed prominently in those windows were four Greco-Roman busts on pedestals, two on each side of the door. The floor was made from large dark green veined marble tiles, and the walls were covered in discreet black-painted wood panels. Along both walls stretching towards the back of the gallery were arranged a number of artefacts, each one placed inside a glass display box sitting on a solid-looking tapered marble-clad pedestal. There were plenty of busts and reliefs, but also a few ornate vases. Each artefact had an engraved brass plate mounted on its pedestal, describing the item and listing its provenance. The brass plates were cheap to make, especially considering some of the sums being paid for the artefacts themselves, but they helped give the gallery an air of seriousness and trustworthiness that was impossible to put a price on. Above each artefact was a carefully positioned spotlight, bathing the relics in soft golden light and making them stand out like beacons in the otherwise dark and moody space.

Over the next hour or so, Yassin politely entertained two prospective customers, one of which might have some potential, the other just another one of those people who liked to pretend to be wealthy for fifteen minutes of their otherwise uninteresting lives. Yassin had learnt to accept these people as an unavoidable part of doing business, but he was always relieved when they finally ended up leaving.

At one point, the door to the street opened, and in walked a stunning woman who looked to be in her early thirties. She had long dark hair, wore immaculate makeup and was dressed in an understated but elegant dark purple dress under a long black coat. Her gold jewellery completed the ensemble.

Yassin pretended to be busy behind the small reception desk located on the left just inside the gallery. Out of the corner of his eye, he watched as the woman approached, one black high-heeled shoe at a time as she strode calmly and confidently across the green marble floor towards him.

'Hello,' she said sweetly in a genteel accent, just as he straightened up and raised his gaze to look straight at her.

Very nice, he thought to himself.

'Good morning, Madam,' he said with a faint Arabic accent and giving her a well-practised smile that was somewhere between obsequiousness and an eagerness to please.

Her reaction would tell him what sort of person she was. A time-waster without the funds to back up her presence in his gallery, or someone who could genuinely afford his wares.

Fiona nodded courteously, smiled and held his gaze without replying, clearly expecting the man behind the reception desk to make more of an effort to make her feel welcome and attempt to accommodate her wishes. Yassin smiled inwardly. This woman was the real deal.

'Please,' continued Yassin, stepping out from behind the reception desk and offering his hand. 'My name is Nadeem Yassin. How may I help you today?'

Fiona took his hand and then lifted it ever so slightly upwards, signalling to him that he was expected to kiss it. Yassin dutifully complied, instantly sensing her delicate perfume. Rose petals?

'Nadeem,' said Fiona, maintaining her cut-glass accent and smiling warmly. 'My name is Scarlett. Very nice to meet you.'

'And you, Madam' said Yassin, returning her smile, but not daring to be so presumptuous as to use her name.

'It's Miss,' said Fiona amiably.

'Very well, Miss Scarlett,' replied Yassin, and gave a tiny bow of the head.

'What a gorgeous gallery,' said Fiona appreciatively, taking her time to turn slowly and look at the gallery's interior. 'I don't think there is anything quite like it anywhere in London.'

'Thank you,' said Yassin fawningly, giving a small bow and genuinely feeling flattered. 'I designed it myself. I wanted something sumptuous and sufficiently opulent so as not to put these magnificent pieces of art to shame.'

He gestured to the many glass display boxes lining the walls.

'Well,' smiled Fiona, gently tossing her hair to one side. 'I dare say you succeeded. It's lovely, and it really does do these amazing artefacts justice. How long have you owned it?'

'I bought it and refurbished the whole thing three years ago,' replied Yassin. 'We used to be near Regent's Park, but we wanted a more prominent location in London, and I thought this would fit the bill very nicely.'

'So, you bought it?' asked Fiona, sounding impressed. 'It must have been very expensive.'

'Yes,' said Yassin and nodded. 'We bought the property outright. No sense in paying a landlord every month, and potentially being kicked out at the end of every rental period. We needed stability, and we had the funds to make sure that we acquired just the right place for what we need.'

'Yes, that makes sense,' said Fiona, smiling at him and holding his gaze for just a little bit too long. 'Do you have somewhere we can sit? I would like to discuss a specific type of artefact that I am looking to acquire.'

'Certainly,' said Yassin and motioned towards two identical forest-green chaise longues that had been placed around a small and shiny brass coffee table halfway along one of the gallery's walls.

You can stay for as long as you like, he thought.

The two of them sat down on one of the chaise longues, and as Fiona made herself comfortable, she crossed her legs first one way and then the other, making sure to allow Yassin to see her lower leg through the slit in her purple dress.

'Before we begin,' said Fiona, now sounding very business-like and causing Yassin to sit up and pay careful attention to what she was saying. 'I need to ask you about what procedures you have in place for ensuring that you don't accidentally end up selling either stolen goods or forgeries.'

Yassin nodded gravely and took a moment to appear pensive.

'I understand,' he said. 'Your concern is, of course, very valid. I am sure we have both read stories about forgeries and stolen artefacts being sold at auction right here in this very city. Well, let me assure you that we carry out exhaustive research into the provenance and previous ownership of every piece you see in this gallery. To this end, we make use of an international database of stolen objects, but we also employ independent investigators to track down all available information about an individual piece, and we obviously use experts in their fields to ensure that we are not dealing with forgeries. And naturally, all the relevant paperwork from those efforts is available to prospective buyers.'

'Very well,' said Fiona, looking somewhat placated. 'I have a growing collection of Assyrian art, and as you can imagine, I would be horrified to discover that one of those had been looted from an archaeological site.'

'We have a private little mantra here,' said Yassin. '*Provenance is paramount*,' he continued, looking pleased with his alliteration, which he clearly thought made him sound clever and educated. 'Without reliable and trustworthy information about the provenance of a piece of art, we wouldn't have a business at all.'

He's an amazing liar, thought Fiona.

'So, tell me,' she said with a demeanour that indicated that she was now happy to move on to specifics. 'Would you happen to have anything from

Palmyra? I was keen to purchase a funerary relief from there at an auction at Christie's last year, but I was abroad at the time and missed out. Something a bit like this perhaps?'

Reaching into her handbag she extracted her phone. She quickly swiped across the screen a few times and showed Yassin a now closed auction listing from the highly reputable London auction house Christie's. It showed a detailed limestone relief of the head and torso of a woman. She was draped in what was clearly a thin garment that was attached to her left shoulder with an elaborate brooch. Her hair was covered by a headdress with a diadem holding it in place, and her face looked serene and youthful. Her right hand was held raised in front of her with the palm facing out, which is a gesture frequently seen on funerary portraits from Palmyra, possibly as some sort of protective gesture. Underneath the image of the relief was a small piece of text saying 'North Syrian Limestone Funerary Relief of Young Woman. 1st or 2nd century BCE. Estimate: 16,000 - 12,000 GBP.'

'Marvellous,' said Yassin, studying the image. 'As I am sure you are aware, hundreds of these reliefs have been recovered from Palmyrene communal tombs, but I must say that this is a most exquisite piece. So well preserved. And what a beautiful subject she was.'

Yassin glanced up at Fiona with a smile, looked back down at the image on her phone and then back up at her, seemingly studying her face for a moment.

'Not unlike yourself,' he smiled sycophantically. 'You two happen to look very alike.'

Fiona was momentarily thrown by the directness of the attempted compliment, but she quickly regained her composure and smiled shyly at Yassin.

'Thank you,' said, fluttering her eyelashes a couple of times, pretending to be flattered. 'So, do you have anything similar to this that might be going up for auction soon?'

'Possibly,' said Yassin, looking up at the ceiling for a moment, as if trying to remember what might be lined up for his next auction. 'Or perhaps…'

He paused and glanced at her with a conspiratorial smile. 'Perhaps we can source something, just for you.'

'You mean, without going through the auction process?' asked Fiona, sounding surprised but intrigued. 'Is that possible? I mean, are you allowed to do that?'

'I can do as I please,' replied Yassin, gesturing to the gallery. 'This is my gallery, and I am not obligated to sell anything to anyone I don't like. Similarly, I can sell my pieces through auction, or I can sell them directly to my customers if I like them and if I think we might be able to do more business in the future. Some customers also prefer to deal directly with me on a per-item basis so as to avoid publicity. I am sure you understand.'

'Oh, of course,' nodded Fiona. 'Some things are best kept private.'

'Absolutely,' said Yassin, seemingly content that they understood each other.

'If I give you an email address, could you keep me updated?' asked Fiona. 'I am very keen not to miss out again.'

'Of course,' replied Yassin, taking out his phone from his suit pocket. 'Let me just write it down.'

'Sorry, one moment,' said Fiona, reaching into her handbag to extract her own phone once again, but before she did so, she snapped the small black device she had taken from Andrew's safe onto it. 'I just need to make sure I give you the right one.'

Yassin waited patiently as Miss Scarlett swiped the screen on her phone a number of times, seemingly trying to find her own email address. As she did so, Yassin took the welcome opportunity to admire her features.

Gorgeous, he thought. *I might ask her out.*

Suddenly Fiona's face changed, and she placed one hand on the seat next to her as if to steady herself.

'I am suddenly not feeling so well,' she said, sounding drowsy and disorientated. 'Is it very hot in here?'

'Uhm, no Miss,' replied Yassin, looking confused, then placing his phone on the coffee table and moving closer to her. 'Are you all right?'

Fiona creased her forehead and looked anxious. 'I really don't feel well at all. Do you have a restroom I could use?'

'Certainly,' said Yassin and got to his feet, offering her his hand to steady herself with. 'This way please.'

Fiona allowed him to lead her through the long gallery towards the back of the building. She made sure to walk slowly and to look unsteady on her feet, so as to allow the device to connect to Yassin's phone which was now lying right next to hers. Within a few seconds, the snooping app should connect to his phone via Bluetooth, spoofing it into behaving as if it was talking to a backup server. Once her app had established a connection, it then spent less than ten seconds hacking the access codes by running through millions of possible password combinations. As soon as it had found the right password, the app then cloned the entire contents of Yassin's phone in less than a minute. Every file, photo, text message and email Yassin had ever sent or received was copied onto a separate partition on Fiona's phone for later analysis. When Fiona returned to the chaise lounge, flanked by an anxious-looking Yassin, her phone had finished its task and had terminated the Bluetooth connection.

'Thank you for your help,' said Fiona, picking up her phone and swiping the screen. 'I don't know what that was all about.'

'That's quite all right,' said Yassin.

'Anyway, here is my email address,' she said and showed Yassin a fictitious address she had typed into her phone before leaving home.

'May I… call you?' asked Yassin clumsily. 'I mean, just to make sure you are all right.'

'That is ever so kind of you,' said Fiona. 'I think I am all right now. Thank you for your time today. It was nice meeting you. Hopefully, I will hear from you soon about another funerary relief.'

Then she turned and walked out of the galley, leaving a frustrated yet composed Yassin to watch her as she swept out onto the pavement where the wind momentarily caught her perfectly conditioned hair and made it billow out behind her. She continued along Ludgate Hill towards the west. After a few minutes, she began to feel more relaxed. She was quite pleased with her own performance as Miss Scarlett, and as she walked along the pavement, she had a small spring in her step.

I could get used to this cloak-and-dagger stuff, she thought.

SEVEN

Andrew drove west along Charles Helou Avenue past Beirut's container port for just over five minutes, after which he turned right onto the Beirut to Damascus International Highway, also known as Route 30. This quickly took him out of the city centre, and then the highway began winding its way gently upwards and almost due east across the foothills of the Mount Lebanon mountain range. After about two hours, during which he regularly looked in the rear-view mirror and made a mental note of the cars behind him, Andrew drove over the low mountain pass that led into the Beqaa Valley, which is a flat and fertile valley approximately fifteen kilometres wide. It represents the northern end of the Great Rift Valley that stretches more than 500 kilometres from northern Syria towards the south through Israel to the Red Sea. It was dusk as he passed through the large but sleepy-looking town of Bar Elias situated in the middle of the valley, with the Mount Lebanon range to the west and the Anti-Lebanon Mountains to the east, behind which lay the border with Syria.

After less than ten kilometres, he turned off Route 30 and continued south. As he did so, he was able to see the busy Masnaa border crossing sitting at the foot of the hills a few hundred metres away to his left. The sun soon disappeared behind the Mount Lebanon range to the west, and he continued south along the mountains for about five kilometres, passing through the village of Hammarah, after which he took a left turn towards the small town of Mazraat Deir al-Ashayer which was only a couple of kilometres from the border. As the road snaked its way further up the Anti-Lebanon mountain range towards the town and the Syrian border, the green and fertile Beqaa Valley gave way to an increasingly arid, pale orange and rocky terrain.

When he reached the town, he quickly found his intended destination. It was a petrol station on the outskirts of the eastern part of the town, and as he pulled into the car park, darkness was descending across the dry and rocky landscape. Behind the car park was open ground with sparse vegetation stretching away towards the foothills several hundred metres away towards the east. The sky was now rapidly changing colour from orange into a washed-out blue, to dark indigo to almost perfect black. There was a streetlight just next to the petrol station entrance and a floodlight mounted on a pole at the back of the car park. The petrol station was open, but there were no customers. Inside stood a single staff member hunched over the counter and seemingly reading something. He either did not notice or did not care to look as the white Honda Corolla pulled into the car park and came to a stop in a bay at the very back, out of view of the shop.

Andrew remained in the car for a few minutes to observe the sparse traffic on the road. Satisfied that he had not been followed from Damascus, he then grabbed his backpack and exited the car. He left the keys in the ignition, the driver's side door slightly open, and the interior light on and easily visible from the road. He was hoping that some kindly but criminal soul would steal the car at some point over the next several hours, preferably driving it far away and taking it apart to sell for spare parts. The odds of that happening were not bad, and Jones would no doubt come up with a suitable cover story for the rental company.

Andrew walked briskly towards the door to a customer toilet that was part of the petrol station's main building. He went inside and checked the three cubicles. All empty. He entered the one furthest from the door to the outside and began changing out of his suit and into clothes that he felt infinitely more comfortable in. Black trousers and a tight-fitting jacket. Boots. Tactical vest. Belt with holster and the loaded Glock 19 with its mounted suppressor. He left the MP5SD with its stock folded inside the backpack. There was no need to equip that just yet. After less than five minutes he was ready.

He exited the cubicle, walked to the door and peeked outside. The car park was empty. Then he grabbed the Glock 19 from its holster, brought it up, aimed at the floodlight at the back of the car park and fired a single suppressed shot. The pistol produced a muffled thwack and only a small amount of recoil. A fraction of a second later the 9mm bullet tore through the floodlight's hard transparent plastic cover and blew apart the light bulb. The light immediately winked out, and then the car park was plunged into almost complete darkness.

Andrew put the pistol back in its holster, stepped outside and put the backpack onto his back. Then he vaulted adeptly over the low fence at the back of the car park and began jogging across the open weed-covered ground towards the low hills in the distance.

He knew that his average speed across even terrain with personal pack and weapons was about two klicks per hour. It was called 'tabbing', a TAB being the acronym for Tactical Advance to Battle. It was probably one of the best-rehearsed training activities in the Regiment, which was always keen to cultivate the quality of endurance, both physical and mental.

More than anything, this type of situation reminded him of that formative period during SAS selection in the UK around the Brecon Beacons in South Wales, hauling a fully laden Bergen across the peaks, and navigating the terrain using only a map and a compass. The recruits would carry heavy loads and push their bodies to the limit, making the physical exertion he had previously experienced in the regular army look like a casual stroll in Hyde Park. Later on, they had been sent on simulated escape and evade missions, where they were tasked with traversing the countryside from A to B during the night. This would happen whilst trying to evade the aptly named *Hunter Force* of SAS officers tasked with finding and capturing him and his aspiring candidates. Capture, as it turned out, was inevitable, after which the simulated captivity and interrogation by Arabic-speaking instructors had proven remarkably realistic. After several days without food or sleep, it became difficult to hang on to reality, and some of the candidates were simply unable to hack it and ended up quitting. For Andrew, it was an experience that gave him a clear sense of where his own limits lay, both physically and psychologically, but he managed to hang on and he eventually graduated. It was not an experience he was keen to repeat.

As darkness had fallen over the foothills of the Anti-Mount Lebanon range, the temperature had dropped and the humidity in the air had begun to rise noticeably as the moisture in the ground escaped and filled the air with a sweet smell. It was as if the land was breathing a sigh of relief after another scorching hot day.

Traversing the landscape in the pale light from the half-moon in the sky above, the regular crunch-crunch of his boots on the dry rocky ground, as well as his elevated but steady breathing and heartbeat, soon put him back into a mode that his body knew well. The rhythm of his feet was almost like a trance that was regulated, not by his brain, but by his body as it ambulated steadily across the terrain. After all these years in the Regiment, he knew his own body exceptionally well, and he was now pushing it hard, but without making the needle go into the red. Like all the other successful SAS selection candidates, he had long ago learned to push to an optimal level of exertion, where he would make the best progress on a cross-country tab for the smallest amount of energy expenditure. On a scale of 0 to 100, he needed to be around the 80 mark, and he was able to gauge if he was slipping even slightly below or above that level. He was in 'the zone'.

As his body switched to autopilot and did what it was trained to do, his mind invariably drifted to other thoughts. To Fiona. She was probably at home on the sofa right now, reading one of her archaeology books or watching a movie. In many ways, the two of them were exceptionally compatible, and yet at the same time, they often had fundamentally different outlooks on life and the world at large. She believed that people were inherently good and that only circumstances could conspire to make them do evil things. Andrew had always seen the world differently, believing that some people were just hardwired to be violent and unscrupulously selfish in their pursuit of what they wanted. But what if she was right? Could anyone be able to transform into a monster if presented with a sufficiently toxic cocktail of chaotic circumstances? Could he?

Nearing the ridge up ahead, he stopped for breath for a few minutes. He turned to look back down at the town of Bar Elias around eight kilometres away, that at this time of the evening seemed to be lit up brightly. Facing forward again, he could see the ridge up ahead. The unmarked border with Syria ran along the ridgeline itself, which had steep slopes on both sides. He was unlikely to come across patrols up here, simply because there was no way to lay down a road. He checked his location on the GPS tracker and decided to adjust his course slightly south in order to make sure he hit his pre-determined waypoints. A quick time check told him that it was now 23:52. He was supposed to make contact with Faisal in thirty-eight minutes.

Pushing on, he finally made it to the top of the ridge. It was noticeably cooler at this altitude, but he was still sweating from the ascent. There was an overgrown walking trail running along the ridgeline, but it did not appear to be well travelled. It might even have been an animal track. After another thirty metres of walking along the track towards the east and down a gentle slope, he found himself with a view down into Syria. The faint city lights of Damascus in the far distance gave the hazy sky above it a pale orange hue. Scanning the landscape, Andrew could not see a single residential building nearby. The whole area near the border was barren and lifeless. Perhaps no one wanted to live in what might again become an open conflict area if Syria decided to invade Lebanon as it had done once before in 1976.

Down the slope directly in front of him was the Beirut to Damascus highway that curved north and then west to the border crossing in the pass roughly three kilometres northeast of his position. On the far side of the highway, he could make out the service station that was to be his rendezvous point with Faisal. He estimated that it was about a kilometre away. At this time of night, it would be practically deserted since the border crossing had closed at 5 p.m.

He suddenly heard the characteristic sound of helicopter rotor blades in the distance. It was very faint at first but gradually became louder. After a few seconds, he spotted red and green navigation lights flashing in the dark sky several kilometres away. The chopper was flying north to south, parallel to the border and quite low. Andrew tracked it with his eyes until it disappeared behind the mountaintops to the south, the warbled thudding sound echoing across the mountains and fading slowly until he could no longer hear it.

He proceeded carefully down the rocky slope ahead of him. His eyes had adjusted to the darkness soon after leaving the car behind, but he still needed to be careful. Breaking a leg now and needing medical assistance just might be sufficiently embarrassing to make Colonel Strickland deny ever having heard of anyone called Sterling, and Andrew wouldn't have blamed him.

Once he had descended the steep slope on the eastern side of the mountain range and proceeded into a relatively flat wadi with sparse vegetation in the form of bushes and tufts of grass, Andrew got out his detachable scope and knelt behind a large rock. He trained his scope on the service station which was now about 200 metres away. He could see one driver standing by a pump next to his vehicle as he filled it up, and there were a couple of other cars parked off to the side. One of them was a white Toyota Land Cruiser that looked like it had seen better days. He watched and waited while the man filled up his car, went inside to pay and then drove off east along the highway towards Damascus. Then he pulled out a flashlight from his backpack and pointed it at the Toyota. He pressed the button twice in quick succession. After a few seconds, the Toyota flashed its headlights twice in reply. It was Faisal.

As agreed, Andrew pulled back around thirty metres and got himself in between the dry bushes and out of sight of the highway. He took off his backpack, knelt down and waited. After a couple of minutes, he heard the faint crunching sound of tyres approaching on dry gravelly ground. Then he spotted the Toyota parking up near him on the other side of some bushes. Its headlights were off, but he could just make out the silhouette of a man inside. With his pistol out, Andrew moved through the bushes towards the car as the man exited.

'As-Salaam-Alaikum', said Andrew calmly, raising his left hand in greeting whilst still gripping his suppressed pistol, safety off.

The man had not heard Andrew approach, so the greeting made him jump and turn around to face the black-clad figure that was now only a few metres away and directly behind him.

'Wa-Alaikum-Salaam,' the man replied, sounding nervous.

'Faisal?' said Andrew, trying to sound relaxed and friendly.

'Yes, Faisal,' said the man in slightly accented but otherwise good English, stammering slightly. 'Sorry. They did not tell me your name.'

'It is probably better for you if you don't know anything about me,' said Andrew evenly, holstering his weapon.

As he got closer, he was struck by how young the man was. He couldn't have been much more than twenty. How had he become one of the UK's human intelligence assets in a country like Syria? How had he been recruited, and by whom? Andrew decided that those were questions for another time. Right now, they needed to get moving.

Faisal stuck out his hand in greeting, and Andrew took it and gave it a firm squeeze.

'Nice to meet you,' said Faisal. 'I am happy to help you.'

'Glad to hear it,' said Andrew, struck by the young man's earnestness. 'How far to Damascus?'

'It is about 20 kilometres,' replied Faisal. 'Maybe half an hour.'

'Any roadblocks or checkpoints?' asked Andrew.

'No,' said Faisal shaking his head. 'It is late now. Everything is fine.'

'All right,' said Andrew and nodded. He liked the young lad. 'Let's get…'

Suddenly the whole area was bathed in cold white light. Less than fifty metres away, a car had turned on a set of four powerful headlights pointing directly at them. As they came on, a brief *whoop* and a couple of blue flashes came from the vehicle. Then the sound of car doors opening beyond the blinding light, boots on gravel and the distinct sound of weapons being cocked.

Shit, thought Andrew. *Here we fucking go.*

Faisal stood frozen to the spot for a couple of seconds but then raised his hands in surrender, turning slowly towards the lights. Andrew, however, was already moving around the Toyota towards the driver's side, opening the passenger door and slinging his backpack onto the seat.

'Get back in!' he shouted and slammed the door shut. 'Passenger side. Now! I am driving!'

After a brief moment of hesitation, Faisal scrambled into the car and Andrew jumped in behind the wheel of the left-hand drive vehicle. He turned the key and the engine of the old but powerful four-wheel-drive car roared to life. Andrew immediately slammed the gear lever into first, revved the engine and let go of the clutch. The Land Cruiser's wheels spun in the dirt, kicking up dust as the car leapt forward and fish-tailed slightly on the loose gravel.

Soon they were racing along a dirt track, which Andrew guessed ran roughly in a south-easterly direction away from the highway and more or less parallel to the ridge to their right. Andrew had switched on the long beam and was pushing the car as much as he dared, mindful that he wasn't exactly on home turf and that skidding off the road and into a ditch at high speed right now would be very bad indeed. Faisal was holding on to the armrest on the passenger side door, and steadying himself against the dashboard as the Toyota Land Cruiser lurched this way and that way along the dirt track. His face was a mask of terror. This was clearly more than he had bargained for. Then there was the familiar dry pop-pop-pop of semi-automatic gunfire from behind them. The passenger in the police car was leaning out of the window and firing on the move.

Bloody hell! The police have automatic weapons? thought Andrew, as he grimaced and glanced up into the rear-view mirror. *Maybe they are not police. Did they know I was coming?*

Faisal did not seem to realise what was happening, as he was pointing ahead of them out through the windscreen and indicating a left turn.

'Down that way', he shouted over the noise from the roaring engine and the gravel slamming up into the wheel hubs. He was pointing at a small road that led back towards the highway.

'Are you sure?' shouted Andrew, not convinced that driving onto the highway would be the best idea right now.

The first few volleys from the shooter in the patrol car went wide, or perhaps they had been intended as warning shots, but the third volley connected with the rear of the Land Cruiser, peppering it with bullets. One of them punched loudly through the rear window, shattering it and sending small pellets of glass cascading onto the backseat, after which it hit the roof above their heads at a shallow angle and lodged itself somewhere between the plastic covering and the metal. Faisal yelped, suddenly realising what was happening, and then he produced a panicked stream of words that were a barely comprehensible mix of English and Arabic.

Andrew swerved the car from side to side as he raced along the dirt road, trying to make it harder for the shooter to land his shots. It also has the effect of throwing up clouds of dust behind them, which partly obscured the Land Cruiser as the pursuer's headlights lit them up in the darkness.

After a couple of moments with no firing, the shooter apparently became frustrated, because he let loose with fully automatic fire, spraying bullets into the dust cloud head of him until his submachine gun clicked and the magazine was dry. Several of the bullets smacked into the rear of the Toyota with loud metallic pings. Then the firing stopped.

'Bloody hell!' shouted Andrew with an almost maniacal grin on his face, gallows humour being part of the standard special forces toolkit.

'Are you all right?' he said, turning his head to look at Faisal. The young man sat unmovingly and looked straight ahead. At first, Andrew thought he had gone into shock, but then his head lolled forward and slumped down onto his chest, blood dripping out of his mouth. A high-powered bullet from the submachine gun had hit Faisal's headrest, expanded like a hollow-point bullet and continued into the back of his head where it had slammed into his brain, causing terminal damage during the final part of its journey.

'Fuck!' exclaimed Andrew, his eyes locked on the young man's face for a moment.

Opting against going back towards the highway, Andrew instead decided that the Land Cruiser's four-wheel-drive system was his best shot at getting away. He yanked the wheel to the right and the Land Cruiser swerved off the dirt road and through a clump of low bushes. It continued across the uneven terrain, its suspension system working overtime to keep the car level and the tyres connected to the rough ground underneath. As hard a job as that was, Andrew could see in his rear-view mirror that the pursuing car was having even more trouble. Its headlights were bouncing and swerving wildly behind him. Either the men following him were in a regular car, or the driver had received no training in high-speed driving across terrain like this.

Up ahead, at the foot of a steep incline leading up to the ridge above, Andrew spotted a collection of huge boulders lit up by the Land Cruiser's headlight. The several-metre-high boulders must have tumbled down from the ridge long ago, and they had now settled firmly in the flat wadi below. Andrew swerved again and headed straight for them. He drove as close as he dared to the nearest one, opening the driver's side door as he passed. Then he put the car into neutral and jumped out, rolling rapidly across the ground as the Land Cruiser continued forward without him under its own momentum. He banged his left elbow on a rock and swore at the pain. As soon as he was able, he scrambled to his feet and bolted for cover in the darkness behind the boulders. Pulling out his Glock 19 and panting heavily, he now felt much more comfortable. This was *his* home turf. They were now playing by *his* rules.

The pursuing car braked hard as soon as its driver saw Andrew exit the Land Cruiser and head for the boulders. There was a moment of relative calm, and then the pursuing car moved forward a couple of metres, turning slightly to the left to allow its headlights to bathe the boulders in their bright light. Two men got out, both of them carrying automatic weapons. They said nothing as they advanced towards the boulders with their weapons up.

Inside less than a second, three suppressed shots were fired from somewhere behind the boulders, all three of them finding their mark in a tight grouping in the chest of one of the men. He dropped his weapon and staggered before toppling over and falling face-first onto the rocky ground where he lay completely still. A small cloud of dust whirled up around him as he dropped directly in front of the patrol car's powerful headlight. His companion quickly scrambled back towards the vehicle and took cover behind it. He was breathing heavily, aiming his weapon at where he had last seen the black-clad man.

Suddenly he thought he heard footsteps off to his side, so he swung his weapon around and aimed into the darkness. The night was almost completely silent, apart from a few cicadas producing their characteristic rapid clicking sound. A small rock landed a few metres behind the man, clacking into a larger boulder and bouncing off to roll a couple of times across the ground. The man spun around and let out an involuntary grunt of fear and frustration at being toyed with in this way. Then he thought he heard the soft crunch of a boot on the ground directly behind him, and as he spun around once again, he raised his weapon and prepared to open fire.

He only managed to get a brief glimpse of the black-clad figure out of the corner of his eye before a single suppressed shot rang out. The bullet slammed into his forehead and jerked his head back. His knees instantly gave way and he fell onto his back in an ungainly fashion, his knees bent all the way back and his arms splayed out to the sides.

Andrew walked up and stood over him, still pointing the Glock 19 at his face. Then he lowered it and studied the man's black border patrol uniform. He exhaled slowly and evenly.

That'll do, he thought and began removing the uniform from the dead border guard, making sure not to get any blood on it.

He put the uniform jacket over his own black shirt, donned the guard's cap and rolled the man's shirt and trousers up into a bundle. Then he walked back to where the Land Cruiser had come to a stop. Faisal's body was now slumped fully forward, blood-matted hair dangling from his forehead and a large red pool in his lap and on the seat. Andrew pressed his lips together regretfully. This was not how things were meant to go.

He briefly considered trying to find an old well or some other way to dispose of the three bodies, but then decided against it. There was no time, and he would have to leave the Land Cruiser here anyway since he couldn't afford the risk of being seen driving a car full of bullet holes into Damascus. He would have to take the border guards' patrol car and hope for the best. Wearing the black uniform and the cap on his head, he figured he could pass as the real thing as long as he kept moving and didn't get too close to anyone.

He got behind the wheel again and moved the Land Cruiser back to the boulders where he parked it so that it couldn't easily be spotted from the highway which was a few hundred metres away. As he did so, Faisal's body moved around slightly, his head lolling from side to side. Rigour Mortis was yet to set in, and it was a grizzly sight. Andrew quickly rummaged through Faisal's pockets and soon found what he was looking for. The keys to the Damascus safe house, along with a small note with the address. Then he grabbed the backpack from the backseat of the car and placed it on the ground. Finally, he dragged the two dead guards over to the boulders and left them next to the Land Cruiser.

The patrol car was a black Toyota Rav4 with a broad white stripe painted down its side, and الحدود حرس written in black on top of it, which means Border Guard. Andrew got in behind the wheel and adjusted the seat and the mirrors. Then he started the engine and drove slowly along the dirt road and back towards the highway, headlights still off. Without Faisal, he would have to make his way to Damascus and find the warehouse on his own. He had the precise coordinates, so he would just have to use his map and the GPS. It wouldn't be the first time.

No plan survives contact with the enemy, he thought to himself as he pulled onto the nearly deserted highway, switched on the headlights and drove off towards Damascus.

Eight

Wearing the black uniform of the dead Syrian border guard, Andrew drove the Toyota Rav4 along the highway towards Damascus. It was now just after 1 a.m., and there wasn't a single car on the road. After around five kilometres, the highway skirted the small town of Al-Dimass. From there it went due south for another eight kilometres to the town of Al-Saboura, which was off to the left of the highway as it curved its way through the arid hills down towards Damascus. As he approached the Syrian capital from the west, he could see Mount Qasioun which lies immediately to the north of the city centre, and which towers more than a kilometre above the city.

As soon as it enters the suburbs of Damascus, the highway continues on through the entire city after which it curves north to become Highway 5 which stretches all the way to Homs 150 kilometres to the north. Andrew did not venture inside the city itself, but took an exit on the western outskirts and followed it north towards his destination - the warehouse where the chemical agent had been stored, and whose precise coordinates he had marked on his map.

On the way there, he passed through several of the city's suburbs, now all virtually dormant as almost everyone seemed to be at home and asleep. He saw no pedestrians, and the only vehicles he passed were a couple of trucks and a police car. He wasn't sure whether to acknowledge its presence, but before he could decide, the moment was gone and the police car had moved past him, seemingly paying him no attention. He and the RAV4 looked for all the world like any other border guard on the way home after a late shift.

He allowed himself a moment to look at the various suburban buildings. Virtually every one of them was constructed in a two or three-storey brutalist architectural style. They appeared to be concrete pre-fabs. Most of the ground floor windows had iron bars across them, and every house seemed to have been painted in either an off-white or a pale brown colour. There were a few shops dotted here and there, but there was nothing that resembled the type of shopping streets that he was used to. At least not in this part of town. He got the feeling that this was a relatively down-at-heel neighbourhood.

He slowed down as he drove into the industrial estate on the northern outskirts of the city. It looked deserted, and directly across the street from it was possibly the least well-equipped playground he had ever seen. Rusty swings and slides with paint peeling off and tufts of grass poking up through the dry soil.

Wonderful place to store chemical weapons, he thought, caustically.

Inside the industrial estate, there were several concrete buildings, each one set on individual plots behind barbed wired chain-linked fences, and many of them also contained adjacent corrugated sheet metal warehouses of all sizes.

The warehouse he was heading for was at the end of the road furthest from the entrance to the estate. It was set back about fifty metres on an otherwise disused-looking plot, and the chain-linked gates by the road were closed and locked with a metal chain and a padlock. He was somewhat surprised to see the plot completely unguarded, but then a handful of guards would only draw attention to it, which he was sure was probably the last thing the owners wanted.

He drove up close to the gates so that the front of the RAV4 was just touching them. Then he put the car into first gear and feathered the clutch, making the vehicle inch forward slowly and putting more and more strain on the metal chain. The RAV4's tyres ground hard against the gravel beneath them, making the odd pebble shoot out and skid across the ground, but after a few seconds the chain broke and the gates swung open amid a long drawn-out and forlorn-sounding squeaking noise as they swivelled on their rusty hinges. Andrew quickly checked behind him to make sure no one had seen him, and then he slowly drove through the gates and stopped the car around halfway to the warehouse.

He wasted no time in grabbing his backpack from the passenger seat and extracting the gasmask and the small pack containing the one-time-use hazmat suit.

Inside the pack, there was also a small spray can that contained aqueous sodium hydroxide, which is a simple water-based chemical solution that very effectively neutralises nerve agents like VX through the process of hydrolysis. If there were still traces of a nerve agent inside that warehouse, he would need to spray himself down before taking the hazmat suit off again after his visit.

He assessed the risk of exposure to be very low, since VX and similar compounds have a half-life of around six to ten hours, often much shorter in hot dry climates like Syria. In addition, VX persists for a relatively short amount of time on porous surfaces like concrete and wood. What this meant was that 99 percent of any aerosolised agent inside the warehouse would have dissipated over the past two days alone, and much more than that would have gone since the suspected incident over a week ago. However, because of its extreme toxicity, whereby it only takes a miniscule amount of exposure to cause serious neurological effects, Andrew had decided that he couldn't be too careful. With some difficulty, and worried that it might rip, he managed to wriggle into the hazmat suit while still inside the car. He then donned the gasmask and placed the atropine injector inside a small hip pocket that had been glued onto the suit's exterior.

Leaving the headlights on to try to illuminate the warehouse's interior, he opened the car door and stepped out, grabbing the LCAD sniffer from the front seat. Then he closed the door and began walking slowly towards the warehouse.

It was hot and humid inside the suit and the mask. He was already sweating, and his vision and hearing were severely impaired. The only sounds he could hear were his own heavy breathing and the crunch of the gravel beneath his feet. He was suddenly beginning to feel vulnerable walking around here by himself. If for some reason he were to end up exposed to the VX agent, there would be no help to call on, and he probably wouldn't be found for weeks or even longer.

He fired up the LCAD and cautiously approached the tall sliding double doors to the windowless warehouse. He had already spotted that they were unlocked and that there was a small gap between them. Had this been done on purpose to ventilate the place? Or perhaps the warehouse was completely empty and there was nothing to find. Or was it because Syria's infamously ruthless and violent military intelligence directorate, the Mukhabarat, had somehow been warned of his arrival by Lebanese intelligence, and was already lying in wait inside?

Andrew walked up to the entrance and grabbed the handle on one of the double doors, pulling it aside. It rolled slowly along its rail amid a faint metallic juddering sound. Andrew stood still for a moment, looking inside the warehouse. It was empty except for a forklift parked off to one side on the concrete floor, a stack of wooden pallets piled on top of each other in one of the far corners, and two large concrete blocks placed side by side near the middle of the room. In shape and size, they looked vaguely like stone sarcophagi.

Andrew walked inside the warehouse holding the LCAD out in front of himself. Its digital display showed a small animation similar to a radar scope, sweeping 360 degrees around itself as it worked to pick up any traces of chemical agents in the air. So far, it was finding nothing.

He continued towards the two concrete blocks, wondering what they had been used for. Perhaps they had simply served as places to pack the chemical weapons into other containers for onward shipping to some other location. Next to one of them was a dark discoloured area on the concrete floor. Andrew knelt down to study it and was almost immediately convinced that what he was looking at was remnants of a pool of blood that had been left to dry there. It was slightly smeared on one side as if something had been dragged through it.

He glanced at the LCAD. Still nothing. If the mercenaries had become exposed to a chemical agent similar to VX inside this warehouse, then it would have dissipated almost entirely over the past week, but the LCAD should still have been able to pick up tiny trace amounts nonetheless. The fact that it had picked up nothing meant that the soldiers who turned up in the hospital had to have been exposed somewhere else. But then, what was this warehouse for? He looked again at the concrete blocks, now convinced that this place had only ever served as some sort of short-term repackaging location for the weapons before they were sent to their final destination. But why was there a pool of dried-up blood? He walked around the blocks and soon discovered another blotchy dark stain. A few feet away was an empty shell casing from a small calibre weapon, most likely a pistol. He searched the area but there was only one casing to be found.

Walking first to the forklift and then to the stack of wooden pallets, it was clear that they had played no part in whatever had gone on inside the warehouse, as they were both covered in a thin layer of dust, and there was no sign of anything having been moved around for a long time.

The LCAD was still picking up nothing, so Andrew decided that he had found all there was to find. As he was making his way back towards the car, his eye caught something lying on the ground halfway between the warehouse and the car. It was small and reflective, but he hadn't seen it on the way into the warehouse because the light from the car had come from behind.

He walked over to it and knelt down. It was a piece of hard plastic the size of a credit card, and it had been pushed partly into the gravel. He wiped the dirt from it and held it up in front of his face. Looking through the gasmask visor, which was now beginning to steam up on the inside, it looked like some sort of ID card.

He quickly sprayed himself down with the sodium hydroxide and then took off the mask and the hazmat suit. The clean and dry evening air felt like a glass of cold water on a hot day. Packing up his equipment, he got back into the car and looked at the plastic card again. The writing was in Arabic, and it was definitely not a credit card. It had a picture of a man wearing what looked like a hospital uniform, possibly that of a porter or some other service staff. Next to it were several lines of text, most likely the man's name, and in the opposite corner from the picture was an emblem and the name of a hospital in both Arabic and English. Somehow this hospital particular employee had ended up here in this warehouse. Whatever he had been doing here, he must have dropped his hospital access card without realising it. But why had he been here? And could the access card still be working?

Using his phone, it took Andrew only a couple of minutes to identify the hospital's location. It was a military hospital simply called Hospital 601 on the northern edge of the Shikh Saad neighbourhood. He seemed to remember that it had played an extremely unsavoury role in the Syrian government's brutal crackdown on democracy protesters during the Arab Spring. According to Strickland, it also just happened to be where the report about the chemical agent exposure of Russian mercenaries had initially come from. It was less than three kilometres from his current location. Whatever had produced the now dried-up pools of blood inside the warehouse was somehow connected to Hospital 601.

Andrew decided that he needed to get there without delay. The night was his friend, but it would only give him another two or three hours of assistance. After that, the city would be waking from its slumber and that would make his investigation much more difficult. He started the engine, turned the car around and exited the warehouse plot, leaving the gates open.

* * *

By around 2:30 a.m., Andrew had arrived at Hospital 601. It was located next to the circuitous 7th April Road that winds its way up from the most northerly suburbs of Damascus towards the enormous presidential palace compound at the top of the plateau, which itself towers over the capital. Directly opposite the military hospital, the plateau rose up increasingly steeply towards the palace and there were no buildings on that side of the road, no doubt for security reasons. As he looked up towards the high plateau, Andrew reflected on the fact that there was probably nothing quite as paranoid as a ruthless dictator who belonged to a sect constituting a small minority of the population.

He was beginning to feel the effects of not having slept for around 16 hours and having been on the move for much of that time. Being in a firefight had also drained some of his energy. However, he had to push on and get this done well before dawn if possible.

He decided to first drive casually past the hospital in order to get the lay of the land, and also to determine the level of security at the gates. As it turned out, there was only a small guardhouse with a single occupant. At this time of night, the hospital seemed deserted, so he decided to gamble and simply drive straight in. On his second pass, he calmly drove the car off the main road and past the guardhouse, giving the guard a nod as he passed. The guard got to his feet and seemed to observe Andrew's car as he entered, but then he sat down again. He must have spotted that the car was a border patrol vehicle and that Andrew had been wearing a black uniform with various golden insignia on the shoulder and a black cap with gold trim. In a country like Syria, there is rarely ever any upside to accosting strangers in black uniforms, even if they arrive unscheduled at a military hospital in the middle of the night. Especially if you are a lowly army conscript tasked with the night shift at a sleepy military hospital.

Andrew calmly continued to the parking lot behind the main building and drove the car into a bay where he stopped. He turned the engine and the headlights off but remained in the vehicle for several minutes, waiting to see if the guard would follow him and attempt to verify his credentials. After a while, he concluded that the guard had decided discretion to be the better part of valour, so he opened the door and stepped out. The night air was surprisingly cool, and he found himself involuntarily shuddering after having sat in the warm car. When he looked up at the four-storey hospital building, he could see that most of the curtains were drawn, and the lights were on in only a couple of the windows.

He scanned the building for a back entrance and soon spotted a door with a single light bulb mounted above it. This was his best option, so he grabbed his backpack and began walking across the parking lot towards it. There were only a handful of cars parked there, and they were all civilian and most likely belonged to the skeleton crew manning the hospital at night.

Andrew swiped the access card from the warehouse across the reader next to the door, and it dutifully beeped as the lock snapped open. He grabbed the door handle and entered, making sure to move purposefully and look as if he had business there, just in case anyone spotted him. He found himself in a corridor with two offices on the right and a set of stairs and an elevator on the left. There was no sign of anyone being around. He quickly checked the offices. They were both empty, but the lights were on, and so were the two computers on the desks. The stairs opposite went both up and down from the ground floor. If there was one thing he knew about dead people, it was that it was always better to store them in a cool place, preferably underground, so he decided to take the stairs down to where he guessed the morgue would be.

After descending two flights of stairs, he was soon proven correct. At first, he couldn't put his finger on what had convinced him that he was standing in front of the entrance to the morgue, but then it hit him. It was the faint smell. It was a particularly sterile yet pungent chemical smell, not unlike formaldehyde. Perhaps it was a special cleaning product that was used in places like this, but it was the same the world over.

In front of him were a set of double doors that were painted a washed-out green. Each door had a small frosted window and a metal push plate, and beyond them, he could see light coming through the glass. Taking a deep breath, he then proceeded through the doors and found himself in a small room with another set of double doors opposite, and a small desk occupied by a young man in a military uniform who was looking down, seemingly reading a book. From the look of his uniform, Andrew instantly clocked that this was almost certainly another young conscript who had been given the graveyard shift, quite literally. He looked up in surprise at being approached at his late hour.

'Masaa al-khayr,' said Andrew curtly, using the Arabic greeting for *"Good Evening"*.

Acting on pure instinct, he then immediately began walking briskly towards the young soldier. Keeping his head down so that his face was partly obscured by his cap, he reached inside his uniform as if about to extract some sort of document for the soldier to inspect.

'Masaa an-noor,' replied the young soldier uncertainly, using the standard reply to Andrew's greeting, literally meaning, *"This evening is full of light"*.

Clearly used to being told what to do, the young soldier just sat there, waiting for the black-clad officer to state his business.

As Andrew stepped up to the desk, he pulled out the access card he had found in the warehouse and smacked it down on the wooden desk, causing the soldier to look down to inspect it. It was enough to distract him for the couple of seconds it took Andrew to continue walking swiftly past the desk and then place himself next to and slightly behind the soldier. In a lightning-fast move, he reached down and wrapped his right arm around the soldier's neck, holding him in an iron-like vice and beginning to squeeze hard. The soldier immediately began to produce wheezing noises as Andrew tightened his grip, and then he grabbed desperately at Andrew's arm. Realising that Andrew was much too strong and that it was a useless endeavour, and with his legs kicking frantically under the desk, the panicked young soldier tried to claw at Andrew's face, but he was too uncoordinated and stricken with terror to manage.

Andrew could easily have killed him by snapping his neck, but he simply couldn't justify that to himself. This young lad was a conscript, and he would probably rather have been just about anywhere but right here right now. His arms were flailing around clumsily, and he produced a weak nasal grunting noise. After less than a minute, the lack of oxygen to the soldier's brain made him pass out, and as his arms and legs went limp, Andrew lowered him gently onto the floor and placed him in the recovery position which would allow him to breathe freely. He would most likely regain consciousness within the next few minutes, so Andrew had to move fast.

Andrew pushed through the next set of double doors and found himself in front of a huge polished steel door mounted on two heavy-duty hinges on the right-hand side. It looked more like a bank vault than anything else. He stepped up to the door, turned the oversized handle to unlock it and pulled it open. Beyond was a room about five metres wide and fifteen metres deep. It was cold, probably around 15 degrees Celsius, and the smell of chemicals was even stronger here. The room was neatly tiled in a pale green and black checkered pattern, and on the walls on either side were two sets of ten smaller metal doors with handles arranged on two levels. On a shelf that was mounted on the wall next to the door was a thin dark green binder. Andrew grabbed it and opened it up. It contained a document for each of the twenty cold lockers, listing the details of their respective deceased occupants.

Bingo, thought Andrew, and begin leafing through it.

He quickly found what he was looking for. Russian names, probably lifted from papers found on the dead mercenaries. Everything else was in Arabic, but that didn't bother him. All he needed to know was where to find them, and that part was easy since each document had a number written in red pen inside a small box, corresponding to each mercenary's cold locker. For each one, a tick had also been made in a small box next to the word, *Haraq*. "Incineration". These bodies had seemingly been scheduled to be destroyed here at this hospital, thereby erasing all traces of their existence or what had happened to them.

This lent a certain urgency to Andrew's visit, but what really threw him was that there were six Russian names, not four as he had been led to believe. They were in lockers 8 through 10 on the left side of the room, and 11 through 13 on the right side. All six lockers were at the back nearest the far wall. If six mercenaries had been brought to the morgue, but only four had been killed by the nerve agent, who were the other two and how had they died? There was only one way to find out. Andrew placed the binder on a small metal table under the shelf and walked briskly to the back of the room.

He grabbed the handle on locker 8, twisted it and pulled to open. There was a gentle hiss. Faint wisps of condensation escaped from the locker as the cold air inside it met the slightly warmer air in the room.

Inside the locker was a large metal tray fixed onto side-mounted rails, and on top of the tray was a black zipped-up body bag. Andrew pulled out the tray and looked at it for a couple of seconds. He was suddenly wondering if he had made a mistake coming in here without wearing his hazmat suit and his gas mask. He considered it for a brief moment but then decided that since the bodies had already been examined and catalogued, and because of the simple fact that they were stored here in a standard morgue, they would no longer pose a threat.

He unzipped the body bag and spread out the sides to allow him to look inside. He had a rough idea of what he was going to find, but nothing could have prepared him for what he saw, and he almost retched at the sight. The only thing he was sure about was that what he was looking at was human, or at least it had once been human. Beyond that, he was struggling to make out features, except perhaps where the eyes, nose and mouth had been. The skin on this poor bastard's face was disturbingly puffed up and looked as if it had blistered aggressively. It was as if it had partially melted off him. A sticky-looking mix of brown foam and coagulated blood caked the man's mouth. There were bodily fluids with varying colours and consistencies that had oozed out from dozens of deep lesions in the badly discoloured and cratered skin. The lips were black and severely swollen, and the eyes looked as if they had been almost eaten away by whatever diabolical substance this man had been exposed to. His hair was oddly patchy, and several clumps of it seemed to have spontaneously fallen out but were still clinging to his sticky skin. Walnut-sized lumps covered his neck, and several of them had burst and were leaking a milky liquid. A disturbing amount of thick frothy yellow fluid had oozed out of his ears and pooled onto the large metal tray below. The pungent smell of chemically burnt and rapidly decomposing human flesh was overpowering.

'Jesus!', breathed Andrew as he pulled his head back and turned it slightly to one side, only just managing to clamp down on his own voice lest anyone should hear him. *What in God's name happened here?*

He turned back and slowly leaned in over the body. Whatever had killed this man had done so in gruesome and spectacular fashion, and it had almost certainly not been a quick death. Even as the chemicals had begun decomposing his skin, he would have understood what was happening to him, and that there was no way for him to be saved. A bad way to go out. In fact, probably one of the worst ways imaginable to die.

Andrew extracted the LCAD unit and switched it on, moving it from the man's head and down over his chest. The small radar animation spun for a few moments and then the unit beeped, showing a piece of text on its display. Andrew turned it around to look closely at it. The display read:

Vesicating agent: Present (Type unknown)
Nerve agent: Present (Type unknown)
Analysis inconclusive.

Shit, thought Andrew and produced a small wince.

This man had been subjected to a massive amount of a hellish cocktail of two high-grade chemical agents. One had been a blistering agent and the other a nerve agent, but the LCAD's analysis software was clearly unable to determine their precise nature based on the chemical signature of the residual molecules from the now broken-down chemical agents. And this was despite the sniffer unit having a comprehensive and up-to-date built-in library of known chemical weapons in its memory bank. This could only mean one thing. The two agents had to have been newly developed exotic weapons that had not yet been characterised and classified by the chemical weapons scientists in the UK's Defence Science and Technology Laboratory at Porton Down near Salisbury.

Whilst looking at the LCAD's display, it suddenly occurred to Andrew that this man could not possibly have been exposed to the chemical weapons inside the warehouse that Andrew had visited just a few hours earlier. If that had been the case, there would have been trace elements still inside it, given the extreme dose that this man had clearly been exposed to. So where had it happened? The only logical explanation was that the exposure had resulted from some sort of accident during the removal of the weapons from whatever secure storage unit they had originally been kept in, either Russian or Syrian. But why had the weapons been moved to the warehouse, and what was their ultimate destination?

After a couple of minutes of inspecting the dead man and battling the urge to vomit at the sight of his horribly disfigured face, Andrew was finally able to see past the sickening vista and notice that the man was wearing something akin to a Russian Army uniform, although not quite the same. He was not regular army. In fact, Andrew quickly noticed that he was not from any part of the Russian Federation's armed forces at all. On the shoulders of his uniform, he wore a small badge with the image of a white skull inside a red cross-hairs. Above it was written 'PMC Wagner Group', and below it was the same text but in Russian, 'Группа Вагнера'. Strickland had been right. These guys were mercs from Russia's most infamous mercenary group, or Private Military Company as they liked to call themselves. The unofficial attack dogs of the Kremlin.

The Russian Federation was not the first country to use mercenaries in large-scale government-sanctioned military operations in recent history. That honour went to the United States, which used PMCs extensively during its occupation of Iraq. The logic was simple. Replace regular US Army personnel with private contractors, and the official US Army body count from its involvement in Iraq suddenly falls dramatically. In essence, the PMCs were paid to do the dying so that regular US soldiers didn't have to.

This business model was then replicated in Russia, with Wagner being by far the most successful PMC, partly because of its founder's close ties to the Kremlin. Wagner had been deployed in Chechnya, South Ossetia, Libya, Syria and Ukraine, as well as several hotspots in Africa where Russia was keen to exert influence, but was unable to do so using either financial means or regular military assets. In doing so, Wagner had developed a reputation for being effective but also poorly disciplined and absolutely brutal in its dealings with the local civilian population. However, as with all things in the Russian Federation, there was no such thing as a truly private corporation. Private ownership of businesses and the ability to operate and make a profit was only ever something that happened with the consent of the Kremlin. This was also true for the PMC industry, and soon Wagner Group effectively became the unofficial rapid response force of the Russian Federation, offering the Kremlin full deniability and making Wagner's owners spectacularly rich in the process.

Andrew glanced again at the man's face and wondered what town or village in Russia this mercenary had grown up in. Or perhaps he was from one of the former Soviet republics. He couldn't help but wonder how difficult it might be to identify a body like this using its DNA after such a massive exposure. Was that even possible? Perhaps some of the internal organs would still be undamaged.

He decided to unzip the body bag fully and take a couple of photos to send back to Strickland. The colonel would be able to have them analysed along with the readings from the LCAD. Even if it had not been able to determine the exact types of the two chemical agents, it would hold a list of the chemical traces that it had picked up. Perhaps that would provide the boffins at Porton Down with enough clues to be able to infer precisely what weapons they were dealing with, and how much of a risk to the public that might represent. Just because a chemical weapon had the potential to wreak havoc on anyone exposed to it, did not necessarily mean that it was particularly useful as a terrorist weapon. The other half of a chemical weapons attack, apart from the weapon itself, was the storage constraints that it might have, such as stability, temperature and pressure. On top of that came the issue of delivery. If the weapon was particularly difficult to deliver over a sufficiently large area, then it might well be that other less potent weapons would be better suited. But all of those questions would have to be examined at Porton Down. What he needed to do now was to collect as much evidence as possible in the form of pictures and LCAD readings, and then send those back to London as soon as possible.

He zipped the body bag back up, slid the tray with the dead mercenary back into the locker and closed it. Then he repeated the exercise with the next three lockers. They all contained similarly disfigured corpses with Wagner badges on their uniforms, although the last two seemed to be slightly less badly afflicted. The real surprise was when he opened lockers 12 and 13 and then unzipped the body bags within them. They contained the bodies of two men, but apart from the fact that they were also dead, they bore no resemblance to the previous four. They were both wearing what at first appeared to be hospital uniforms, although Andrew soon noticed that they also wore the Wagner Group badges. Perhaps they might have been part of a section of Wagner involved with chemical weapons handling. Perhaps they were bona fide Russian scientists from the research facility at Leonidovka. More importantly though, was that the cause of death had not been a chemical agent, but rather an acute case of cranial lead poisoning, also known as a bullet to the back of the head.

What the hell? thought Andrew as he inspected the two dead men.

Then it all clicked into place. The two men were almost certainly Wagner Group chemical weapons experts who had found themselves caught up in a plot by Mikhail Tokarev and Major Zahir Obaid to steal a batch of chemical weapons, either from the Army of the Russian Federation or from the Syrian Army. Having served their purpose, they had then been callously terminated inside the warehouse as soon as the weapons had been secured and inspected. This was what the dark stains on the warehouse floor had been all about. It was dried-up blood from their headwounds. Evidently, the entire operation had been shrouded in secrecy to the point where its instigators had been prepared to kill several of their own co-conspirators at the earliest opportunity in order to prevent any leaks.

If this theory was correct, and if what Strickland had told him turned out to be accurate, then the bottom line was that Tokarev and Obaid had succeeded in acquiring one of the most potent and dangerous chemical weapons in existence from under the noses of the Russian or Syrian army and that this weapon was now in their hands. It was a chilling prospect. What did they intend to do with the weapons?

Andrew finished taking LCAD readings and pictures, and then he pushed the metal trays with the bodies back into their lockers and headed for the door. As he did so, he grabbed the dark green binder from the metal table and left the morgue's cold storage. When he re-emerged through the double doors to where he had choked the young soldier unconscious, he was stunned to find the room empty. Somehow the young man had regained consciousness and managed to flee without making a sound. Andrew winced. He should have tied him to the table or to a radiator. Or perhaps he should have killed him? Either way, it was a rookie mistake. The soldier might be on his way to his barracks by now, or he might already be on his way back to the hospital with a truck full of Mukhabarat state security officers. Or perhaps more likely, he had run off home to decide on the best way to get out of completing his conscripted military service. Whatever the case, Andrew had to get out of there as soon as possible.

After exiting the building, he grabbed his backpack from the car and decided to leave the vehicle where it was. No doubt, the authorities would be looking for it soon, and he knew that he was less than a twenty-minute walk from the safe house to which Faisal had handed him the keys. He quickly checked the map on his phone to get his bearings again, and then he jogged south towards the centre of the city.

The safe house was in a narrow street in a sleepy down-market neighbourhood near a set of rail tracks. The whole area seemed completely deserted, but Andrew could see that the dark night sky was beginning to take on an amber hue towards the west, so it would not be long before the local residents emerged from their houses. Still wearing his jet-black border guard uniform, Andrew walked calmly along the street where the safe house was located. It was supposed to be just a couple of metres down a small alley up ahead.

Just as he was about to turn down the alley, a woman came around the corner roughly fifteen metres further along the street. She stopped, clearly surprised to see him there. Perhaps she knew everyone who lived on this street and was wondering who this stranger was. Andrew turned his head sharply towards her, projecting the authority that he thought the uniform probably gave him in the eyes of most ordinary Syrians. The woman instantly averted her eyes and began crossing to the pavement on the other side of the street. Andrew continued down the alley and quickly found the alley and the front door to the safe house. It was old and the paint was peeling off, but it was made of hardwood and seemed very sturdy.

He fished the key out of his pocket and inserted it into the lock. To his relief, it slid in easily. He reached into his jacket and pulled out his Glock 19, silently pulling back the slide to chamber a round. One smooth counter-clockwise turn of the key later, the door was unlocked and swung open on its well-oiled hinges. Beyond it was a single square windowless room, and it was almost completely empty except for a bed, a table with a chair, a kitchenette along one of the walls with a small fridge, and what looked like a small toilet and shower room in a corner. He stepped inside and closed and locked the door behind himself. Then he hit the light switch and walked over to the table where he put down the gun and the backpack. He suddenly felt the pent-up tiredness wash over him. He had been on the move for much too long without a rest, and it was now catching up with him fast.

The fridge contained a decent assortment of bread and fruit as well as several soft drinks, so he sat down at the table and wolfed down as much as he could manage, whilst sending an encrypted message back to Colonel Strickland containing a written debrief of what he had seen, and attaching the pictures from the morgue. He relayed how Faisal had been killed, and how he suspected the Syrian authorities would soon be looking for him. Also included in the message were the LCAD readings for the scientists at Porton Down. As soon as it had been sent, he suddenly felt as if a great weight was bearing down on him. As if gravity had suddenly increased tenfold. All he wanted to do was give in to it, lie down and sleep. He went over to the bed and threw himself onto it. A few seconds later, he was out cold.

Nine

Back in her studio in the house in Hampstead she shared with Andrew, Fiona sat down at her desk and plugged her mobile phone into her PC using a USB cable. She then fired up an application that would allow her to extract Nadeem Yassin's cloned phone content from her own phone and display it on her PC monitor. She clicked the 'Go'-button to start the process and went off to the kitchen to make herself a cup of coffee. When she returned a few minutes later, the transfer was complete.

A large stylised mobile phone had now appeared on her monitor, showing her the contents of Yassin's phone the way it would be displayed to him if he was holding it in his hand. Fiona took a few moments to flip through the various home screens and menus in order to familiarise herself with the layout and the various apps that had been installed. It soon became apparent that Yassin's phone was a dual-SIM phone, but not in the conventional sense of allowing one mobile phone to operate with two SIM cards and giving the user control over which SIM to use at any given time. Yassin's phone was much more advanced. It allowed him to swap between two entirely separate operating systems, each with its own settings, email, messaging and other apps. It was effectively two phones in one, between which it was possible to swap seamlessly. Glancing at the settings for the swap-over controls, it seems that the software was from some software developer in China.

Fiona frowned and began swapping between the two, trying to understand what she had found, and it soon became apparent what the purpose was. Yassin was using one of the two phones for all of his communications, contacts and appointments related to his legitimate business through Malakbel Gallery & Auctions. It all looked very normal and above board.

The other phone, however, was a treasure trove of information about what seemed to be an extensive art smuggling operation through which Yassin sourced ancient artwork primarily from Syria, but also from Lebanon, Egypt, Iraq and Iran. There were reams of emails listing shipments through ports and airports from a multitude of locations across the Middle East, each one detailing the contents of the shipment, the various handlers involved along the way and how much they were paid. There were also details about which customs officials had to be approached in order to ensure that shipments could clear the customs checks unmolested, and how much money was paid into the private accounts of these officials to facilitate the transfer. It was a highly complex and seemingly costly logistical operation, but recalling having glanced at some of the price tags associated with the art pieces being sold in London, Fiona realised that those costs were tiny compared with what they were sold for at Malakbel.

She continued going through Yassin's emails and discovered several digital paper trails detailing communications between Yassin and a man named Zahir Obaid. She sat back for a moment, looking into the middle distance. This was the man Andrew had mentioned. Clearly, and as she had already suspected, he had to be related to Nadeem Yassin Obaid, and somehow Zahir was involved in sourcing the illegal art for Yassin to sell in London.

But sourcing the ancient pieces of art was only the first step in a long sequence of events that was required for Yassin's business to function. Fiona thought back to her meeting with Yassin. He had clearly been less than truthful about the nature of his business, but one thing he had said that was beyond doubt was that the provenance of an ancient piece of art was a prerequisite for being able to sell it, especially at the prices being paid in his auction house. This was something Fiona had first-hand experience with from her work at the British Museum.

There had been huge growth in demand for ancient artefacts from the Middle East over the past many years, and anyone who was serious about their art knew better than to do business directly with people in the countries from which the art originated. For that reason, artefacts almost always went through a series of middlemen, whose purpose it was to launder the looted items and create a document trail that made it look legitimate. The most common approach was to obfuscate the item's origin by fabricating records falsely showing that an item has been in an old family collection for many decades and that it had finally been released as part of an estate following a death. The criminals would even go as far as to falsify obituaries to lend credibility to the whole fictitious scenario. It was precisely this sort of extensive obfuscation effort that Nadeem Yassin seemed to be coordinating from his gallery on Ludgate Hill in London.

Fiona decided to dig into a shipment involving a statue unearthed from the ancient site of Palmyra. It was comprehensively documented and seemed to have been excavated and processed by a team of competent archaeologists several years ago, but there were no official records of its existence anywhere else on the internet. In other words, it seemed as if Obaid and Yassin were running an under-the-radar team of archaeologists. Those archaeologists had somehow gained access to Palmyra and were excavating there illegally and then selling their finds in London through Malakbel.

After some more digging, Fiona found that one name kept popping up repeatedly as she skimmed the many documents related to shipping information. It was a company called Crescent Logistics, and it seemed to be at the centre of all of the illegal art smuggling activities. It apparently had legal operations in both the UK and several other European countries, but she was unable to find out anything about its ownership structure or precisely what the company's activities were.

As she looked through Yassin's calendar, Fiona discovered that Crescent Logistics had carried out regular shipments from Damascus and also from Baghdad going back several months. There seemed to be a fairly regular pattern to them, but then she saw that the pattern was about to be broken. Soon a shipment from Pakistan of a batch of ancient Afghan art would arrive in London. It appeared to be several statues from around the 5th century CE before Afghanistan became dominated by Islam. Perhaps Zahir and Yassin Obaid were branching out to other markets. The shipment was scheduled for less than a week from now, although unusually, there were no details about the precise route that it was expected to take.

After spending another hour sifting through the hundreds of emails and attached documents contained on Yassin's phone, she came across a reference to an upcoming meeting between Zahir Obaid and Mikhail Tokarev at a place called Porok. This name didn't mean anything to Fiona, but she instinctively felt that this had to be important. Why else would Yassin have it in his phone when he was in London and therefore clearly not going to be attending? The meeting was scheduled for the 14th at 10 p.m. Fiona did a doubletake and then glanced down to the lower right-hand corner of her monitor. The 14th was today. The meeting was happening this evening.

Still looking at her computer screen, she grabbed her coffee and took a sip, only to discover that it had gone cold. She bit her lip and stared at the calendar in front of her. There was definitely something here that might be really significant, but she also knew that her own efforts had hit a dead end. Unless she could somehow find a way to dig much deeper, this would be as far as she would be able to take her investigation.

Then she had an idea. She was slightly hesitant about it, but because Andrew had asked her to look into this, and because he had said that it was somehow connected to what he was doing right now, she decided that it would be the right thing to do.

She picked up her phone and dialled a number that Andrew had given to her a long time ago, but that she had never used. Not until today. The phone rang a couple of times before it was picked up.

'Hello,' said a friendly but clipped voice.

'Oh, Colonel Strickland?' said Fiona nervously. 'This is Fiona Keane. I hope it is all right for me to call you directly like this.'

'Fiona,' exclaimed Strickland cheerfully. 'Yes, of course. How are you? What can I do for you?'

'Well,' said Fiona. 'Andrew asked me to look into two people whom he said were connected to something he was working on. Tokarev and Obaid.'

'Ah, yes,' said Strickland knowingly. 'Those two characters.'

'I came up empty on Tokarev,' said Fiona, 'But I've managed to discover certain things about Obaid that I think I need to share with you since Andrew is off the grid right now. And I think I need some help to get to the bottom of all this. Can I come to your office and show you what I have found?'

'Certainly,' replied Strickland. 'As it happens, I just received a secure message from Andrew a few hours ago. He is all right and progressing with his mission. I can't tell you where he is, of course. For your own safety, you understand.'

'Is he all right?' asked Fiona.

'Oh yes,' said Strickland calmly. 'Nothing to worry about. He can handle himself. Anyway, why don't you come to my office this afternoon, and then we can have a chat about what you have discovered. Say 2 p.m.?'

'Sounds good,' said Fiona, sounding relieved. 'See you then.'

★ ★ ★

It was late afternoon in Damascus when Andrew woke up to the sound of a car horn blaring somewhere nearby. He had been asleep for more than ten hours, but he had needed it. He went into the bathroom and took a long shower, decided against shaving and then changed into some clothes that had been left for him in a wardrobe next to the bed. There were several options, but he went for an elegant grey suit with a white shirt, a black tie and a pair of black leather shoes. It all fit him surprisingly well. He looked rather suave if he did say so himself.

Sitting down at the desk, he extracted his mobile phone from the jacket he had worn the night before and saw that a message had come through from Colonel Strickland. Its contents were both intriguing and slightly concerning. Apparently, Fiona had decided to go all in on his request to look into Tokarev and Obaid. Having found nothing on Tokarev, she had identified what appeared to be a relative of Zahir Obaid. He was a London art dealer by the name of Nadeem Yassin Obaid, and with the help of GCHQ, Strickland had determined that he was the nephew of Zahir Obaid. The two of them seemed to be illegally sourcing ancient art from Syria and selling it in London using falsified provenance records.

Fiona had also discovered that the art smuggling operation was carried out using an international logistics company called Crescent Logistics, and Strickland had then been able to find out that the company was part of a complicated web of businesses in a number of different countries, but that they were all ultimately owned by Mikhail Tokarev. It seemed that Tokarev had built himself a small business empire after leaving Wagner Group. Even more intriguing was something else that Strickland had uncovered with the help of MI6. The warehouse that Andrew had visited the previous evening was owned by a front company also controlled by Tokarev.

Andrew sat back for a moment considering what he had just read. Something about this just didn't seem right. It was clear that Tokarev and Obaid had been working together to facilitate the smuggling of ancient art from Syria. This was the sort of graft that Andrew would have expected to find in a corrupt dictatorship like Syria, especially when there was involvement from a former member of the Wagner Group. But why had the two men suddenly changed tack to raiding a chemical weapons storage facility? That was an infinitely riskier endeavour, both in terms of the actual risk of accidental exposure, but also in terms of the very real risk of running afoul of the powers that be in Syria.

Andrew guessed that the duo would have needed to oil some important wheels inside the Syrian power structures in order to pull off an operation like that. As evidenced by the six dead Russians in the morgue in Hospital 601 in the Shikh Saad neighbourhood, something clearly had not gone according to plan. However, he had no doubt that the chemical weapons were now in Tokarev's and Obaid's possession.

Was it just that those chemical weapons were a more lucrative source of revenue, or was there some larger purpose afoot that Andrew did not yet understand? Where were the weapons now? Who were they planning to sell them to, and was there a specific purpose for acquiring them? Or could it be that Tokarev and Obaid were planning to use them themselves?

He shook his head at the multitude of different possibilities, none of them very appealing. All he had at this point was speculation. What he needed were facts. He needed proof. And the nightclub Porok was his best bet.

Strickland had ended the message by telling Andrew that Tokarev and Obaid appeared to be scheduled to meet again at Porok that same evening. Andrew looked at his wristwatch and decided to get himself ready. He raided the fridge one more time to make sure that he would have enough energy for what might end up being a long night, and then he donned a white dishdasha that was hanging inside the wardrobe. The long cotton robe with its high collar completely covered his suit and shoes, but it had concealed openings in the hems at the front, allowing the wearer to reach through it to access a wallet or in

Andrew's case, a gun in an under-arm shoulder holster. He also put on a pair of sunglasses and a white keffiyeh. Along with his dark full beard and the sunglasses, the traditional middle eastern headdress would make it difficult for the casual observer to identify him as anything other than a well-heeled local businessman. Perfect for where he was going.

As he exited the safehouse just after 8 p.m., the sun was going down again and the temperature was slowly dropping from unbearably hot to almost pleasant. However, inside his dishdasha-covered suit and tie, it was a lot warmer than he would have liked. He felt decidedly overdressed for the rundown area the safe house was located in, but as soon as he was back on one of the main roads going towards the centre of Damascus, he had the sense that he was blending in nicely. He swapped to the shady side of the street and made sure to walk along calmly, occasionally pretending to check his phone.

As he approached the city centre, there was a noticeable change in the types of buildings around him. They became increasingly modern-looking and there were more glass and steel facades mixed in with tall residential buildings and office blocks. He walked around the perimeter of the enormous Umayyin Square, which is a giant roundabout that connects to most of the major traffic arteries in the western part of Damascus. From there he strolled past the Ministry of Defence which sits on a large wedge-shaped plot immediately next to the square. Then he took a right down a road by the name of Moussa Ibn Noussair, where Porok was supposed to be located.

After another ten minutes of walking, he spotted it. The nightclub was located in a former cinema. It was set back from the street, and in front of it was a horseshoe-shaped paved area where VIPs could arrive and step out of their cars before the valet would take their car keys and park their vehicles. Above the main entrance was a wide black awning with the name 'Porok' written in both Roman and Cyrillic, in large lit-up golden letters. It made the place look both exclusive and expensive.

During daylight hours it probably looked quite dull and uninteresting. However, now that the pink and purple swirls of neon lights that covered most of the outside of the building had been switched on and the western pop music was coming out of the main entrance, it was a very different story. Compared with anything else he had seen in Damascus so far this was like a colourful tropical fish inside a grey shoal of cod. It stood out like a beacon in the night, and some of the first punters were already arriving. Some came in official-looking limousines, others drove flashy brightly-coloured sportscars. Porok was very clearly attracting exactly the right kind of clientele for the type of business opportunities that Tokarev seemed to be cultivating in Syria.

Andrew had no doubt that these were the movers and shakers of the country's military and civilian elite, all mixing with each other in a decidedly non-Arab setting. He did not see a single female enter the nightclub, but he noticed three large and brawny Caucasian-looking bouncers at the front door. They were almost certainly some of Tokarev's former colleagues from Wagner Group. They had short-cropped hair and looked like they were suffering from serious anabolic steroid addictions. On one side of the nightclub was a small alley leading down to a parking garage under the building, and on the other was a much narrower alleyway.

It was still more than an hour until Tokarev and Obaid were supposed to be meeting, so Andrew decided to keep walking past the nightclub. Instead, he kept going for another thirty metres where he then entered the lobby of the Dama Rose Hotel on the opposite side of the road. It was an ostentatious place with walls and floors covered in high-gloss marble, ceilings strewn with tiny spotlights giving the place a warm soft ambience, and dark wood furniture with intricate ornamental carvings. The staff were wearing dark blue uniforms and they moved around swiftly and efficiently, tending to the needs of a small handful of guests.

Andrew walked to the bar and ordered a drink, and then he placed himself by the floor-to-ceiling windows where he could look out onto the street and see diagonally across to Porok on the other side. Observing the Russian muscle at the front door for a couple of minutes, Andrew decided that attempting to walk in through there would prove too risky. There was bound to be a membership requirement that he would be unable to blag his way past. Worse than that, he had his suppressed Glock 19 strapped to his chest under his left arm, so if they decided to search him, there was going to be trouble. But he would never consider entering without it. What he needed was a covert entry. It would either have to be the parking garage or the narrow alley next to the building, which he figured was bound to have a service entrance.

After another twenty minutes of watching the main entrance and making mental notes about the characters arriving, he placed his half-finished drink on the table in front of him and exited the hotel lobby. It was now completely dark, the temperature was balmy and pleasant, and traffic on the street had dwindled to almost nothing. He watched as a police car slowly drove past Porok, its two uniformed occupants ignoring the nightclub. Syria's alcohol laws are much more relaxed than those of most other middle eastern countries, but licences are still required. However, Andrew had no doubt that the two officers in the police car would rather kneecap themselves than attempt to enter a place like Porok to check whether its license was valid. With someone like Major Obaid backing him up, Tokarev had this scene completely sewn up, and no one was going to rock this particular boat.

Andrew crossed the road and walked casually towards Porok's main entrance. Instead of walking to the door, he veered off towards the alley where he stopped and extracted his phone, pretending to make a call. The muscle at the door had almost certainly spotted him but they seemed to be ignoring him. When another limousine arrived, depositing yet another VIP in front of the entrance and thereby briefly distracting the Russian door crew, Andrew seized the opportunity to slip down into the alley and out of sight. Being used to doing covert work whilst wearing black tactical clothing and being kitted out with weapons, mags and grenades, he felt vaguely silly skulking around in the shadows wearing the white dishdasha. He couldn't wait to ditch it, but that would have to wait.

The alley was only about three metres wide and the sides were lined with dumpsters that stank to high heaven having sat outside in the sweltering heat for the whole day. About fifteen metres along the wall was a single door, and just as Andrew approached it, it suddenly burst open amid the noise of drunken laughter and the gleeful squeal of a female voice.

Andrew immediately moved over to hug the wall next to a drain where he then stood completely still, watching the scene in front of him. Out of the door had come a tall and scantily-clad woman with long blonde hair wearing an extremely short skirt and disconcertingly high heels. She seemed intoxicated and was giggling and staggering slightly as she exited and turned around to face her companion. He was a short podgy-looking man with a moustache, wearing a black uniform that Andrew immediately recognised as that of the Mukhabarat, the feared Syrian secret police. He was doing a better job of hiding his drunkenness than she was, but he had clearly had a few drinks too many himself already, even though the evening had barely begun.

The woman regained her balance and took a few steps back towards the officer, and then she pressed herself against him. It looked quite ridiculous since the man was now looking almost straight up at her, her breasts virtually level with his eyes. He grabbed her arse and pushed her backwards until they were both pressed against the wall on the other side of the alley. Then the two of them began kissing, his hands frantically groping her body whilst she made giggling noises that sounded like she was enjoying it. They also sounded decidedly fake to Andrew. These were not two people escaping through a back entrance to have a moment to themselves. This was a paying Porok customer getting handsy with the merchandise, and the merchandise was being paid to pretend to like it. This was simply a transaction, and it suddenly became very obvious to Andrew what kind of establishment Porok really was.

He also knew instinctively that this was his moment to strike. He pulled out his Glock 19, slipped out of the shadows and walked swiftly but silently towards the couple, covering the distance in less than five seconds whilst holding the pistol down behind himself. The two did not notice him until Andrew was right behind the Mukhabarat officer, grabbing the back of his collar and throwing him sideways onto the concrete where he fell onto his front. As he fell, Andrew stepped towards him and brought out his gun to aim down at him. He fired two suppressed shots which both slammed into the back of the officer's head, causing him to slump onto the ground, his body instantly going limp.

Andrew heard the woman produce a whimper and then a sharp intake of breath, but before she could scream, Andrew had shoved her roughly against the wall with his left hand covering her mouth and the pistol's suppressor pointing at her forehead at a distance of just a couple of centimetres. She froze instantly, her eyes wide with fear. She was very attractive and suddenly seemed a lot younger than she had first appeared. She might have been in her mid-twenties. As they stood there, Andrew thought he saw a brief moment of realisation on her face, as it became clear to her that despite Andrew's white garb, he was not an Arab but a westerner.

'Do you speak English?' asked Andrew in hushed tones, adding a hard and intimidating edge to his voice.

The woman nodded frantically under Andrew's hand. She looked terrified. Perhaps he had overdone it slightly, but he needed this woman in order to get inside the nightclub, and he had to make sure she didn't screw things up for him.

'All right,' he said menacingly, his eyes tightening as he glared at her. 'I am going to remove my hand. You are going to stay quiet and do exactly as I tell you. Do you understand?'

The woman nodded again, tears of fear welling up in her pale blue eyes.

'I am not going to hurt you if you do as I say,' continued Andrew, calmer this time. 'What's your name?' he asked, lifting his hand slightly from her mouth.

'Irina,' said the woman timidly, her Slavic accent coming through as she spoke.

'Ok, Irina,' said Andrew. 'Where are you from?'

'Belarus,' she replied. 'Minsk.'

'You're a very long way from home,' said Andrew, his tone softening further. 'All right, listen to me, Irina. There are some very dangerous men in there who might be about to kill a lot of people. I am here to try to stop them, and you are going to help me.'

Irina stared blankly at him, unable to speak and clearly overwhelmed by the sudden violent turn of her evening, so Andrew continued calmly.

'You and I are going to walk back inside,' he said, looking intently into her eyes. 'You are going to pretend that you have been with me the whole time, and you are absolutely not going to speak to anyone else. Got it? You just stay close to me.'

Irina nodded again. Andrew pulled back from her, and after fixing her with a brief look, he re-holstered his weapon.

'Ok. I am going to trust you,' he said, 'but if you try anything, you end up like him.' He jerked his head in the direction of the dead Mukhabarat officer.

'You can trust me,' said Irina weakly, clearly now persuaded that she did not have a choice in the matter.

Andrew quickly searched the dead officer. He was carrying no weapons, but he had a big wad of dollars in a golden money clip that seemed as if it was about to burst, a set of car keys and a Mukhabarat ID card with his name, photo and section number, all in expensive-looking gold stencil.

Andrew opened the lid of one of the reeking dumpsters, picked up the officer and dropped him into it. He didn't feel bad about it in the slightest. He was pretty sure that on balance, the Syrian people would be better off with one less Mukhabarat officer in their midst. And besides, at this point, there was hardly any price that was too high to pay for being able to track down a batch of chemical weapons that had the potential to kill thousands of innocent civilians in just a few minutes.

'There,' he said, wiping his hands against each other as if to wipe dirt off them. 'Good riddance.'

He looked over at Irina who had just stood there silently watching Andrew doing his macabre work. She did not appear to have understood exactly what he had said, but she seemed to get the gist of it, and Andrew saw no sense of regret on her face. He walked back to her, holding the money clip in his hand.

'If all goes well,' he said, 'you can have the money from that arsehole.'

He held up the wad of cash in front of her. He watched her look at it, the cogs in her head clearly turning as she tried to work out precisely how much money there was and what it could do for her back home in Minsk.

'Deal?' asked Andrew, his tone making it abundantly clear that even though it sounded like a question, it was not up for negotiation.

'Ok,' said Irina, nodding with a long sigh, and visibly steeling herself for what she was being asked to do.

Andrew found himself impressed with her sudden change in attitude and demeanour. She looked for all the world like just another bimbo, but she clearly had guts. With her obvious gumption and determination, she suddenly reminded him of Fiona, and he found himself briefly wondering what other unpleasantries she might have had to put up with inside Porok during her time working there, whether that had been weeks or months or even years. Then he forced himself to clear his head of thoughts of home, and instead looked Irina in the eyes again.

'Good,' he nodded. 'Just stay calm and do as I say, and you'll be fine. Come on. Let's go.'

Irina seemed to instantly switch into escort mode as her long legs transported her elegantly to the side door of the nightclub where Andrew had stopped with his right hand resting on the door handle. She nodded and activated a well-practised, calm and slightly aloof smile. She was ready, so Andrew opened the door and the two of them entered.

Inside was a small room with access to a hallway leading to the nightclub itself, as well as two doors to the restrooms - one for men and one for women. They made their way along the hallway to the main bar area. The walls were wood-panelled and the carpet was a dark navy blue with subtle swirly magenta patterns glowing faintly under the UV light that was mounted everywhere. There was a soft thumping of music that grew louder as they approached the end of the hallway.

At first glance, Porok looked and felt vaguely like most western nightclubs Andrew had been to. But on closer inspection, there were some subtle differences. It didn't have music blaring aggressively out of the speaker system, and there weren't throngs of young people bouncing loudly all over a crowded dancefloor whilst variously holding and spilling their drinks. This was a strange cross between a regular nightclub and a West End gentleman's club. There was western pop music playing at a not-too-loud level, a well-stocked bar with improbably good-looking male and female staff in crisp black uniforms, private booths where punters could withdraw with their female companions, and a small dancefloor in the corner. However, the only people dancing there were a handful of scantily clad and intensely bored-looking women who all looked to be in their twenties, and not a single one of them appeared to be local. They were all tall and blonde with distinctly Slavic features, and most of them seemed to have undergone various types of surgical enhancements.

Andrew caught sight of one of them leaving the dancefloor and walking over to a middle-aged Arab man dressed almost identically to Andrew. She gently sat down on his lap with a big smile, flicked her hair back and thrust her breasts forward in an attempt to secure the man's attention, and then she leaned back slightly with a quizzical look on her face as if to say "*Don't you like me?*". The man clearly wasn't interested in her. Perhaps he preferred someone a bit larger or shorter or heavier, or perhaps he was simply into redheads today. Whatever the case, his face remained impassive as he waved a hand dismissively, barely looking at her.

The young woman shrugged almost imperceptibly, got to her feet and walked away with an expressionless look on her face. To her, this was just another day at the office, and being rejected curtly was just part of the job. She might even have preferred it that way, even if it meant she would miss out on a large tip. At any rate, there were bound to be more opportunities for her as the night progressed.

As Andrew looked around, it became clear to him that every single female in the nightclub, except for the staff, was essentially here as entertainment. There was a skinny one. A fat one. An impossibly gorgeous one. A tall one. A short one. A selection of brown, blonde red and blue hair. There was a great deal of variety and something for everyone, and that was by design. This wasn't just a bunch of young women. It was a carefully curated menu. And it worked. There were punters everywhere, all of them seemingly eyeing up the women. There were what looked like officers from the Syrian army. There were lots of middle-eastern men dressed in white or black dishdashas and various types of headdresses. There were also a couple of loud brutish-looking Caucasians wearing colourful open shirts, and Andrew assumed that they were most likely Russians. There were two Asian men in business suits engaged in a deep conversation whilst their two respective female companions pretended to busy themselves with their nails.

Virtually every customer in Porok was being tended to by at least one woman wearing skimpy clothes and holding their drinks, lighting their cigars or simply serving as a temporary trophy for the men to look at and enjoy for as long as they were there. From the perspective of the mainly Arab clientele, this certainly wasn't a nightclub in the conventional sense. This was an amusement park for powerful men, most of whom probably suffered from raging mid-life crises, and it was clearly doing a roaring trade. Business was good. So good, in fact, that no one seemed to notice Andrew walk in with Irina on his arm and make his way towards the bar. Walking along calmly and wearing his dishdasha, his sunglasses, a full three-day stubble, and with a tall blonde woman in high heels and a short skirt on his arm, he looked exactly like the other men in there.

Andrew stopped a few metres inside the nightclub to survey the scene in front of him, and Irina dutifully did the same whilst taking the opportunity to extract a small mirror from her handbag to inspect her make-up. Andrew noticed a couple of the men who were already there glancing in his direction, but they clearly weren't looking at him. Irina had already slotted into her usual role, skilfully directing attention away from him and towards herself, and giving Andrew the cover he needed. Scanning the crowd, Andrew saw no sign of either Tokarev or Obaid. He checked his watch. They were supposed to meet in just under thirty minutes.

In the far corner next to the bar was a set of stairs curving up towards the first floor. One of Tokarev's suited musclebound goons was standing in front of it with his feet slightly apart and one hand gripping his other wrist in front of him. He stood there calmly, but his face was set in an expression that told everyone to stay clear. It was immediately obvious that he was making sure no one walked upstairs without the permission of the boss. Andrew instantly knew that the stairs led to Tokarev's office and that he had to find a way to get up there.

He led Irina to the bar where she propped herself up onto a barstool and ordered two cocktails from the barman. A Cosmopolitan for herself served in a wide cocktail glass and a Martini for him. They arrived quickly, and Irina obsequiously slid Andrew's drink over to him. As she did so, she stroked his shoulder gently in a perfectly credible and well-practised but utterly faux show of subservience. She was good.

Sipping his drink, Andrew noticed that no one else was watching them anymore. He leaned in towards Irina.

'I need to get upstairs,' he said in a hushed voice, jerking his head gently towards the stairs a couple of metres away.

Her flawless smile didn't waver, but her eyes widened for a split-second, the fear returning.

'That's Mikhail's office,' she whispered, her voice trembling slightly.

'I know,' said Andrew. 'And I need to get inside it. Is there a way to get rid of the guard by the stairs?'

Irina looked past Andrew towards the goon and pressed her lips together. She seemed to think for a moment, and then she nodded.

'I will try,' she said and grabbed her drink from the polished hardwood bar top.

She slid off her barstool and sauntered casually towards the guard, balancing perfectly on her high heels and swaying her hips from side to side as she walked. Andrew was watching her out of the corner of his eye, and the stairwell goon didn't seem to take any notice of her. He was standing in front of the bottom step on a small raised platform, and as Irina stepped onto it holding her drink, she made an impressive show of tripping clumsily, lurching forward towards the goon and spilling the entire contents over the front of his jacket. Even from where Andrew was sitting, he could see the sugary red liquid running off the fabric and glistening in the soft lighting of the nightclub.

The goon growled something angrily in Russian, which Andrew thought might have been '*Suka*', the ubiquitous and versatile term for 'bitch'. He was about to slap her with the back of his hand, but then seemed to think better of it. Tokarev probably handed out severe penalties for damaging the merchandise. Irina appeared to degenerate into a torrent of profuse apologies, attempting to wipe the guard's jacket with her hands but only succeeding in smearing the drink all over it. He pushed her away roughly and stomped off towards the restrooms, Irina following close behind him like a puppy, apparently desperate to make amends.

Damn, she's good, thought Andrew.

Having turned their heads to observe the brief moment of commotion, the other punters now returned their attention to their drinks and their entertainment. This was Andrew's chance.

He left his drink on the bar top and walked casually away from it towards the stairs, holding his phone up and pretending to be making a call. He muttered some incoherent gobbledygook into the phone, and as he turned around briefly it was clear that no one was watching him. Moving swiftly but trying not to look like he was in a hurry, Andrew ascended the curving stairs to the landing above. It seemed that no one had spotted him walk up. He found himself in a short corridor with a solid-looking wooden door at the far end around five metres away, and another door halfway along. The door at the end was ornate and had a gold handle.

That has to be it, thought Andrew and strode purposefully towards it.

The other door was partially open, and Andrew briefly glanced through the gap. Inside was what appeared to be a small storage room.

Upon reaching the ornate door at the end of the corridor, he was relieved and slightly surprised to find it unlocked, but then Tokarev was probably the sort of man no one would dare cross by trespassing in his private office. The consequence of that transgression for his staff was probably of a corporeal nature. All the more reason for Andrew to get in and out as quickly as he could. He figured he could just about handle himself against the Russian goons if it came to it, but he would rather not cause a violent scene inside the nightclub if he could avoid it.

He reached for the door handle, and for a brief moment considered the possibility that Tokarev had arrived much earlier and was already inside his office right now. It was a chance he had to take. He had not come this far to turn around now. He pulled out his Glock 19 and gripped the door handle. Then he opened the door.

TEN

Andrew slipped inside Tokarev's office and closed the door quietly behind him. There was no one there, so he quickly slotted his pistol back into its holster. The windowless office was roughly four by four metres and furnished with a strange mix of modern and traditional furniture. There was a large mahogany desk in the middle of the room, and behind it were bookcases with very few books but plenty of what appeared to be paraphernalia from Tokarev's days of active duty. Badges from the VDV. Several medals. Several spent 50-calibre bullet casings which probably had some dramatic story attached to them. A couple of handguns mounted on wooden plaques for display purposes. Tokarev was obviously keen on regaling his visitors with his war stories. On a console table in the far left corner was a table lamp with a square piece of mirror lying beneath it. It reflected the light from the lamp up onto the ceiling, but the reflection was distorted, and when Andrew took a closer look, he realised that there were two lines of white powder lying on the mirror. Cocaine. Tokarev liked to party.

There was a laptop sitting on the mahogany desk and Andrew momentarily considered snatching it and secreting it under his dishdasha, but that would have given the game away. If Tokarev's laptop went missing, the Russian would know that the information it contained had been compromised. That might make him change his plans for the chemical weapons, whatever they were.

He pressed the laptop's power button, and because it had only been in sleep mode it sprang to life almost instantly to display a black desktop background with the morbid white skull and red crosshairs logo of Wagner Group in the middle of the screen. Tokarev evidently still thought of himself as being part of that fraternity. Perhaps it was like any other mafia organisation. You can go off and do other things, but you never really leave.

Andrew reached inside his suit jacket under the dishdasha and extracted a small memory stick. These days, he never went on a mission without one of those. He inserted it into one of the laptop's USB ports and proceeded to copy the entire documents folder to the stick. He also quickly located the laptop's local email repository and began copying those files too. It was several gigabytes altogether, so it took a few moments. The lads back in London would need to sift through it all, but Andrew felt confident that it would provide at least some insight into the disappearance of the chemical weapons.

He glanced at his wristwatch while the files were being copied. He had only been inside the office for five or six minutes, but he knew he would need to get out sooner rather than later. Tokarev had to be on his way to Porok by now, and Andrew did not relish the idea of being cornered up here in his office with only one exit and a bunch of ex-VDV or Spetsnaz types blocking his way out.

The files finally finished copying themselves over, and Andrew yanked out the memory stick. As he walked back towards the door, he spotted a collage of framed photos on the wall to his right that he had not noticed before. He stopped for a moment to inspect them. They all had Tokarev in them, although each one was of him alongside different people in different locations. Andrew studied Tokarev's face for a few moments. He recognised him from the single photo he had been shown by Jenkins before setting out. Tokarev seemed to have a permanently sly and calculating yet somewhat detached look on his face. Andrew figured he would ring the bell very loudly on the psychopath meter.

There were photos from several different cities, including London, Paris and Moscow, as well as some that appeared to have been taken on hunting trips in what was almost certainly somewhere in Russia. Then Andrew spotted a grainy photo that had yellowed slightly. The backdrop was mountainous and arid-looking, and Andrew instantly recognised Mikhail Tokarev. It wasn't just the *telnyashka* VDV undershirt. It was the way he stood bolt upright with his chest out and looking self-important, obviously trying to compensate for his diminutive stature.

However, it was the second person in the photo that really caught Andrew's attention. He was a tall man with a large frame, broad shoulders and a full black beard, and he was wearing a loose-fitted brown two-piece that looked to Andrew like a *Peraahan Tunbaan*, the traditional buttoned shirt with vest and pants attire that was worn by most Afghan men. On his head was a black turban to match his beard, and in front of him, he was holding the easily recognisable AK-47 in his hands. Despite the low quality of the photo, Andrew could see that he appeared to have a large scar running diagonally across his face from his left forehead across his nose to his right cheek, and his left eye was covered by an eyepatch.

From what little of his face Andrew could see behind the large beard, the eyepatch and the turban, he seemed heavily weathered and most likely in his late forties or early fifties. If Andrew had to make a guess, he would have said that this was an Afghan warlord or a Taliban commander. It was exactly the type of person Tokarev would cultivate a relationship with. Could this be the drug-manufacturing Afghan warlord that Jenkins had mentioned? It was a distinct possibility. Was he also connected to the theft of the chemical weapons? Were those weapons about to be used in Afghanistan, perhaps to settle scores against other warlords? The latter somehow did not seem likely.

After a few moments, Andrew was able to see past the poor quality of the photo and study its details, and that was when he suddenly saw it. It took him a couple of seconds to fully register what he was looking at, but then there was no doubt in his mind. Around the neck of the tall bearded Afghan was a large circular medallion on a strap. It seemed slightly warped, and even though the photo was grainy, he knew exactly what it was and who it had belonged to. He was absolutely certain. It was a £5 Millennium Crown and it was Frank Malone's.

Andrew blinked a couple of times, suddenly feeling slightly lightheaded and having to steady himself against the wall. This was Frank's bloody medallion. No doubt about it. Who the hell was this Afghan, and why was he wearing Frank's talisman? Was he the same Taliban commander who had killed Frank all those years ago? Andrew's eyes narrowed and bored into the bearded man's face as he tried in vain to remember the commander's appearance, but the twelve years had muddled the memory of what he had looked like. Had this sick bastard taken the medallion as some sort of trophy so that he could brag about having killed a UK special forces soldier? It was a very likely scenario in a lawless country like Afghanistan, where violence in pursuit of power was the order of the day, and where weapons were worshipped with almost the same fervour as Allah. Burning anger began to rise inside Andrew.

Then an even darker possibility bloomed insidiously inside his mind. What if Frank was still alive? What if he had somehow survived that day twelve years ago? What if he was still being kept prisoner in some hellhole in the mountains of northern Afghanistan? A mentally broken slave, forced to work the poppy fields. A mutilated pet on a chain to be shown off by a psychopathic Taliban commander. Andrew wouldn't put it past the Afghan warlords who were infamous for their brutality, and who would use any means available to demonstrate their power.

Andrew felt sick. He shook his head to try to recover from the shock of what he had seen, and then he pulled out his phone to take a picture of the framed photo. He quickly checked the picture on the screen to make sure it was in focus, and then he shoved the phone back into his suit pocket.

Deeply shaken by what he had found, he suddenly realised that he was sweating, and it wasn't only because he was wearing three layers of clothing. He looked at his wristwatch again. It was time to go. There wasn't much more he could achieve by hanging around, other than increase the likelihood of getting caught.

He opened the door to the corridor slightly to make sure no one was there, and then he stepped out and began walking back towards the stairs. Just as he was approaching them and drawing level with the door to the small storage room, his eyes caught an almost imperceptible change in the shadows and light spilling up through the staircase from the nightclub below. Someone was coming up the stairs.

His only option was the storage room. He quickly slipped inside and silently pushed the door to, but without closing it completely lest it made a noise. As soon as he had done so, he heard the sound of heavy footsteps on the last few treads of the stairs, and then the sound of someone heavy lumbering towards him along the corridor. He caught a brief glimpse of a large person passing the storage room and continuing towards Tokarev's office. It was the goon that Irina had drenched with her Cosmopolitan.

Andrew only had a few seconds to make a decision about what to do. The goon was clearly on his way to check on Tokarev's office, so Andrew could either wait for him to enter and try to slip out and down the stairs, or he could wait for him to come back and then solve the problem with a more permanent solution in the form of a bullet. Andrew decided against the latter because a dead goon inside Porok would make it abundantly clear to Tokarev that something was afoot. Even if there was a small chance that Tokarev might not connect it with the chemical weapons and instead assume that it had something to do with his weapons and drug smuggling business, Andrew preferred to leave quietly if possible.

He slipped out and walked briskly but silently towards the stairs, but he had barely taken more than a couple of steps when a gruff voice called out from behind him.

'Hey!' said the goon loudly. 'Stop.'

Andrew stopped but did not turn around. As far as the goon was concerned, Andrew might just be some local Arab who had got himself lost while the stairs had been left unguarded. But if he turned around to show him his face, the goon would almost certainly smell a rat. Andrew could hear the footsteps of the large man approaching him.

'What you do up here?' asked the man in broken and heavily Russian-accented English.

'I am sorry,' replied Andrew, turning his head slightly to the left but careful not to reveal too much of his face. 'I needed the men's room.'

'Toilet downstairs,' said the goon irritably. 'No customer up here.'

The goon placed a large hand on Andrew's right shoulder and grabbed his left arm with his other hand. It was at that moment that his fingertips bumped against the Glock 19 sitting inside its holster under Andrew's jacket. Andrew could practically hear the alarm bells go off inside the goon's head, and he could sense a sudden tension in his movements as he realised what he had just discovered. The Russian produced a short surprised-sounding noise, took a step back and began reaching for his own weapon, which was sequestered under his own jacket. But Andrew was too quick.

He spun around and slammed a clenched fist into the throat of the Russian, instantly sending him staggering backwards whilst clutching his throat and trying to shout out. The only sound he was able to produce was a hoarse rasping noise as he struggled for breath. An instant later, Andrew was on him again, pushing him backwards into the storage room and shoving him as hard as he could against the concrete wall opposite the door. The back of the goon's head smacked loudly into the wall. This disorientated him for a brief moment, but it was long enough for Andrew to pull out his silenced pistol, aim at the man's forehead and pull the trigger. Blood and brains exploded out of the back of his head and onto the wall behind him with a wet slapping noise, and then the large man crumpled onto the floor in a heap.

'Shit,' growled Andrew.

He stood over the Russian for a few seconds, trying to work out if there was a way to dispose of the body, but he decided that his only option now was to leave it here and hope that no one came up to find him before he could manage to leave Porok. He holstered his weapon and stepped back out into the corridor, closing the door behind himself. He then walked back downstairs where Irina was sitting at the bar with a fresh cocktail. Andrew walked over to the bar and sat down on the barstool next to her.

'Everything ok?' she asked quietly, her perfect smile not betraying the tension that Andrew could sense in her posture.

'Sure,' said Andrew, doing his best to look and sound calm and in control whilst lifting his cocktail off the bar. 'Everything is just fine.'

Only then did he spot the two men in a booth on the opposite side of the club. It was Mikhail Tokarev and Zahir Obaid. Tokarev was wearing a light grey pin-striped suit with a blue silk cravat, and Obaid was in his uniform, obviously keen to make sure no one forgot how important he was. They must have arrived while Andrew was upstairs, and they appeared jovial and seemed to be making small talk and putting away their first round of drinks. There were two more Russian goons standing in front of them, shielding them from the punters and creating a private space for them to talk in.

'See that guy in the suit over there?' said Andrew, leaning towards Irina and looking towards Tokarev.

'That's the boss,' replied Irina in a hushed but strained voice, looking nervous. 'That is Mikhail Tokarev.'

'I know,' said Andrew. 'Get me into the booth next to him. I need to hear what they are talking about.'

After a brief moment of hesitation, Irina got off her barstool, picked up both of their cocktails and walked confidently towards the booth next to the one occupied by Tokarev and Obaid. Andrew followed her, and together they slid onto the booth's horseshoe-shaped seat on the side nearest the adjacent booth with the two men. Andrew caught one of the goons performing a cursory inspection of the new arrivals, but he clearly did not deem them a threat, because he turned to face forward again and ignored them.

'Pretend to snog me,' said Andrew.

'What?' said Irina, looking perplexed.

'Kiss,' said Andrew. 'Pretend to kiss me.'

Irina did as he asked and made a good show of looking like she was all over Andrew, when in fact she was just nuzzling her head close to his and allowing him to listen to the conversation in the next booth.

Tokarev and Obaid were speaking in English, which Andrew was sure irked them both significantly, but it was clearly the only language they shared, and having a translator sit in on this meeting was no doubt considered too risky. After a few seconds, however, it became clear to Andrew that he would be unable to hear what they were saying because of the ambient noise in the nightclub and also the fact that the two of them were speaking in relatively hushed voices. Perhaps they were intentionally using the background noise of the club as a sort of audio camouflage to prevent anyone from eavesdropping.

'I can't hear a damn thing,' said Andrew, pulling back slightly from Irina.

His frustration was building. He had come all this way and had managed to get lucky and be right next to the two main targets of this operation, and now he was unable to listen in on their conversation.

'I have an idea,' said Irina quietly, maintaining her playful demeanour to help mask what she was saying.

He looked at her quizzically, somehow not actually feeling surprised by her remark, but still impressed that she had offered her assistance.

'I can use my phone,' she said. 'I will set it to record and put it next to Mikhail.'

Andrew's forehead creased as he was trying to decide whether to let her help him, or stop her from putting herself in harm's way.

'All right,' he said finally and nodded.

It was his best shot, and if things went sideways, then he would just have to make sure that both of them got out of there in one piece. Irina tapped on the voice recorder to activate it and then turned the screen off.

'Wish me luck,' she said and winked at him. Then she slid out of the booth.

It was an incredibly risky plan, but it was also incredibly brave. Irina clearly had an axe to grind with Tokarev, or perhaps it was just pent-up anger from her time working in Porok, which Andrew felt sure had done very little for her sense of self-esteem, even if it might have made a big difference to her bank balance.

Hell hath no fury…, he thought.

Irina stepped around the nearest of the two Russian goons as if he wasn't even there, and then leaned down to give Tokarev a peck on the cheek. He barely acknowledged her. Then she walked back out of the booth and made her way towards the restrooms. What

Tokarev had not noticed was that she had placed her phone behind a cushion on the seat next to him, just out of sight. With any luck, it would be able to pick up enough of his conversation with Obaid to allow Andrew to make sense of it.

Andrew shifted deeper into the booth so that he could observe the two men out of the corner of his eye. He pretended to busy himself with his phone whilst keeping both the adjacent booth and the door to the restrooms in his peripheral vision. After a few minutes Irina emerged, but she did not return to Andrew. Instead, she walked to the bar where she appeared to be ordering drinks. When they arrived in front of her, she placed them on a tray and then simply stood next to it, clearly waiting for something.

After several more minutes, Andrew was beginning to worry that she was overplaying her hand and risking the whole thing by leaving her phone there for so long. Suddenly there was movement in the booth next to his. Andrew glanced over and it was clear that the meeting between Tokarev and Obaid had now finished. Immediately, Irina picked up the tray from the bar top and made her way swiftly to the booth where the two men had now got to their feet and were shaking hands. Irina swept past the two goons again, put the tray on the table in front of Tokarev and sat down on the seat next to him to place the newly mixed cocktails in front of the two men. This elicited an annoyed scowl from Tokarev and a wave of the hand that told her in no uncertain terms to get lost. She bowed her head deferentially, got back up and walked the drinks back to the bar as Obaid made his way towards the exit and Tokarev headed for the bar where he began talking to a Caucasian man who was probably a regular. They seemed to know each other already.

Irina soon came back to Andrew's booth and slid in next to him. She handed him her phone with a confident yet slightly self-conscious smile.

'Bloody good work,' said Andrew, genuinely impressed. 'I should call MI6 and have them hire you.'

'I'm sorry,' said Irina, looking at him curiously. 'I don't understand.'

'Never mind,' smiled Andrew. 'Give me a second.'

He got out his own phone and paired them up using Bluetooth. Then he transferred the audio recording from her phone to his, and then made sure to delete it from hers. Not only was it nothing to do with her, but if Tokarev ever found that recording, she would be likely to end up as pig feed on a farm on the outskirts of Damascus, never to be seen in Minsk again.

Just as the Bluetooth transfer completed, Andrew spotted Tokarev making his way towards the stairs next to the bar. He was heading for his office upstairs.

'Time to go,' he said hurriedly and slid out of the booth. 'Where are the stairs to the parking garage?'

'There is a lift that way,' replied Irina and motioned to a corridor close to the exit. 'Come with me.'

She led Andrew along the corridor and into a small lift that happened to be waiting with its doors open, and the two of them quickly stepped inside and pressed the button with a down-arrow. The lift only serviced the parking garage, and it did not provide access to the first floor above them.

After a few seconds, the doors opened and they stepped out into a cool and humid parking garage that had a faint smell of petrol exhaust. Andrew quickly ripped off his headdress and dishdasha, and then he fished the car keys he had taken from the Mukhabarat officer out of his trouser pocket. He pressed the unlock button, and from their right about fifteen metres away they heard a chirp and saw headlights and orange indicator lights flash twice. As they walked over to the car, a sly smile spread across Andrew's face. The car was a lime green Lamborghini Spyder convertible. Tokarev clearly wasn't the only one in Damascus with money to spare.

'Quick,' said Andrew. 'Get in.'

He was keen to get out of there, not just because it would be a question of time before someone discovered either the Mukhabarat officer in the dumpster or the dead goon in the storage room, but also because Andrew wanted to try to follow Obaid. The major was bound to be making his way to his home, and Andrew was already formulating a new plan in his head. Tonight was the best chance he was going to get at uncovering where the chemical weapons had gone, and he wasn't about to waste it. He also felt sure that he would have only a few hours to get the information he needed.

He pressed the glowing ignition button, after which the Lamborghini's V10 engine roared to life with such force that Irina jumped slightly in her seat. Then she grinned at him. The Italian thoroughbred had an automatic gearbox, no doubt designed to allow the driver to focus on steering the car and managing its 602 BHP. Andrew put the gearstick into 'Drive' and feathered the accelerator. The car nudged forward and he soon had a good feel for it. He pressed the button to raise the convertible roof in order to obscure who was behind the wheel, and then he drove slowly up the curving concrete ramp towards street level, the car's engine growling expectantly. When they emerged, several people outside Porok turned to look, but all they saw was yet another performance car with yet another punter taking his entertainment with him as he left the nightclub.

It was just after midnight as Andrew pulled up by the exit onto a virtually deserted Moussa Ibn Noussair Road, the engine of the Lamborghini growling behind them. Looking first left and then right, he instantly spotted a black limousine driving away towards Umayyin Square.

'That's got to be Obaid,' said Andrew.

He depressed the accelerator and the car leapt forward enthusiastically amid the roar of its engine. Had he opened up the throttle fully, the car could have accelerated to 100 km/h in 3,2 seconds, but it would also have carried the risk of it spinning out of control, and it would certainly have drawn unwanted attention from the limousine in front of them. He kept his speed low, matching that of the limousine and staying on its tail at a distance of about one hundred metres. He wasn't worried about losing it since he could easily catch up if he needed to, so he allowed the distance between them to open up to where he felt confident that the driver of the limo would not suspect that he was being followed.

After a twenty-minute drive northeast through the city centre and out the other side, the limo turned down what looked like an exclusive tree-lined private road with large houses set back on massive grounds, all of them built in a distinctly European style. A couple of minutes after that, the limousine stopped outside a gated property with a huge renaissance-style house on a suitably big plot. It was surrounded by a three-metre-high brick wall that was painted white. As Andrew saw the limo pull over and stop up ahead, he immediately took the first left to get out of sight. He waited there for a few minutes and then turned the car around and stopped again to look at Irina.

'All right,' he said. 'Listen, Irina. You can't go back to Porok.'

She nodded as if she already knew what he was about to say.

'I had to take out the goon by the stairs,' continued Andrew. 'Right now, he is lying dead in the storage room upstairs next to Tokarev's office. There is bound to be lots of CCTV inside that place. When they find out that you helped me, and trust me, they *will* find out, and if you then go back in there, you won't be leaving alive. Do you understand me?'

'I understand,' said Irina calmly, seemingly already having concluded the same thing.

Andrew got out his phone and spent a few moments looking up Damascus International Airport departures.

'I am going to take you to the airport,' he said. 'There's a SyrianAir flight leaving for Kuwait at 03:35. There are bound to be seats still available at this hour. Make sure you are on it. It doesn't matter where you go after that, as long as you get out of Syria.'

'I understand,' she repeated. 'I always carry my passport in my handbag. Just in case. And I have nothing of value in my apartment in Damascus. Just clothes like these.'

She looked down at her outfit, and Andrew thought he caught a flicker of regret on her face.

They drove to the airport in silence. Andrew did not want to burden her with a barrage of awkward questions about her personal life, and he himself did not feel like small talk. He just needed to help her get out of the country as soon as possible. Tokarev's goons would eventually put two and two together and start looking for her, and that would mean that the Mukhabarat would be looking for her too, and that would be a very bad situation.

Irina found some music on the radio. It was a piece of classical music that Andrew did not recognise, but she seemed to enjoy it. At one point, as he glanced over at her, he thought he saw her hands spread out on her lap, individual fingers moving gingerly up and down in unison with the musical notes. He realised that if he had put her in front of a piano, she would probably have been able to play the piece they were listening to.

After just under twenty minutes, they pulled up in a short-stay parking bay outside the airport's departure hall, and Andrew killed the engine. Several other travellers glanced in their direction, but he was pretty sure they were looking at the Lamborghini and not at them. He reached inside his suit jacket pocket, extracted the Mukhabarat officer's bloated golden money clip and gave it to her. He estimated it held perhaps as much as thirty thousand dollars.

'You've earned this,' he said, meaningfully. 'Use it wisely.'

She nodded once, took the money carefully from his hand and placed it inside her handbag.

'This is no place for you,' he said gently. 'Go somewhere else and make something of yourself. You did amazingly well tonight. You're so much better than this shithole.'

'I know,' replied Irina quietly, looking down into her lap with a self-conscious smile and suddenly seeming like a completely different woman from the one he had first seen stumbling out of the side entrance of Porok earlier that night. 'Thank you,' she whispered.

'Good luck,' he said.

She looked up and smiled at him. Then she got out of the car and walked purposefully towards the entrance to the departure hall. Andrew was pleased to see that she didn't look back as she disappeared inside.

Eleven

Driving back to Obaid's house in the exclusive neighbourhood in northern Damascus, Andrew connected his phone to the Lamborghini's speaker system and listened to the recording of the meeting between Tokarev and Obaid. The audio quality was good enough for him to make out most of what was being said, and he felt sure that once he was able to listen to it in a quiet room, he should be able to make sense of it. He did, however, pick up several references to a shipment out of Syria to Pakistan, and some talk about subsequent payments in the form of heroin. There were also references to a location in Peshawar. He couldn't make out exactly what was said, but it sounded like they were talking about a warehouse and some merchandise that was to be handled by Crescent Logistics, the shipping company that Strickland had mentioned in his message the night before, and which Fiona had determined was also involved in extensive smuggling of illegal art from the Middle East to London. Andrew finished listening to the recording, noting how it ended with the rustling sound of Irina grabbing the phone from Tokarev's seat. He hoped she would manage to get to Kuwait, and then perhaps find her way to somewhere safe to start a new life.

As he drove, Andrew began to contemplate what he had learned so far. Tokarev was buying weapons cheaply and illegally from the Russian military to sell to a Taliban warlord in Afghanistan. He was then using the proceeds to buy heroin from them, shipping it via Syria into Europe along with illegally excavated ancient art, which then seemed to end up in a London auction house after having had its provenance falsified. Tokarev had used his connection with Obaid to acquire the illegal art, but the two of them had subsequently conspired to steal a cache of one of the most dangerous chemical weapons ever developed, from a Syrian storage facility. Not only that, but they seemed to be preparing to ship it to Afghanistan, possibly via Pakistan, where it then appeared to be destined for some warlord. Most disturbingly, the warlord just might be the same Taliban commander who had murdered Frank Malone all those years ago.

It was a lot to take in, and as he thought about the complex web of activities that surrounded Tokarev, Obaid and now this mysterious Afghan warlord, Andrew was beginning to feel like he needed to sketch it all out on a mental map, and then draw lines between each person or entity to try to visualise how and in what respect they were all connected. It was the only way to make sense of it all.

Arriving back in the upmarket neighbourhood where Obaid's house was located, Andrew parked the

Lamborghini some two hundred metres away under a tree and away from the streetlights. He took a brief moment to prepare himself, and then he got out of the car and began walking towards the house. The tree-lined street was completely deserted, and of the handful of huge houses that he was able to observe through the foliage of their enormous grounds, only one of them had the lights on.

Arriving at the tall black metal gates of Obaid's estate, Andrew kept on walking until he was under a tree that was right next to the white-painted perimeter wall. Checking again that there was no one around, he adeptly climbed up the tree, over the wall and jumped down on the other side, landing almost silently on the soft and freshly mown lawn. He sat still for a moment, listening out for noises or movement near the house, but all he heard were the mating noises of dozens of cicadas sitting in the trees and bushes. The imposing house itself was quiet, and the only lights still on were near the front door. The moon was out, and Andrew felt somewhat exposed out in the open like this, but surprisingly, there didn't seem to be any CCTV cameras overlooking the grounds. There was one camera mounted on a pole near the gate facing away from him, and another on the house itself but pointing down towards the path leading to the enormous front door. Andrew was well outside of its field of view as he made his way quietly along the edge of the estate towards the back of the house.

He passed quietly through an unlocked wooden gate set into another brick wall and found himself in a separate section of the garden with a large lit-up swimming pool and a generous entertainment area extending up to the back of the huge house. The only sound he could hear was the gentle hum of the pool's water circulation system. He spotted several sun loungers near the edge of the pool along with a couple of folded-down parasols. Andrew was pleased to see that there was nothing to indicate that any children lived there. That would make what he was about to do significantly more straightforward.

He grabbed a seat cushion from a chair and moved silently up to the house where he placed himself next to a door with eight small glass panes. On the other side of the door was what appeared to be a living room. Holding the cushion against the pane closest to the door handle, he pressed the barrel of his suppressed Glock 19 into the cushion and fired a single shot. There was barely a sound as the bullet punctured the cushion and went through the glass. He grabbed the cushion where the bullet had gone through and forced it slowly through the now shattered glass, pushing shards out of the way and catching most of the fragments in the cushion as he did so. Only a few pieces fell onto the wood floor inside, and they barely made any noise. Having pushed the cushion all the way through, he let it go and reached over to unlock the door. This was the moment of truth. If there was an alarm system active, things were about to get a lot more interesting.

He gently pushed the door open, grimacing slightly as he did so. Nothing. No alarms. He exhaled. So far so good. He made his way across the elegant and contemporary living room, continued into a hallway with white marble flooring and then up a wide winding staircase with a black metal handrail to the first floor. He felt confident that he would find Obaid's bedroom upstairs, and he was soon proven correct. At the end of a corridor that seemed to be running the length of the house, he came to a door that was slightly ajar. He stopped and listened. He could hear the sound of snoring. Tilting his head slightly to one side and listening intently, he realised that what he heard was the sound of two people snoring. One of them had to be Obaid. Who was the other? Andrew had no intel on Obaid's private life.

He checked his pistol and then slowly pushed the door open, stepping inside the bedroom without making a sound. The room was huge, at least ten by ten metres, and its large windows overlooked the grounds and the pool at the back of the house. Moonlight shone in through them, bathing the bedroom in cool white light.

There were two people sleeping in a large double bed, white silk covers draped loosely over them. One was a shapely-looking dark-haired woman, perhaps in her thirties. She was naked and lying on her front. She could have been Obaid's wife, his girlfriend or someone he had hired for the night.

Next to her was the podgy and exceptionally hairy Major Zahir Obaid lying flat on his back with his large belly protruding up into the air, his head back at an angle and his mouth open. His snore mostly drowned out that of his female companion, and, like her, he was lying completely naked with his legs splayed out slightly to the sides. It was a sight Andrew had no desire to commit to memory.

He walked up to stand a couple of metres from the bed. Close enough to take control, but not so close as to give any of them an opportunity to lunge at him. Not that he thought it was likely to happen.

'Zahir!' he shouted, and the flabby major instantly awoke, sitting up and producing a confused yelp.

'Don't move!' commanded Andrew, pointing his pistol at Obaid's forehead, the major's drowsy brain trying to make sense of what was happening.

Obaid shuffled backwards for a couple of seconds until his back was pressed against the headboard. His eyes looked fearful, but also full of contempt.

The woman next to him slowly came to with an annoyed-sounding groan. She obviously still hadn't realised what was happening. Turning over to face Andrew, her expression instantly contorted into terror when she saw the gun. Then she screamed something in Russian.

'Shut up, bitch,' growled Obaid angrily in English, his drowsiness now quickly abating.

'Is she your wife?' asked Andrew, looking at Obaid.

The major nodded once but said nothing.

'Get up,' said Andrew menacingly and looked at the woman. 'Go to his wardrobe and get some of his ties, and then come back here and tie his hands behind his back.'

The woman hesitated, her eyes darting quickly to Obaid as if looking for guidance.

'Now!' barked Andrew, sounding as threatening as he could.

That did the trick. The naked woman immediately slid off the bed and went to pull out a large wide drawer from where she grabbed several neatly folded ties. As she did so, Obaid was staring unflinchingly at Andrew, studying him and probably trying to work out who he was dealing with and what his options were.

'What do you want?' he demanded, his voice having now regained some of the arrogant and pompous quality that Andrew had noticed from the audio recording.

Andrew shifted the Glock slightly to the left and fired. The gun spat out a single 9mm bullet that covered the distance to Obaid in a fraction of a second. It slammed into the headboard a couple of centimetres from his head, and his body jerked involuntarily, making his flabby skin wobble. His eyes were now squeezed tightly shut, and Andrew could hear the trembling in his breath.

'I said, shut up!' snarled Andrew.

The woman flinched at the shot, but she came back towards them looking terrified. Andrew flicked the barrel of the gun in Obaid's direction. She immediately understood the gesture and knelt next to the major, beginning to tie his hands together behind his back. Andrew was unable to see exactly what she was doing, but he was in no doubt that the woman presented no threat. Once she was done, she stood up and faced Andrew, seemingly unfazed by the fact that she was wearing nothing at all. Standing there in the light, Andrew could see from her face that she was perhaps not even thirty years old yet, but that her body had been surgically altered to the point of grotesqueness. Her breasts looked stuck-on and were much too big for her slight frame, and her lips were so pumped full of silicone filler that it looked as if Obaid had been violently slapping her around.

'Walk towards me,' said Andrew sternly, his gun still pointing at them. 'Then turn around and kneel.'

She did as he asked, and within a couple of seconds, Andrew had pulled a black cable tie from his pocket, knelt behind her and slipped it around her wrists.

'Go back and sit on the bed,' he ordered, and she immediately did as he asked.

He followed her around to the other side of the bed, Obaid tracking him with his eyes the whole time, a frightened but disdainful look on his face. As the woman sat down, Andrew grabbed another one of Obaid's ties and secured her wrists to the bedpost. Then he placed the pistol's suppressor under her chin and pushed upwards and to the side to make her look straight at him.

'Listen to me,' he said icily. 'Any sound. Any attempt to leave, any attempt to raise the alarm, and your hubby here gets it. And if you tell the authorities anything about me later, I will come back for you. Are we clear?'

The woman nodded vigorously without a word. She was shivering, and it wasn't because it was cold. Clearly representing no threat whatsoever, Andrew had no qualms about leaving her here. Her best bet was to do exactly as she had been told, and she knew it.

'Good,' he said, and then he turned his attention and his weapon back towards Obaid. 'Get up and walk downstairs. You and I are going to have a little talk.'

There was a brief moment of hesitation, but then Obaid rose from the bed and began walking out of the bedroom and into the corridor. Andrew followed a couple of metres behind him, and as he walked through the doorway, he turned around to look at the woman. She had not moved a muscle, but Andrew still decided to drive home his point. He brought up his left hand and placed his outstretched index finger over his mouth. Then he moved it down slightly and mimed a cutting motion across his own throat. The woman had clearly got the message and nodded.

Andrew led Obaid outside to the swimming pool and forced him to kneel near the edge of it. He was shivering in the cold air. Without warning, Andrew kicked Obaid square between his shoulder blades so that he fell forward onto the edge of the pool, his head and upper torso in the water. Andrew grabbed his hair and held his head under for around twenty seconds. Obaid wriggled and writhed, his panicked screams muffled by the water. Andrew yanked his head up and out of the water, and the major immediately began spluttering and heaving for breath. He was just about to say something when Andrew dunked his head back in, holding it underwater for another ten seconds. Then he pulled him roughly back up onto his knees, still facing the pool. Obaid was coughing and retching violently, trying to get the water out of his lungs. After about half a minute he was almost breathing normally again.

Andrew placed the gun's muzzle at the back of Obaid's head. He knew that he had to put the thumbscrews on and that things might get messy in order for him to get what he needed, but the stakes were too high to play nice. He leaned down so that his head was close to Obaid's.

'Let's play a little game I like to call, *Tell Me The Fucking Truth*,' he said Andrew. 'You only get one life, and a lie means your brain ends up sprayed across this lovely pool of yours. A hell of a mess for your expensive wife to clean up. Do you understand the rules?'

Obaid nodded and coughed.

'Yes,' he squeaked, the arrogance now entirely gone from his voice. 'I don't understand what this is about?'

'Oh, I think you do,' said Andrew frostily. 'I know about your little side business with the stolen artefacts from Palmyra. And I know you have a nephew in London who facilitates the sale of these artefacts.'

'It's just business!' said Obaid after a moment's hesitation, sounding slightly surprised, as if the looting of ancient artefacts was just a bit of harmless fun that anyone would have done if they were given the opportunity.

Andrew pressed the suppressor harder against the back of Obaid's head.

'I also know that you and your friend Mikhail Tokarev have stolen a batch of chemical weapons from a storage facility southwest of this city.'

Obaid's body went rigid.

'As I am sure you know,' continued Andrew. 'Several of Tokarev's Wagner mates died in the process. Nasty deaths, I might add. I know, because I saw them myself. Not a pretty sight. Bad way to go.'

He paused for a couple of seconds before continuing, now speaking slowly and with venom in his voice.

'Where are the fucking weapons, and what are you planning to do with them?'

'I don't know,' blurted Obaid, sounding frightened.

'What the hell do you mean, you don't know?' snarled Andrew. 'You orchestrated the whole fucking thing. Without you, Tokarev and his Wagner goons would never have got their hands on those weapons.'

'I just provided the paperwork for the storage facility,' stammered Obaid. 'They paid me a lot of money. Tokarev took control of the weapons immediately. They took them away somewhere. They are supposed to be flown out from Mezzeh Military Airport, but I don't where they are going!'

'Bullshit!' shouted Andrew, pressing the pistol against Obaid's head so hard that it was forced forward and the Syrian ended up with his chin on his chest.

'It's true. I swear it!' squealed Obaid.

Andrew decided to change tack. He extracted his mobile phone from his pocket and found the picture he had taken of Tokarev and the tall Afghan.

'Who is this man?' demanded Andrew, holding the phone in front of Obaid's face.

'An Afghan warlord,' blathered Obaid nervously. 'That's all I know. I have never met him. He is Tokarev's business partner.'

'Business partner,' repeated Andrew sarcastically. 'That's a lovely fucking way of putting it. Tokarev is shipping the weapons to Afghanistan. He is delivering them to this man, isn't he?'

'I am not sure,' said Obaid. 'Maybe, yes.'

'What's his name?' asked Andrew, gripping Obaid's hair and yanking his head backwards.

'They call him *Al Naji*', replied Obaid nervously.

Andrew ran the name through his mind for a couple of moments. He had never heard of it before.

'And what is this Al Naji character going to do with the weapons?' he asked.

'I don't know!' said Obaid. 'I never dealt with him. Only Tokarev talks to him. They trade drugs and guns.'

'So, you *do* know something about him,' said Andrew, anger building in his voice again.

He was beginning to lose patience with the chubby naked man in front of him.

'Listen, you fucker,' he snarled, grabbing Obaid's hair roughly and twisting his head back and to the side to look him in the eyes. 'Those weapons have one purpose and one purpose only, which is to indiscriminately kill as many people as possible. You helped a psychopathic Russian mercenary get hold of them, and now he is selling them on to an even bigger Afghan psychopath who is planning to use them God-knows-where. So, as far as I am concerned, you've already murdered thousands of innocent people. It just hasn't happened yet. So, where the hell are the weapons right now?'

'I do not know,' repeated Obaid insistently. 'I swear!'

Andrew sighed and lowered his gun. He was considering whether he might have to do something more drastic to Obaid to make sure he told him all he knew. Perhaps kneecapping him would make him spill the beans. He was about to yank the naked man to his feet when Obaid suddenly threw himself at him with surprising speed and agility for someone who looked so out of shape. Worse still, Obaid had managed to snap the cable tie. His wrists were bleeding where the sharp plastic had cut into his skin, but he had freed himself nonetheless, just before jumping to his feet and barrelling hard into Andrew. The major's pathetic form and demeanour had lulled Andrew into a false sense of security. Rookie mistake. This momentary lapse in concentration and his lowering of the gun had given the major an opening, and his lunge had caught Andrew completely off guard.

The two of them toppled over. Obaid was on top of Andrew, frantically scrambling for the gun while Andrew was trying to keep it out of his reach. Andrew headbutted Obaid hard on the bridge of his nose, and there was an instant crack as it broke. Blood gushed out and down onto Andrew's face, and at that moment Obaid's hands gripped Andrew's neck and began to squeeze with surprising strength. Obaid's eyes were bulging, his jowls were quivering and he grimaced maniacally as he tried to choke the life out of Andrew. Barely able to see and struggling for breath, Andrew grabbed Obaid's neck with his left hand and brought the Glock up to press the muzzle to the side of Obaid's head.

'Let go or you die,' croaked Andrew, completely taken aback by the sheer recklessness of the major.

Instead of letting go, Obaid just tightened his grip and squeezed even more tightly, a crazed look in his eyes as the blood continued to pour out of his nose. Andrew couldn't believe the strength of this man.

He pulled the trigger and the Glock produced a quick muffled cough. The bullet tore through Obaid's brain and exploded out the other side of his skull taking tissue, blood and brain matter with it. It splattered noisily onto the white pool tiles next to where they lay, as Obaid's overweight body slumped heavily down onto Andrew like an obese ragdoll. Andrew immediately pushed it off and rolled to one side. Then he scrambled to his feet and stood panting heavily over the lifeless corpse.

Bloody hell, he thought. *Didn't see that coming.*

Then he winced. What else could Obaid have told him? He was convinced that the Syrian knew more than he had let on, but now he would never know.

He used the water in the pool to wash the blood off his face and out of his hair. Remarkably, his suit and shirt only had minor blood spatters on them. Then he glanced up towards where he knew Obaid's bedroom to be. If his wife had any sense, she would stay exactly where she was. He briefly considered topping her too but decided that there was no justification for it, even if she might help identify him. He needed to get himself to the military airport as fast as possible, and he just had to hope that she had listened to him earlier and that she wouldn't reveal anything to the police that might help them track him down. At this point, with Obaid dead, there was no upside for her in assisting the authorities.

He decided to drop the ID card that had belonged to the dead Mukhabarat officer at Porok next to Obaid's body, to try to ward off any serious investigation from local police. At least for a short while. He suspected that they would be too scared to get involved in something which, on the face of it, looked like a Mukhabarat hit. If local investigators found the ID card, he felt confident that it would scare the crap out of them and at least cause a delay in the investigation. He knew full well that a forensics team would eventually work out that the 9mm bullet had come from a Glock 19. They would then instantly know that it could not possibly be connected to the Mukhabarat, but by then he would be long gone. Or so he hoped.

He went back into the house and proceeded to the front door where he disabled and reset the CCTV system including its video recordings. Then he left the house through the front gate, jogged back to the Lamborghini and got in behind the wheel. He figured he would have just a few hours before the police would be looking for him and the Lamborghini, and at any rate, the sun would come up soon. He started the engine and accelerated down the street, driving fast southwest through the centre of Damascus towards Mezzeh Military Airport.

* * *

Andrew drove the Lamborghini back towards the centre of Damascus, swinging past the safehouse where he darted in and grabbed his backpack. Then he got back in the car and headed south to Umayyin Square. From there he proceeded southwest along the four-lane Fayez Mansour Road which eventually exits the capital and becomes Highway 7, and then it extends all the way to the Israeli border and the occupied Golan Heights some 65 kilometres away. Along the way, he barely saw any other cars. It was now just after 4 a.m. and still very dark except for the faint light of the moon from behind a few clouds high up in the atmosphere. The only traffic on the roads was a few large trucks with images of fruit and vegetables on their sides.

He stayed on the highway for about five kilometres, and then the city petered out and morphed into more industrial zones and open and arid disused-looking land, bushes and tufts of long grass dotted everywhere, but not a tree in sight. There were a couple of half-finished large-scale building projects underway on both sides of the highway, most likely residential blocks, but they seemed far from finished. They might even have been scrapped halfway through. He knew that the population in Syria was falling and that the number of people living in Damascus was flatlining at best, so perhaps the construction of these apartment blocks had been abandoned.

He slowed down and took the offramp towards the airport and found himself in a tired-looking semi-industrial neighbourhood where he immediately began looking for a place to dump the car. Arriving at a target in a lime green Lamborghini was definitely not in the SAS handbook for covert operations. In approaching the military airport, he would need to cover the final several hundred metres on foot in order to make sure he wasn't spotted.

The engine of the Lamborghini growled softly as he drove slowly along, trying to find a place to get rid of the vehicle. He eventually spotted an abandoned petrol station that had a double garage. It had most likely been used by the resident mechanics when the petrol station was operational, but they were empty now and the roller shutters on one of them were up. Andrew drove the car into the garage and turned off the engine. He stepped out of the car, walked to the roller shutters and used a greasy rope hanging by the side of the entrance to pull them down, thereby concealing the Lamborghini from anyone driving past out on the street.

He took off his suit, shirt and tie, and dumped them in an old open oil drum that had doubled as a rubbish bin. Then he changed back into the black clothes he had arrived in just over 24 hours ago. They already reeked of sweat and dirt, and it had a faint smell of cordite from when he had fired his MP5 at the two border guards. He thought of Faisal and pressed his lips together in regret. That kid deserved better. He wondered whether the bodies had been found yet. Checking his wristwatch, he knew he was on borrowed time and the clock was ticking ever more loudly now.

Having changed clothes, inspected his weapons and strapped the MP5SD and the Glock 19 to his tactical vest, he exited out of the back of the petrol station into an overgrown backyard full of rusting cars and piles of spare parts. He spent a few seconds looking at his compass and getting his bearings, after which he jumped over the low chain link fence at the back of the plot and made his way through a warren of narrow alleys between dilapidated buildings and sheds until he arrived at the edge of the military airport by a large open area covered by tall wild grass.

Opposite him and roughly twenty metres away was a four-metre-tall barbed wire fence that surrounded the airport. There were floodlights mounted on tall pylons along the fence every fifty metres or so, but there seemed to be no guards or patrols anywhere in sight. About three hundred metres away he could see several large aircraft hangars, and one of them had its huge metal doors slid aside. From his position, he was unable to look inside the hangar, but he could see light spilling out and a couple of vehicles parked outside. There were also several people milling about. Further away on an apron in front of a set of smaller hangars were parked two attack helicopters. Russian Ka-52s.

He looked towards the east where the sky just above the horizon was taking on a faint orange tinge. Then he then glanced down at his wristwatch again. 4:35 a.m. The sun would come up in just over an hour. It was time to go. He crouched as he made his way swiftly to the fence. Here he knelt down and extracted a pair of wire cutters, quickly snipping enough of the chain link fence to make a hole large enough for him to squeeze through. Once on the other side, he folded the cut-out piece of the fence back to where it had been so that a casual observer would not notice that a hole had been made.

He made his way swiftly down into a dry drainage ditch that ran all the way along the nearest taxiway. This would allow him to approach the large open hangar without being seen. After around five minutes he was less than fifty metres from the hangar. He crawled halfway up and lay down on his front, raising his head above the brow of the ditch. From his vantage point, he was able to see a cargo plane guarded by at least five armed men. At the plane's rear, its cargo ramp was down and several soldiers in brown uniforms were busy unloading pallets loaded with contents that was wrapped tightly in semi-transparent plastic sheeting. He was unable to see exactly what they might contain, but each pallet looked like it held a large number of smaller packages or bags. A forklift was driving up the plane's rear ramp and transporting the pallets down and out.

Outside and next to the plane were two Syrian army trucks, and next to each of them stood two men, presumably the drivers and their armed escorts. Each truck had another two armed men standing at the rear, overseeing the transferral of the cargo from the plane and onto the trucks. There were orders being shouted as the soldiers hurried to get the cargo off the plane, and one of the drivers seemed to be pacing back and forth impatiently. Andrew could have sworn the shouting was in Russian. Through his binoculars, he examined the men by the trucks more closely. They had Wagner Group badges on their shoulders. These were Tokarev's men being assisted by what looked like Syrian Army conscripts, no doubt ordered by Major Obaid to help the mercenaries transport their illegal goods.

Andrew slid back down into the drainage ditch and made his way another thirty meters further along to the point where the distance to the hangar was only around twenty metres. Several low but thick bushes grew there which provided him with the cover he needed to climb out and make his way crouched to the side of the hangar, out of view of the men by the hangar doors.

Attached to and sticking out from the main hangar was a smaller structure with a single door to the outside. He decided to leave his backpack in a bush since it would be cumbersome to wear, and it would also make him much more visible. Then he slipped inside. He found himself in what appeared to be an office with a short corridor leading to a lavatory and a small storeroom. Just as he entered and closed the door behind him, a soldier entered through the door to the hangar itself and headed straight for the toilet without spotting Andrew who was crouched behind a desk next to the door to the outside. As the soldier strode purposefully along the corridor towards the toilet, Andrew clocked that he was carrying a pistol in a holster on his belt.

He immediately knew that this presented an opportunity. Still crouched low, he made his way silently across the office floor and along the corridor. He could hear the soldier whistling a tune, and as he entered the lavatory, he immediately spotted the soldier standing in front of the urinal with his back to the door, about to unzip his trousers. Distance, three metres.

The soldier must have somehow sensed movement behind him because he turned his head to look. But Andrew was already moving fast. He 'covered the distance in less than a second and used his own momentum to ram into the soldier, causing his forehead to slam hard into the tiled wall directly in front of him. Andrew heard his nose break as his face smacked into the tiles, and the soldier produced a shocked grunt. Andrew immediately grabbed the back of his collar and yanked him forcefully backwards across the room, sending him through the door to the cubicle opposite the urinal. The soldier was instinctively moving his hands to his face as blood spurted out of his nose, but before he could regain his senses and put up a fight, Andrew was on him again, kicking him in the chest and making him stagger backwards to slump onto the toilet seat. The soldier reached for his sidearm, but Andrew had already anticipated this, whipping out his suppressed Glock and aiming at the man's head. He fired a single shot, and the bullet slammed into the soldier's head causing blood to spray onto the wall behind him with a wet slap. The soldier went limp and slumped down onto the toilet seat, leaning back against the wall with his chin on his chest.

Andrew knew what he had to do, and he worked quickly. He dragged him onto the floor and stripped the uniform off him. There was now blood on its front, but there was nothing Andrew could do about that. After less than a minute, Andrew had stripped the uniform off the soldier and put it over his own clothes. He had also donned the man's brown cap which had fallen to the floor as his head had smashed against the tiled wall. He pulled it down as far as it would go to conceal his face. Then he closed the cubicle door from the inside and climbed over it. That just might buy him a few valuable seconds if someone came in there soon after he had left.

Andrew cautiously made his way back to the office and was able to briefly peek out into the hangar as he did so. It looked like the crews were still unloading the pallets from the aircraft. He slipped outside to fetch a small plastic case with a set of standard-issue listening devices and a GPS tracker from his backpack. Then he moved to the doorway that led to the hangar, beads of sweat forming on his forehead despite the night air being cool. He peeked out through the door and into the hangar. The cargo plane and the soldiers were about twenty metres away, and taking another look at the plastic-wrapped contents of the pallets, he was in no doubt that he was looking at heroin worth tens of millions. It was almost certainly coming from Afghanistan. From this Al Naji character, whose name Obaid had revealed before getting himself killed by his own swimming pool.

Near the hangar's back wall was a long row of tall and sturdy multi-level steel shelving units containing pallets with oil drums and several other packed items. The shelving stretched almost all the way to the other side of the hangar. By the looks of it, this was a major hub for Tokarev's Crescent Logistics and its operations in Syria.

On the far side of the hangar was a single pallet loaded with what appeared to be a dark reinforced case that looked like it might have been made from a dull carbon fibre composite material. It bore no markings, but Andrew instantly knew exactly what he was looking at. It could only be the chemical weapons, ready to be loaded onto the plane. He had to move fast. Once those weapons were on that plane, he would have no way of tracking them.

He waited a few seconds until no one was looking in his direction, and then he slipped out of the doorway and hurried into cover behind the first section of shelving. Keeping low behind the contents of the many pallets arranged in the shelving units, he quickly made it to the far end without being spotted. He was now directly behind the pallet with the chemical weapons, and for a moment he almost felt their presence as his hair stood on end. What he was looking at, sitting there less than five metres away, was enough neuro-toxin to kill tens of thousands of people if delivered effectively. It was truly a weapon of mass destruction. If he could have brought sufficient firepower in the form of a team of SAS soldiers, he would have preferred to hit this place hard, eliminating all of the soldiers and securing the weapons. But as it was, he had to work covertly, place the GPS tracker, and then hope to be able to arrange for the shipment to be intercepted at a later stage.

Once again, he waited patiently until no one was looking in his direction. Then he slipped out from behind cover and moved up next to the pallet with the chemical weapons, out of view of most of the soldiers. Moving casually so as not to attract attention, he reached into his pocket and extracted the black matchbox-sized GPS tracker. He peeled the thin plastic film off the self-adhesive strip on the back, and then stuck it to the back of the carbon fibre case. The tracker was so small and innocuous-looking that no one was likely to spot it unless they were looking for it. Having secured the unit to the case, he then walked behind the shelving units again to make his way back towards the office.

Suddenly there was a shout behind him, and for a few seconds, he thought he might have been spotted. However, when he peeked over the oil drums he was concealed behind, he saw one of the Wagner mercenaries remonstrating with a soldier driving a forklift. The soldier seemed to have clipped a bag on one of the pallets, and a white powder had spilt out onto the hangar's concrete floor. The Wagner mercenary was in the middle of a minor tirade, causing everyone else in the hangar to look in his direction, and Andrew used this to his advantage by moving swiftly to the other side of the hangar and slipping back into the office without being spotted.

He returned to the outside the same way he had come in, grabbed his backpack and slung it over his shoulder, and then he walked behind the back of the hangar away from the point in the perimeter fence where he had entered the airport. He briefly considered leaving the same way and getting back to the Lamborghini but decided that it would be too risky. The authorities would be looking all over for that car now, and they might already have collated CCTV footage from Porok, Obaid's house and perhaps even the international airport where he had dropped Irina off. There was no way he would be able to drive that car without ending up in a Syrian jail cell, most likely for the rest of his life. Or perhaps they would just drag him out of the car and shoot him in the middle of the street. Either way, what he needed was an alternative mode of transportation.

As he came to the back corner of the hangar, he could see across to another identical hangar around fifty metres away. There were no lights on inside, so he made his way over there as quickly and quietly as he could. As he walked, he glanced back over his shoulder a few times to make sure he wasn't being followed. Having successfully managed to place the tracker on the shipment of chemical weapons inside a hangar crawling with soldiers, he now had the distinct feeling that he was rapidly running out of both time and luck.

He entered the dark hangar by a side door. The huge main hangar doors were closed, but the hangar itself was not empty. Immediately in front of the doors was what appeared to be a mid-sized commercial twin-engine turboprop aircraft. It was about fifteen metres long with a wingspan of about the same. He walked closer to inspect it and realised that it was a Beechcraft's King Air B200, one of the most sold workhorses of small-scale commercial passenger aviation. He studied the aircraft for a few seconds and then smiled. This would do nicely.

He opened the aircraft's door, which was located towards the rear of the fuselage. Quickly climbing inside, he made his way forward through the passenger cabin to the cockpit where he flicked the switch to power up the avionics. Then he checked battery power, oil levels and the fuel gauge. All good to go. The fuel tank was almost full, and he knew that RAF Akrotiri in Cyprus was only about 300 kilometres away. With a bit of luck, he might be able to make it there in as little as an hour.

However, first, he had to get the plane out of the hangar, and then he had to get it airborne without being shot. After that, he needed to somehow evade the Syrian radar systems and its air force. Finally, he had to hope that the fast and manoeuvrable modern Russian fighter planes based at Khmeimim Air Base near Latakia on the Mediterranean coast would not be scrambled to intercept and shoot him down. It was a hair-brained plan, it was nonetheless his best shot at getting out of the country fast.

TWELVE

Andrew was just exiting the Beechcraft to go and investigate how to open the hangar doors when he heard the distant but distinctive harsh rasping sound of diesel engines starting and revving up outside. The two trucks had clearly now been loaded with the pallets packed with heroin, and they were now preparing to leave the airport. He reckoned they would soon be on their way to the port city of Tartus, where the heroin would be loaded onto a ship for the journey to Europe, no doubt camouflaged amongst innocuous Syrian agricultural products like cotton, olive oil and spices from the country's farms.

It turned out that the hangar doors were operated manually, so he grabbed onto the large metal handle on the door to the right and began pulling at it. Each door weighed many tonnes, and at first, he thought he would be unable to move them. He gripped the handle with both hands and pulled as hard as he could, and finally, the door began to move slowly to one side along its rusty metal track, creating an opening that was just wide enough for him to stick his head through. The sky outside was now a pale yellow, but the sun had not quite cleared the hills to the east. He looked out and to one side just in time to see the two trucks drive off, their red tail lights and black diesel exhaust disappearing behind the hangar as they headed along a service road towards the airport's main exit several hundred metres away.

Suddenly he heard the whine of a jet engine starting up, and then a few seconds later another engine. The cargo plane was getting ready to depart. It was taking the chemical weapons to their destination, where ever that was. The pitch and level of the engine noise increased dramatically, and then he saw the front of the aircraft begin to emerge from the hangar. Two armed soldiers were walking calmly along on each side of the aircraft, escorting it out of the hangar and onto the taxiway towards the runway. After a couple of minutes, the cargo plane was taxiing towards the end of the runway roughly five hundred metres away, and shortly thereafter it was accelerating rapidly along the military airport's only runway, which was orientated almost perfectly from west to east.

The cargo plane lifted off smoothly and gracefully into the early morning sky, and Andrew tracked it with his eyes for as long as he could before it disappeared into the morning haze. It had kept climbing gradually without changing its heading, and it seemed to be flying almost directly east. If it had needed to change its heading, it would already have banked either left or right and settled on a new course, but it had not done so. It just kept flying straight east.

Afghanistan, or perhaps Pakistan? thought Andrew. *What the hell is going on?*

He hoped the tracking device had not been detected, and that British Intelligence would be able to pick it up when the plane landed. If not, they would lose track of the weapons, and the next time they would hear about them again would probably be after the death of thousands of people. He briefly wondered if there was a way to get word to London and engineer a rapid response plan to shoot down the aircraft, but that had the potential for a different kind of disaster. The carbon fibre case would probably survive the plane being shot down by an air-to-air missile, but there was a risk that it would be ripped open upon impact with the ground. If this happened in a populated area, this could result in a truly catastrophic scenario involving a huge number of civilian deaths. The only thing he could do now was to put his faith in the GPS tracker and simply hope for the best. His least favourite option when it came to doing anything.

He heard the sound of a car engine starting up and looked over towards the hangar where the cargo plane had been loaded. There he saw a jeep pull out of the hangar and drive off in the same direction as the trucks. This would be the Syrian Army soldiers leaving for their barracks. There were four men inside the jeep. He couldn't remember how many he had spotted when he first arrived, but he felt sure that there had been more than four. He waited for a few moments to see if another jeep would emerge, but the airport had now fallen silent.

Deciding that he could wait no longer, he began opening the two hangar doors, pulling first one and then the other huge door along their metal rails to create an opening wide enough for the wingspan of the Beechcraft to fit through. They produced an uncomfortable amount of metallic screeching noises, but he had to keep going. Once the doors were open, he walked back to the Beechcraft and began taking off his stolen brown uniform.

He had just picked up his backpack to climb back up into the aircraft when he heard a voice calling out from behind him. It had come from the direction of the door to the exterior that he had come through about twenty minutes earlier. It was a man shouting something in Arabic. Andrew slowly turned around to see two Syrian Army soldiers approaching him with Kalashnikov assault rifles. They held their weapons in front of themselves, but they were not aiming directly at Andrew. Had they been part of the loading team in the other hangar? Had they spotted him and followed him here? Or were they part of a regular airport perimeter patrol?

From their facial expressions and the way in which they strode towards him, Andrew could tell that they had the swagger and easy confidence, arrogance even, that holding an automatic weapon invariably gives young men in uniform. He had seen it in abundance in Iraq and Afghanistan amongst both militants and local security personnel. But holding a weapon was not the same as being able to use it. And being able to fire it, was not the same as being able to use it well. Only a tiny select group of people in the world could be classed as firearms experts, and Andrew was one of the best of those people. He had fired hundreds of thousands of rounds in his military career, and to him, it was second nature, like walking or breathing. These two looked like they had only ever fired their guns on a firing range. Most likely, they would have their fire selectors on 'Safe'.

Andrew's backpack was at his feet, his Glock was in the chest holster at his side, and he had taken out the MP5SD and placed it just inside the aircraft on the floor by the door. As he began turning, he slowly moved his hands out to his sides, palms facing towards the two soldiers. The soldier nearest him shouted something in Arabic, which Andrew thought might have included the word '*silah*' meaning 'weapon'.

He raised his left hand further and reached slowly towards the holstered pistol with his right hand.

'Ok,' he said loudly but calmly. 'I'll put the gun on the floor.'

He released the leather strap and made a show of pulling his pistol out of the holster using only his thumb and his index finger as if it had been too hot to grip in his hand. He knelt down and placed it on the smooth concrete floor in front of him, and then he flung it forward, sliding it across the floor towards the two soldiers. During the couple of seconds that their eyes were fixed on the suppressed Glock 19 sliding and spinning towards them, Andrew, still kneeling, reached up behind himself and grabbed the MP5 from inside the Beechcraft. Before any of the two soldiers knew what was happening, he had brought the silenced submachine gun around to his front, pressed it into his shoulder, flicked the fire selector to burst fire mode and aimed at the first soldier. He squeezed the trigger and the MP5 spat out three bullets in quick succession, all of which hit the soldier in the neck and the head. His head whipped backwards from the force of the impacts and his knees buckled. As he was dropping to the floor, the other soldier panicked and raised his weapon. But it was already too late. Andrew's next volley smacked into his chest, all three bullets finding their target in a tight grouping square in his centre mass. He produced a strange cough as if he had taken a hard blow to the stomach, a surprised look on his face. Then he staggered back a couple of steps and fell onto his back, slamming the back of his head into the concrete floor with a loud crack. Then he lay still. Andrew rose from his crouched position and disengaged his weapon. Then he walked over to the two soldiers. They were both very dead.

He swiftly recovered his pistol, turned and walked back to the aircraft where he flung his backpack inside, climbed up and closed the door. He moved forward to the cockpit, and after a couple of minutes, he had familiarised himself with the aircraft to the point where he felt confident that he would be able to fly it, having piloted several similar aircraft over the years.

To his relief, the two turbo-prop engines sprang to life happily amidst a loud roar and copious amounts of black exhaust filling the back of the hangar. After a couple of seconds, they were idling smoothly, the engines having warmed up and the black smoke dissipated. He did not switch on the headlights or the navigation lights, since he wanted to remain as stealthy as possible. He disengaged the brakes and pushed forward on the throttle. Soon the Beechcraft was slowly rolling out of the hangar. Steering it along the taxiway towards the start of the runway, Andrew kept his eyes peeled for more soldiers, but the coast was clear. Driving the aircraft slightly too fast towards the end of the taxiway, he was finally able to feather the brakes, depress the left rudder pedal fully and steer the plane onto the runway. He didn't bother to stop before proceeding, but simply opened up the throttle to full as soon as he was able, and then flicked the lever to set the flaps to being fully extended.

The Beechcraft, carrying no passengers and no cargo, leapt forward and accelerated rapidly towards its takeoff speed of just over 200 kilometres per hour. Andrew pulled back gently on the yoke and the aircraft lifted off effortlessly. He banked right almost immediately, flying first south and further away from the city centre, and then turning to a heading of around 290 or west-northwest towards Cyprus. Retracting the flaps and raising the landing gear, the aircraft's airspeed indicator quickly nudged upwards to around 450 kilometres per hour. Ahead of him, less than ten kilometres away, the Anti-Lebanon mountains rose up to around 1500 metres. Anyone inside the military airport would no doubt have seen the Beechcraft take off, but he still stayed as low as he could in order to avoid being picked up by either military or civil aviation radar systems.

After almost 20 kilometres, which took only about six minutes to cover, he flew over the border with Lebanon. Through pure chance, he ended up flying almost directly over the village of Mazraat Deir al-Ashayer, from where he had initially crossed into Syria. He couldn't quite believe that it had not even been 36 hours since he had left the Toyota Rav4 at the petrol station down below.

Momentarily feeling a sense of relief at having made it into Lebanese airspace, his calm was suddenly shaken and his hair stood on end as he picked up a dark shape in his peripheral vision on the left-hand side of the aircraft. When he turned his head, his heart sank. Flying alongside him less than thirty metres away was a Syrian Air Force MIG-25 in desert camo livery, with the red, white and black bullseye logo emblazoned on its two vertical tail wings.

Designated *Foxbat* by NATO, this old Soviet interceptor aircraft dating back many decades, and its angular form revealed that it had been designed well before radar-defeating stealth technology had become mainstream in military aviation design studios. But its age did not mean that the aircraft wasn't able to pack a punch. Far from it. Andrew spotted the four air-to-air missiles mounted under its wings, and a single one of those fired at the Beechcraft would send it falling to the ground as thousands of burning pieces of wreckage.

The MIG-25 performed a quick wing-waggle, moving its wingtips up and down several times in quick succession. Andrew squinted and looked inside the cockpit where he could see the pilot looking back at him. He was wearing a grey helmet with markings and he had his hand raised. He was pointing down towards the ground. The message was clear. He wanted Andrew to land the plane immediately, and he clearly did not care that they were now in Lebanese airspace. For a moment, Andrew was wondering why he had not already been shot down, but then he realised that the pilot was almost certainly unaware of what had happened at the Mezzeh military airport just twenty minutes earlier. He had most likely just been on a regular combat air patrol when he had been directed to intercept an unauthorised flight from there.

Andrew needed to think fast. He obviously could not outrun the MIG and it was also much more manoeuvrable than the Beechcraft. But then he had an idea. He pulled the throttle back and the aircraft immediately began to lose speed. The pilot in the MIG attempted to match him, but Andrew was sure that the stall speed of the MIG, which is the speed below which the wings lose lift and the aircraft suddenly and dramatically begins to plunge belly-first towards the ground, was much higher than that of the Beechcraft. In other words, this meant that he would be able to fly much slower than the MIG.

He kept reducing the airspeed, and when it had dropped to around 230 kilometres per hour, the MIG was still next to him but with a very high angle of attack, its nose pitched steeply upwards as the pilot tried to compensate for the reduced lift generated by the MIG's wings. His gesticulations now looked decidedly angry. Andrew knew that he did not have much time, so he set the autopilot to fly straight ahead on a heading of 295, and he then locked the airspeed at 210 kilometres per hour. Slow, but still comfortably above the Beechcraft's stall speed. He figured there would be no way the MIG could match that speed without dropping out of the sky.

He grabbed his backpack and hurried back to the rear of the passenger cabin where he yanked the handle on the door downwards. He then pushed the door out and slid it aside, the cold air immediately rushing inside the cabin and tearing at his clothes. When he looked outside, he could already see the MIG beginning to inch ahead. Its pilot was simply unable to fly this slowly, but he was clearly also unwilling to veer off. Within another ten seconds, the MIG had moved ahead of the Beechcraft by about thirty metres, exposing its engine exhausts. They were huge. The MIG-25 had been designed purely as an interceptor and had been given two extraordinarily large and powerful engines to help it carry out that task, able to push the aircraft to a top speed of 3,500 kilometres per hour. But it had never been designed to fly this slowly.

Andrew wasted no time. He extracted his MP5SD from the backpack and slammed in a fresh 30-round magazine. He then took aim and held his breath. He knew he would only get one opportunity to get this right, and that his chances of success were slim. But right now, this was the only option he had if he was going to get out of Syria.

With the wind whirling around him causing his eyes to tear up, and using the doorframe to steady his aim, he then fired the submachine gun in short bursts, aiming at the exhaust of the MIG's right-hand engine. He was under no illusion about being able to shoot down the fighter plane. 9mm bullets packed nowhere near enough of a punch to do that, but all he had to do was damage one of the engines. The MIG, like most Soviet-designed aircraft, was built to take a beating. However, a jet engine is a fragile thing if it sustains damage to the delicate and extremely fast-spinning fan blades inside it.

He soon emptied the magazine. Aiming proved difficult because of the continuous movement of both aircraft, but Andrew sensed that several of the 30 bullets had found their mark, and he was soon rewarded with a big puff of smoke, a brief yellow flare of jet fuel burning brightly inside the exhaust of the engine, and then a lot more smoke shooting out of the back of the MIG. After a few seconds, during which time the MIG wobbled slightly as the pilot tried to figure out what was happening, the engine suffered a flameout and shut down, residual smoke still billowing out of its exhaust.

Down one engine, unable to determine what the problem was and clearly having lost his confidence, the MIG's pilot veered off and banked to the left, losing altitude as he did so. Right now, he would have several warning lights flashing amber and red inside his cockpit, and so his priority was no doubt now to get the damaged aircraft back to an airstrip as soon as possible.

Andrew grabbed the door again and was straining to pull it back towards himself. He was only just able to do it, and when it finally slotted back into the frame of the fuselage, thereby sealing the cabin off from the howling wind, Andrew was sweating and panting. He hurried back to the cockpit where he strapped in, disengaged the autopilot, shunted the throttle all the way forward again and began pushing the controls forward too. The Beechcraft immediately began to lose altitude but it also rapidly picked up speed. After less than thirty seconds, the needle on the airspeed indicator was pushing 560 kilometres per hour, near the aircraft's maximum safe speed.

Pushing the aircraft to its limits and flying west as low as he dared in order to avoid radar detection, Andrew crossed over the Mount Lebanon range. He could now see the Mediterranean Sea about thirty kilometres away. Ahead of him and to his right, he could make out the city of Beirut. He followed the contours of the valleys and ravines down the western side of the mountain range until he was barrelling over the hills just south of the capital.

As he approached the coast, the terrain flattened out and there were more and more houses and villages. When he finally roared over the rooftops of the coastal village of Naameh some fifteen kilometres directly south of the centre of Beirut, he felt relief for the second time during this flight but was quick to clamp down on it given what had happened earlier. For all he knew, there could be another squadron of Syrian Air Force fighter planes right behind him with their missiles locked on.

He adjusted his heading to 297, which is what the onboard navigation system told him he needed to do in order to fly straight for Cyprus and RAF Akrotiri. Distance, 243 kilometres. It was now a clear morning with hardly any wind, and the sea was calm as he skimmed the surface of the water, desperately trying to stay low enough to make sure he would not be picked up by shipborne radar systems mounted on Russian warships to the north near the port city of

Tartus, which was less than 100 kilometres away. The curvature of the Earth should just about be enough for him to stay hidden from them below the horizon.

He glanced down at the aircraft's instruments. There was still plenty of fuel left, and all the temperature and pressure gauges were still in the green, although several of them were flirting with yellow. He was pushing the aircraft to its limit, but as long as he made it to Akrotiri, he didn't care if the Beechcraft never flew again. He figured that it would be a question of time before modern Russian interceptors such as the SU-34 would be scrambled and sent south, and with their advanced look-down radar system, they would be able to pick him out on their scopes no matter how low he was flying.

The flight to Cyprus felt like the longest 20 minutes of Andrew's life. The entire way there, he couldn't shake the feeling that high above him there were Russian fighter jets having already locked on to the Beechcraft, and that at any second now he could be blown to smithereens by air-to-air missiles that he would never even see coming. Perhaps the missiles were already in the air and just moments from hitting him. Each second was another second where he found himself mildly surprised to still be alive.

He remained as low as he dared, skimming across the ocean until he was a few kilometres from Akrotiri. Then he recovered a few hundred metres of altitude, extended the flaps and lowered the landing gear to begin his final approach. He did not bother to try to raise the control tower. This was going to be an unauthorised landing, and regardless of what he did or how he did it, he could expect an armed welcome committee surrounding his aircraft with guns drawn as soon as it came to a stop. But right now, he could barely imagine a more welcome sight.

★ ★ ★

MES AYNAK, LOGAR PROVINCE, AFGHANISTAN

Doctor Xiao Yi was a long way from home. Hailing from the port city of Guangzhou, China, about 125 kilometres northwest of Hong Kong, he was used to a very different climate. As the capital of Guangdong province and located at the mouth of the Pearl River, Guangzhou had one of the warmest and most humid climates of any of China's major cities, and Yi was struggling badly with the parched and arid climate of central Afghanistan. His skin felt permanently dry and itchy, his lips were prone to becoming cracked, and no amount of facial moisturiser seemed to do anything other than make him look like a freshly basted pig about to be shoved in an oven. This somehow seemed appropriate, since the temperatures at the excavation site felt hot enough to cook with, and rarely seemed to drop to a tolerable level during the day. Only at night did he feel comfortable, but since there was virtually nothing to do at the small camp during the pitch-black evenings, he tended to go to bed early.

Working as a consultant for one of China's largest mining and metallurgical companies, Yi had been sent to Mes Aynak to oversee the archaeological excavation of a number of ancient Buddhist temples that were scheduled for destruction once the new copper mines opened. Settled by Buddhists in the 2nd century, Mes Aynak had already been inhabited for centuries, going back as far as the Bronze Age. Covering a combined area of upwards of half a million square metres, it was a large sprawling city during its heyday, and it had served as an important hub on the Silk Road from China to Europe for more than a thousand years.

Nowadays, its attraction was of a different kind. This mountainous area of Afghanistan, some 30 kilometres southeast of Kabul, held large copper deposits, and the Chinese company he worked for had secured the mining rights for the entire area. It was estimated that the copper deposits in the ground could be worth as much as one hundred billion dollars, and in the face of that much profit, concerns about the cultural heritage of Afghanistan counted for very little.

The excavation site that Yi was working on sat atop a long ridge. The sun was searingly hot, and the light breeze did little to cool him down. He was wearing dark linen trousers and a white shirt with suspenders, which he thought made him look sophisticated. He had black, short-cropped hair and wore small round glasses that gave him the appearance of squinting at everything. Beads of sweat had formed on his face, which combined with his generously applied moisturiser to make his forehead glisten in the sun, and his white shirt had large sweaty patches down his back and under his armpits.

Down in the valley below, he could see the long white pre-fab buildings with their blue-painted corrugated metal roofs, which constituted the initial outpost of the mining company. Bulldozers and huge trucks were busily re-sculpting the entire valley floor to prepare it for the new railway line and the small city that was about to be built there to serve to copper mine and its hundreds of workers. The mine was scheduled to open in four months, and Yi was part of a team of archaeologists that had been hired to excavate and remove as much of the ancient Buddhist site as possible before the ridge was sheared off the terrain to be replaced by a several-kilometre-wide pit, dug about 500 metres deep into the Earth. The archaeological effort had received international funding and employed tens of workers spread across dozens of individual sites throughout the valley. It had been a pre-requisite for the Afghan government signing off on the contract for the mining rights, and so Yi and a handful of other archaeologists had been brought in as consultants to oversee the effort.

Despite the site's clear connection to ancient Chinese culture and history, he had the distinct impression that the Chinese mining company was thoroughly disinterested in the Buddhist temples here. They were constantly pushing to wrap up the excavations that would allow them to begin the work of burrowing down into the ground for the precious resources hidden there.

The site on the ridge had been discovered using ground-penetrating radar, and today Yi was overseeing the packaging up of eight intact one-metre-tall Buddha statues that had been unearthed inside the temple. The ancient terracotta statues were most likely from the 3rd century and they were in remarkably good condition. Like the other artefacts that had been excavated at Mes Aynak, they had been carefully cleaned with soft brushes, wrapped in fine bubble wrap, and placed securely inside large bulky polystyrene boxes. Those boxes had then been sealed inside wooden crates for their onward journey. Unlike the previous batches, though, these eight statues were not going to the National Museum of Afghanistan in Kabul for processing. Yi had instead arranged for them to be loaded onto a truck and driven the 250 kilometres through Jalalabad and the Khyber Pass to Peshawar in Pakistan. Here they would be handed over to the buyer, who as far as Yi had understood it, was an anonymous private collector.

The deal had been agreed through a mysterious but extremely persuasive middle-man who had one day simply turned up at the dig site and presented Yi with an offer he couldn't refuse. The offer included an eye-watering number of zeroes. The middle-man had told Yi that the private collector was very keen on obtaining ancient Afghan art before it was ruined along with Mes Aynak after the opening of the mine. The middle-man had also pointed to the additional risk of the ancient artefacts being sent to Kabul, where they could end up being destroyed by zealous Taliban fighters who objected to any form of spirituality that did not conform to their narrow interpretation of Islam.

Whatever the case, Yi was not bothered either way. He just wanted the whole excavation project wrapped up as quickly as possible so he could get out of this backwater hellhole. All he wanted to do now was to go back to China to continue teaching at the Department of Archaeology at Sun Yat-Sen University in the Haizhu District of Guangzhou. The only reason he was here was that he had been paid a lot of money to put up with the appalling conditions, the insufferable climate, the awful food, and the barely literate locals who only spoke English. So, if he could hit two birds with one stone and speed things up whilst also taking a *finder's fee* from the private collector in Peshawar, then why shouldn't he? He just wanted to leave this place behind and go back to civilisation as soon as possible.

Thirteen

Mikhail Tokarev sat brooding in his soft leather chair inside his office on the first floor of the former cinema which now had the name *Porok* emblazoned on its façade in gold lettering. He was running his fingers through his short-cropped dark hair and scratching his stubble as he watched the footage on his laptop. His stocky frame was hunched over as his eyes narrowed and bored into the screen in front of him.

It was 5 a.m. The nightclub had closed its doors an hour earlier, and downstairs the regular cleaning staff were tidying up and getting the club ready to open again the next evening. In the storeroom a few metres from his office door, a specialist cleaner was busy scrubbing the blood and brains from the floor and the back wall where a member of his security team had been shot in the head by an unknown assailant several hours earlier.

The dead man's name was Pyotr, and Tokarev had known him since they had both joined the Wagner Group many years earlier. Pyotr was not the sharpest knife in the drawer, everyone knew that, but he was a good soldier and he was loyal. So, when Tokarev had struck out on his own after a number of years on the Wagner payroll, Pyotr, along with a handful of others, had joined him on rolling short-term contracts. Now he was dead meat, or what the Russian military officially designates 'Cargo 300'.

When Tokarev had initially joined Wagner Group after a career in the Russian airborne VDV, the PMC was still a relative newcomer on the international scene. Like all of the other men joining the company at that time, he had been attracted by the idea of being sent on exciting and dangerous missions to different parts of the world where the Russian Federation had vital interests. However, the main draw had been the prospect of being paid multiples of what he would have earned if he had remained with the VDV.

He and the other new Wagner recruits, all of whom were already experienced special forces operators, had been stationed at Wagner's main base near the village of Molkino, which is about 30 kilometres southeast of Krasnodar in the North Caucasus region of southern Russia some 70 kilometres from the Black Sea. The base happens to be right next to another base that is home to the Spetsnaz special forces, which are under the control of Russia's military intelligence agency, the infamous GRU.

Tokarev knew that technically speaking, mercenary businesses are both illegal and unconstitutional in the Russian Federation, but all this really meant was that the Kremlin had absolute control over their operation. They could imprison any of Wagner's people at any time over any perceived transgression against the Russian leadership, and its status as an illegal entity also ensured that the group would never present a threat to the Kremlin.

His deployment to Syria had happened just a few months after he had joined, and he and his fellow mercenaries had spent the first several months protecting the Syrian regime from multiple rebel groups who were attempting to overthrow the Syrian government in the wake of the Arab Spring. Eventually, the situation had degenerated into a chaotic civil war, with Russia supporting the Syrian regime in their fight against the rebel groups, many of whom were religious fundamentalists. The United States, which was in the middle of its own fight against ISIS in northern Iraq and eastern Syria, similarly had a significant military presence there in support of the mainly Kurdish SDF forces who were also battling ISIS.

It was during this time that the Wagner Group had been thrust into the limelight in Syria, and not for the reasons Tokarev would have wanted. With the Kremlin's approval, Wagner had signed a contract with the Syrian regime which stipulated that its Russian owners would be entitled to 25 percent of the output from any oil or gas fields they managed to recapture from the SDF. This resulted in a misguided and ultimately disastrous assault on a natural gas field controlled by the SDF. The gas field was located near the city of Deir al-Zour on the Euphrates River in eastern Syria near the border with Iraq some 400 kilometres northeast of Damascus. It became known as the Battle of Khasham, and it involved several hundred Syrian Army and Wagner Group mercenaries attacking the gas plant, which at the time was under the protection of a small contingent of Delta Force operatives and U.S. Marines who were working with the SDF against ISIS.

Watching the Syrians and the Russians approach the sprawling gas facility with infantry, artillery and tanks on their drone feeds, the US operations centre in Qatar used the deconfliction line to Russia to warn them to stay away, but the Syrians and the Russians kept coming. Eventually, the attacking force opened fire with T-72 tanks and artillery, after which the US responded with overwhelming force from stealth fighter jets, bomber aircraft, AC-130 gunships and Apache helicopters. The result was utter mayhem and destruction, and when the fight was over about four hours later, the Syrian and Russian forces had fled, leaving between 200 and 300 soldiers dead on the battlefield. There were no US casualties.

Tokarev had been part of that attacking force, and at the time, he and his comrades had no idea what they were about to go up against. All they had been told was that they were going to take over a gas field from the rebels and that they would get a large bonus payment upon completion of the mission. He was now convinced that the Kremlin had used the incident as an experiment. It was a simple way for the Kremlin to test the US military's commitment and willingness to fight in Syria, without putting any regular Russian Army forces in harm's way. Wagner mercenaries did not just offer Russia plausible deniability. They were completely expendable, and news about any resultant deaths could easily be controlled inside Russia by a news media that had been entirely co-opted by the Kremlin.

There was no doubt in Tokarev's mind that the Kremlin had callously sacrificed the Wagner mercenaries on the geo-political chessboard. He understood that this was part of the deal of being a mercenary and that their lives did not matter to the decision-makers in Moscow, but it still stung. After having served in the army of Mother Russia for decades, those soldiers had been sent off to certain death just so the Kremlin could test the resolve of the US over some desert outpost.

The ultimate insult had been when, after the intense battle where several hundred Wagner operatives and Syrian Army soldiers had been killed, the Kremlin had still denied that Russia had anything to do with it and had then refused to evacuate the dead and wounded. They had to make their own way back to Syrian government-controlled territory and only then were they airlifted back to Molkino on Russian military transports.

It was at that moment Tokarev decided to go private. He was sure he could do better by operating on his own, and he had established good relations with several Syrian Army officers such as Major Zahir Obaid and several others. This would end up greatly facilitating his transition to private enterprise. But his exit from Wagner did not mean that he would cut ties with the group entirely. He still had relationships with several of the senior officers there, just like he had maintained contact with people in the Russian army and the intelligence community. He had always known that those sorts of relationships might prove useful one day, and today was such a day.

He had just finished looking at the CCTV footage from inside Porok for the third time, and he suddenly realised that he could feel his own pulse in his carotid arteries. He was furious. Not only had this intruder co-opted that stupid bitch Irina and killed Pyotr. He had also taken out a Mukhabarat officer in the alley next to the nightclub and thrown his body into a dumpster. This was more than just irritating. It was bad for business since he and the Mukhabarat officer were planning to enter into an extortion scheme together, where Tokarev would supply the muscle to make sure certain local businesses paid protection money to the Mukhabarat officer, which Tokarev would then receive a cut from. And the last thing he needed was the secret police asking questions about the details of his operations in Damascus.

But worse still was the fact that the intruder had been inside his office and seemed to have looked at his laptop for several minutes. Because of the placement of the CCTV cameras, Tokarev could not see precisely what the man had been looking at, but there was literally nothing on that laptop that Tokarev did *not* want to hide from the outside world. For that reason, it was never even connected to the internet. From the angle of the camera, he wasn't completely sure if he was imagining things, but it looked as if the man had inserted a memory stick into the laptop. This was extremely concerning. Continuing to watch the footage for several more minutes, Tokarev was also puzzled as to why the man seemed to have studied the framed photos on his wall for such a long time.

He had tried to call Zahir Obaid to get him to mobilise the Mukhabarat and hunt down this little shit ASAP, but the Major had not picked up the phone all night. Perhaps he was with one of his mistresses again.

Tokarev scrubbed through the footage one more time to try to find moments where he could get a clear look at the intruder. The image quality was less than perfect, and the still images he was able to extract were grainy and slightly out of focus, but he nevertheless managed to secure two images that he thought were acceptable. Then he got on the phone to an old friend at the GRU who was based at their headquarters on Grizodubovoy Street back in Moscow.

A few minutes later, the images had been encrypted, emailed to his friend, received and decrypted, and then fed into the GRU's artificial intelligence-enhanced facial recognition software. Along with an algorithm built around a sophisticated convolutional neural network, it contained a huge database of images from known foreign military and intelligence operatives. Tokarev was confident that if the intruder was known to the Russian military intelligence services, then the algorithm would come up with a match eventually. All he had to do was wait.

* * *

When Andrew opened his eyes, it took him a few seconds to remember where he was. The past couple of days had been so eventful that it took him a moment to reassure himself that he really was at RAF Akrotiri, and that the images flashing through his mind of being shot down over the Mediterranean Sea inside the flaming wreckage of the Beechcraft had merely been a bad dream from which he had just woken up.

He sat up in the small but surprisingly comfortable bed inside the basic and utilitarian officer's room that had been provided to him at the barracks. He had been taken there earlier in the morning, once the resident MPs had been on the phone with Colonel Strickland in London and been reassured that he really was who he said he was.

It was now late afternoon, and he grabbed his phone to call London. The first number he dialled was Fiona's. She picked up almost immediately, and he relayed the events of the past couple of days since he had left London. She in turn relayed the details of what she had discovered about Nadeem Yassin and his connection to Zahir Obaid and Tokarev.

'It is amazing what you can cram into a few days if you make an effort,' he said, attempting to sound cheerful, but Fiona failed to see the humour in the situation.

'You could have got yourself killed several times over,' she said. 'Chemical weapons. Gunfights. Fighter planes?'

'Well, it's part of the job. And I got out, didn't I?' said Andrew, slightly defensively.

'By the skin of your teeth, by the sounds of it,' replied Fiona, clearly anxious. 'So, what now?'

'I am going to call Strickland and tell him that I need to head to Pakistan. I think the weapons are almost certainly there if they haven't already arrived in Afghanistan. Either way, my gut tells me that we don't have a lot of time. Whoever bought them is almost certainly intent on using them sooner rather than later. They must know that there will be efforts underway to recover them, so every day they sit in some storage facility is another day when their plan to deploy them might be foiled.'

'I don't suppose there is anything I could say to make you reconsider,' Fiona sighed. 'If you roll the dice enough times, eventually you are going to lose.'

'I'm afraid not,' replied Andrew. 'I'm already in too deep for me to suddenly pull out and let someone else take over. I'm the best man for the job.'

'Fine,' said Fiona, sounding resigned and anything but fine. 'Just… be careful. These people are clearly serious. They wouldn't think twice about sending someone like you to an early grave.'

'I know,' said Andrew. 'I am used to that by now. Anyway, I will call you when I can.'

'All right,' she said. 'Goodbye, Andy.'

Putting down the phone, Andrew wondered, and not for the first time, whether he was putting Fiona in an impossible situation. It was always much easier to be the one out in the field rather than the one staying behind wondering what was happening. But Fiona was strong, and she knew what she had signed up for when she moved in with him after their relationship had become serious. He then rang Colonel Strickland.

'Andrew,' said Strickland. 'Good to hear from you. I was glad to hear that the boys at Akrotiri didn't shoot down your plane after you suddenly popped up on their radar and headed straight for the airbase.'

'I was just happy to set foot on British soil again,' replied Andrew. 'Can't say I was too concerned with how I was greeted. Anyway, it was all sorted out quickly. Thanks for taking the call from the base commander.'

'No problem,' said Strickland. 'So, what did you find out in Damascus?'

Andrew proceeded to deliver a full debrief, including the details about the weapons storage facilities, his visit to Porok, how he had been forced to kill Zahir Obaid, and his suspicions about the destination of the chemical weapons. Strickland appeared unphased by it all and sounded like he was taking notes as Andrew spoke.

'What is your next move,' he asked. 'Sounds like we need to get you to Pakistan as soon as possible.'

'My thoughts exactly,' said Andrew. 'Although I will have to make my own way there using civilian transportation.'

'I agree,' said Strickland. 'You should go to Islamabad before you do anything else. Let me make a few calls first. When you arrive, you should head straight for the British High Commission. It wouldn't be safe for you to stay anywhere else in the city.'

'Who is in charge there?' asked Andrew.

'A chap called Philip Penrose,' replied Strickland. 'He's MI6 and head of station, so you'll have to run everything by him.'

'Everything?' asked Andrew hesitantly.

'Well,' said Strickland. 'Within reason, operational security allowing and all that.'

'All right,' replied Andrew, satisfied that he would have control over how much to share with the local intelligence people in Islamabad.

'Just, don't underestimate him,' said Strickland admonishingly. 'He might come across as a bit of a bumbling toff, but he's razor sharp and he likes to know everything that goes on in his station.'

'Got it,' said Andrew. 'I will keep that in mind. And I will try to keep you updated whenever possible. I might be off the grid for a while, depending on how things go.'

'I understand,' said Strickland. 'I am always here if you need me. Good luck.'

* * *

Later that evening, Andrew was walking to the gate at Larnaca International Airport and boarding a Qatar Airways flight to Doha, where he had a two-hour layover. Then he would continue on a connecting flight to Islamabad. Both legs of the journey were around three and a half hours long, which meant that he would be in Pakistan by late morning the next day.

He was travelling under his own name this time. Since he was going to be heading straight for the offices of the British High Commission in Islamabad, and since Pakistani intelligence would almost certainly be watching him as soon as he touched down, he saw no point in trying to hide his identity. In addition, travelling under his own name and using a diplomatic passport would allow him to skirt the regular luggage checks. This, in turn, meant that he would be able to bring a secure diplomatic case with the equipment

Matt Jones had issued to him in Beirut, rather than having to try to obtain new kit in Islamabad.

After stretching his legs and grabbing a cup of coffee in the transit area at Doha International Airport, he boarded the second aircraft where he had a window seat on the left-hand side of the aircraft. It took off and flew over the Persian Gulf, across southern Iran and then into Pakistan. After about two hours, just as the sun was coming up, the inflight map showing the position of the aircraft indicated that they were now skirting the southern border with Afghanistan by less than 20 kilometres. Andrew gazed out of the window and down on the hazy desert landscape. What was in front of him was a huge swathe of land that he and many of his comrades in the Regiment had come to appreciate for its raw beauty, and which had been populated by Pashtuns for millennia. But the border between Afghanistan and Pakistan was a completely artificial creation. The 2,600-kilometre-long border was known as the Durand Line, named after the British diplomat who drew it on a map in 1893, thereby changing the fate of tens of millions of people for centuries to come, and dividing their land into two separate parts. One was British India to the south. The other was the Emirate of Afghanistan to the north. A little over half a century later, the Islamic Republic of Pakistan broke away from India, inheriting this border with Afghanistan in the process.

This region of the world, situated as it was on the Silk Road, had always been a crossroad between east and west. It had once been conquered by Alexander the Great. It had been coveted for centuries by generations of Persian rulers, and it had been squeezed for yet more centuries between the colonial powers of Russia to the north and the British in India to the south. It had rarely ever known peace. As the fortunes of the global powers waxed and waned, this land had been buffeted by their respective armies as they battled the locals and each other for control. It was called the Graveyard of Empires for a reason.

Looking down, Andrew knew that he was looking at Helmand Province, where most recently more than four hundred British soldiers had been killed fighting the Taliban. From an altitude of about ten kilometres, it looked deceptively peaceful, beautiful even. But this was a case of appearances being deceiving if he had ever seen one. The Taliban had held a tight grip on power in both Helmand and the neighbouring province of Kandahar, and this had made it an extremely dangerous place for British troops to be deployed. His own memories of his time there were as clear as ever. The Taliban, who seemed to be everywhere and nowhere at the same time, had a particularly powerful hold over the local population in those provinces, and there was a very good historical reason for that fact.

Most people tended to think of Afghanistan as a chaotic and violent place, but as a keen student of history, Andrew knew that this had not always been the case. Far from it. Not even during modern times. In the 1960s the government instituted constitutional reforms designed to secularise the country and transform it to become a modern democracy. A parliament was elected and a new supreme court was established, both of which challenged the old order of religious leaders being the centre of decision-making and conflict resolution. In the major cities, women entered the workforce and the bars served alcohol to foreigners and Afghans alike. This transformation could have been the beginning of a new and modern era for Afghanistan, but it proved a step too far too fast. The rapid changes to Afghan society and the increasing influence of western culture created tensions between the urban Afghans and the rural tribes. On top of these tensions, the government reforms would invariably also be costly, and the central government's finances at the time were shaky, to say the least. The Cold War was well underway, and so the Afghan government decided to open the country up and attempt to play both sides. In the early 1970s, they let American companies enter the country, with all the effects that this had on local culture and attitudes, and at the same time, they invited the Soviet Union to come in and help modernise their military. Tensions in Afghan society between cities and the rural population increased.

Another source of tension was the fact that many of Afghanistan's military officers had received their training in the Soviet Union, and had come back firm believers in Marxism and Communism. When the civilian government ordered the arrest of communist sympathisers in April 1978, who by then were perceived to be a growing threat to the country's stability, parts of the military took power in a coup, almost certainly with Soviet backing. The result was the creation of a new socialist Afghan government backed by Moscow, which instituted several ideologically led reforms that were disastrous for the country's economy and general society. When dissent broke out in Herat and a number of Soviet advisors were killed, the Soviet Union responded in brutal fashion by carpet bombing the entire city, killing at least twenty thousand people. This extreme act of violence, which was to become a hallmark of Soviet and Russian foreign policy and military intervention, was most likely an attempt to send a signal to the Afghan people that dissent would not be tolerated. In the end, the Soviet Union launched a full-scale military invasion in December 1979 and they quickly took control of Kabul, where they installed a puppet government.

This was when the Mujahideen, a highly decentralised insurgent military force, began to take shape. They fought the Soviet occupation for a decade, pulling in fighters from other Muslim nations to take part in what they saw as a Jihad, a holy war, whilst increasingly being supplied by the United States who sought to limit Soviet expansion. In particular, the supply of the newly developed Stinger missiles to the Mujahideen ended up becoming a major factor in the war. Because of the difficult terrain in Afghanistan, tanks and soldiers were difficult to use effectively, especially against the Mujahideen who were experts at asymmetrical warfare and insurgent tactics. The only ace the Soviet Union had up its sleeve was heavily armoured Hind attack helicopters, but as soon as the Stinger missiles arrived, that advantage was taken away from them. Eventually, in 1989, the Soviet Union withdrew from the country, having been badly humiliated and having suffered the loss of around fifteen thousand men.

The war against the Soviet Union and the subsequent civil war between rival warlords through the 1990s had a devastating impact on the country. Large numbers of Afghan women and children fled to Pakistan where they were housed for years in refugee camps. Here, young boys were inducted into religious madrassas where they were taught very little except to recite the Koran in Arabic, a language they did not speak. When the thousands of boys from that generation became young men, they returned to Afghanistan, particularly the city of Kandahar. In that region, a new religiously inspired group was growing and beginning to take power in response to the increasingly chaotic situation in the country where rival warlords were still fighting for control. This new group was called the Taliban, meaning 'The Students', because of their strict adherence to Islam, and because most of them came from the madrassas in Pakistan.

The most prominent institution in the indoctrination effort was the Darul Uloom Haqqania seminary located halfway between Islamabad and Peshawar. Its thousands of alumni were given a fundamentalist view of Islam and of society, and during this period Pakistan's military intelligence, the Inter-Services Intelligence agency or ISI, provided the Taliban with broad support. The reason for this support, which included military, financial and logistics, was partly an attempt to exert control over neighbouring Afghanistan, and partly an effort designed to prevent certain India-backed Mujahideen groups in the north of the country from taking power.

One of the most impactful products of the ISI's involvement was the Haqqani Network, which was named after the Haqqania seminary. Considered an offshoot of the Taliban, and now designated a terrorist group by the West, this network was initially one of the Mujahideen groups that received the most CIA funding during the Reagan administration in the 1980s.

The Taliban were predominantly of the Pashtun ethnic group, which gave them a lot of local support amongst the overwhelmingly Pashtun population in the country's southwest, and this made it easy for them to take over neighbouring provinces. Expanding north and then east after the Soviet withdrawal, they variously defeated and bribed local warlords to join them, and eventually, they would rise to take over almost the entire country. They entered Kabul in 1996 and formed a government that followed an extremely strict Pashtun-inspired interpretation of Islam.

Suddenly, women had to be accompanied by a man at all times. Men had to grow beards. It even prohibited basic activities such as watching TV, listening to music and flying kites. Having succeeded in taking over most of Afghanistan and fulfilling their ambition of creating a state ruled in accordance with Islam as they interpreted it, they then made the fateful decision to give shelter to Osama Bin Laden after September 11, 2001.

Andrew had read most of what there was to read about the Taliban, and although it was often said that the Taliban was created by Pakistan's ISI, he realised that it was slightly more complicated than that. It was equally true that American dollars sent to Pakistan had so corrupted that nuclear weapons-armed country, that it caused the ISI in many ways to be the de facto ruler of Pakistan. In this manner, the Taliban was ultimately nurtured and grown using US funds. Benazir Bhutto, who was Pakistan's Prime Minister in the early 1990s, warned President George W. Bush that the US was "creating a Frankenstein monster" with its funding of the Mujahideen. The warning went unheeded, and the covert CIA programme codenamed Operation Cyclone which funded the Mujahideen through the ISI, continued.

There was another unforeseen effect of these enormous sums of money flowing into Pakistan. The arrival of billions of dollars from the US over the course of several decades had fostered corruption on a truly massive scale. The army was now one of the biggest real estate owners in Pakistan, and its generals were some of the wealthiest men in the country. This represented a threat to the system, but not in the way most people would assume.

The reality was that the single biggest threat to the status quo in Pakistan, and thereby to the ISI, was the eradication of terrorism and the Taliban. The reason was that the defeat of the Taliban would lead to the turning off of the faucets that had poured huge sums of American taxpayer money into Pakistan. For this simple reason, the ISI had an ongoing incentive to assist the Taliban, to help them to remain in power so that they could continue to present a perceived terrorist threat to the West. Pakistan, through the ISI, was playing both sides.

This complicated dynamic had eventually made the ISI by far the most important player in Pakistan, and Andrew suspected that he would have to engage with them at some level in order to make progress in his investigation. He was not expecting them to provide direct support, but he was hoping that they would allow him to continue his attempts to track down the chemical weapons. Surely, it would be in the ISI's own interest to make sure that those weapons were never used, either in Afghanistan or inside Pakistan itself.

With about thirty minutes to go before landing, Andrew leaned close to the window and looked out into the distance. He thought he was able to spot the famous Khyber Pass, which connects Pakistan with Afghanistan across the section of the Hindu Kush called the Spin Ghar mountain range, and which had been one of the most important and challenging points along the Silk Road. During more recent times it had served as a veritable highway for the Taliban as they shuttled back and forth between the madrassas and training grounds in northern Pakistan and the battlefields in Afghanistan. Knowing how many of his fellow soldiers, both from within the SAS and from the regular army, had lost their lives in Afghanistan at the hands of the Taliban, he couldn't help but feel a sense of bitterness at the duplicity of Pakistan and its intelligence services. But he knew he had to put those emotions aside and pretend to play nice with them. At least for now.

FOURTEEN

Xiao Yi was in his temporary accommodation inside one of the basic pre-fab units built in the valley of Mes Aynak. The evening before, he had made sure to personally oversee the departure of the truck carrying the eight ancient Buddha statues. After a surprisingly good night's sleep, he had now just come back from breakfast, such as it was, at the staff canteen. As he sat down on his bed, a message pinged in on his phone. It was from the Pakistani middleman.

The transfer of the payment for the statues had come through. It was not exactly a life-changing sum of money, but it equated to around six months' worth of his regular salary at the University back in Guangzhou.

Easy money, he thought and smiled, suddenly finding himself wondering if somehow there might be similar opportunities for him out there. He would have to dedicate some time to research that. Perhaps this could be the start of a new and more interesting life.

He also checked his emails and discovered a message which appeared to be from the mining company's HQ in Beijing, although he did not recognise the name of the person that had sent it. However, it did have the right email suffix, and there were hundreds of people working at HQ, so the fact that he had never heard of this person was not particularly surprising.

He read through it and couldn't quite believe what it said. Apparently, the head office was so pleased with his work that they had decided to allow him to return to Guangzhou if he should wish it, without suffering the usual financial penalty for early contract termination, and even with a nice bonus to boot. His replacement would arrive within a few days, but he would not be asked to stay on for a handover of responsibilities. A car had been arranged for him that afternoon, which would take him to Kabul International Airport for a flight to Guangzhou late that same evening.

Yi sat back, staring into the middle distance for a moment. This was incredible news. He had been paid by the middleman and now he was free to leave this objectionable place. No more dry heat. No more crappy food. No more having to listen to the locals mumbling incomprehensibly in Pashto. No more having to be woken up every morning by that bloody call to prayer. He was going back to China. Back to civilisation. He got to his feet and went off to pack his things for the car ride that afternoon. This was one trip he did not want to miss.

When the car arrived later that day, Yi was surprised to find that it was an old white jeep and not an official car from the mining company's fleet of vehicles. But even more irksome was the fact that the driver stepped out and handed him the keys. After a brief exchange in broken English, the driver shrugged, pointed at the car and walked away. Apparently, the man had business here at the site, and Yi would have to drive the roughly 40 kilometres to the airport by himself.

Yi was highly irritated. He had been used to chauffeur-driven cars, and now he had to get behind the wheel himself. He produced a huff as he watched the driver walk away, but then he got into the jeep. There was no way he was going to let an administrative cock-up get in the way of him leaving this shithole and returning to his home town. He started the engine, put the car in gear and drove north out of the valley towards Kabul. Up ahead several kilometres away, he could see the mountain pass that he would need to traverse in order to make his way back down onto the plain in between the Hindu Kush mountains where the Afghan capital was located.

* * *

Up on a ridge three kilometres north of the Mes Aynak Valley, a young lean man wearing a brown kameez and a dark green turban dismounted his horse and detached a satchel from the horse's saddle. He walked over to a spot where he had a full view of the valley below. Here, he knelt down. Extracting a pair of binoculars from the satchel, he directed his gaze along the road whose hairpin bends wound their way up one side of the pass and down the other. In the distance, he could see a small cloud of dust that was moving slowly in his direction. After a couple of minutes, he was able to make out the vehicle through the shimmering haze. It was the white jeep.

Waiting patiently for the vehicle to make its way up past all the hairpins to the pass, he watched as it traversed the brief flat saddle point between the two nearby mountain peaks. Then it began making its way down the other side towards Kabul which was just visible in the far distance.

The man reached inside the satchel again, this time extracting an old Nokia phone.

* * *

Xiao Yi was nervous. The drive up towards the pass had been laborious, with all the hairpin bends requiring him to constantly wrestle the wheel left and right. Without power steering, it had been a strenuous task for someone who wasn't used to any form of physical exercise. However, the drive down towards Kabul made him even more anxious. It was not quite as steep as the road he had just travelled up, but there were at least as many hairpin bends, and he would have to use the engine as well as the brakes to try to reduce speed on the steepest stretches. Yi had never been a confident driver, and this old jeep felt more like a tractor than a modern car. Still, if this was what it would take for him to leave this place, then so be it.

As the Jeep entered the first turn, it left a small trail of fluid on the road behind it. The bleeder valves on the car's brakes had been opened slightly before the vehicle had been handed over to Yi, but there had been no need to use the brakes driving up towards the pass. Only now that he needed to apply pressure to the brakes did the brake fluid begin to flow out of the valves.

Between two hairpin bends, Yi glanced down at the dashboard. The engine temperature was flirting with the red area, and every time he let go of the clutch in order to use the engine to bleed off speed, the engine would whine unnervingly and the revs displayed on the car's tachometer would spike well beyond what he was comfortable with.

He hauled the wheel over to one side to take the next turn, whilst keeping his foot on the brake, and that was when it happened. The firm resistance he had felt through his right foot as it rested on the brake suddenly disappeared, and he instantly sensed the car beginning to accelerate. Looking down into the footwell with a panicked expression on his face, he began frantically pumping the brakes, but nothing happened. It was as if the brakes had been completely disabled.

He reached down and grabbed the handbrake, yanking it upward as hard as he could, but as he did so he felt the metal wire connected to the brakes snap. Suddenly the handbrake felt like a flimsy lightweight doorhandle.

The car picked up more and more speed as it continued down the slope towards the next hairpin bend. Yi looked ahead, and while producing a panicked moan he positioned the car all the way over on one side of the road, trying to give himself as wide a turn as possible. Timing it almost perfectly, he wrestled the steering wheel to one side and somehow miraculously managed to keep the car on the road as it negotiated the bend. His reward was another bend less than fifty metres away. The car was now travelling dangerously fast and Yi briefly considered opening the door and launching himself out and onto the road, but he simply did not have the courage to do that. At fifty kilometres per hour, it would be like landing on a cheese grater. But if he stayed in the car, he could end up seriously hurt as well. Before he could reconsider, the next bend was upon him.

Through force of habit, he pressed down on the brake once more, only to sense how the brake pedal felt completely disconnected from the rest of the car. This momentary distraction caused him to misjudge the bend and enter it too late, which resulted in the Jeep tipping onto two wheels as it made the turn.

As soon as the two inside wheels lifted off from the road, Yi panicked and instinctively began to correct by turning the wheel the opposite way. The car straightened up and the two inside wheels slammed back down onto the road again. However, the car was now inexorably heading for the flimsy-looking stone barrier that had been set up along the road. On the other side of it was a cliff edge with a fifty-metre plunge down to the bottom of a narrow ravine.

Yi cried out in terror as the Jeep smashed through the stone barrier. He felt the hard jolt as the car impacted the barrier, but within a couple of seconds, he then experienced the confusingly tranquil weightlessness as both he and the vehicle accelerated towards the ravine below at exactly the same speed. The car began to turn over in the air as it fell, and his vision was a blur of sky, then rocks, then sky again.

He only just had time to look out of the side window before the car spun again and then smashed down violently onto the bottom of the ravine. His head slammed hard against the side door as the car crumbled and deformed. Then everything went dark.

When he came to, his ears were ringing and he was unable to work out where he was. His eyes were closed and felt strangely puffy when he tried to open them. He reached up to his bruised face and felt it covered in sticky blood. But somehow the blood was dripping upwards. That was when he realised that the car was upside down and that he was still strapped to his seat. Incredibly, the seatbelt and the sturdy old chassis had saved his life. He was alive. He was going to make it. He just had to get out of the car and then hope his phone was undamaged. Then he could call for help and leave this hellhole for good.

His shaking hands found the buckle and pressed the release button. He instantly crashed down onto the inside roof of the overturned and mangled Jeep, a sharp pain shooting through his back and his legs. He looked down and saw that his right leg was bent at an unnatural angle, and as he watched it, he was struggling to fathom that it was his own. For some reason, the pain had not hit him yet, and he just stared at it for a moment. Then he realised that he was still in danger. He could smell petrol. If the car caught fire, he would be burnt alive. He had to get out. He reached for the door handle next to him, and in that instant, Xiao Yi's life ended.

The explosive device had been attached to the car's fuel tank and connected to a mobile phone taped to the device. It detonated with a powerful crack that rolled down the ravine and could be heard many miles away. In an instant, the vehicle became enveloped in a huge orange fireball. An angry-looking column of black smoke roiled up from the explosion.

A couple of seconds later, the soundwaves from the explosion reached the man on the ridge, momentarily startling his horse. However, it soon calmed down again. It had been bred to be used in skirmishes in the Afghan mountains, and gunfire and explosions had been a regular occurrence throughout its life. The man took one last look at his handiwork, and then he mounted the horse and rode off slowly down the trail towards the east. His job was done. Now he had to report back to his master, the Emir.

* * *

When Andrew arrived in Islamabad mid-morning and took a taxi from the airport to the British High Commission in the Ramna 5 neighbourhood of the city, it initially reminded him of Cairo. There was the same crowded bustle of life and noise, similar-looking buildings, the same heat and the same chaotic traffic that left him happy to have a competent local driver rather than having to navigate the maze of streets himself. The biggest difference was the smells. Every so often the taxi would pass a food vendor or a restaurant, and it would immediately become clear that the smells of herbs and spices here were very different from those in Egypt. And whenever the taxi slowed down at an intersection, he was able to hear fragments of conversations between locals walking along the pavement, either talking to each other or on their phones, mostly in Urdu or Pashto.

The British High Commission was located in a large brutal-looking concrete structure inside the diplomatic enclave on the north-eastern outskirts of Islamabad. It was next to the Embassy of Thailand and the High Commission of Malaysia, and it was a small and almost self-contained piece of the UK inside Pakistan. Andrew was met at the gates by a tall well-groomed man who looked to be in his mid-thirties. As he got out of the taxi, the man approached with his hand outstretched and a friendly smile on his face.

'Mr Sterling,' he said. 'My name is Chris Saunders. I am Philip Penrose's deputy. Very nice to meet you. Did you have a good flight?'

'And you,' replied Andrew, shaking Saunders' hand. 'Yes, it wasn't too bad.'

'Please come with me,' said Saunders, who looked exactly like someone might expect a young British diplomat to look, but Andrew knew that for all intents and purposes, Saunders was an intelligence operative. 'The high commission is in the main building over there. We're over this way.'

He motioned towards another concrete structure set back about fifty metres from the main gate on a neatly manicured lawn between a number of cedar trees. It was three storeys tall with dark tinted windows and a main entrance guarded by two armed security guards – both Caucasian.

'I take it you'll want to get cracking as soon as possible,' continued Saunders. 'So, I will take you straight upstairs and introduce you to Philip Penrose, our head of station. He might come across as a bit eccentric, but he knows what he is doing. Very well connected at all levels here in Pakistan.'

'Very good,' said Andrew. 'Please, lead the way.'

They entered the building and walked across the polished stone floor of the reception area to the elevators which took them up to the top floor of the building. As they exited the elevator, Andrew picked up the faint smell of cigarettes, and as he looked around there was an unmistakable air of Britain's colonial past about the place. Perhaps it was the ornate furniture or the large oil paintings on the walls. Whichever it was, there was a distinct sense of this place existing with one foot in the past.

They walked past a small reception with another pair of armed guards and then along a carpeted corridor to a door at the far end. Saunders knocked gently, and immediately a voice came from the other side.

'Come!' it said.

Saunders opened the door and turned to Andrew.

'This way, please,' he said, motioning for Andrew to enter ahead of him.

Philip Penrose's office was sizeable, with ample room for a large desk overlooking the gardens of the High Commission through large windows dressed with Venetian blinds that were made of light-coloured wood. There were also a couple of sofas and a coffee table arranged next to a section of wall with bookcases crammed full of literature, and a large open floor area, at the end of which stood a man who appeared to be in his mid-fifties. The first word that popped into his mind when he laid eyes on the station chief was 'suave'. He was wearing light khaki trousers, a white shirt with cufflinks and suspenders, and on his feet were a pair of perfectly polished dark brown dress shoes. Penrose was tall and sported neatly trimmed reddish blond hair with a side parting, and as Saunders and Andrew entered, he briefly looked up, but then reverted his gaze to the floor by his feet where he was about to hit a golf ball with the putter he was holding in his hands.

'One moment,' he said in a clipped accent. 'Please do sit.'

Saunders looked at Andrew, gestured towards the sofas and nodded. Andrew shrugged and walked over to the nearest one, unbuttoned his jacket and sat down.

Penrose took his time to hit the ball gently with the putter, and as he did so it rolled in a perfectly straight line along the short-piled grey carpet to a small green plastic putting cup that had been placed near the sofas. It then rolled up the shallow ramp and came to rest inside the putting cup, which played the first ten notes of 'Rule Britannia'.

As Penrose watched the ball roll along the floor, Andrew in turn watched Penrose. He was handsome, but he seemed to have a slight curl of his upper lip on the left side of his mouth, giving him the appearance of having a permanent condescending sneer on his face. Strickland had told him that he was the great-grandson of some 'Lord Penrose' whose exact claim to fame Andrew could no longer remember. Something to do with South African cotton production. He exuded the easy and slightly arrogant confidence that comes with growing up as an aristocrat in England with at least one silver spoon in his mouth. Andrew had no doubt that this chap would have had a trust fund and several nannies by the time he was three, and that his time at Cambridge, followed by a stint at the Foreign Office and then MI6, had been helped along at least to some extent by his surname. Apparently, he had been stationed in Paris and then Moscow before being sent to head up MI6's operation in Islamabad.

Penrose held up the putter in front of himself and studied it for a few seconds, a sly smile spreading across his face to reveal a perfect set of teeth.

'Bloody marvellous,' he crowed. 'Titanium shaft. Head milled from a single piece of high-grade steel. Perfectly counter-balanced pentagonal grip. It might cost a bomb, but that's a small price to pay to ensure that I beat that tremulous Bancroft on Saturday. He's the Deputy High Commissioner, but for the life of me, I will never understand how he ended up in that job. If it were up to me, He'd be scrubbing the toilets of the toilet cleaners.'

Penrose's locution reminded Andrew of how someone had once described that particular way of speaking as sounding less like speech, and more like modulated yawning.

'Anyway,' continued Penrose as he walked to the sofa and sat down opposite Andrew. 'You're Andrew Sterling. correct?'

'That's right,' replied Andrew.

'SAS?' asked Penrose nonchalantly.

'Technically, yes,' replied Andrew. 'I sometimes need to get my hands dirty, but I spend a lot less time in the field than I used to.'

'Intriguing,' smiled Penrose, clearly tickled by Andrew's ambiguous answer.

'Anyway, thanks for seeing me,' said Andrew evenly with a business-like demeanour. 'I take it Colonel Strickland has already briefed you on why I am here?'

'More or less,' said Penrose with an air of vague indifference as he draped one arm over the armrest and swung one leg over the other. 'I understand that you believe you're tracking a shipment of Russian chemical weapons obtained from Syria, is that right?'

'Yes,' replied Andrew. 'I have reason to believe that they have made their way either here to Pakistan or into Afghanistan.'

Penrose regarded Andrew for a few moments with a dubious expression.

'Hmm,' he said, sounding unconvinced. 'I must say, that sounds slightly far-fetched, but then so did the idea that Osama Bin Laden was living in a house next to the Pakistani Army's officer academy. You never know, these days. In hindsight, it all seems tediously obvious, of course. If you assume that the Taliban is an operational extension of the ISI in Afghanistan, and if you reflect on the fact that the Taliban was responsible for the safety of Bin Laden because of the ancient custom of Pashtunwali, then it isn't really a great leap to end up concluding that the placement of Bin Laden in that safehouse was an ISI operation. Anyway. Water under the bridge now.'

'If I may,' interjected Saunders, raising one hand slightly from his lap and looking at Andrew. 'As you might know, Pashtunwali is the ancient custom of showing ample and virtually unquestioning hospitality towards travellers, even if they are perfect strangers. This is taken very seriously in this part of the world.'

'Yes, I am familiar with the concept,' nodded Andrew politely.

'I must say,' exclaimed Penrose with a look of surprise mixed with amusement as if he had forgotten that Saunders was in the room and that he was even able to speak. 'I do marvel at your perspicacity, young Saunders. Why you haven't yet been made head of this station, thereby sending me off to my well-deserved pastures, is truly beyond my ability to comprehend.'

Saunders shrank visibly back onto his seat on the sofa, a look of embarrassment but also mild annoyance on his face.

Andrew watched Penrose impassively, as the station chief asserted his authority. He clearly had a large and fragile ego, and while he might have come across as being indifferent to Andrew's mission and to the possible presence of chemical weapons in Pakistan, Andrew somehow also got the distinct impression that he was less than thrilled to have Andrew poking around on what he no doubt very much regarded as his own turf. He decided to steer the conversation in a different direction.

'I take it you work completely independently of the High Commission?' he asked.

'Between you and me and the lamp post,' said Penrose, 'I wouldn't trust those people any further than I could throw them. They like to pretend that everything here is rosy and that if the UK just focuses on promoting trade between our two countries, then eventually everything will be all right. They haven't got the foggiest idea of the kinds of threats this country represents to the West. Without the intelligence gathering operation that my department undertakes, there would have been untold numbers of attacks against British interests both here and in the UK. They think everything can be reduced to business and British Pounds, but trust me when I tell you that information is the only currency that matters here. And control of information translates into influence, and that is the ultimate game we play here.'

'So how do you procure this information?' asked Andrew.

'Well,' said Penrose, adjusting his silver cufflinks. 'We have an extensive signals intelligence operation here, and we are obviously fully plugged into 5-Eyes. But the really valuable stuff comes from human intelligence sources. The bloody ISI is flush with cash and therefore profoundly corrupt, and that in turn causes predictable power struggles inside that agency. This ultimately paves the way for us to exploit personal grievances and internal power struggles, in order to obtain information about their current operations and overall policy-making. Many of those operations are of a highly clandestine nature, and they mostly have the objective of supporting religious and political groups inside Afghanistan.'

'You will understand this much better than I do,' said Andrew, 'but it is my impression that the ISI seem to think of Afghanistan as their backyard and that they are somewhat obsessed with the Taliban.'

'Oh absolutely,' replied Penrose. 'They created the damn thing to begin with. But like most parents, they can't seem to accept that their child is now fully grown and wants to decide things for itself.'

'Have you been able to penetrate the Taliban with human intelligence operatives?' asked Andrew.

'We're constantly trying to develop sources inside the various religious seminaries, not least the Darul Uloom Haqqania,' replied Penrose, 'but it is extremely challenging, to tell you the truth. Most of those people can't be tempted with money, and they are ideologically locked into the Haqqani way of thinking. We've had several instances where we have been cultivating nascent relationships with people there, only to have them disappear under mysterious circumstances, or even turn out to be ISI operatives placed to spy on *us*.'

'Double agents?' asked Andrew, somewhat taken aback.

'Yes, you might call it that.'

'So, essentially the ISI is still trying to run Afghanistan remotely?' asked Andrew.

'Oh yes, they are as active as they have ever been,' replied Penrose. 'To them, Afghanistan is not a project they cultivate for a decade and then move on from. Afghanistan's future is potentially an existential threat to Pakistan, so they are in it for the long haul. Their planning stretches across many decades. There is even talk that their aim is to persuade the Taliban to attempt to take Kashmir from India. I wouldn't put it past them.'

'How would you rate the ISI?' asked Andrew. 'Are they competent? Do you take them seriously?'

'Well,' shrugged Penrose with a slightly annoyed demeanour. 'We have to. And they are quite effective, if that's what you mean. They tend to get things done. But they're bloody lunatics if you ask me,' he continued, producing a chortle and sounding as if he meant it but really didn't care. 'They are less of an intelligence agency and more of a covert operations outfit these days. A state within a state, and with absolutely no political oversight. We have countless examples of them spending a significant amount of their resources on tracking down and assassinating Pakistani dissidents that have fled abroad. They have murdered dozens of their own citizens in several western countries, but always with enough layers of people separating them from the perpetrator to credibly claim that it had nothing to do with them. And as you know, their funding of the Taliban is legendary. Let me tell you, those bastards seem to have more money than God.'

Penrose sounded almost envious as an odd smile formed on his face. Then he continued.

'As I am sure you know, the Americans had been funding them to high heaven, quite literally!' Penrose produced a high-pitched laugh, clearly amused by his own joke. 'Seventy-two virgins and all that?' he continued.

'Yes, I got it,' said Andrew, indulging the station chief.

'There are obviously some good eggs in there as well,' continued Penrose. 'But the agency itself is rotten to the core. Still, it all keeps us busy, eh?'

'How about sources on the inside?' asked Andrew. 'Have you been able to develop anything there?'

Penrose paused for a moment as if pondering how much to tell Andrew.

'Well, I have several contacts on the inside,' he said in his somewhat snobbish accent and sounding as if he was now mildly bored with the topic. 'However, I am obviously not privy to the strategic aims of the organisation. All I know is that you can't trust the bastards. And frankly, in this world of fragile and ever-shifting allegiances, I must say that I prefer it that way. The Pakistanis are uniquely reliable in the sense that they are always absolutely and completely unreliable. So at least we know where we stand, and we should interact with them accordingly. Once you accept that reality, this whole game simply becomes about getting the most out of any given situation.'

'Game?' asked Andrew.

'Oh, come now,' said Penrose superciliously. 'It's all a game, old chap. They spy on us. We spy on them. We shake hands in public and stab each other in the back behind the scenes. Oldest story in the spy book. I mean, let's not pretend that we're all friends here. The intelligence business is ruthless. It is all about getting an edge on your counterpart and then using that to squeeze them as hard as you can to get as much out of them as possible. You can't be sentimental about these things, my boy. There is no such thing as trust in this business.'

'Sounds lonely,' observed Andrew. 'So why are you here, if I may ask? What do you get out of this?'

'Me? Well, it certainly isn't the money,' chortled Penrose almost scathingly. 'I suppose I just love the chase.'

Listening to Penrose, Andrew thought he had the air of someone who had grown up with a silver spoon in his mouth, and he genuinely didn't seem to care whether the whole world went to hell. To him, it was all just a game he played for the sake of amusement. A way of passing the time between checks from his trust fund. Checks that no doubt made his monthly salary from MI6 look like charity.

'I might need your help in establishing some sort of contact within the ISI,' said Andrew. 'Perhaps find out if they have picked up anything about these chemical weapons shipments.'

Again, Penrose looked dubious. He leaned forward slightly and made a steeple with his hands in front of himself, whilst taking on a ponderous look. Then he shrugged and spread out his hands.

'I will see what I can do,' he finally said. 'Saunders and I will have a chat about this later. I can't promise anything, of course. You don't just call up the ISI and ask them for information.'

'I understand,' said Andrew. 'Any help you can arrange would be appreciated, not just by me but by London. I would expect Pakistan to take this as seriously as we do.'

Penrose nodded slowly, studying Andrew for a moment.

'Right,' he finally said, glancing at his wristwatch. 'Well, it was nice to meet you Mr Sterling, but I must get on with things.'

At that, Saunders rose and Andrew followed suit.

'Thank you for your time,' said Andrew, offering his hand.

'No problem,' said Penrose and shook it, somehow managing to convey a sense that he thought Andrew now owed him a favour. 'If you need anything else, Saunders here is your man.'

Andrew and Saunders exited Penrose's office and made their way back along the corridor to the small reception area before speaking again.

'Quite a character,' said Andrew, raising one eyebrow and glancing sideways at Saunders as the two of them rode the elevator back down to the ground floor. Saunders smiled the sort of smile that betrayed not only complete agreement but also the notion that this was a generally accepted truth here at MI6 in Islamabad.

'He is not always the easiest boss to work for,' he said, almost apologetically. 'But he is a force to be reckoned with. He has developed an extensive network of contacts inside the Pakistani army and the ISI, and it has yielded real results on several occasions, including some fairly high-profile cases on the other side of the border with Afghanistan. He's quite enmeshed here, and he is very well-connected. Some people here think he will never return to England.'

'Really?' asked Andrew. 'Why is that?'

'Rumour has it that he has gone native,' said Saunders with a knowing look.

'What do you mean?' asked Andrew evenly.

'Well,' said Saunders furtively. 'According to local chatter, he has got himself a local lover whom he sees regularly. She is supposedly much younger than he is. She could be an ISI operative for all I know.'

'Where did that rumour come from,' asked Andrew. 'And couldn't that represent a security risk? I would expect him to be vetted and monitored on an ongoing basis, precisely to avoid a scenario like that.'

'Oh, we all are,' replied Saunders. 'But all that stuff is above my paygrade. I have to assume that there isn't a problem.'

'Right,' said Andrew ponderously as they left the building and exited out into the pleasant grounds of the High Commission compound.

'Let me show you to your digs,' said Saunders. 'They are over in the main building. A bit basic, but perfectly comfortable.'

'I am sure I have seen worse,' said Andrew.

'How long do you expect to stay for?' asked Saunders breezily.

'I really couldn't say at this point,' replied Andrew. 'It all depends on whether I can pick up the trail of those weapons. Speaking of which, I am going to need a PC and a secure line back to London. I am waiting for them to provide me with some SigInt.'

Andrew was referring to the GPS tracker he had planted on the chemical weapons in Damascus, whose signal he hoped British intelligence would have located by now. But he was reluctant to reveal more than he needed to, even if Saunders seemed trustworthy enough.

'One more thing,' he continued. 'I would also appreciate it if you could provide me with whatever information you have on an Afghan warlord we have in our sights. Goes by the name of *Al Naji*. Ever heard of him?'

'I believe I have,' said Saunders, looking up and to the left as if trying to recall the information. 'I will have a look and see what I can dig up. I think he is a fairly important player inside Afghanistan, but I will have a look in our files. Give me about half an hour.'

'Excellent,' said Andrew. 'Thank you.'

FIFTEEN

The white Mercedes sedan with the tall bearded passenger sitting in the back had skirted Kabul several hours earlier. It had passed through Jalalabad about thirty minutes ago and was now approaching the border between Afghanistan and Pakistan. Up ahead was the Khyber Pass and the busy Torkham border crossing where thousands of people were queueing in vans, cars, motorcycles and on foot. It was just after midday, and the sun was beating down on the dry pale brown and mountainous landscape. As the driver approached the border crossing, he slowed down and peeled away from the main road towards a VIP lane manned by a handful of Afghan government border patrol officers. Having already been notified about the arrival of the Mercedes, the most senior officer stepped forward, double-checked the number plates and performed a quick visual inspection of the car and its passengers. There were two people sitting in the backseat. A youngish Taliban fighter directly behind the driver, and next to him was an older man with a full black beard. The older man was wearing a brown kameez and a black turban, and he had a grizzled weatherworn face with a large scar running diagonally across it. Over his left eye was a black eyepatch.

Although the guard did not know the older man's name, he instantly recognised him, and so he nodded deferentially and swiftly moved on to inspect the escort vehicle which had stopped directly behind the Mercedes. He asked for no passports or other paperwork, and after a few seconds, he simply waved the two cars through.

A minute later the driver of the Mercedes stopped again on the Pakistani side, where another group of border guards awaited them. The driver rolled down his window and handed one of the guards a document with a dark green circular logo printed in the top left corner. It was emblazoned with an eagle spreading out its wings underneath a crescent moon and a star. Written in a semi-circle around the edge of the bottom half were the words 'Inter-Services Intelligence'. The driver also handed the guard a bulging envelope. Giving the document only a cursory glance, the guard then took possession of the envelope with a demeanour that indicated that he had been expecting it. He quickly opened it and inspected its contents. Then he nodded, stepped back from the Mercedes and waved it through.

In the back of the car, the tall bearded man sat impassively as the vehicle proceeded to leave the border crossing area and proceed along the N-5 National Highway and down into Pakistan's Khyber Pakhtunkhwa province towards the city of Peshawar. During the entire crossing, he had been looking straight ahead, seemingly taking no interest in the interaction with the border guards on either side of the border. He had crossed over at Torkham more times than he could remember, and he had complete confidence that every cog that needed to be oiled for his operation to function, had been oiled more than sufficiently for his transport trucks to pass the border without being inspected. The same was obviously true for his personal vehicle, and whereas most people would end up queueing for hours to cross over, he only ever spent a few minutes here. It would be another hour or so before he would be arriving at the compound in Peshawar. Here he would meet two of his most trusted associates who were both permanently stationed in Pakistan. They would then escort him to the compound's secure warehouse where the prize he had been seeking for so long was now being kept.

As the warlord sat absentmindedly looking out of the window at the Pakistani half of the Khyber Pass, his right hand found its way up to his chest, where it began toying with a large silver coin on a leather strap.

* * *

In London's West End, Fiona was again sitting at her desk with her laptop. The sun was spilling in through the window in front of her, and next to her on the desk was a steaming cup of hot chocolate and a muesli bar. In the kitchen, the large TV that was mounted on the wall was switched on, the sounds of a news show coming through the doorway to where she was sitting.

She was studying the website of the City of London's Planning Department, which is in charge of reviewing and evaluating plans for new construction projects and refurbishments inside the City of London's local government district, which is just a small part of Greater London. What she was interested in was a plot on Ludgate Hill just opposite St Paul's Cathedral. The location of Malakbel Gallery & Auction. She had decided to try to find out as much as she could about the business, and having already pulled all of the pertinent information from Companies House about the business itself, including its published financial records and its ownership structure, she now wanted to see what was available regarding the property itself.

Nadeem Yassin had said that he had bought and refurbished the gallery himself, so Fiona had managed to find the publicly available historical planning applications lodged with the planning department before any of the construction work had begun several years earlier.

The architect's drawings and construction plans had been submitted roughly a year before work had begun, and they had been drawn up by an architectural firm that Fiona discovered no longer existed. The plans themselves included various CAD drawings showing the proposed internal layout of the property, including floor plans and elevation drawings from several angles, including the street view, pipework, electrical wiring and all the other aspects of complete refurbishment project. There were also several 3D renderings to help the planning department visualize the final results before either accepting or rejecting the proposal.

It all looked very professional and convincing, and Fiona was not surprised that permission had been granted for the work. It was only when she took a closer look at the top-down floor plan of the entire footprint of the property that she noticed something odd. The interior walls of the gallery itself seemed to have been hugely over-specified in relation to the purpose they served. They were much thicker than she would have expected, and they had been constructed with steel-reinforced concrete on top of the original brickwork. Granted, some of the buildings in central London were old and perhaps not quite up to modern standards, but even so, what Fiona was looking at seemed excessive. On top of that, it was obvious from the floor plans that the walls of the long gallery were tapering as they extended from the street towards the back wall. Casting her mind back to her visit there, she did recall a slight but noticeable sense of disorientation when she had first entered the gallery. As if her sense of perspective had been playing tricks on her when she looked towards the back of the gallery's interior. At the time she had thought nothing of it, but now that she was looking at the tapering walls on the planning application, it was clear to her that she had not been imagining things. The gallery really did have an odd skewed shape.

She discovered yet another mystery when she looked at the specifications for internal components such as support beams, doors and door frames. She had not noticed when she had been inside the gallery and had feigned illness and a need to go to the restroom, but along the way, Nadeem had led her through a wide door at the back of the gallery, which was the only access to the rear of the property. What was strange about the door and the frame it sat in, was that it seemed to be much thicker and bulkier than it needed to be – almost as if it had been conceived as a way to stop burglars from accessing the gallery's interior via the back of the property. When Fiona examined the listed supplier of the door, she discovered that it had been sourced from an American company specialising in panic rooms, bank vaults and airlocks. In other words, heavy-duty equipment designed to take a beating.

Creases formed on Fiona's forehead as she slowly leaned back in her chair, her eyes still locked on the laptop's screen.

What is all this? she thought. *Malakbel has definitely not been built as an average gallery. But why?*

Still gazing at the floor plans, she reached for her cup of hot chocolate, only to realise that she had already emptied it. She got up and made her way into the kitchen to get a refill. The TV was now showing a news segment about the situation in Afghanistan and the increasingly violent confrontations between different warlords and Taliban factions. The presenter was saying that during the past many years these warlords had fought over control of heroin production as much as they had fought against the US-led international force in the country, but because many of the warlords were located in different regions of the country, the conflict was beginning to take on a more regional and even sectarian nature. Apparently, there were now fears of an escalation of the fighting over the coming weeks. Then the presenter moved on to a segment about the upcoming annual Remembrance Day ceremony on the 11th of November, to mark the end of the First World War. The event was taking place in just under a week, and Commemorations were planned all across the country and the world. At the Cenotaph near Whitehall in London, it was expected that much of the royal family would be in attendance, along with the Prime Minister and most of the Cabinet.

Fiona had never been very interested in military commemorations of that sort, often thinking that there was an excessive degree of soldier worship in the UK that she felt uncomfortable with. However, being involved in a relationship with Andrew and having seen first-hand what he and his comrades were prepared to risk in order to keep the public safe, she had gradually changed her perspective. Every year, young British soldiers lost their lives in operations in far-flung parts of the world, many of them taking part in covert anti-terrorism operations, and therefore never receiving the public recognition that they rightly deserved.

Whilst looking at the end of the news report, Fiona pondered this for a few moments and then decided that perhaps she would attend the ceremony at the Cenotaph this year after all.

★ ★ ★

There was a quick knock on the door to Andrew's temporary accommodation inside the British High Commission's main building in the compound in

Islamabad. It was a small but comfortable room arranged not unlike a small hotel room. Andrew was lying on the bed but sat up at the sound of the knock.

'Come in,' he said.

The door opened and Saunders popped his head through and smiled.

'Is this a good time?' he asked.

'Sure,' said Andrew and got to his feet. 'Did you find anything on Al Naji?'

'I did,' replied Saunders and entered, closing the door behind himself.

He was holding a folder with documents in his hands. The two of them sat down across from each other at a small table next to the room's kitchenette.

'It's not much, but we do have a rough idea who he is,' said Saunders, opening the folder and laying out the documents in front of Andrew.

'The headline is that he is this pretty notorious warlord. Been on the scene for at least a decade, apparently. A real ruffian. He has established himself as one of the primary heroin producers in the north of Afghanistan, and has grown his turf steadily by essentially killing off the competition.'

'Sounds friendly,' said Andrew flatly.

'Yes, a rather ruthless character,' continued Saunders. 'Apparently leads from the front whenever there are open hostilities between his organisation and other warlords. Supposedly unkillable, if you believe the locals. That's how he got his *nom de guerre,* 'Al Naji'. It literally means 'The Survivor' in Arabic. It's all nonsense, of course, but the Afghans seem to be fond of those sorts of ideas. Or perhaps he has cultivated that notion himself. At any rate, he has been wounded on multiple occasions, so he has a slight limp and he always wears an eyepatch. I am not sure exactly how he lost an eye, but it certainly helps him look intimidating. Have a look here.'

Saunders placed a grainy photo of Al Naji on the table. It appeared to have been taken from an elevated position, looking down and across a busy street where Al Naji was in the process of entering the back seat of a car. He was much taller and broader than any of the armed men around him, and he exuded a natural authority which would leave no onlooker in doubt about who was in charge.

'This is the best one we have,' said Saunders. 'Not exactly great image quality, but I am sure it would be enough to ID him if you saw him walking down the street. Quite an imposing character, if you ask me.'

'What do we know about his drug operation?' asked Andrew.

'Not a great deal,' replied Saunders. 'As I said, he has successfully taken over the heroin business in large parts of the north and even has operations inside Pakistan in the area around Peshawar. It is possible that he uses Peshawar as his main hub for distribution to Europe, which is where most of the Afghan heroin ends up. As I am sure you know, Peshawar has a large international airport that would be perfect for that purpose, especially if you have the means to bribe local officials, which I am sure he does. It is even said that somehow certain elements inside the ISI are involved, offering protection for his drugs business in return for a cut. We have no evidence of that of course. It's just rumours.'

'Is there any indication that he is involved in the arms trade?' asked Andrew.

'Some,' replied Saunders. 'Like a lot of warlords, he has cultivated relationships inside several of the neighbouring former Soviet republics such as Turkmenistan and Tajikistan. All of those countries still have large stockpiles of ancient Soviet weapons, but a lot of it still works, especially small arms. Al Naji has apparently been buying up all kinds of weapons and using them against his rivals.'

'I am sure none of the warlords have ever acquired chemical weapons in the past,' said Andrew. 'Have you seen any indications that this might be on the cards?'

'Never,' said Saunders resolutely. 'I don't think any of them have an appetite for that sort of thing. Not only are they very difficult to get your hands on, but using them effectively without accidentally killing your own men is extremely difficult.'

Andrew nodded pensively.

'Is there anything else I should know about him?' he asked. 'Anything that might help me track him down?'

Saunders thought for a moment.

'Well,' he finally said. 'As I said, he is an absolutely ruthless bastard. One of the things he is known for is using forced labour inside his heroin production facilities. Apparently, he forces his workers to become addicted to the drugs, thereby ensuring that they stay in line and never leave. There are rumours of several foreigners being caught up in that whole thing. He supposedly keeps some of them as trophies, and blackmails others to work as couriers using false identities, under threat of Al Naji tracking down and harming their families back in Europe or the US.'

'Bloody hell,' said Andrew, his thoughts instantly turning to Frank Malone. Could this have happened to him? Could he be chained up inside a drugs factory, forced to work day and night for this Al Naji? 'He sounds like an absolute psychopath.'

'Yes,' replied Saunders. 'We obviously don't know exactly how much of this is true, but there is no doubt that he is an extremely violent and unpleasant character.'

Andrew thought for a moment and then folded his hands on the table in front of him, looking straight at Saunders.

'I am going to let you in on some information I picked up in Damascus,' he said. 'But I need your word that this stays between us. Ok?'

'Absolutely,' replied Saunders and nodded with an earnest look on his face.

'There's this Russian ex-mercenary from Wagner Group who we know is involved in the drugs trade, but who has now branched out to acquiring and trading some pretty nasty chemical weapons. I can't tell you all the details, but I have reason to believe that a shipment of those weapons may already be here in Pakistan, most likely Peshawar, and that they could be headed for Afghanistan, possibly to be used in the wars between rival warlords.'

'Crikey,' said Saunders, visibly concerned. 'That would be a disaster. Thousands of civilians would be killed. Have we informed the Pakistanis?'

'Not yet,' replied Andrew. 'Not until we know who exactly we are dealing with. We suspect that somehow this Al Naji character is involved, although we don't yet understand who or what the weapons might be intended for. Anyway, we think the weapons have already made it to a warehouse in Peshawar. I have the name of the district, but I don't know the exact address. Do you have any human intelligence on the ground there that I might be able to use?'

'Possibly,' said Saunders hesitantly. 'Given that Peshawar is a major recruiting ground for the Taliban, we obviously have several sources there. However, they are mainly focused on the Haqqani Network, so I don't know if they would be able to assist. But I will give it a try. I've actually got someone in mind. A young chap by the name of Tahoor Qureshi. He's a junior officer with the local police at the Gulbahar Police Station just east of the city centre. Good egg. Wants to do the right thing for his country. Paranoid as anything though. I won't be able to discuss this with him over the phone. He is convinced the ISI is listening in on his calls, so I would have to go and meet him in person. It's only a couple of hours' drive from here.'

'Is that really necessary?' asked Andrew. 'I don't want to put you in harm's way. These are some very serious people we're dealing with. To be blunt with you – I have the sort of training and experience needed for this sort of thing. You probably don't.'

'I am sure it'll be fine,' shrugged Saunders. 'There isn't a hope in hell of my source agreeing to meet with you. He only ever meets with me. Anyway, I have lived in this country for four years now, and I have been to Peshawar quite a few times. I know how to handle myself. I don't take stupid risks, and I never put my assets at unnecessary risk either.'

'All right,' nodded Andrew reluctantly. 'If you're sure. But please keep in touch with me on a regular basis.'

'I'll do that,' said Saunders. 'I can be there by late afternoon today. I am going to send my source a text with a codeword so he will know when and where to meet me. We've done this a number of times before.'

'Thanks,' said Andrew. 'I really appreciate this.'

After Saunders had left, Andrew lay back down on his bed, staring up at the ceiling. His thoughts returned to the almost unimaginable scenario of Frank having been kept prisoner inside a drugs factory. He forced the thought out of his mind. Frank was dead. He saw him get shot at close range. He saw his broken body fall to the ground. He couldn't possibly have survived that. Could he?

* * *

It was mid-afternoon when the white Mercedes arrived at the fenced-off warehouse in the large western suburb of Peshawar called Hayatabad. A heavily industrialised area, especially in the westernmost part, there were factories and warehouses crammed together on irregularly shaped plots. There were ceramics and kitchenware manufacturers, food packaging facilities, paper mills, stone and marble suppliers and various transport and logistics companies. The entire area was conveniently located next to the N-5 National Highway just six kilometres from Peshawar's Bacha Khan International

Airport close to the city centre. It was also close to several rail links, allowing for easy access to both domestic and regional markets.

The Mercedes stopped briefly outside the gate as a guard approached. After a quick exchange of words, two other guards opened the chain link fence and allowed the car inside. The driver proceeded through the gate and stopped just outside the main entrance to the warehouse. There were no signs or logos on the building to indicate which type of business was located there.

As soon as the vehicle had come to a stop, one of the guards, who had been jogging alongside the Mercedes as it entered, stepped up and opened the left-hand passenger door. Al Naji stepped out and slowly drew himself up to his full height. He was a tall broad-shouldered man as it was, but with the black turban on his head, he towered over the now diminutive-looking guards. He winced slightly from the pain in his leg. It was his most prominent battle scar, and it had been with him for a long time now. He had learned to live with it, and just like all the other injuries he had suffered along the way, it reminded him of how he had survived countless violent encounters where lesser men would have perished. He reached up with his left hand to adjust his eyepatch and then smoothed down the front of his kameez.

He was flanked by a shorter bearded man wearing dark loose shalwar trousers, a brown knee-length kameez shirt and a dark green waskat waistcoat. His name was Abdul Wasiq, and he had been by Al Naji's side during his rise to power in Northern Afghanistan.

He was the money man, in charge of finances and most of the transport logistics related to the shipping of heroin across international borders, as well as the purchase of weapons from former Soviet republics.

Al Naji began walking slowly towards the door to the warehouse. Wasiq gestured for one of the guards to run ahead and open the door, whilst making sure to stay a couple of steps behind the warlord at all times.

The door was opened and the imposing figure of Al Naji entered first, followed by his small entourage. Inside, he was met by a short bespectacled man wearing a light-coloured shalwar kameez. He had the bookish look and demeanour of a scientist, and he was clearly nervous about meeting the notorious warlord for the first time. As the warehouse door clanged shut behind the group, he hurried up to him. He gently took the towering figure's outstretched hand, bowing low to kiss it and doing his utmost to convey his respect and deference.

'Good day, Doctor Anwar,' said Wasiq, nodding at the man with the glasses.

'Emir,' said the man meekly, using the ubiquitous honorific term for someone worthy of the highest respect. 'We are privileged to have you here.'

Al Naji withdrew his hand and nodded silently.

'Take us to the weapon,' said Wasiq.

Doctor Anwar took a short step back, nodded and began to turn around.

'Come with me please,' he said and started walking towards the back of the warehouse where a wide concrete ramp led down to a set of steel double doors.

From the outside, the warehouse might have looked old and slightly dilapidated with its peeling paint and partly rusted corrugated roof, which was how it was intended. However, this belied its interior, which revealed it to have been constructed relatively recently. There were vehicles and storage units as well as a couple of forklifts parked to one side, and the ramp down to the double doors was smooth and clean.

The small group of people descended the ramp where the bespectacled man unlocked the doors with an electronic keycard and led the group inside. They walked along an underground corridor and emerged into a large low-ceilinged space where groups of people surrounding a grid of tables were busy packaging up packets of heroin inside a range of different household and industrial products that had been sourced from a variety of manufacturers in the local industrial area.

Each type of product, selected specifically for this purpose, had been bought in large batches because of the ease with which packets of heroin could be concealed within them. Once the packets had been placed inside specially created cavities, they were then replaced alongside the rest of the original batch, sprayed with a chemical solution that dissolved traces of heroin, and then finally repackaged for onward shipment, mainly to Europe.

It was a laborious process, and there was a whole team of quality assurance staff to check each item before it was shipped. But the markup between the negligible production cost inside Afghanistan and the ultimate street value in Europe was so enormous that the investment in time and effort paid off to a spectacular degree.

The operation in this particular warehouse had been ongoing for a number of years now, and it was one of Al Naji's main earnings streams. The profits, with the help of the creative and financially astute Abdul Wasiq, were funnelled through a web of front companies in various tax havens all across the world, until they finally ended up in Al Naji's personal investment fund that was managed from a small and discreet asset manager in the British Virgin Islands. Along the way, Wasiq was also given a generous cut. At this point, Al Naji had amassed very significant wealth, but apart from weapons and salaries for his small army, he had very few things to spend it on, and even less desire to do so – at least not at this time. He had much loftier goals than that.

The small group proceeded swiftly to the very back of the packaging floor, the workers eyeing them as they went. A visit from the Emir was far from an everyday occurrence, although it had been known to happen in the past. The group finally arrived at a large metal door which required a passcode to open. Wasiq stepped up and punched in the code, after which the lock beeped and the door unlocked. They proceeded through it to a small dimly lit room which was empty except for a large charcoal grey case sitting on a sturdy metal table in the middle of the room. It had arrived two days earlier from Bacha Khan International Airport and had been sitting inside this room since then, awaiting the arrival of the Emir.

Al Naji stepped up to the case, placed his hands on the lid and opened it. Inside were 24 baseball-sized glass spheres with a slightly luminescent blue liquid inside each of them. Together, they produced a faint blue glow that bloomed out of the case and seemed to envelop Al Naji as he stood there by himself inspecting his prize. The blue glow was reflecting dully off the large coin that was hanging around his neck. The talisman that had once belonged to a man called Frank Malone.

The rest of the group stood silently near the door behind the warlord, barely daring to breathe. A vague but grim smile slowly spread across Al Naji's face as he looked down into the case with his one good eye. Finally, he had acquired what he had been seeking for so many years. These mesmerising and beautiful blue glass spheres would at long last allow him to carry out his plan, and finally set things right.

SIXTEEN

Andrew was standing outside the entrance to the main building in the British High Commission compound. Philip Penrose had come good on his promise to arrange for a meeting with an ISI representative by the name of Major Shahid Khan, and Andrew was waiting for one of the high commission's resident drivers to arrive with a vehicle to take him to ISI headquarters less than two miles away. He could easily have walked there, but he had been advised not to. It wasn't that Islamabad was necessarily unsafe for westerners. It was just that it was likely to be unsafe for British special forces personnel like him arriving in the country for opaque reasons. He had no doubt that the ISI already knew exactly who he was and that they had him under surveillance, which could also mean that other interested parties would already know of his presence here.

As Penrose had said, ISI is less of an intelligence-gathering organisation, and more of a covert operations division that is deeply enmeshed in Pakistan's various radical Islamic groups. It is often regarded as highly paranoid and sees itself and Pakistan as being under threat from all sides. India to the south, assisted by the UK and the US. An increasingly assertive China to the east. And Afghanistan to the north, which Pakistan considers its own backyard but whose wars inevitably spill over into Pakistani society. At one point, the ISI was famously referred to as a state within a state by a former Pakistani prime minister.

Andrew had already received the brief file that MI6 had put together on Major Khan, and he had been reading through it in preparation for the meeting. Khan was from a wealthy family in Islamabad. His grandfather had founded one of Pakistan's first telephone companies in the 1960s, generating huge wealth and placing the family at the centre of power and political influence in the country. Shahid joined the ISI early in his career after having completed his military service. Among other things, he was now tasked with managing relations with the various madrassas inside Pakistan who were funded by the ISI, and which since the 1980s and through the 1990s had indoctrinated countless child refugees from the civil war in Afghanistan, in order to send them back to Afghanistan to join the nascent Taliban which the ISI had always hoped to control.

The paradox of the ISI's involvement with the Taliban, and its continuous efforts to control the organisation after having helped give birth to it, was that ISI agents eventually developed sympathies for their Taliban counterparts. Initially, this happened only in the lower ranks of the organisation, but as time passed, those junior officers became senior officers, eventually turning the ISI into what was effectively a partner organisation for the Taliban. This gave the Taliban political access inside Pakistan, and it became very much a co-dependent relationship and a two-way street in terms of who relied on whom. By 2001, the ISI was generally on the back foot with the Taliban, realising that they had created a monster that they could no longer fully control.

MI6 estimated that Khan was most likely close to the Taliban's Pakistani leadership, and also heavily involved in internal Taliban politics, no doubt trying to manage it in a way that would benefit the ISI first, and Pakistan second. The brief on Khan also mentioned that he had liaised with MI6 staff in Islamabad in the past, and that he had now offered to help locate the chemical weapons shipment, if it was indeed in the country. MI6 seemed to think that the Major travelled to the tribal areas of both Pakistan and Afghanistan on a regular basis.

The car taking Andrew to ISI HQ arrived quickly, and he got into the backseat. The driver then took him along Khayaban-e-Suhrwardy Road, which runs along the northern edge of the large and wooded Shakarparian National Park. Less than five minutes later, the driver took a right onto Muhammad Mansha Yaad Road where the main entrance to the ISI complex was located. Just as the car made the turn, Andrew spotted a sign at the intersection pointing south towards the newly built Pakistan-China

Friendship Center. Andrew had no doubt that this large exhibition and trade centre had been funded entirely by the Chinese state, and that it was part of an effort to use China's increasing economic power to cultivate influence in this part of the world at the expense of the US and Europe. It was yet another chance for the ISI and the Pakistani government to play off different foreign parties against each other, as it had done many times before. He felt sure that the location of the centre just a few hundred metres from ISI HQ was no accident.

The ISI headquarters comprises a large centrally located angular concrete three-storey building with a large semi-circular section facing the road – not unlike The White House in Washington DC. The main intelligence-gathering entities, as well as the leadership of the organisation, reside in this building. To the side and behind it are a number of separate buildings for additional staff and functions.

There was a palpable sense of hostility as Andrew got out of the car, entered the building and walked across the lobby to the reception. He could practically feel the eyes of the security guards and the other staff boring into him as he walked. A white European walking into the HQ of the most secretive and powerful organisation in Pakistan was clearly not an everyday occurrence.

He proceeded up to the front desk but did not get a chance to introduce himself before a young man in an olive-green military uniform stepped up to him and addressed him in a strangely detached tone of voice.

'Mr Sterling,' he said, stating it as a fact rather than a question. He clearly already knew exactly who

Andrew was. 'Please come with me. I will take you to your meeting.'

Andrew was about to introduce himself, but then simply nodded and gave a slight shrug. He would have preferred a more friendly approach but wasn't about to let this overt hostility throw him. He wasn't really here to make friends.

He was led along a wide polished marble corridor to an elevator which brought himself and the nameless ISI officer up to the first floor. They stepped out into another corridor and walked along to a dark wooden door with a brass plate mounted on it which read 'Major Khan'. The officer opened the door to reveal an office with a view out over the national park. Next to the wall on the right-hand side was a dark wooden desk and a comfortable-looking leather chair. There was a distinct smell of cigar smoke in the air. The junior officer gestured for Andrew to enter and sit down in the single chair that had been placed opposite the desk. Then he closed the door and left Andrew there by himself.

Andrew walked over to the window and looked out across the busy Khayaban-e-Suhrwardy Road and down into the national park. It was a pleasant view. Then he sat down in the chair and waited. The wall behind the desk was full of books, and a laptop was sitting on the desk flipped open but switched off. Andrew noticed what looked like an ancient Afghan knife sitting on display in a small stand on the desk. It looked very similar to knives he had seen on a previous trip to Herat in western Afghanistan. Both the handle and the sheath were made of a dull metal but they were richly decorated, wreathed in depictions of ornamental flowers and with gems set into the metal. It looked old. Very old.

A couple of minutes later, the door opened again and in walked a broad-shouldered man in his fifties with a weatherworn face, a large curved nose, black bushy eyebrows, a thick moustache and short dark and neatly combed hair gleaming with oil. He was wearing a military uniform similar to the one worn by the officer who had picked Andrew up in the lobby. However, from the display of commendations on his chest and the way he carried himself, Andrew could tell that he was much more senior. On the lapels of his camouflaged shirt were crescent moons with a star inside them.

'Mr Sterling,' he said flatly, with a distinct sub-continental accent. 'I am Major Shahid Khan. S wing.'

It took Andrew a couple of seconds to grasp what the Major had said, but then he recalled that the ISI's roughly ten thousand employees are divided into lettered sections, the most notorious being S wing. Unlike the more conventional information-gathering sections of the Pakistani intelligence community, S wing is responsible for managing the organisation's relationships with Islamist militant groups such as the Taliban, sometimes even assisting them in attacks against perceived common enemies, although they would never admit to this. Most of their active operations occur in other countries, chiefly Afghanistan, but since the border areas are so porous, and because the Taliban operate almost freely across the Afghan-Pakistan border, S wing also conducts significant operations inside Pakistan itself.

From the way Major Khan had introduced himself, seemingly emphasising his affiliation with S wing, Andrew immediately got the feeling that this man was here reluctantly, and that he was keen to make it clear to Andrew that this was his turf, and people like Andrew were less than welcome. He wondered how Penrose had managed to arrange this meeting, given the obvious reluctance of this man to be here. He also found it strange that the meeting had not been set up with someone from C wing, which primarily liaised with foreign intelligence services, and which even included a CIA-funded counter-terrorism unit. From what he had understood, reading his brief about the ISI, from the perspective of foreign intelligence services it was often the case that C wing would say one thing, while S wing would do another – sometimes the exact opposite.

'Nice to meet you,' said Andrew, reading the Major's body language and making no attempt to shake his hand.

The two of them sat down across from each other, and Major Khan folded his hands on the table and looked straight at Andrew, clearly expecting him to initiate proceedings.

'Right,' said Andrew. 'Thank you for seeing me. As I am sure our station chief Penrose has already advised you, we believe that a shipment of highly potent chemical weapons may have been smuggled into Pakistan, possibly with the intention of transporting them to Afghanistan to be used in tribal clashes there. Needless to say, any use of such a weapon on any civilian population anywhere in the world would have catastrophic consequences.'

'Obviously,' nodded Khan.

'So, let me come straight to the point,' continued Andrew. 'Have Pakistani intelligence, either the ISI or any of the other agencies, picked up anything at all about that? I would imagine it would be a pretty big deal if it had arrived here.'

'No,' replied the Major and shook his head slightly. 'I have seen no evidence of such a shipment. Is your intelligence credible?'

'I feel quite sure it is solid,' said Andrew, thinking back to watching the transport plane lifting off and disappearing in the mist over Damascus several days earlier.

'What is your source?' asked Khan.

'I am afraid I can't divulge that,' replied Andrew. 'But we know for a fact that these weapons were stolen somewhere in the Middle East, and that they are highly likely to have arrived in Pakistan already.'

'Where exactly do you believe they entered Pakistan?' asked Khan, sounding unconvinced. 'Which city?'

'We're not sure,' lied Andrew. He was still waiting for the MI6 unit liaising with 5-Eyes back in London to pick up and locate the signal from the GPS tracker he had placed on the weapons case, and he wasn't about to offer everything he knew to the ISI at this stage. 'Have there been any indications, either recently or in the past, that the Taliban or perhaps other Islamist groups were trying to acquire this type of weapon?'

'No,' replied Major Khan dismissively. 'I think you know as well as I do that these weapons are extremely difficult to handle, and even more challenging to deploy. Why use something as complex as a VX-agent when simple Semtex will do the job?'

Andrew hesitated for a brief moment. Why had Khan mentioned VX? As far as he knew, Penrose had not divulged anything about the nature of the weapons Andrew was attempting to locate. Then he shrugged.

'I think it would be a mistake to ascribe too much rationality to those extremist types,' he said. 'Just because a sane person who values his own life might steer clear of using chemical weapons, doesn't mean that a religious zealot would do the same. I think you probably know this better than I do.'

Khan regarded Andrew impassively for a couple of seconds.

'Perhaps you are right,' he finally said. 'But as I said, we have not picked up any chatter about this sort of thing, and I am sure that would have been the case if such weapons were really here in Pakistan and in the hands of warlords or terrorists. Someone always talks, and we are always listening.'

'I am sure that's true,' said Andrew. 'Are you familiar with an Afghan warlord by the name of Al Naji? We believe he might be involved somehow.'

'I know of him, yes,' replied Khan. 'He has become quite powerful in the tribal areas in the north-east.'

'Have you ever dealt with him directly?' asked Andrew. 'Perhaps assisted him with money or weapons?'

Khan's face took on an annoyed and somewhat offended look.

'Mr Sterling,' he said. 'Pakistan does not deal with drug dealers and warlords. Our aim is to bring peace to Afghanistan and to help the Afghan government transition the country towards a prosperous future. Warlords and terrorists can play no part in that.'

Andrew knew that Khan was lying, and Khan knew that Andrew knew. But there was nothing Andrew could do, except perhaps call out the lie, but that would have been profoundly counterproductive. So, he simply nodded and pressed his lips together.

'Well,' he said. 'If you don't have any information, then I won't be taking any more of your time today. Thank you for seeing me. I appreciate it.'

Major Khan rose and Andrew followed suit, but then he turned back towards the desk.

'I am sorry,' said Andrew, 'but I couldn't help but notice the knife on your desk. May I ask how old it is and where it is from?'

Khan picked it up and turned it over in his hand,

'It is quite old,' he replied. 'Several centuries. It is from Afghanistan. A gift from a friend.'

'May I see it?' asked Andrew.

Khan handed it to Andrew who gently pulled the blade out from its sheath. As he held the knife in his hand, he could feel how perfectly balanced it was. The craftsmanship was exquisite. He placed the tip of his thumb on the edge of the blade. It was still very sharp.

'Very nice,' he said. 'Must be worth a fortune.'

'Not for sale,' said Khan, clearly not finding the prospect of selling it appealing.

He reached down to the desk and pressed a button. Almost immediately the door to the office opened and the junior officer, who must have been waiting outside in the corridor the whole time opened the door and looked at Andrew with slightly raised eyebrows.

'Well, I guess I will be going then,' said Andrew as he handed the knife back to Major Khan. 'Thank you again.'

As Andrew left the building and got back into the car that had been waiting for him outside, he wasn't quite sure what to think of the brief meeting. It had been a slightly surreal and fairly fruitless experience, and now he almost felt as if Khan's motivation for taking the meeting to begin with had been to assess Andrew, and to find out what he knew about the chemical weapons. But did that mean that Khan knew more than he had admitted? Had the ISI picked up information about the shipment? It was almost inconceivable that something as momentous as that could have slipped past the organisation's extremely extensive and ubiquitous network of assets and informants in Pakistan.

As Andrew sat looking out of the window of the car on the way back to the High Commission compound, he couldn't shake the feeling that there was something familiar about Major Khan. He had the uncomfortable feeling that he had definitely seen him before, but he just couldn't place him. It was only when he was walking back towards his room along a footpath inside the main building of the High Commission that it suddenly hit him. He hurried back to his room, sat down on the bed and got out his phone. He flicked through the stored images until he got to the picture that he had taken in Tokarev's office inside Porok in Damascus. At the time, he had only intended to take a picture of the framed photo of Tokarev standing next to the tall bearded warlord. However, in his haste, he had also, entirely by accident, captured some of the framed photo next to it, showing Tokarev posing in one of the booths inside Porok with a man wearing a dark suit and a white shirt. He was of stocky build and had short dark hair, thick eyebrows and a moustache, and an unmistakable hooked nose. It was definitely Shahid Khan. Incredibly, the ISI Major must have visited Tokarev in Damascus, and he had clearly had the confidence to allow himself to be photographed there.

Andrew couldn't believe what he was seeing. Somehow Tokarev and Khan were working together. This also meant that everything Khan had told him was likely to be a lie. In all likelihood, Khan knew of the chemical weapons and of their arrival somewhere in Pakistan. In fact, he might well have been instrumental in making sure they arrived safely and did not have to undergo any kind of inspection by Pakistan's border force or customs inspection team. For all Andrew knew, the aircraft used to transport the weapons could have been an unmarked Pakistani Airforce transport plane.

This was an unexpected turn of events and one that he felt he needed to discuss with either Saunders or Penrose. Saunders was in Peshawar to meet his intelligence asset there, so Andrew would not be able to reach him for several hours. He was about to get to his feet to go and see Philip Penrose when he suddenly thought better of it. It was Penrose who had arranged the meeting with Khan, so was Penrose also somehow compromised?

Just then Andrew realised that a text message had arrived on his phone while he had been in the meeting with Khan. It was from Saunders.

> Andrew. I met my chap in Peshawar. No info on the WMDs, but said he has a possible lead on a drug packaging hub here that could be Al Naji's operation. Said he needed time to find out more. He also said that he had picked up the possible location of a westerner (possibly a soldier) that was captured years ago in Afghanistan, and who is believed to be held hostage by the Haqqani Network somewhere in the city. I am going to look into it. Will message again later with an update. Chris.

Andrew involuntarily furrowed his brow as he read the message.

Shit, he thought, pressing his lips together. Saunders was now getting himself into very deep water. He clearly trusted his asset in Peshawar, but what if that trust was misplaced? And going to "look into" a location that was potentially used by none other than the notorious Haqqani Network to secrete a western hostage sounded downright foolhardy.

Taking a moment to consider his options, Andrew reluctantly accepted that he had no real choice. He had come to Pakistan to try to track down the chemical weapons, but right now there was no way he could just let Chris Saunders fend for himself, especially since everything he was doing was effectively an effort to help Andrew in his investigation. He knew that he had to get himself to Peshawar as soon as possible.

★ ★ ★

Inside the warehouse in Hayatabad just west of Peshawar's city centre, two of Al Naji's armed fighters were standing guard at the top of the ramp leading down to the underground facility. At the back of the facility were another two men standing guard at the entrance to the room holding the large charcoal grey case. Al Naji and Abdul Wasiq were in an adjacent room that was hermetically sealed, looking in through a one-way mirror. The tall bearded warlord was standing immobile close to the glass, keen to observe the procedure up close.

On the other side of the glass, Doctor Anwar and two of his assistants were huddled around the case, which had now been opened, allowing full access to all 24 of the glass spheres containing the blue liquid. Next to the case was a long-wheeled table that had been brought into the room a couple of hours earlier. Placed on top of it were eight wooden boxes, each with a roughly one-metre-tall Buddha statue inside. The statues had been brought in from Mes Aynak in Afghanistan. Each one had been drilled through and hollowed out from the bottom up, allowing for the insertion of three glass spheres in each. The spheres were to be separated inside the statues using bespoke laser-printed semi-spheres to hold them in place and prevent them from knocking into each other.

The drilling process had been overseen by Al Naji himself and it had been going on for most of the day. Each one of the ancient and irreplaceable statues had to be carefully hollowed out, to make room for the spheres. Once the spheres had been placed inside, they then had to be sealed up using a special mixture that would conceal their contents and allow them to pass a cursory customs check upon arrival at their destination.

Doctor Anwar and his two assistants were all wearing bulky yellow rubber hazmat suits with their own breathing apparatuses, and they had been moving around awkwardly inside the room, looking vaguely as if they were submerged underwater. Now, they were all stationary around the grey case, getting ready to transfer each of the 24 spheres into the Buddha statues. Doctor Anwar was directing proceedings through the wireless comms equipment that was part of the hazmat suits, and on his mark, one of his assistants carefully lifted the first sphere from the foam interior of the case using two gloved hands. The other assistant then slid a specially designed set of tongs with a rubberised grip underneath the spheres and then waited for his colleague to gingerly place the sphere inside it. Once secure, the sphere was then inserted into the first statue and carefully pushed to the far end of the drilled hole. After this, one of the laser-printed semi-spherical spacers was pushed in to hold the sphere in place. Then followed the second sphere, then another spacer, and then the third and final sphere. An endcap was then pushed into the drilled hole, holding the third sphere in pace. Finally, the special mixture, which had been designed to work as a hard glue and to dry roughly in the same colour as the stone the Buddhas were made from, was used to seal up the statue. The whole process took roughly ten minutes per statue, and by the time the eighth statue had been sealed up and all 24 spheres had been secreted away inside, Doctor Anwar and his two assistants were sweating profusely. The heavy hazmat suits had no ventilation beyond the fresh air supply coming from the air tanks mounted on their backs, and the temperature had quickly risen inside them as the three men worked to finish their task.

Doctor Anwar breathed a sigh of relief as the final Buddha was sealed up and placed safely back in its wooden case, securely enveloped by polystyrene pieces to hold it in place during its journey. He had been running Al Naji's heroin packaging facility for almost five years and considered himself a trusted employee, but he had been extremely reticent about today's extraordinary event. However, he wanted to serve his Emir well, and he was now immensely relieved that everything had gone as planned. He did not know exactly what was in the spheres, except that it was a toxic substance that had to be handled very carefully. His two assistants had been told nothing about their contents, although they would obviously have guessed its potency from the requirement to wear a hazmat suit. He used the suit's internal comms system to thank the assistants and then he began walking slowly towards the closed door.

At that moment, the door opened and Al Naji stepped inside. Doctor Anwar's two assistants had just begun following the doctor towards the door, but all three men had now stopped. Al Naji walked a couple of steps into the room, raised the suppressed pistol he was holding in his hand and pointed it straight at Doctor Anwar's forehead. Without hesitating, he pulled the trigger and a bullet tore through Anwar's faceplate and slammed into his head, sending blood and brains exploding out of the back of it and into the back of the hazmat suit's hood. From the outside, it looked like a small explosion had happened inside the suit, sending a spray of blood whirling and splattering around inside it.

Without hesitation, and with a speed that betrayed serious weapons training, Al Naji shifted the pistol to fire at first one assistant and then the other. The two men had stood frozen to the spot, petrified by the sight of their esteemed boss being executed. By the time all three bodies had slumped heavily onto the floor where they had stood, Al Naji lowered the gun and stood there for a moment, observing the bodies of the men who until a few seconds ago had been working loyally for him. Then he turned and exited the room. As he did so he turned briefly to Abdul Wasiq.

'Get this cleaned up,' he said calmly in Pashto. 'And find people to replace them.'

'Yes, Emir,' said Wasiq obsequiously.

'Inform me when the statues have been loaded onto the plane,' said Al Naji.

Then he exited the underground facility and proceeded outside to where his white Mercedes was waiting. He got into the left rear passenger seat and closed the door. Without a word, the driver immediately set the car in motion and drove out of the gates, proceeded out of the industrial area to the N-5 National Highway where he turned left and headed towards the Torkham border crossing and Afghanistan.

SEVENTEEN

Later that evening, Andrew went up to the third floor of the MI6 building in the British High Commission's compound and knocked on Philip Penrose's door.

'Come,' came the reply from the other side.

Andrew opened the door to find Penrose sitting at his desk with his feet resting on the corner of it and reading what looked like a report of some kind that had been stapled together in the top left corner. He peered over the edge of the report and then lowered it.

'Sterling,' he said, with vague surprise and a hint of annoyance in his voice. 'I thought Saunders was taking care of you.'

'Well, that's what I came to talk to you about,' said Andrew and closed the door behind him, walking up to Penrose's desk as he continued speaking. 'He has been very helpful, but he seems to have gone off the grid. He went to Peshawar earlier today to have a chat with an asset there. He messaged me earlier and indicated that he would contact me again later in the day. It is now almost 8 pm, and he still hasn't been back in touch. I would like to ask you to have your guys here try to pinpoint the location of his phone.'

Penrose placed the report face down on the desk, lifted his feet off it and placed them back on the carpet. Then he straightened himself up in his chair.

'I am sure he is all right,' said Penrose in his upper-class drawl, sounding entirely unconcerned. 'It is not unusual for our people to be held up from time to time. It's a rather chaotic country, you know.'

'I understand,' said Andrew, 'but I am concerned that he might be getting in over his head. 'Does he have much field experience? I mean, has he ever been in combat?'

Penrose looked slightly perplexed for a moment, but then produced an insincere half-smile.

'Andy,' he said somewhat condescendingly. 'This isn't the army, old boy. We do things under the radar, as it were. Covertly, you see? We don't go in all guns blazing and leave a trail of destruction. Our modus operandum is somewhat more refined than that.'

Andrew decided to ignore the dig at him and his soldier background. As far as he was concerned, Penrose was a sheltered toff who would last about fifteen seconds on the battlefield. Instead, he just nodded sagely.

'I understand that too,' he said. 'However, these are very serious people we are dealing with, and I simply don't think Saunders is equipped to deal with them on his own if things go south.'

Penrose looked unconvinced, and there was no trace of concern for his employee to be found in his passive facial expression.

'I could put you in touch with Colonel Strickland in London, if you'd like?' added Andrew.

Penrose's demeanour changed immediately. He clearly did not relish the idea of even more outside interference on his patch, and he did not appreciate the implied threat of bringing London into this. Out here, London might as well have been on a different planet. This was his little kingdom.

For a moment Penrose looked as if he was about to produce an indignant outburst, but then his demeanour changed in an instant once again.

'Well played, old boy,' he said and produced a reptilian smile. 'I shall ask our electronic surveillance team downstairs to locate Saunders' phone. They can hack into the local mobile phone networks as easily as you and I could light a cigar. As long as the phone is switched on, they should be able to triangulate its location and pinpoint it to within a few yards. I am sure Saunders will turn out to be in a nightclub somewhere.'

His attempt at levity fell flat. Andrew suddenly got the distinct impression that Penrose was only ever interested in what benefitted Penrose. Displaying no concern for his colleague in the face of a very real danger of physical harm made Andrew's esteem for the man plummet through the floor. This sort of indifferent and cavalier attitude amongst officers to the lives and wellbeing of men in the field was what got soldiers killed. This had happened on countless occasions in the British Army and beyond.

'Thank you very much,' said Andrew affably. 'I appreciate that. When can I expect a result?'

'Shouldn't be more than thirty minutes,' said Penrose, now back to his somewhat disinterested and bored-sounding self.

'Very well,' said Andrew and began walking towards the door. 'Would you ask them to email it to me ASAP? Thank you.'

Then he left Penrose's office and walked back along the corridor.

What a weasel, he thought. *I guess I can't expect much help from him going forward.*

Inside his office, Penrose was seething, his eyes boring into the door that Andrew had just closed behind himself, and a scowl now having spread across his usually perfectly composed face.

You jumped-up little shit, he thought, loathing and disdain rippling through his whole body. *Who the hell do you think you are?*

* * *

'Hello Andrew. It's Fiona. I wanted to speak to you, but I guess you're busy, so I will just leave you a quick voice message. I've discovered that Nadeem Yassin is scheduled to take receipt of a collection of ancient Buddha statues from Afghanistan via Peshawar in a couple of days. I haven't been able to find out precisely where they came from though, but I guess it is safe to say that they were obtained illegally. Not sure if Obaid was involved, or if any of this helps you in any way, but I thought I'd let you know. I also decided

to have a closer look at Malakbel Gallery & Auctions, which you will remember acts as the front for Nadeem Yassin and his uncle's art smuggling business in London. I downloaded the planning application for the gallery and noticed something odd. I am not a structural engineer, but it just seems like the proportions are weird, and the walls don't meet at 90-degree angles. And they put a massive steel door at the back of the gallery – almost like an airlock or something. Really weird. Once again, I really don't know if any of this is even remotely relevant to what you are doing, but it just seemed strange to me, so I thought I would mention it. Anyway, I hope you are all right and that you are keeping safe. Hopefully I will hear from you soon. Love you. Bye.'

★ ★ ★

Philip Penrose stood up resolutely from his desk, walked to a cupboard and extracted a brown leather holdall. Then he exited his office and proceeded downstairs to the lobby. Here he headed for the main exit out onto the lush High Commission compound grounds where his black chauffeur-driven Audi carrying diplomatic number plates was just pulling up in front of the building. As he walked outside and passed between the two armed guards, they shared a look and a knowing smirk. Penrose was off to see his mistress again, or was it a male lover? It was a running joke among the security staff who had little else to do than to notice who came and went at what times, and where they might be off to.

Penrose got into the back of the car and gave the driver directions. He then took off his grey suit jacket and his white shirt and grey tie, unzipped the holdall and extracted a dark blue long-sleeved top and a black leather jacket. Having put those on, he finally reached into the holdall and donned a black cotton baseball cap, pulling it down low in front of his face.

Ten minutes later, the Audi came to a stop on Kohistan Road in Islamabad's F-8 Sector, near the huge Fatima Jinnah Park which occupies an entire sector quadrant in the middle of the city. He was in a relatively heavily built-up area due west of the park, with multi-storey apartment buildings, shopfronts and restaurants lining the road on both sides. It was a relatively wealthy area of the city, and there were plenty of people milling around. He usually only ever came here much later at night, but today would have to be an exception. As soon as he closed the door, the Audi pulled back out onto the road and drove off.

Keeping his head down and giving the impression of someone who felt at home in this area and knew exactly where he was going, he traversed the wide pavement and disappeared down an alley next to a busy restaurant. He then proceeded through a warren of narrow streets and alleys, until he arrived at the back entrance to a nondescript house halfway down a dimly lit street that was too narrow to allow cars to drive along it. He pressed a button next to the door and glanced furtively up at a security camera that was mounted above the door. A couple of seconds later the lock buzzed for a few seconds and Penrose then pushed the door open and disappeared inside. The door clicked shut behind him, and then the street was quiet again.

* * *

Andrew woke up with a start just as the taxi was making its way through the centre of Peshawar and out the other side towards the east. The drive to the major city in the west of the country had taken roughly two and a half hours, and had brought him through Islamabad's city centre and onto the M-1 motorway. The taxi had then driven north-west across the Indus River, past the city of Mardan, and then back down towards the south-west over the Kabul River. From there it had been a fairly straight road across the fertile plains leading to the foot of the low mountains where Peshawar was situated. On the other side of the city, the N-5 National Highway led up through the Pakistani side of the Khyber Pass to the border with Afghanistan some 20 kilometres away.

During the trip, Andrew had managed to slump down into his seat and sleep for about an hour. Before dozing off he had briefly wondered whether the taxi driver could be trusted, but had then decided that excessive paranoia would be unhelpful. He was already fairly well rested, but he had a feeling that things might get interesting over the next few days, so he would need to get sleep whenever he could.

He reached into his pocket to check his phone. There was a voice message from Fiona which he listened to, whilst looking out of the window at the city as it rolled by. He wasn't sure how a shipment of

Buddha statues from Afghanistan might have a bearing on what he was doing, and the same could be said for Fiona's puzzlement about Malakbel's past planning applications, but he was grateful for her efforts nonetheless, and perhaps they would prove fruitful in time. But right now, he needed to focus on his mission of trying to locate Chris Saunders.

As the taxi approached the eastern outskirts of the city, it was just before midnight and the streets were almost empty. Andrew sat up and leaned forward slightly, keen to get a feel for the local area. It was clearly some way away from the city centre, with low buildings everywhere and an increasingly industrial feel. In the distance, he could see tall chimneys and cranes sticking up from what appeared to be a number of factories near the edge of the city.

He had plotted the last known location of Saunders' phone on a map on his own phone. Then he had asked the driver to drop him a couple of hundred metres away. It had turned out that roughly twelve hours earlier, the signal from Saunders' phone had stopped abruptly at a location that appeared to be right in the middle of the infamous Karkhano Market. The market was established in 1985, and its name means 'industries' in Pashto. It is, however, also known as *Smugglers Bazaar*, because of the often illicit nature of goods being traded there due to its close geographical proximity to the border with Afghanistan. Guns and drugs in particular are never difficult to come by in Karkhano. There is also ample opportunity to buy electronics, clothes, watches and even smuggled petrol in bulk. The enormous value of the goods traded illegally represents a significant amount of lost tax revenue for the Pakistani government, but so much money flows through the market that local police authorities can easily be bribed to look the other way or even partake in the illegal businesses operating there. There have been several past attempts to clean up the market and crack down on the illegal trade, including the bulldozing of a section of the market. However, that particular section was then quickly rebuilt, and two weeks later the police officer in charge of the raid was found murdered.

As Andrew exited the taxi, he was wearing the same black clothes he had used in Syria, and his stubble had now grown into a short dark beard. In the dark and with his head down, he might just get away with moving around the almost empty market area without anyone taking too much notice of him. He also had a black backpack slung over his shoulder, which contained the folded-up MP5SD, his suppressed Glock-19, some ammunition, a couple of grenades and a few other things he thought he might need.

As the taxi did a U-turn and headed back towards the centre of Peshawar, he brought out his phone and looked at the map. The last known location of Saunders' phone was about 120 metres to the north-west. He would have to make his way down one of the main thoroughfares of the market and then take a left towards an area that looked like it was comprised exclusively of narrow alleyways.

He began walking along the side of the main road, making sure to look both as if he knew where he was going, and as if he wasn't in a hurry. Turning down the main thoroughfare, it became obvious that the entire market area was now effectively shut for the day. Most storefronts had shutters and metal bars across them, and only a couple of the grocery shops were still open. The street was about five metres wide, but the tired-looking two-storey buildings on either side made it feel significantly narrower and more claustrophobic. Overhead, there was a dense and chaotic-looking network of powerlines reaching across the street, indicating that much of this area had sprung up in a haphazard and uncoordinated fashion over the years.

He walked past one of the few shops that was still open, sensing that the shopkeepers and the handful of customers inside it were eyeing him suspiciously as he walked along. However, he decided to press on and continue as if he hadn't noticed that they were taking an interest. Soon, he was able to peel off down one of the alleyways, and after another couple of minutes, he came to a small dark courtyard. It was surrounded by more two-storey buildings, and looking up towards the starry night sky he felt like being down at the bottom of a well. The courtyard was no larger than perhaps five by eight metres, and as he looked around, he struggled to see what purpose it could possibly serve, other than allow for rear access to the surrounding buildings and shops.

He checked his map again. The last signal that had been picked up by the local mobile phone network had been triangulated to a location on the northern edge of the courtyard. However, triangulation was never an exact science. Atmospheric disturbances can have tiny but significant effects on the travel time of the electromagnetic waves that constitute the phone signal, and that in turn can mean that the true location of the signal source is several metres from where it was thought to be.

Andrew pulled out his pistol from the backpack and walked cautiously across the flagstone-covered courtyard. The only noises he could hear were the sound of a car passing the market area out on the main road, and the distant murmur of voices belonging to the shopkeepers bidding their last customers goodnight out on the main thoroughfare. At one point, a dog in a nearby alley began to bark, but that only lasted a few seconds and then there was near silence again.

He proceeded to the northern edge of the courtyard but could see nothing out of the ordinary. He checked the buildings backing onto it, but none of the houses at this end of the courtyard had any doors on this side. For a moment he wondered if the last known location had been inside one of the buildings, but looking again at the map on his phone, it seemed clear that the courtyard itself was the last place the phone had been switched on. This was definitely the place, but there was no trace of Saunders, and no trace of a struggle or anything else untoward having happened here. Had Saunders been kidnapped? Was he now being held hostage somewhere nearby? Or was he in some hole inside Afghanistan?

Looking up at the façade of one of the adjacent buildings, Andrew felt something shift slightly underfoot, accompanied by a dull metallic clonk. He looked down. It was a drain cover. It was square and had long straight slits in it to allow rainwater to run down into the sewage system below. He stood immobile for a couple of seconds, looking down at the drain cover, and then an uncomfortable feeling began to spread throughout his body. Clenching his jaws, he kneeled down and inspected the metal cover. It was dirty and caked in dry mud, but at two points around the edge he could see the metal underneath, and there were clear signs on the rim around it that it had been moved recently.

He looked up and around, checking that he was alone and straining his ears to make sure no one was in the vicinity. Then he tucked the pistol into his shoulder holster under his jacket and stuck his fingers through the slits in the cover. Gripping the metal and straining for a couple of seconds, he managed to pull the cover free and lift it up, placing it on the flagstones as quietly as he could. He then pulled out a small torch from his backpack and shone a light down into the hole. It stank of faeces mixed with the smell of some sort of petroleum product that he couldn't quite identify, yet it looked virtually dry down there.

Leaning down towards the opening, he shone the torch around the space below. It seemed to be a circular tunnel roughly one metre in diameter. The drop from the courtyard down to the bottom was less than two metres. The stench was so overpowering that he was about to pull back and reach for the drain cover to seal it back up. But then he spotted something that made him stop dead in his track. It was the tip of a black shoe. The type of shoe someone might wear at the office. In an instant, his mind raced back across the events of the past few days, as if he was rewinding a film and watching it backwards. He stared intently at the small part of the shoe he could see from where he was sitting. It looked a lot like the type of shoe Saunders had been wearing.

Steeling himself, Andrew swung his legs down into the hole, gripped the torch between his teeth, placed his hands on the edges of the hole and dropped down. He landed adeptly on both feet, took the torch from his mouth and pointed it at where he had spotted the shoe. It was a shoe just like Saunders', and it was attached to a foot. Moving the torchlight slightly further along, it became clear that what he was looking at was a dead body that had been dumped down here, probably in anticipation of it being carried away the next time there was a downpour. He stepped over next to it and knelt. Shining his light on the corpse's face, he felt a knot form in his stomach. It was Chris Saunders, and his pale face was screwed up in a disturbing grimace, as if his death had been painful. Andrew let the light of the torch sweep over the dead MI6 operative. His clothes seemed surprisingly clean, considering where he had been lying, but he was located away from the small trickle of sewage that ran along the bottom of the tunnel.

Andrew quickly shone the light along the tunnel in both directions to make sure he understood the nature of his immediate environment. In one direction the tunnel disappeared in a straight line into the darkness, and in the other direction it curved left and out of sight. He then returned the torchlight to Saunders, and placed two fingers on the side of his neck, just to be sure. For a moment he thought he could feel something, but then he realised that it was his own pounding heartbeat creating the sensation of a pulse in his fingertips. However, he also noticed that

Saunders' skin felt like the exact same temperature as the ambient air. In other words, he had been dead for long enough for all of his body heat to have dissipated away.

Searching Saunders' jacket pockets for his phone, Andrew found nothing. This could only mean that whoever had killed him had also taken it with them. Once again, Andrew's mind flashed back to when he had received a text message from Saunders. Whoever had taken his phone would now also have access to that message, plus any other messages Saunders might have sent. He had to relay this back to Penrose as soon as possible. The man might be an arrogant arse, but he was still Saunders' boss, and if Saunders' death had the potential to put other MI6 assets at risk, then that left Andrew no choice but to report it without delay.

Saunders' body lay inside the sewage tunnel in something not unlike the recovery position, partly on his front with his left knee drawn halfway up and his left hand close to his face. Once again, Andrew was puzzled by how relatively clean he looked. It was almost as if he had been carried down here rather than simply dumped. Perhaps his killers had wanted to place him out of sight, in case someone opened the drain cover.

Shining his torch at Saunders' face once again, Andrew noticed bruising near his larynx. He pulled back the collar of Saunders' shirt to reveal a dark purple bruise that extended all the way around the front of his neck. He had been strangled. Why strangle someone in a part of Pakistan where guns are more commonplace than cars?

Then something else caught Andrew's eye. There seemed to be a dark substance smeared onto two of Saunders' fingers and nails on his left hand. Andrew gently took Saunders' cold hand and lifted it up slightly to study it more closely. It looked like dried blood. Had Saunders been fighting back as he was killed? Had he been able to scratch his assailant, and was this then the blood of his murderer?

Andrew did not hesitate. He reached into his backpack and extracted one of the small plastic bags he had brought along in the expectation of taking heroin samples. With the right equipment, individual shipments of heroin could potentially be traced back to where they had been produced, which might help in identifying the network of producers and sellers that surrounded Al Naji. Now, however, the bag would serve a different purpose. He brought out his hunting knife, and, using its sharp tip, he gingerly scraped the dried blood from under Saunders' fingernails. It was a very unsettling thing to have to do, given that he had been spending time with this man just hours earlier. But Saunders was dead, and this was now the best way Andrew could serve him. If he could help identify his killer, there just might be a small chance of the bastard being brought to justice one day, even if that seemed like a tall order right now.

Just as he was putting the plastic bag back in the backpack, he thought he heard voices. He froze, turned and tilted his head slightly towards the opening above him and then held his breath for a couple of seconds. They were faint, but he could definitely hear at least two men speaking in hushed voices. He reached for his pistol again and extracted it silently from the holster. In that moment, a male voice from above shouted something loudly in Pashto, and then something small and spherical dropped down through the opening and landed almost at Andrew's feet with a metallic clonk. He stared down at it and instantly knew what it was. A hand grenade.

His instincts immediately took over, and without wasting even a fraction of a second he reached down to the live grenade with his right hand, grabbed it and hurled it along the sewage tunnel in the direction where it curved left. Then he threw himself against the wall with his hands over his ears and his eyes squeezed shut. No sooner had his shoulder made contact with the concrete wall than the grenade detonated with a dry ear-splitting crack that echoed and reverberated along the tunnel for several seconds. As the grenade exploded, he felt the force of the blast in his guts. Had he not been shielding his ears, it might well have ruptured his eardrums.

With his ears still ringing, and the characteristic smell of gunpowder from the roughly 60 grams of TNT inside the grenade already in his nostrils, he slowly opened his eyes. At his feet he saw that Saunders' body had shifted slightly from its previous position due to the shockwave created by the explosion in the confined space. The tunnel was now filled with dust swirling around in the air, and the stench was even worse than before. Instinctively, Andrew understood that he only had one option now, and that was to go on the offensive and surprise his attackers. They would without a doubt be expecting him to either be dead or to have attempted to flee down one end of the tunnel. The very last thing they would expect, was for him to come at them right now. It was by far the best strategy, and with a murdered Saunders at his feet, he also felt a deep primeval impulse to exact revenge for his fallen countryman.

Blinking the dust from his eyes, he switched off the torch and then brought up his suppressed Glock-19 and moved to stand immediately below the opening roughly two meters above him. He pointed the gun upwards and waited without moving a muscle. He didn't have to wait long before one of his assailants did the predictable thing and stepped close to the drain to look down into the sewer. As soon as his head appeared, Andrew fired a single shot. The gun coughed, and in a split second the bullet exited the sewer opening, struck the man under his jaw and then tore up through his head and exploded out of the top of his skull, taking blood and brains with it. His body instantly collapsed on the edge of the hole like a ragdoll whose strings had all been cut at the same time. The AK-47 he had been carrying clattered loudly onto the courtyard's flagstones.

Andrew wasted no time. He jumped up, grabbed the edge of the opening, and pulled himself up. Another man was shouting something in an agitated voice, and as soon as Andrew appeared, several shots rang out and at least two bullets slammed into the body of the dead assailant. Andrew used all his strength to pull himself up and out of the hole, and then launch himself sideways towards the nearest building, hoping to find some cover. As he did so, he could see the muzzle flashes of the second assailant's gun. It sounded like a pistol. The man appeared to be firing from behind the corner of a building by the narrow alley that led back to the main market thoroughfare.

Andrew scrambled into partial cover behind a large metal garbage bin, and immediately, several more shots rang out and a couple of bullets struck the bin with loud metallic clangs. He leaned out from behind it and fired twice in quick succession, unsure if he had managed to hit anything. A couple of seconds later he was rewarded with the dull thud of a body hitting the ground heavily. Then he heard the sound of a pained groan.

Peeking out from behind the garbage bin he saw the body of a man lying motionless on the ground by the corner of the building where the alley began. Pistol raised in front of himself and ready to fire again, Andrew moved forward swiftly like a confident predator hunting down its weak and injured prey. As he approached his wounded attacker, the man began to move slowly, attempting to crawl back along the narrow alley. His pistol had slipped away from him as he fell, and it was now lying out of reach a couple of metres away. Andrew ignored it and kept his own weapon trained on the man's head as he covered the final few metres to where he was.

When he reached him, he grabbed hold of his shoulder, lifted him partially off the ground and slammed him hard against the adjacent wall so he was half sitting and half lying against it. He groaned loudly.

The man was probably in his early thirties and had a short shaggy beard and a leathery sun-damaged face. He breathing was shallow and laboured, and his eyes were burning with contempt as he grimaced from the pain. Andrew realised that his two bullets had both found their mark. One had hit the man in the left shoulder, possibly shattering the clavicle or the joint itself. The other looked to have gone clean through his right thigh.

Andrew whipped out the knife from its holster in his belt, and slammed it hard down into the man's leg wound. At that, his attacker produced a noise that was half-way between a cry and a moan, but he was clearly intent on not giving Andrew the satisfaction of seeing him in pain. He barred his teeth and wheezed angrily through them.

'Who sent you?' shouted Andrew furiously.

The man simply stared at him, hatred burning in his eyes.

'Who the fuck do you work for?' roared Andrew. 'Al Naji?'

The man's expression remained unchanged, and there was even a small hint of a contemptuous smile at the corner of his mouth.

'Fuck you!' he breathed, in heavily accented English.

'Tell me who is paying you!' shouted Andrew, tightening his grip on the knife's handle and twisting it a full 180 degrees, causing an unpleasant liquid sucking sound as the blade twisted through the wound in the man's thigh muscle.

He groaned loudly, and Andrew could see that he was now well beyond his pain threshold. His eyes were filled with pain, terror and disdain.

'Who?' shouted Andrew. 'Was it Shahid Khan? Was it the ISI?'

At that, the man's eyes instantly and involuntarily locked onto Andrew's and widened with a strange mix of fear, suspicion and surprise. Andrew immediately understood that he had touched a nerve.

Fucking Major Khan, he thought bitterly.

Then he yanked out the knife from the man's leg and rammed it hard into his chest between two ribs just where his heart was. The assailant's whole body spasmed slightly and then he froze in terror as the realisation of what was happening hit him. He looked down at the knife handle and gripped it with his right hand, but Andrew kept it locked in place, and for some reason the man did not attempt to move his body. He seemed paralysed by fear, and he appeared to understand that this was the end. He turned his eyes up to look at Andrew again for several long seconds, and then his head lolled forward and his breathing stopped. He was dead.

Andrew looked down at the dead man on the ground in front of him and felt nothing, except for a fleeting sense of satisfaction that on some level, justice had been done. This man was clearly involved in the murder of Chris Saunders, and Andrew was almost certain that it had been at the instigation of Major Khan of the Inter-Services Intelligence Agency. But why? And who were these two men? Freelancers or ISI agents on the Pakistani government's payroll? If it was the latter, then he had just stepped in an enormous hornet's nest. But how would Khan have managed to arrange for a hit on Andrew?

A cold chill ran down his spine. The only person who knew that he was going to Peshawar was Philip Penrose. But why would he even consider doing something like this? He and Penrose clearly didn't like each other much, but that could never be enough of a reason. What on earth could be sufficiently important that he was prepared to risk his career and ultimately his freedom in order to try to assassinate a serving member of the SAS? It just couldn't be true, could it? None of it made any sense.

Andrew shook his head to try to clear his mind. He had to stay focused and get on with his mission objectives. The first order of business was to get the blood he had retrieved from under Saunders' fingernails analysed. His only option was to get the sample back to MI6 in Islamabad. He had no doubt that they would have the capability to analyse the DNA contained in the blood without having to send it halfway around the world to London. However, this left him with another problem. The only way to get the sample to Islamabad was to find a courier. But how was he supposed to do that from the Karkano Market just after midnight? There was just one possible way to do it, and that was to spend a lot of money hiring a local taxi driver.

He quickly searched both bodies but found nothing that could help identify either them or their paymaster. There was also no trace of scratches or other injuries that might have been sustained in a fight with Saunders. In other words, none of these two men had actually killed Saunders themselves, even if they might have been involved somehow.

Andrew made his way quickly but quietly through side streets and back alleys to the main road where he flagged down the first taxi he saw. The driver was a portly man who looked to be in his forties. He had a friendly round face and a small but thick moustache, and his taxi had several pieces of paraphernalia hanging from the rear-view mirror. Out of the car's speakers was blaring what Andrew assumed to be Pakistani pop music. It seemed surreal in its blithe cheerfulness, given what Andrew had seen and experienced just a few short minutes earlier.

Luckily, the man spoke good English, and within about five minutes Andrew had conveyed to him that he would pay him 500 US dollars in cash right now if he took the plastic bag straight to the British High Commission in Islamabad. He also promised him that he would get another five hundred upon successful delivery. The man initially looked somewhat dubious about the idea, but once he was holding five hundred dollars in his hands he very clearly began thinking ahead to when he would get another five. In the end, he and Andrew shook hands and then he set off on the two-and-a-half-hour drive to Islamabad.

As soon as the taxi had disappeared east along the N-5 National Highway, Andrew got out his phone and sent a message to Colonel Strickland, asking him to liaise with MI6 to ensure that the sample was received and that its analysis would be expedited. It also had the added benefit of ensuring that there was a paper trail that went via London, so that someone like Penrose couldn't interfere with Andrew's investigation, should he feel tempted to do so. Andrew still couldn't quite believe that Penrose was involved in this whole thing, but it was the only logical explanation for what had happened. There was clearly enough at stake for him to make him roll the dice and try to take Andrew out. But he had gambled and lost.

Andrew wanted to go back to Islamabad himself and beat Penrose to a pulp, but he knew that he had no actual evidence. All he could do now was to wait for Strickland to come back to him with the analysis results. This was likely to take many hours since the DNA sequencing would first have to be completed in the MI6 lab in Islamabad, and then the results would have to be sent to London where MI6 and most likely also GCHQ would run them through their databases, looking for a match. The chances of finding one and thereby identifying the killer were probably extremely limited, but it was still worth a shot. And even if no match came up, the results might be able to help bring the perpetrators to justice at some point in the future.

After what had just happened, there was now something else that he wanted to do here in Peshawar. He needed to find Saunders' asset. The young police officer named Tahoor Qureshi. He might have information on Al Naji, and Andrew also needed to know everything he could tell him about the western hostage that was rumoured to be held right here in the city. If there was even a miniscule chance that the hostage was Frank Malone, then Andrew could not leave this city until he had done everything in his power to find him.

He looked up at the sky, and then down at the clock on his phone. It was just after 1 a.m., and he suddenly felt utterly exhausted. He had to find a place that was out of sight where he could get some rest and think things through.

EIGHTEEN

In a sprawling and heavily guarded compound nestled in the foothills of the Hindu Kush mountains above the small town of Nahrain, which itself is roughly halfway between Kabul and Kunduz, Al Naji was sitting in his sparsely furnished office inside the main building. The compound was constructed from prefabricated concrete segments brought in from Peshawar, and although the barracks for his fighters, as well as Al Naji's own private residential building were basic, they were comfortable and a significant step up from the one-storey mudbrick buildings that dotted the mainly agricultural land surrounding Nahrain.

The large bearded man was looking at his laptop, inspecting drug shipment reports and payment schedules for his web of operations in Afghanistan and Pakistan. As he was working his way through the reports, his right hand moved up towards his neck and he absentmindedly ran his fingertips across the scar where the MI6 operative had scratched off a small piece of his skin, causing a light trickle of blood. At a very visceral level, he had enjoyed squeezing the life out of the spy with his large powerful hands. This suited little British lackey had stuck his nose into things he should have left well alone. The fact that he was from MI6 made it all the sweeter, and Al Naji had barely noticed the injury to his neck until the man's lifeless body had slumped down at his feet. However, the death of this man, Chris Saunders, had been just a small start to Al Naji's campaign. In a few days, he would be able to strike a devastating blow at the heart of the arrogant, duplicitous and treacherous British power structures. Something he had been planning for and dreaming about for over a decade.

There was a knock on the door to his office, and Al Naji commanded whoever was on the other side to come in. The door opened and a gaunt studious-looking man with a greying beard wearing a beige kameez and thin-rimmed round glasses, entered the room holding a mobile phone in his hand. Without a word, he approached Al Naji's desk and placed the phone on it with a short bow.

'Emir,' he then said deferentially. 'It has already been recharged and cloned. If I may - the most recent text message may be significant.'

Al Naji nodded and gestured for the man to leave. As the door closed, Al Naji picked up the phone and turned it over in his hand. Then he switched it on. This was likely to be a treasure trove of information about British intelligence operations in Pakistan, but also in Afghanistan. However, he went straight to the messaging app and opened the last message Saunders had sent before going to meet his maker. As he read through it, deep furrows began to crease his brow. Somehow this Saunders' character had managed to uncover part of his plan and had been on the trail when he had been caught in Peshawar. But how?

Al Naji couldn't care less about the reference to a western hostage held by the Haqqani Network in that city. As far as he was concerned, those Quran-thumping zealots could do whatever they liked as long as they didn't interfere with his business. But the reference to WMDs was extremely concerning. Somehow MI6 seemed to have got wind of the plan.

He looked again at the name at the start of the text message, a mildly perplexed expression on his face.

'Andrew,' he whispered.

* * *

It was mid-morning when Andrew woke up in the tiny hotel room that he had paid for with cash roughly eight hours earlier. The hotel seemed to have only one member of staff, and he was lethargically slumped into an old leather office chair at what passed for the reception area, whilst drinking coffee and watching a cricket game on his small TV. It was located in an old building down an alley, and it was clearly run-down, tired and extremely basic. In fact, it was more akin to an unloved budget self-service motel than anything else. Andrew guessed it probably only had around ten rooms, none of which had a separate bathroom. However, its basic nature and relatively obscure location were exactly what he was looking for. He needed to keep as low a profile as possible, at the very least until daybreak when he would need to get on the move again.

He was unable to shower, and his stomach was grumbling. As he was putting his clothes back on, his phone rang. It was Colonel Strickland.

'Andrew,' said Strickland affably. 'How are you?'

Andrew proceeded to tell him about what had happened the night before and relayed his fears that somehow Philip Penrose was involved.

'I don't have any proof, though,' said Andrew. 'And I am not sure I will be able to find any. At least not at this time.'

There was a long pause on the other end of the line.

'What you are telling me is extremely concerning,' said Strickland finally. 'If you are correct that Penrose was somehow implicated in the attempt on your life, then I think it stands to reason that he was also at least partly responsible for the murder of Chris Saunders. This is about as serious as it gets.'

'I know,' said Andrew, trying to arrive at a plan for what to do next. 'We just can't move on him. There's no evidence, and with his connections inside the ISI, he is virtually untouchable until an independent team of investigators can come in and look into all of this. Meanwhile, there is no chance of me being able to recover Saunders' body. All we have is the sample I sent back to MI6 in Islamabad.'

'Well,' said Strickland. 'I am happy to tell you that the sample arrived safely and is now in the hands of the lab people. I've already been in touch with them very early this morning your time, and again a couple of hours ago. I did not reveal the source of the sample, but they understand the importance of getting this analysed, and for the results to be sent back to London ASAP. Interestingly, they also told me that Penrose has not shown up at the office this morning, and no one seems to have heard from him since he left yesterday evening. Apparently, he is almost always the first person to arrive, and the last person to leave at night.'

Andrew clenched his jaw.

'Something definitely isn't right with this chap,' he said.

'I agree,' replied Strickland. 'Anyway, Andrew. There is another important issue that I need to relay to you.'

'All right,' said Andrew and sat down on the only chair in his room. 'What is it?'

'We briefly picked up the signal from the GPS tracker you placed on the weapons in Damascus. It was first identified at Bacha Khan International Airport in Peshawar. We were then able to track it to a location in an industrial area in the western part of the city, relatively close to your current location if I am not mistaken. But then the signal suddenly disappeared again.'

'Finally. When was this?' asked Andrew perplexed. 'That plane left from Damascus a couple of days ago. Why are we only hearing about it now?'

'Apparently, there was some sort of screw-up with the reporting,' said Strickland. 'MI6 in Islamabad is responsible for collecting and sifting through signals intelligence which this falls under, and for some reason, there was a delay of at least twelve hours between the signal being picked up and when it was identified and then reported back to us.'

'Penrose again?' asked Andrew suspiciously.

'I guess we can't entirely rule that out,' replied Strickland. 'Although I fail to see how he could cause such a delay without arousing suspicion.'

'He's very much the king of that particular castle,' said Andrew. 'He likes to be in charge of virtually everything, so I wouldn't be surprised if he could have easily pulled that off.'

'Perhaps,' said Strickland. 'Anyway. I will send you the last known location of the signal. Be aware that we don't have a precise location. It could be anywhere inside an area of roughly one square kilometre, so you will have to do some digging.'

'Roger,' said Andrew. 'I will pay the area a visit. I also want to locate Saunders' contact here in Peshawar. A chap called Tahoor Qureshi. He might be able to help, although I will have to persuade him first.'

'Very good,' said Strickland. 'Please report back to me only. We can't risk going through MI6 in Islamabad.'

'Of course, Sir,' said Andrew. 'Speaking of which, I have a request. I need someone - possibly our counter-intelligence boys, to intercept Penrose's phone communications. I would bet anything that he is collaborating with Khan, and that Khan is somehow involved with this Al Naji character. And it is almost certain that Al Naji is in possession of chemical weapons. If Penrose is involved with Al Naji, then we need to know about it.'

There was a long pause on the other end.

'We're going out on a bit of a limb here,' said Strickland. 'But given the gravity of the situation, I think it is warranted. However, this is obviously also an extremely delicate matter. If it had been anyone else, I wouldn't have gone along with this. I hope you know that. But I agree, we need to make this happen, even if we have nothing in the way of proof.'

'I guess I shouldn't have killed that bastard in the Karkhano Market,' said Andrew. 'Perhaps I could have got more out of him.'

'Don't worry,' said Strickland matter-of-factly. 'You couldn't have taken him to the police, and you couldn't let him go. He made his choice when he attempted to kill you. Anyway, I will request an urgent call with the head of MI6 here in London to make sure we can listen in on Penrose's phone and have a look at his emails. They are not going to like it, but it is quite clearly in their best interest to root out this problem.'

'I really appreciate this, Sir,' said Andrew. 'I understand that this is dicey, but if Penrose has any hand in the theft of WMDs in any way and we fail to act, then the consequences could end up being impossible to live with.'

'I agree,' said Strickland.

'I will press on and report back to you,' said Andrew.

'Very well,' replied Strickland. 'Take care of yourself, and tread carefully.'

'Will do, Sir.'

* * *

It was just before dawn when the Airbus A330-200F rolled to a stop at the end of the taxiway at Bacha Khan International Airport in Peshawar. In its cargo hold was a pallet containing eight securely packed ancient Buddha statues from Afghanistan. Their paperwork had been arranged by an employee of Pakistan's border force who in reality was working for the ISI's logistics division. This would ensure that no inspection would be carried out as the pallet left the country.

The civilian freighter aircraft was fully loaded with almost 65 tonnes of trade goods, mainly textiles, cotton, leather products as well as fruits and nuts grown on the agricultural land around Peshawar. The pilot switched from the airport ground service frequency to the flight controller in the tower and asked for permission to take off. Permission was granted almost immediately since there was virtually no other traffic at the airport at that time. Passenger planes would not begin arriving and departing until several hours later, so transport aircraft like this rarely had to queue to take off. The pilot pushed the throttle forward and steered the 58-metre-long aircraft onto the runway, and as soon as it was lined up, he pushed the throttle to max and the aircraft began accelerating along the runway. Within a couple of minutes, it was airborne, gaining altitude as it proceeded in a northern direction and then began to bank to the left and head northwest towards Europe.

Almost six thousand kilometres and about eight hours later, the Airbus touched down on runway 27 at Heathrow Airport west of London. Shortly thereafter, it came to a stop on its assigned parking apron at

Heathrow Cargo Terminal in the southwestern corner of the airport. From here the pallet that had been loaded onto the plane in Peshawar was extracted from the aircraft's cargo hold and taken past the usual customs inspections. A large and well-targeted bribe had made sure of that. After this, the pallet was loaded into a large van using a forklift and then taken east via the Southern Perimeter Road towards Central London.

The shortest route took the driver along the M4 to Kensington, then Belgravia and then past Buckingham Palace and Whitehall where Remembrance Day preparations were now well underway. As it made its way towards Westminster Bridge, the truck passed within 100 metres of the Cenotaph where the main ceremony was scheduled to take place in just over 36 hours. Unusually, Armistice Day and Remembrance Day this year both fell on a Sunday, which meant that both the two minutes of silence and the wreath-laying by the attending dignitaries would take place on the same day.

Roughly half an hour later, the van arrived at a warehouse in East London where the eight Buddha statues would be unwrapped. After this, their deadly contents would be taken to their final destination.

* * *

A couple of hours after his conversation with Colonel Strickland, Andrew was making his way along Gulbahar Road which runs adjacent to the N-5 National Highway in the eastern part of Peshawar. During their discussion inside the British High

in Islamabad, Chris Saunders had
nich police station the young officer
shi was attached to, and he had given
hin. description. Tall, lanky with no facial hair. He wa also supposed to have a large hooked nose and green eyes, the latter of which was no doubt a genetic echo from when Alexander the Great's army conquered these lands more than two thousand three hundred years ago in around 330 BCE.

On the way there, Andrew had stopped at a men's clothes shop and bought a mud-coloured shalwar kameez to try to blend in. His almost black beard was now getting fuller, and he figured he would, at least superficially, be able to pass for being a local as long as he didn't have to talk to anyone.

He took a seat at an outside table of a tea house opposite the Gulbahar Police Station. The station was an unusual building, to say the least. Built entirely of red brick it was shaped like a castle, complete with faux turrets and battlements. Andrew raised an eyebrow when he first spotted it. Whoever had approved the building's design at the local city authority had clearly been keen to make sure the police were respected or even feared. Nothing says "We are here to help" quite like a castle. Above it, raised on four separate flagpoles was Pakistan's national flag, with the white crescent and star on an olive-green background fluttering lazily in the light breeze.

He ordered a cup of Kahwah green tea, which is the predominant type of tea drunk in the Khyber Pakhtunkhwa region. It is flavoured with cinnamon, cardamom and saffron, and aside from being delicious, is also said to improve metabolism. In addition, he made sure to order four NanKhatai shortbread cookies, which he had enjoyed in the past.

As he sat there at the corner of the outside area of the tea house with his back against the wall and watching the world go by, he had arranged his phone on the table so that it pointed across the street at the police station's main entrance. The phone camera was zoomed in almost to its maximum, allowing Andrew a clear view of who was entering and exiting. Sitting quietly at the table sipping his tea, he was able to surveil the police station without looking like he was doing exactly that. It was almost midday, so it would be a question of time before the resident police officers would be making their way out of the building to visit the various food stalls and small eateries that were located nearby.

As it turned out, he didn't have to wait long. After less than half an hour, a very tall and skinny man who looked to be in his early thirties or perhaps even younger, exited the building. He was wearing the standard uniform worn by the Peshawar police officers, comprised of a crisp black shirt with white insignia, light brown trousers tucked into high black boots, and a black beret. Andrew immediately looked down and focused intently on his phone. The man looked to have short dark hair, no beard or moustache, and his nose was large and curved.

That's got to be him, thought Andrew.

He casually finished his tea and stuffed the remaining NanKhatai shortbread into the pocket of his kameez. Then he left a tip on the plate and left the teahouse, jogging casually across the road to the other side. Thirty metres further along, the man he was now sure was Tahoor Qureshi made a left turn down a street that led away from the main road. He was walking along calmly, clearly just on his way to his preferred lunch place for the day.

Andrew followed him at a distance of about twenty metres, whilst observing his surroundings and attempting to come up with a plan for how to approach the man. He needed to try to get him on his own, but he could not afford to do so out in the open. It would be too risky – both for him and for Qureshi, who had already put himself at considerable risk for Chris Saunders. The thought of the murdered MI6 operative made Andrew wince inwardly. He had deserved much better than ending up dead in a sewer in Peshawar.

At one point, the tall man appeared to glance furtively over his right shoulder, and a few seconds later he suddenly darted down a small alley on the right and out of sight.

Shit, thought Andrew. *Did he spot me?*

Andrew broke into a slow jog, careful not to draw attention to himself, but also keen not to lose track of Qureshi. When he had almost arrived at the corner the young police officer had disappeared behind, he reverted to walking although at a brisk pace. As he reached the corner he was still walking forward as casually as he could, but he turned his head slightly to the right. He just caught sight of Qureshi disappearing once more around another corner of a building, so he immediately began to make his way down the alley in pursuit. He was running now. He did not feel like engaging in a pursuit on foot through unfamiliar streets and alleys in a city where westerners were not always safe. The fact that Qureshi was a police officer, also complicated matters. He had to catch up with him and get him to talk quickly.

As he arrived at the spot where he had last seen Qureshi, he turned the corner and found himself in a tiny courtyard with a couple of bicycles leaning against a wall and copious amounts of laundry hanging on several layers of washing lines above him. But that was not what he was looking at, because in the middle of the courtyard, pointing a gun straight at him was Tahoor Qureshi. Andrew froze and instinctively brought up his hands.

'It all right, mate,' he said as calmly as he could manage. 'Easy now. I am a friend of Chris Saunders. Are you Tahoor Qureshi?'

Qureshi did not move a muscle. In fact, he did not seem to react at all to what Andrew had said. He just kept the gun trained at Andrew's head, his features locked into a mask of suspicion, and his pale green eyes boring into Andrew's. A few seconds passed, and Andrew's brain was racing, trying to come up with a way to diffuse the situation.

'Who are you?' Qureshi then asked with a thick accent and still holding the gun completely still despite the fact that he must have been feeling tense.

'My name is Andrew Sterling,' replied Andrew, forcing himself to speak calmly and confidently. 'I was working with Saunders on recovering a shipment of chemical weapons which I believe he told you about. I am here because Saunders has been killed. Murdered. I found him in the Karkhano Market last night. I know you worked for him. Or at least helped him.'

At that, Qureshi's eyes seemed to first narrow and then soften as he appeared to be processing what Andrew had just told him. He took on a concerned expression and glanced briefly back in the direction Andrew had come from.

'Are you alone?' he asked, now more subdued.

'Yes,' replied Andrew, slowly lowering his hands to his sides. 'It's just me. I am sorry to put you in this position, but I need your help to find Saunders' killer. And I am also trying to find the chemical weapons. I believe they are in the possession of a man calling himself Al Naji.'

Qureshi kept staring intently at Andrew, but he slowly lowered the pistol. Clearly able to keep his cool, he did not seem to be nervous or tense. Andrew was impressed, especially considering the police officer's young age.

'Is Chris really dead?' he asked, a pained expression spreading across his face as he placed his pistol into the holster attached to his belt.

'I am afraid so,' said Andrew. 'He was a good man. Did you know him well?'

'We met several times,' said Qureshi, taking a couple of steps towards Andrew. 'I trusted him. He was trying to help me against all the corruption here. I gave him whatever intelligence I could find about Taliban operations here in Peshawar, as well as rumours about tribal matters inside Afghanistan. In return, he helped me acquire information about the corrupt local politicians and police officers here in the city. His team in Islamabad had very good electronic surveillance. We were getting close to gathering enough evidence to charge a local police chief at the

Hayatabad Police Station. He is in charge of the western part of the city, including the Karkhano Market. It would have been a big scandal in this city, but I believe it would have been a very great thing.'

Andrew remained where he was but stuck out his hand. Qureshi took another couple of steps forward and gripped it, giving it a firm squeeze.

'I will trust you too,' he said, holding onto Andrew's hand whilst looking at him with his piercing green eyes.

'Thank you,' said Andrew and gave a small nod. 'I am by myself in this city, so I think I could use a bit of local knowledge.'

'Tell me what you need, and I will try to help,' said Qureshi with an earnest look on his face. 'I want to see the corruption in this city rooted out. I have a pregnant wife, and my child will grow up here. I want it to live in a city free of corruption. I have seen too many good people here be cut down by crooked officials. Some of them in the Gulbahar Police Station where I work. It has to stop. We can't go on like this. The Taliban and the drugs have ruined everything.'

'Thank you,' said Andrew.

'What can I do to help?' asked Qureshi.

'I am trying to find a lead on the chemical weapons that Saunders told you about,' replied Andrew. 'They were stolen in Syria, but we now know that they are here in Peshawar - somewhere in the industrial district on the western outskirts of the city. I have a rough location, but I need to get a closer look at the area to try to pin down exactly where they might be located. And I can't just walk around looking for it. That would look suspicious and make me stick out like a sore thumb.'

Qureshi nodded gravely.

'I see,' he said. 'I can take you there in my patrol car. No one will harass you as long as you stay in the car with me. And as long as we don't stop anywhere for too long, no one will know what we're doing.'

'That would be a great help,' said Andrew. 'I also have another thing that I need to look into.'

'Ok,' said Qureshi. 'Tell me.'

'Well,' said Andrew, his forehead creasing. 'You mentioned to Saunders that you might have intel on a western hostage being held by the Haqqani Network in that part of town.'

'Yes,' said Qureshi. 'That is correct.'

'And Saunders told me that you thought the hostage might be a soldier captured in Afghanistan?' asked Andrew.

'That is the rumour. Yes,' replied Qureshi.

'I need to try to locate that hostage,' said Andrew.

'I see,' said Qureshi, looking slightly wary. 'You must understand that I have no real evidence. It is just rumours, but people say the hostage has been kept there for years while its captors wait for an opportunity to exploit the situation. But if it is true, I think I may have an idea about where the hostage might be held. The Haqqani Network run several religious madrassas in Peshawar affiliated with the Darul Uloom Haqqania seminary. One of them is known to receive visitors from Afghanistan. Usually high-ranking members of the Taliban. It is a very well protected compound with dozens of fighters guarding it. The police never go anywhere near it. I am convinced that the local police chief is taking money from them. Anyway, if they are holding a hostage here in this city, then it will almost certainly be inside that compound.'

'Is there a way in?' asked Andrew.

'Not without a fight,' replied Qureshi. 'The guards are well armed, and there are constant patrols. It is like a fortress.'

Andrew nodded sagely.

'Well,' he said, darkly. 'I will have to come up with a plan. There is a chance that the hostage is an old friend of mine. I need to get in there.'

'I see,' said Qureshi. 'It will be very dangerous.'

'No doubt, it will,' said Andrew with a determined look. 'I really appreciate you doing this, but are you sure you want to get involved? Whoever killed Saunders has his phone, so they may have identified you already.'

'I only use burner phones,' said Qureshi darkly, 'but you may still be correct. Anyway, if that is really the case, then I am already involved. I might as well help you take on those people. The local police chief will never do anything, so you are my best option. And if I can help bring justice to the men who killed Saunders, then that is what I will do.'

'Very well,' said Andrew, impressed with the man's mettle. 'Let's move out then. Do you have wheels?'

'Come with me,' said Qureshi. 'My patrol car is parked back at the station.'

The two men began walking back the way they had come, and as they drew nearer the Gulbahar Police Station, they peeled off down a small street that led to the back of the building. Half way along was an emaciated-looking old man sitting on the pavement with his head down low in front of himself. He was wearing ragged clothes, and his beard was thin and grey. As the two men approached, he brought his hands together to make a cup and held it up in front of himself, but he did not look up or make a sound.

Qureshi dug into his trouser pocket and extracted a few coins. He then walked over to the old man and placed the coins gently in his hands.

'Starray ma-shay,' he said in a warm and empathetic voice. It was a Pashto greeting meaning 'May you never tire.'

'Khudai de obakha,' replied the old man weakly. 'May God be gracious to you.'

'There is no real welfare state here in Pakistan,' said Qureshi as he returned to Andrew, and the two of them resumed their walk back to the police station. 'There are many people here who need help, so we must try to do what we can.'

'Very admirable,' said Andrew.

'Begging is illegal in the Khyber Pakhtunkhwa,' said Qureshi. 'The provincial government passed a law recently that makes it a crime to beg for money. It also allows police to confiscate any money that a beggar has.'

'Sounds like giving police a license to rob the beggars,' said Andrew.

'Exactly,' said Qureshi. 'That is what happens here. I am very ashamed of it, but I cannot change it. I am sure that soon they will make it illegal to even give money to beggars as well.'

As the two of them arrived back at the police station, Qureshi gestured to a black Toyota Hilux with the word 'Police' written in large white letters on the side and on the front. He fished his keys out of his pocket and pressed the button to unlock the car.

'It is best if you ride in the back,' he said. 'That way you can duck down and stay out of sight if anyone becomes suspicious.'

'Alright,' said Andrew and opened the rear passenger door. 'Good plan.'

Qureshi got in behind the wheel, started the engine and drove out onto the N-5 National Highway and west towards the city centre. Looking out of the window from the back seat, Andrew was struck by the huge gulf between how normal and unremarkable everything looked, and his knowledge that violent extremism was also a part of everyday life here. You would never guess just by moving around the city during the day and watching people go about their lives, but there was an undercurrent of violence and insidious corruption here. It was orchestrated by religious extremists, who with the help of Pakistan's own state security apparatus had managed to subvert an entire neighbouring country just twenty kilometres away. If any city in Pakistan could feel the boomerang that was the ISI's cultivation of the Taliban over many decades, it was Peshawar. And the civilian population was caught in the crossfire. Sometimes this was quite literally true, such as during bomb and gun attacks on elements of the army or the local police force who did not comply with the Taliban agenda. ISI had truly created a Frankenstein monster, which was now haunting the country and its citizens.

'I really appreciate your help,' said Andrew. 'And I admire your attitude. Trust me, I understand the sorts of risks you are taking. You're a very brave man.'

Holding the steering wheel, Qureshi produced a quick smile and a short chuckle as he glanced back at Andrew, and in that moment, he suddenly seemed much younger and much more innocent than when he had been pointing his gun at the SAS soldier just minutes earlier.

'What's so funny?' asked Andrew, returning his smile.

'My wife,' replied Qureshi softly with a slightly embarrassed look on his face. 'Her name is Jinani. She's the most beautiful woman in all of Pakistan. She sometimes calls me 'Bahadur'. It means *Brave One.*'

'Bahadur,' repeated Andrew and nodded. 'It seems like she knows you pretty well. Sounds like an appropriate name for you.'

'She is my light in the darkness,' said Qureshi looking ahead out of the windshield with a dreamy smile on his face. 'We were high school sweethearts, even though we were not allowed to show it. And our child will grow up to be just like her, I am sure. It is a great blessing for me.'

Andrew felt a real affinity for this young man, despite having known him for less than half an hour. There was something very genuine, brave and admirable about the way he carried himself and the way he thought about the world he lived in. When chasing after terrorists and corrupt ISI officials, it was easy for Andrew to forget that the vast majority of people in this country were decent, honest and moral people who only wanted the best for their country and for their loved-ones. Just like people the world over. But it only took a few bad apples to break everything, and Andrew had spent most of his adult life in pursuit of precisely those types of people.

'What do you know about this Al Naji character?' asked Andrew. 'Does he have much of a presence here in Peshawar?'

'It's rumours, mostly,' shrugged Qureshi. 'But nothing good. People fear him. They speak his name quietly. Mostly they just call him *The Emir*, and he controls a large part of the heroin trade coming out of Afghanistan. He is rumoured to have close ties to the ISI.'

'He might even be their creation,' interjected Andrew. 'Much of the Taliban is.'

'Indeed,' nodded Qureshi. 'It is a very troubling situation. The people of Pakistan need to take their country back, but most are too scared to act.'

'Well, I don't blame them,' said Andrew. 'He sounds like just another psychopathic warlord. Ordinary people can't go up against someone like that, especially if the police are bought and paid for.'

'You are right,' said Qureshi ruefully. 'He is very brutal, and he removes anyone who stands against him. Some people say he killed his own brother to take control of the drugs trade for himself. I don't know if that is true. No one seems to know where he is from. As far as I know, he only comes to Peshawar very rarely. I have never spoken to anyone who has actually seen him. He travels with just a handful of trusted and loyal fighters, and all of his business here in the city is handled by his right-hand-man. A fellow named Abdul Wasiq. He is a Pakistani national, but he spends most of his time in Afghanistan. Or so they say. And just like Al Naji, he is thought to have connections in the ISI. I also think he is in charge of paying bribes in this city.'

'Is there corruption in the Gulbahar Police Station where you are stationed?' asked Andrew.

'Of course,' sighed Qureshi, sounding somewhat despondent. 'It is everywhere. But it is worse in the western part of the city, in Hayatabad and around the Karkhano Market. Too much money. Too much temptation. Police officers are always in danger here, and the pay is not very good. So, it is easy for people to be tempted.'

'Makes sense,' said Andrew. 'The same thing happens every day all over the world. Even in the UK, although there it is not wads of cash that change hands, but political influence and lucrative government contracts. Which police station covers the Karkhano Market?'

'That is the Hayatabad Police Station I mentioned,' replied Qureshi. 'It is on the Peshawar Ring Road a couple of kilometres from the market. Lately, you never see their patrol cars around Karkhano. Virtually all of the officers have been bribed, and those that haven't are keeping their heads down. I am sure the chief is taking money from the warlords.'

'What's his name?' asked Andrew.

'Faizan,' replied Qureshi. 'He used to be a local politician, but for some reason he decided to change careers, and then he suddenly ended up as chief of police in Hayatabad. Very corrupt, I am sure. He is known to meet often with local so-called *businessmen*. I am sure they are really smugglers, Afghan tribal leaders and probably Taliban commanders. They supposedly discuss business, but I have no doubt that they are all just making sure that no one interferes with the drug and weapons trade, and that everyone gets paid to look the other way. Anyway, I think Faizan could also have ties to Al Naji, or at least to Abdul Wasiq, his main representative here.'

The patrol car they were travelling in was now making its way through the city centre and back out to the western outskirts near the Karkhano Market where Andrew had discovered Saunders' lifeless body less than 24 hours earlier.

'We are approaching the industrial area,' said Qureshi.

'All right,' said Andrew and reached forward past the passenger seat with his phone. 'Have a look at this map of the area. The shaded circle is the area within which we have very high confidence the chemical weapons are currently located. At least, that is where we last had a signal from our tracking device.'

Qureshi glanced at the phone and nodded. Then he turned left off the highway and south into the industrial area.

'I know that area,' he said. 'Most of the buildings there are derelict, so there are not that many options. I might have an idea about which buildings could have been used. I will take us as close as possible, but I won't stop the car. It's too risky. And it is probably best if you keep your head down.'

'Got it,' said Andrew and slumped down lower in his seat.

Wearing his beard and the shalwar kameez, he did not exactly stand out, but given what had happened inside the Karkhano Market the night before, caution was warranted. He quickly unzipped his backpack and checked his pistol to make sure it had a full magazine, and then he placed it on the empty passenger seat next to himself. If he was able to locate the spot where the tracking device had last been picked up, then there was a good chance that it would be protected by Al Naji's men, and then things could get messy.

He had initially felt torn about heading for the industrial area. Qureshi's intel on a hostage being held for years at the Haqqania seminary compound seemed plausible, and Andrew was unable to rid himself of the thought that there was a chance, albeit only a tiny one, that this could perhaps be Frank Malone. However, in the end, he knew that going for the location where the chemical weapons might be stored was the only option. The risk of those weapons being deployed against civilians was a nightmare scenario that he had to do everything he could to prevent.

NINETEEN

Qureshi drove the car down one of the main thoroughfares that ran north to south through the industrial area, and then he peeled off to the right down a smaller road.

'We are almost at the centre of the circle you showed me,' said Qureshi.

Up ahead on their left was what appeared to be a sprawling factory complex with multiple buildings and several tall chimneys, but it looked completely run-down, and everything that was made of metal was covered in dark orange rust. It was obviously some sort of disused facility that had been lying dormant for a long time. It was sitting on a large plot, perhaps three hundred by two hundred metres in size, behind a chain link fence which ran all along its perimeter.

'What's that?' asked Andrew, indicating towards the facility.

'It is an old metalworks factory,' said Qureshi as they drove past. 'Copper, I think. It has been lying disused for years since the previous owner went bankrupt. I think it was then bought by some Middle Eastern property investment company, but they never did anything with it. It is just falling apart.'

'Circle around,' said Andrew. 'I want to see it from the other side.'

Qureshi did as he asked and turned left at the end of the plot and then left again to arrive near the front of the facility. It was closed off by a tall rusty metal gate with its dark red paint peeling off, but there were no guards in the guardhouse next to it. In fact, it looked like the entire complex was completely abandoned. Through the gate and off to one side, Andrew could see a one-storey building which appeared to be some sort of storage facility. It was dwarfed by the large factory buildings behind it, but it was probably at least thirty by fifty metres in size. Looking at it more closely as they passed by, it struck Andrew that it was in a much better shape than the factory buildings themselves. It had either been built relatively recently, or it had just been much better maintained. But what was it for, and what was inside? Might this be the location from which the GPS tracker had sent its last signal?

'This could be it,' said Andrew. 'It might be Al Naji's drugs packaging facility, and this could be where they took the chemical weapons.'

'It is possible,' said Qureshi. 'It is only about twenty minutes to Peshawar Airport from here, and it is very close to the Torkham crossing.'

'I need to get inside,' said Andrew determinedly. 'Keep driving and go round to the back of the plot again. I will try to enter through there.'

Qureshi nodded and continued on until he was able to turn left once more and then left again to circle back to the rear of the metalworks plot.

'There is a petrol station at the end of this main road,' said Qureshi and pointed out of the front of the windshield. 'I will park there and wait for you.'

'All right,' said Andrew. 'If I am not there in an hour, just take off and go home. I don't want you to put yourself at any more risk than you already have. I really appreciate your help so far, but I need to do this on my own.'

Qureshi pressed his lips together, almost as if he was about to protest, but then he seemed to think better of it. Perhaps he was thinking about Jinani and the dressing down he would receive if he put himself at risk unnecessarily and ended up getting into trouble. The truth was that Andrew could have used the backup, but he did not know how Qureshi would perform in a tight spot, and entering by himself meant a much better chance of remaining stealthy.

'Ok,' said Qureshi as he pulled over and stopped the patrol car. 'I will wait for an hour. Good luck.'

'Thanks,' replied Andrew as he quickly exited the patrol car. 'Go.'

Qureshi sped off and continued down the road towards the petrol station that Andrew could just about make out in the distance several hundred metres away to the south. Immediately on the other side of the perimeter fence was a dirt track that seemed to run the entire circumference of the plot. On the other side of it was a dilapidated wooden building less than ten metres away. The plot itself was criss-crossed by a dozen buildings of different shapes and sizes, making it an ideal area to move through unseen. It was also the sort of environment that would have been perfect for ambushes in an urban warfare situation. It would have taken an entire platoon of SAS soldiers to clear it out properly, but Andrew was just one man. All he could do was hope that the metalworks facility was as abandoned as it looked, and that he would be able to make it to the warehouse near the front of the plot without being spotted.

He quickly cut a hole through the chain link fence and squeezed through. Then he proceeded across the dirt track and through an open doorway in the wooden building on the other side. It was not obvious to him what purpose it might have served when the metalworks facility was still operational. Once inside, he crouched down and extracted his folding stock MP5SD from the backpack. The submachine gun had just been able to fit inside without a magazine. He unfolded the stock, pulled the charging handle back and slotted a fresh 30-round magazine in. It produced a satisfying click as it locked into place. He then slapped the charging handle back into place, and flicked the fire selector to three-round bursts.

Finally, he took off his shalwar kameez, rolled it up and stuffed it into the backpack. The black shirt and trousers he had been wearing underneath since he arrived in Peshawar would hopefully help him remain unseen.

Putting his backpack back on and gripping the MP5, he then proceeded quietly towards the other end of the wooden building. Reaching the door there, he carefully pulled it open and peeked outside. A narrow road ran directly outside the door, and on the other side was another building. This one was built of prefab concrete modules, and Andrew quickly crossed over to it and entered. It was virtually empty. He continued this process, moving cautiously and clearing buildings as he went, until he spotted the one-storey structure near the front of the plot, through the window of a small workshop building. He could also see the red metal front gate. It was locked from the inside with a heavy chain and a large padlock.

Parked at the rear of the building, nearest his location and out of sight of the road where he and Qureshi had driven past just a few minutes earlier, was parked a pickup truck. Inside it were two men sporting full beards and traditional kameez clothing, not security guard uniforms that one might have expected in a commercial facility like this. They were lazily smoking cigarettes, but did not appear to be talking to each other. Clearly meant to be guarding the facility, they had been told to avoid being visible from the road, and were probably only there just in case the facility had unexpected visitors. Visitors like Andrew. However, they did not appear to be alert or vigilant. In all likelihood, no one had ever dared to enter the facility without permission, so these two men were almost certainly bored to death and highly complacent. On top of that, they most likely weren't very well trained. Andrew liked his chances.

He headed back to where he had entered the small workshop and slipped outside again, moving quietly to the corner of the building from where he would have been able to see the pickup truck if he had leaned out. Instead, he picked up an empty and rusty old gas canister that was leaning against the building. He placed it on the ground in front of himself and gave it a firm push with his boot. The canister rolled past the corner of the building and out onto the small road that led to where the pickup was parked. There it stopped, and Andrew held his breath listening for a reaction. It duly arrived in the form of the sound of two car doors being opened and then closed again. The two guards were coming to investigate. He could hear them exchanging a few words in Pashto. They sounded alert and suspicious.

Andrew slipped back into the workshop and crouched down behind two empty fuel barrels. Now he just needed the two men to come inside the building, and then it would be all over. Their eyes would not have time to adjust to the relative darkness before he could dispatch them. All he had to do was wait.

He heard them outside the workshop exchanging a couple of words, sounding perplexed rather than on edge. Perhaps they figured the canister had fallen over by itself and rolled out into the road. Andrew reached down to the concrete floor next to him and picked up a small pebble. He then threw it roughly five metres across to the opposite side of the workshop where it clanged against another rusty fuel barrel.

The response from the two guards was immediate. Their voices ascended into a higher pitched and tense but quick exchange, and then Andrew could hear swift footsteps approaching. He crouched down lower to make sure he was out of sight of the door and sat completely still whilst gripping his MP5, his right index finger resting on the trigger guard.

Then the two men appeared. They had their weapons out, but they were still not behaving as if they were under any real threat, because they both entered the workshop at the same time and bunched up close to each other. No proper soldier ever behaves like that when clearing a building.

Andrew allowed the two men to take a couple of steps inside the workshop, and then he brought the weapon up, aimed it at the man closest to the door and squeezed the trigger. The MP5 produced a quick suppressed triple-burst in about a fifth of a second, and all three rounds slammed into the guard who was instantly knocked back onto his heels and began falling backwards. Before his teammate could react, and before the first target had even hit the dusty floor, Andrew had shifted his aim to the teammate and released another burst. Once again, all three bullets connected with the centre mass of their target, and within less than five seconds, both guards had dropped to the floor, pools of blood beginning to form where they lay. The second guard had fallen forward and to one side and had slammed the side of his head onto the concrete floor. His body spasmed once and he produced a single liquid-sounding cough, and then he moved no more. Andrew waited a few seconds, but both men now lay immobile on the cold concrete floor.

With his weapon still up and trained at the two men, Andrew advanced towards them, ready to deal with the unlikely event of one of them still being alive. It quickly became apparent that they had both expired, so he secured his weapon and began to search their pockets. Unusually for two security guards, they carried no money, no personal items other than cigarettes and lighters, and nothing else that could have helped identify them. Their presence here, guarding a building inside an otherwise disused metalworks complex, meant that there was obviously something worth guarding. The fact that they were carrying nothing that could identify them told Andrew that they were part of a professional unit that was protecting some sort of high value operation. It had to be Al Naji's drugs business. A secure and therefore natural place to store the chemical weapons.

The older of the two men carried a walkie-talkie in a leather pouch attached to his belt. This probably meant that he needed to check in regularly with someone, most likely on the inside of the one-storey building. This implied that it would be a question of time before the next scheduled report, which in turn meant that Andrew had limited time to enter the building covertly before an alarm was raised. Or at the very least, sooner or later someone would come to investigate why the two guards had not checked in as expected.

Searching the younger man's pockets, Andrew found an electronic keycard. It had no writing or logo printed on it. Just a magnetic strip that likely opened the door to the building they were guarding.

Andrew pocketed the keycard and the walkie-talkie and dragged the bodies of the two men into a dark corner of the workshop. Then he exited the way the two men had just entered and made his way towards the one-storey building they had been guarding. He quickly searched the pickup truck but found nothing of any interest.

He went around the back of the building and made his way along a narrow path between it and the perimeter fence, on the other side of which was another much taller factory building belonging to a different business. When he approached the corner, he peeked out but saw no one. He proceeded to the doors and swiped the keycard across the reader. The door unlocked with a faint click, and Andrew pushed inside with his weapon up – fire selector on single shot.

To his surprise, the building was virtually empty, and there was no one guarding it on the inside. There were a few storage units arranged along one of the walls, a couple of stacks of wooden pallets off to one side, and two small forklifts parked next to them. But at the centre towards the back was a wide concrete ramp that extended downwards to a set of double doors.

There was no cover, and Andrew felt exposed in the large open space of the building, so he wasted no time in advancing towards the ramp. He proceeded down towards the double doors and swiped the keycard again. Once more, a lock clicked open. Had it not done so, Andrew would have been stuck excruciatingly close to his objective, but luckily, the dead security guard seemed to have had clearance to pass through both sets of doors.

This was it. This was almost certainly where the weapons would be stored – if they were still here. Wincing, Andrew regretted not having taken the time to get a message to Strickland about his exact location, just in case things went south and he didn't make it out of there in one piece. But it was too late for that now. He had to push on.

★ ★ ★

Andrew carefully pushed open the left-hand side of the double doors just enough to be able to peek through the gap to the underground facility. On the other side of them was a small anteroom with an alcove on one side which was manned by two guards, and a single wide door directly opposite from where Andrew was standing. The two guards, both sporting thick beards and dressed similarly to the two men Andrew had just eliminated outside, were busy playing cards, and so they did not spot the door moving. Unable to see what was on the other side of the room, Andrew had to assume that there could be more guards just out of sight.

He unclipped a flashbang from his tactical vest and pulled the pin. Allowing a single second to pass, he then pushed the door open just wide enough to allow him to toss it inside. Another second later before the grenade had even hit the floor, it detonated with an ear-splitting crack and a blindingly bright flash of light, the combination of which was enough to leave anyone blind, profoundly disorientated and possibly even vomiting from the extreme sensory overload.

Entering the now smoky anteroom with his weapon raised, and amidst the shouts of pain and confusion coming from inside, he immediately released a quick burst of fire into each of the two guards. One was hit several times in the chest and spun partly around from the force of the bullet impacts. The other took at least two of the three rounds to the head, jerking it back and sending his arms flailing out to his sides as he fell. Both men then collapsed in ungainly heaps onto the floor.

With his weapon still up and ready to engage, Andrew quickly swung around in anticipation of there being more guards on the side of the room that he had been unable to see from behind the double doors. However, there was just a wall there with what looked like time schedules for workers. The single large door opposite the double doors had been pushed open just a crack by the force of the flashbang exploding, and from beyond it, Andrew could hear the sound of panicked voices, someone shouting aggressively in Pashto, and the noise of furniture scraping across the floor as the people inside the room scrambled for safety.

Fully appreciating that his main assets right now were surprise and aggression, Andrew knew that his best option was to push through without delay, and hope that whoever was on the other side was too confused, scared or disorganised to react properly to a threat. He ran over to the large door, kicked it open and then took cover inside the anteroom behind the concrete doorframe. In that instant, whoever was inside opened fire and a hail of bullets slammed into the doorframe, producing small clouds of dust and concrete fragments flying through the air. Several more bursts peppered the double doors on the other side of the anteroom.

Andrew yanked his second and last flashbang from his vest and tossed it around the corner and well into what looked like a long and wide space where large metal tables were arranged in a grid with halogen tube lights mounted above them. After exactly two seconds, the flashbang detonated. The defenders fired off an additional couple of bursts of gunfire, but then the firing stopped. They were clearly no longer able to see what they were shooting at. Andrew heard several people screaming and shouting something unintelligible in Pashto. Without hesitating, he moved around the corner and into the room.

It was immediately clear that this was a drug packaging operation, with dozens or perhaps even hundreds of bags full of white powder stacked neatly on the tables next to various types of household products inside which the bags were to be smuggled. Some of the bags had been hit by the spray of gunfire coming from the handful of guards who had been positioned inside the room, no doubt in order to make sure that none of the valuable powder was siphoned off by any of the workers. Clouds of white powder swirled around in the air and were drifting slowly towards the floor. Over to one side along a wall, there were perhaps a dozen of those workers cowering with their hands covering their heads, some murmuring what sounded like desperate prayers. At the back of the room were four guards who Andrew was now sure were all part of Al Naji's resident security crew. Two of them were crouched, clearly badly affected by the flashbang, but the other two were firing random bursts in the general direction of the door that Andrew had just come through. They were panicked and unable to aim properly, but that didn't mean that they couldn't get lucky and hit Andrew or end up killing some of the workers.

He quickly ducked down and took cover behind one of the metal tables that had been knocked over by the workers during their desperate scramble for cover. A few stray bullets slammed into the table, but they only made deep dents and did not carry enough power to punch all the way through.

Andrew had to come up with a plan, and fast. He had not expected to find himself in a gunfight where he needed to try to avoid hitting what were essentially a bunch of civilians. And with the two guards firing indiscriminately, it was a question of time before one of the workers got hit. Andrew was carrying several fragmentation grenades, and they would have taken out the four guards instantly. But a grenade would also risk killing some of the workers, so that option was unavailable.

As the seconds ticked by, the effects of the flashbang on the guards were wearing off, and the two of them who were already standing now seemed to have worked out that their lone assailant was behind the overturned metal table. Aiming their Kalashnikovs, they both opened up on the table, peppering it with bullets that threatened to punch through the metal at any moment. The two other guards now also seemed to be joining in. It was a cacophony of loud reverberating gunfire inside the long room, and the workers were now screaming and wailing in abject panic.

Recalling the layout of the room from when he had entered, Andrew realised that he only had one option, but it was going to take all the composure he could muster. He flicked the fire selector to full auto, took two quick breaths and then swung up and over the edge of the table, releasing a burst of eight or ten rounds. None of them hit any of the four guards, but instead they all zipped through the air to their right and slammed into a section of wall where a large red fire extinguisher was mounted on the wall. Two of them smacked into the highly pressurised metal cannister, and it instantly exploded violently in a cloud of white liquid and gas that immediately enveloped the four men and knocked one of them completely off his feet. They all scrambled to get back up, but it was too late. Andrew now had the initiative, and their fate was sealed. He quickly swapped mags and peeked over the edge of the table to see where the four men where now positioned.

With a fresh 30-round magazine in his MP5 and the fire selector back to three round bursts, Andrew emerged from his cover. Clinically and methodically, he released a burst into each of the four men. The two that had managed to get back up were taken out first, their weapons clattering to the floor. Their two colleagues barely had time to aim their weapons before they too were dispatched – their bodies riddled with bullets from several bursts of gunfire from Andrew's submachine gun.

As the gunfire died down and Andrew advanced swiftly towards the four men, the workers suddenly sprang to their feet and bolted for the door in a chaotic mob of panicked non-combatants. Andrew quickly swung around towards them to make sure that some of the guards had not been hiding amongst the workers, but it did not appear so, and within seconds they had all left the large room and were sprinting up the concrete ramp and out of the building.

Satisfied that they presented no threat, Andrew then continued swiftly forward towards the four guards that he assumed would now be dead. They were all lying on the floor covered in a gooey mixture of fire-retardant foam and heroin. The air reeked of gas and chemicals and was heavy to breathe, and some of the overhead halogen lamps were dangling off the ceiling either completely broken or flickering.

He moved up and gave the nearest guard a kick. His body barely moved. He was just dead meat. The same was true for the next two, but the final guard seemed to still be breathing. He was lying on his front and he had a bad neck wound, from which blood was pulsating out. He wasn't going to last more than a minute or two, but Andrew had neither the time nor the inclination to attempt to save him. Instead, he turned him over onto his back and leaned down to his face. He looked to be in his thirties, and he had deep creases around his eyes and deeply tanned skin. He was barely breathing now.

'Who owns this place?' asked Andrew coldly and placed the muzzle of the MP5 on his forehead. 'I will put you out of your misery if you tell me right now.'

The man locked eyes with Andrew and stared at him for a few seconds. Then his lips moved, but Andrew couldn't hear what he was saying.

'Tell me who runs this place!' he yelled. 'Where are the weapons?'

The man didn't flinch but simply continued moving his lips in what Andrew suddenly realised was a prayer. He clearly understood that he was dying, and he was not going to give his killer the satisfaction of providing him with anything he asked for. Andrew grimaced in frustration, and as the man exhaled for the final time, he thought he could see a hint of a smile at the side of his mouth. Then he stopped breathing and lay still, his eyes staring blankly into space.

'Shit,' said Andrew, wiping sweat from his brow.

He searched all four men, but again found nothing of value and nothing that could definitively prove that this place was owned and operated by Al Naji.

Looking around, he spotted a closed door in the opposite corner from where the now torn-open fire extinguisher had been mounted. He had not noticed that before, and he instantly reloaded the MP5 and brought it up, pushing it into his shoulder and advancing purposefully. He gripped the door handle, pressed it down and pushed the door open whilst standing slightly off to one side and half expecting another group of guards inside ready to overwhelm him. But nothing happened. He stepped forward and peeked inside to see a corridor that was about five metres long. It seemed to split into two at the end, so Andrew pushed forward listening out for any sound of movement.

Reaching the end of the corridor he decided to first go to the left. A few metres along was an open door, and on the other side of it was a small room with a large dark window set into the wall opposite. The lights were on inside the room, but he was unable to see what was on the other side of the window. He found a switch on the wall and flicked it, and immediately the space on the other side of the glass was bathed in cold white light. It was a virtually empty room, except for a metal table in the middle where a chillingly familiar item had been placed. It was the charcoal grey weapons case that he had planted the GPS tracker on in Damascus. But worse than that, it was open and there was nothing inside.

'Damn it,' whispered Andrew bitterly.

The weapons had been here, just as the tracker had indicated. But he was too late. They had clearly been taken somewhere else, and almost certainly to their ultimate destination – wherever that was. He left the small room, followed the short corridor around the next corner and entered the room with the grey case. He was not worried about possible exposure, since any leak of the chemicals would have rendered the entire facility unusable for a long time, and the weapons had obviously not put a stop to the drug packaging operation in the adjacent room.

Inspecting the case, he found that the tracker was still attached and so it had clearly not been detected either by Tokarev's men or by Al Naji's. This meant that there was a good chance that neither of them yet knew that Andrew was in Peshawar. This could prove to be an advantage, even if it was only for a short while. However, the fact remained that the weapons were gone, and Andrew had absolutely no idea where they might be at this point.

He walked back to the large packaging room which looked utterly chaotic after the gunfight. The heroin dust had now mostly settled, and Andrew walked over to one of the metal tables that still had intact bags of heroin and a stack of ground coffee packets. The heroin bags looked to have been hermetically sealed. They had most likely also been treated with chemicals to dissolve any trace of heroin on their exterior, in order to evade any inspection attempts at their final destination, which was most likely somewhere in Europe.

He realised that he was probably running out of time now, and that soon, more of Al Naji's men would descend on his location, possibly trapping him inside the facility. He had to get out soon. He moved out into the anteroom and inspected some of the papers that had been whirled up into the air by the flashbang and had settled on the floor. Everything was in Pashto, so he stuffed some of them into his pockets on the off-chance that there might be useful evidence on them. Then he spotted what looked like a stack of yellow self-adhesive shipping labels, no doubt meant to be stuck to the packages of goods that had packets of heroin concealed inside them. His eyes narrowed as he inspected them.

'Crescent Logistics,' he muttered, reading the name of the international shipping company listed on the labels.

This was the logistics company that Fiona had mentioned was used by Obaid and Tokarev for their art smuggling operation. The one tied to Malakbel Galley & Auctions. Did this mean that the drugs were all destined for London, and could that possibly mean that the chemical weapons were headed there as well? Could they already have arrived?

A chill ran down Andrew's spine as he reached into the zipped-up side pocket of his trousers containing his phone. He had to send a message back to Strickland immediately. So far, it was only speculation with virtually no actionable evidence, but it very much seemed like Al Naji was intending to use the chemical weapons soon, and there was now a real risk that London was the intended target. But the trail here in Peshawar had now gone cold.

TWENTY

Tahoor Qureshi opened the door to his modest house in the north of Peshawar and beckoned Andrew inside. Having listened to him recount what had transpired inside the heroin packaging facility in Hayatabad, Qureshi had decided that Andrew needed to lay low, and the only place he could think of taking him was his own home. On the way there, he had asked Andrew questions about his past and current work, and Andrew had felt no hesitation in replying openly and honestly. Despite having known Qureshi for less than a day, there was something in the young man that engendered trust and confidence. A sense of decency and commitment to values that he clearly held sacred. It was also true that Qureshi was in some respects a naïve idealist, but then perhaps the world needed more of those.

Andrew had not elaborated much on his time in Afghanistan with the Regiment, but he had provided enough information for Qureshi to conclude that he could handle himself if the events at the packaging plant weren't already ample proof. Andrew had also given him a glimpse into the life he had back home in London, and the fact that a special woman was waiting for him there. At that point, Qureshi had prodded him in a good-natured fashion about the prospect of having children, but Andrew had merely smiled, and would not allow himself to be drawn except to say, 'Perhaps one day'.

The young police officer's house was in a quiet residential neighbourhood roughly two kilometres from the city centre. It was tucked between a small group of cedar trees, and it had its own small walled garden where Qureshi said his wife Jinani liked to sit and read whilst stroking her growing belly and talking to their unborn child. He had sent a message to her ahead of their arrival, and when they entered the small but neat and tidy house, a young and visibly pregnant woman appeared with a welcoming smile.

'This is Jinani. My wife,' said Qureshi, his demeanour gentle and tender.

The woman lit up in a friendly smile and waved a shy 'hello'. Andrew decided that Qureshi had been telling the truth when he had talked about how beautiful she was. With her delicate features, her slightly pouty mouth, long black hair and dark almond-shaped eyes, Andrew could see why Qureshi had fallen for her. She was wearing a cream-coloured loose-fitting top with long sleeves and intricate gold embroidery, a similar set of long trousers, and a mint-coloured *dupatta* - which is the large traditional Pakistani shawl designed to cover shoulders and head.

'Very nice to meet you,' said Andrew. 'Thank you for allowing me into your home.'

She gave a small bow and gestured for the two to take a seat in the living room. On the way there, Jinani tugged at Qureshi's sleeve and he turned to face her. She took his hands in hers and spoke a few words to him in Pashto whilst looking up at his face, not exactly with a look of concern, but rather with a sentiment that seemed to want to make sure that he was all right, and that he knew what he was doing. He nodded to what she had said, a look of respect and tenderness on his face. He seemed to have reassured her with his words, because she then placed a hand gently on his cheek and smiled. He returned her smile, and then he joined Andrew in the living room where they sat down on a pair of low burgundy velvet sofas. As they sat, Jinani went into the kitchen to make tea.

'She seems lovely,' said Andrew.

'She is very shy,' said Qureshi. 'And her English is not so good. But she is much cleverer than I am. She is my rock. I am not sure what I would do without her.'

Andrew smiled and thought of Fiona.

'Anyway, I think we should stay here until later this evening,' said Qureshi. 'Then I will take you to the Haqqani seminary. It is on the southwestern outskirts of Hayatabad. We can drive there in about twenty minutes. But I can't come with you. It is too risky. You understand?'

As he finished his sentence, he jerked his head silently towards the kitchen.

'I completely understand,' said Andrew, spreading out his hands. 'Especially with a baby on the way. And

I would never want to put you in that situation anyway. You just point me in the right direction and then you should take off.'

Qureshi nodded. 'Very good.'

When Jinani arrived with their tea, she also placed a large plate full of local delicacies in front of them, mainly cookies, dried fruit and nuts. Andrew particularly enjoyed the *Gulab Jamun*, which are deep-fried balls of thickened milk and saffron, soaked in rose water syrup.

Soon after, Jinani retired to the bedroom, and the two men then spent the next couple of hours talking about all things large and small, until the conversation again turned to the task at hand.

'You should expect there to be lots of guards at the seminary,' said Qureshi, looking slightly concerned. 'Even though it claims to be a school, it is well known that it is often used as a meeting place for high-ranking members of the Haqqani Network. I also think they meet plain-clothed representatives of ISI there. And the local police do what they can to stay out of their way. No one dares interfere with them. This is Pakistani soil, but we might as well be in Afghanistan.'

'I am sure that's true,' said Andrew. 'I will need to be careful, but as you can imagine, I know quite a lot about the Haqqani Network, and I have had my fair share of run-ins with the Taliban. I can handle myself.'

'I believe you,' replied Qureshi. 'I hope you find what you're looking for.'

'Me too,' said Andrew. 'There's a lot at stake here. Anyway, it is almost 11 p.m. We should get moving.'

'Ok,' said Qureshi. 'We will take my own car. If they spot my patrol car, they will get nervous. Let's go.'

* * *

It was a clear but moonless evening as the sleek black corporate Learjet 60 came to a stop on the parking apron at the VIP terminal at Bacha Khan International Airport in Peshawar. The pilot switched off the bright landing lights and shut off the two powerful Pratt & Whitney PW305A turbofan engines. With their combined 9,200 pounds of thrust, they had propelled the aircraft to its cruising speed of around 840 kilometres per hour, allowing it to cover the roughly 3,000-kilometre distance from Damascus in just under four hours.

A few minutes earlier, it had approached the airport south of the city centre from the west, and then performed a long banking manoeuvre to the left in order to line up with runway 35 which pointed almost due north. As it did so, its passengers could look out of the left side of the aircraft and see the street lights of Hayatabad down below. This was their ultimate destination. This was where their target was most likely to be located.

As the engines spun down and their high pitch noise moved lower through several octaves, the pilot engaged the parking brake and released the passenger door lock. The door swung open and the fold-down stairs were extended, allowing the passengers to disembark down onto the tarmac next to the terminal building. As they exited, they were greeted by the warm and humid night air.

There were five of them, all carrying large and heavy-looking holdalls. They were burly, muscular types with short military-style haircuts, and they were all wearing desert camouflaged tactical clothes and heavy boots. None of them spoke as they made their way from the aircraft to the terminal building, and as they entered, the man who appeared to be the leader of the group walked purposefully towards a passport control desk manned by two Pakistani border police officers. He dropped his bag unceremoniously on the grey linoleum floor next to the desk and handed one of the officers his passport. His expression was one of arrogance mixed with impatience.

Under normal circumstances, each man would have needed to have his luggage scanned and inspected by the border police, but these were not normal circumstances. The officer examined the passport for a few seconds and then picked up a phone to place a call to the ISI headquarters building on Muhammad Mansha Yaad Road in Islamabad. After a few seconds and a quick exchange of words, the officer put the phone back down, returned the passport and waved the men through without asking to see any more documents.

'Welcome to Pakistan, Mr Tokarev,' he said.

The Russian did not reply, but simply picked up his holdall, slung it over his shoulder and walked towards the terminal's exit. The other four men followed without a word. They all carried the same steely and detached expression as Tokarev, and they were just as keen as he was to find and eliminate the arsehole who had infiltrated Porok and killed their former comrade from Wagner PMC, Pyotr. This was a job, and a very well paid one, but this time it was also personal. Andrew Sterling would not be allowed to leave Pakistan alive.

* * *

By the time Qureshi and Andrew had driven around the centre of Peshawar and through Hayatabad to the southern outskirts of that suburb, it was getting close to midnight. Qureshi's car was a dark grey Honda Civic, which looked to be at least twenty years old. It would never win any prizes for style or comfort, but it would serve tonight's purpose perfectly, precisely because it was so dull and ordinary-looking.

There was no cloud cover, but because the moon wasn't out it was almost pitch black where there were no buildings or street lights. Most of this part of town was comprised of large open areas with just a few houses dotted here and there, and further away there was nothing but open fields and dry grassland.

When they finally reached a T-junction at what appeared to be the very edge of town with the foothills of the Hindu Kush and the border with Afghanistan straight ahead of them in the far distance, Qureshi pointed to their right along the road.

'About 2 kilometres that way to the north, on the other side of the N-5, is where the Nasir Bagh refugee camp used to be. It sprang up in 1980 after the Soviets invaded Afghanistan. Around 100,000 people living there a few years later. A very large area – like a huge tent city. It was closed down in 2002, but during those 22 years it was one of the most important recruiting grounds for fundamentalist groups like the Taliban and also the Haqqani Network.'

'No doubt with the assistance of the ISI,' said Andrew, gazing along the road towards the north.

'Certainly,' replied Qureshi ruefully and nodded.

He then turned his head and pointed south along the same road, before continuing.

'And right there,' he said, pointing at an imposing-looking compound with high walls about two hundred metres away and set back about a hundred metres from the road, 'is the Haqqani seminary. It was built just a few months after Nasir Bagh opened. Everything is connected here, if you know where to look.'

'I see that it was no accident that the seminary ended up being built right here,' observed Andrew.

'I will drive past it,' said Qureshi and made a left turn. 'It should be very quiet now.'

As they approached the seminary, Andrew tried to map out what he could see of the layout of the compound. He also spotted four guards near the front gate – two sitting on a bench outside and another two in a small shack, and he thought he saw at least two more patrolling on the walls above, although it was difficult to make them out against the almost black night sky.

'They can call it a seminary all they like,' he said, 'but they are guarding it like it is a fortress. And it looks to be built like one too. I am sure there is a lot more than just classrooms in there.'

'It is well known to serve as a residence for prominent scholars,' said Qureshi. 'But with regular high-profile visitors from Afghanistan, there are bound to be a lot of guards.'

As they passed the compound, Andrew was attempting to assess the optimal approach, specifically the one which would have the smallest chance of him being spotted. However, at the same time his mind could not rid itself of the notion that if there really was a hostage in there, then there was a small chance that it could be Frank Malone. There were a number of coalition soldiers that had gone missing in Afghanistan over the years, but almost all of them had eventually turned up either dead or alive. Frank had just vanished without a trace.

Qureshi kept driving past at a speed that would not arouse suspicion and continued on for another kilometre before pulling over by the side of the road under a couple of trees.

'There are two drainage ditches on either side of the approach road leading to the compound,' Andrew said. 'If you drive me back there, I will jump out and make my way to the compound through the ditch that is furthest from the gate.'

'Ok,' said Qureshi and did a U-turn. 'I will stop only for a couple for seconds, and then I will drive away. You will be on your own after that.'

'Perfect,' said Andrew.

As they approached the compound for a second time, Andrew had his hand on the door handle ready to step out as the car was slowing down, when suddenly Qureshi swerved back onto the centre of the lane and accelerated.

‘What are you doing?’ exclaimed Andrew perplexed, turning his head to look at Qureshi who was indicating out of the windshield.

‘Car,’ he said.

Andrew looked ahead and saw two headlights approaching a couple of hundred metres away.

‘Don’t move,’ said Qureshi. ‘We are just going to drive past him.’

As they approached the oncoming car, Andrew suddenly felt incredibly self-conscious sitting in the front seat and being bathed in the light from its powerful headlights. The only saving grace was that whoever was driving it, was likely to also be partially blinded by the Honda’s own lights. Just as the two cars passed each other, Andrew could see that it was a white Nissan sedan with just the driver in it. In that moment, Qureshi swore under his breath in Pashto. Andrew could not pick out what he had said, but it sounded serious.

‘What?’ he asked, looking over at Qureshi.

‘That was Wasiq!’ he said tensely. ‘Abdul Wasiq. Al Naji’s man. I only caught a glimpse, but I am sure it is him.’

‘The guy running Al Naji’s business in Peshawar?’ asked Andrew, attempting to look into the wing mirror on his side of the car.

‘Yes,’ replied Qureshi, lifting his gaze to the rear-view mirror. ‘And he just turned down the access road to the compound.’

‘Shit,’ said Andrew. ‘What the hell is he doing there?’

'I don't know, Andrew,' said Qureshi, shaking his head slightly and sounding worried. 'But it can't be anything good.'

'Turn off the lights and pull over by that old house,' said Andrew, pointing ahead to a dilapidated-looking building by the side of the road. 'Just park up next to it, about ten metres away from the road, and then turn off the engine. We'll observe from here.'

Qureshi did as he asked, and as soon as the Honda's headlights were off, he drove past the building and then reversed in next to it so that they could see the compound through the windshield. As they watched, the compound's gates opened and Wasiq's car entered a courtyard on the other side. Then the gates closed again.

'Probably something to do with money,' said Andrew. 'Or could this be related to the hostage?'

'I am not sure,' replied Qureshi, peering ahead towards the compound a couple of hundred metres away. 'But it must be something important.'

The two men then sat almost silently for just under ten minutes, after which the gates to the compound opened and Wasiq's Nissan re-emerged.

'Get out of sight,' said Andrew, sliding down into his seat as far as he could go. 'And be ready to follow at a distance.'

About a minute later, Wasiq's car drove past the innocuous-looking parked Honda Civic and headed back towards the T-junction where Andrew and Qureshi had stopped about half an hour ago.

'Let's go,' said Andrew. 'Follow him. No lights.'

Qureshi started the engine, pulled out onto the road and then began following Wasiq's car at a distance of about one hundred metres. As soon as they re-entered the suburb proper where there were streetlights along the roads, he put the headlights back on, hoping that even if Wasiq spotted them in his rear-view mirror, he would merely think that the driver of the Honda had forgotten to switch them on when he set out.

Al Naji's top deputy drove his car towards the east through the southern-most areas of Hayatabad to a built-up area containing both residential houses and shops. The traffic was very sparse now. Trees were dotted along the streets in what by Peshawar standards looked to be a relatively well-off neighbourhood, and after a while, Wasiq pulled over by the side of the road in front of a non-descript two-storey residential building. It was surrounded by a high white-painted brick wall, and it had a solid-looking wooden gate that was painted black. The building itself was painted a beige colour, and it was sitting quite close to two similar buildings on the plots on either side of it.

Wasiq did not exit his vehicle, but as Qureshi and Andrew were about to catch up to him, the black gate opened and the car drove into a small parking space in front of the house. As they passed, the gates were just closing again.

'Keep going for a bit,' said Andrew, gesturing ahead of them. 'Maybe pull over next to that ATM over there.'

He pointed to a bank on the other side of the street with an ATM built into its façade. Qureshi did as he asked, slowed down and performed a U-turn that allowed him to park up right in front of the ATM.

Both men got out and walked over to it together. Andrew had grabbed his backpack and had slung it over his shoulder.

'Pretend to be taking money out,' said Andrew as they huddled around the machine.

'Ok,' said Qureshi and looked furtively over his shoulder and down the street. 'I think I will park up at that petrol station down there. I won't be able to wait for more than about an hour. It will look suspicious.'

'Ok,' said Andrew. 'I will go and investigate the house. If I don't see you again, thank you for everything you've done.'

'You are welcome,' smiled Qureshi. 'But this is my city. In helping you, I hope to be helping the ordinary people who live here.'

'Good man,' said Andrew, placing his hand briefly on Qureshi's shoulder. 'Take care, mate.'

Then he began walking back along the side of the road with his head down, the backpack slung over one shoulder and his hands in his pockets. He continued past the house, noting that the gate had an electronic keypad mounted on it. The white brick walls on either side were about three metres high, so there was no way he would be able to scale those from the street.

The next house along also had a wall facing the street, but there was no gate - only an open doorway which Andrew quickly slipped though. Standing in the dark, away from the street lights, he could see that there were no lights in the windows, and that there was a narrow passage to the rear of the property. The walls of the house itself appeared to be less than three metres from the building that Wasiq had just entered next door.

Andrew made his way to the back of the house and looked up. There was a drainpipe running all the way up to the flat roof. He looked up, visually inspecting the drainpipe and trying to gauge whether it could hold his weight. If he could get up on the roof, he might be able to jump onto the roof of the building Wasiq was in. There was bound to be a way down into the house from there.

Pulling the straps on the backpack tight, he gripped the drainpipe and began climbing. It creaked disconcertingly several times on the way up, but eventually he was able to haul himself over the edge and onto the flat roof. He took a moment to listen for noises but picked up nothing, and then he looked across the gap to the roof of the building next door. It suddenly seemed like a much longer jump than it had when he had been looking at it from ground level, but he still thought he would be able to make it. He was more concerned with creating too much noise when he landed, but he had to risk it.

Stepping back a few of metres from the edge, he then ran forward, placed one foot on the edge of the building and pushed off as hard as he could. After flying through the air for a couple of seconds, his feet hit the flat roof of the adjacent house, and he instantly performed a perfect roll, bleeding off speed and reducing noise to a minimum. As soon as he was able, he got to his feet and knelt, once again listening for noise or the sound of voices. Still nothing.

A couple of metres away was a small accessway to the house with a slanted roof that protruded from the otherwise flat top of the building. He moved over to it to discover that it had a small black-painted door that was shut but unlocked. Extracting the suppressed Glock 19 from his backpack, he checked the magazine and flicked the safety off. He would have preferred the MP5, but the spaces inside the house were likely to be too tight to use the submachine gun effectively. The pistol would also allow him to be slightly faster and more nimble on his feet.

He pulled the door open and looked down the stairs leading up to the roof from inside the house. There was a faint light at the bottom where it seemed like there was a hallway or a corridor of some description. He froze for a couple of seconds and thought he could hear faint voices, but it was difficult to tell with the occasional car driving past out on the road. Slipping inside with the pistol pointed down towards the bottom of the stairs, he walked carefully and quietly, taking one step at the time and hoping that the wooden stairs would not creak and give his presence away to whoever was inside.

When he made it down to the bottom of the stairs, he could distinctly hear voices speaking in Pashto, but they seemed to be coming from somewhere below him on the ground floor. Moving silently, he soon reassured himself that there was no one upstairs. All he found was an extremely sparsely furnished office with no office chair, a bathroom with no sign of any personal effects, and a bedroom with a freestanding closet and a bed, but no mattress. Clearly, this house was not a home to anyone. So, what was its purpose, and why was Wasiq here in the middle of the night?

Moving to the top of the stairs, he paused and knelt, aiming his pistol downward towards the ground floor below. The stairs seemed to come down to another hallway. He could now clearly hear voices. They sounded like two men in conversation with each other, and Andrew assumed that one of them was Wasiq. It was now many years since Andrew had been deployed to Afghanistan, so his Pashto was quite rusty. However, during the snippets of conversation he was able to hear, he thought he picked up words that meant 'ransom', 'foreigner' and 'Emir'.

Foreigner? thought Andrew, his heart now pounding in his chest. *Malone?*

Just at that moment, a figure appeared at the bottom of the stairs. Andrew had been so focused on eavesdropping on the conversation that he had not heard the man approach. To Andrew's surprise he was not one of Wasiq's men, and instead of wearing a traditional shalwar kameez, he was dressed in a black police uniform and was wearing a black beret on his head. In his hands was what appeared to be a Type 56 assault rifle, which is standard issue for the Pakistani police force, and he was also carrying a Beretta 92 sidearm in a holster on his belt.

Before Andrew could react, the police officer somehow sensed his presence and turned his head up and to the side. As soon as the two men locked eyes, the officer began to move his rifle around to aim up towards where Andrew was kneeling. He never made it further than halfway before Andrew released two quick rounds from his Glock. The pistol produced two meaty klicks, and both bullets instant slammed down into the officer's chest, making him stagger sideways with a shocked expression on his face, and causing him to drop the rifle and clutch his chest. He barged into the wall behind him and slid onto the floor, leaving a smeared trail of blood on the wall.

Everything had happened in just a few seconds, and Andrew's reaction had been purely instinctive. He did not want to kill police officers, but if he had hesitated for even a second, he would have been the one lying in a bloody heap at the bottom of the stairs right now. The voices downstairs turned from calm to panicked in an instant. There was shouting and the sound of chairs scraping against the floor. Realising that he had to push his advantage and try to exploit the element of surprise and the confusion, Andrew vaulted down the stairs in a couple of large steps and emerged into the hallway in a crouched position with his pistol out in front of himself and ready to engage any additional threats.

The hallway led to an entrance hall near the building's main door at one end, and a sparsely furnished living room at the other end. In the living room was another police officer, who at the sight of Andrew immediately opened fire with his assault rifle. It barked angrily, and a short barrage of bullets tore through the air just above Andrew's head. The officer had clearly not been expecting the threat to emerge so low to the floor, and that gave Andrew the opportunity he needed. Taking a fraction of a second to bring his pistol up, aim and fire, the single bullet punched a neat hole in the officer's forehead, but left a mess of blood and brains as it exploded out of the back of his head. He collapsed like a ragdoll onto the floor.

Andrew kept pushing forward, and as he cleared the corner to the small living room, he saw Wasiq standing with his back against the wall next to a table. He looked terrified, and he was holding a phone in his hand which he seemed to be trying to operate. Next to him was what appeared to be a very senior police officer in a crisp black uniform with copious amounts of decorations and medals. He was also wearing the black beret that his two dead officers had been sporting. He was fumbling awkwardly in an attempt to draw his Beretta 92 from its holster and flick the safety off.

Andrew advanced into the room with his pistol aimed at the senior police officer, whilst Wasiq was frantically trying to operate his phone.

'Put the weapon down!' shouted Andrew in a commanding voice as he moved another measured step closer to the senior officer. 'Put it down. NOW!'

However, the officer ignored him and attempted to bring his gun to bear. Andrew fired twice. They bullets struck the officer on the left side of his chest, just where his heart would be, and he collapsed onto one knee and then fell backwards against the wall with a thousand-yard stare.

At that moment, a small door near the corner of the room flew open, and another man emerged. He seemed to be coming up a set of stairs, and he must have heard the burst of gunfire from the police officer's assault rifle. He was wearing traditional civilian clothes, and he was carrying a modern pump action shotgun which he immediately swung around and fired at Andrew. The shot was deafening inside the small room, but by some miracle none of the pellets in the shell managed to hit him. The shooter had fired too early, probably out of panic or because of bad training or perhaps a bit of both. The roughly 50 pellets ripped into the drywall next to Andrew and tore a chunk out of it in a cloud of dust and debris. Seeing that he had missed, the man pulled the shotgun slightly towards himself and initiated the pump action to load the next shell, but at that moment two more shots from Andrew's Glock 19 tore through the air and hit him square in the face. His head jerked backwards and he folded onto the floor in an ungainly heap, his mangled face smacking into the floorboards with a wet thud.

No sooner had the man dropped to the floor before Wasiq had launched himself towards the dead senior officer, grabbed his pistol and attempted to point it at Andrew. It was a valiant effort, but ultimately reckless and futile. One shot to his shoulder was all it took. Wasiq let out a pained yelp and dropped the gun on the floor.

Andrew wasted no time and advanced on him, punching him as hard as he could on the jaw, at which point his legs gave way and he fell unconscious to the floor, his phone clattering onto the floorboards. Andrew did not want to kill Wasiq. This man would be in possession of a veritable treasure trove of information about Al Naji, and possibly even the chemical weapons. But that would have to wait. Right now, Andrew needed to investigate what was clearly a basement level under the house.

He picked up the phone and put it inside a pocket in his tactical vest. Then he quickly yanked a plastic zip tie from a side pocket in his backpack and secured Wasiq's hands to a pipe on a radiator that was mounted right where the man had fallen. He pulled it as tight as he could, and he could see a trickle of blood where the sharp plastic was cutting into Wasiq's skin, but he didn't care. He could not afford to take any chances right now, and there was no telling how long Al Naji's top lieutenant would be knocked out for. Andrew just needed to make sure that the man stayed exactly where he was until he came back up.

Quickly getting to his feet and moving towards the door to the basement, he released the almost empty magazine of his Glock, slapped a fresh one into the grip and pulled back the slide to chamber a round. Then he peeked around the doorframe and down into the basement. All he could see was a dusty-looking concrete floor that was dimly lit by what appeared to be a single ceiling-mounted light that was perhaps about a metre from the stairs.

He listened for movement but heard nothing, except a sudden moan which sounded like it was coming from a man. Images of a tortured and mutilated Frank Malone flashed through his mind, but then he regained his focus and descended the stairs with his weapon ready. The basement level turned out to be much smaller than the footprint of the house, almost as if it had been dug out after the house had been built. It consisted of a short corridor with a single door at the end, roughly three metres away. Outside it was a light switch mounted on the wall, and there was also a chair which Andrew assumed had been where the shotgun-wielding man had been sitting before he barged upstairs to an ignominious death. On the floor next to the chair was an ash tray brimming with cigarette butts, and on the wall next to the door was a small hook with a metal key.

Andrew advanced towards the door, picked the key off the hook and unlocked it. His heart was racing, and he could feel sweat running down the side of his face, a single bead on the side of his right eyebrow threatening to peel off and down into his eye. He quickly wiped his forehead with his sleeve, and with his pistol held out in front of himself and ready to fire, he pushed the door open.

The room was pitch black, and he was only able to estimate its size as being around two by three metres because of the light spilling in from the corridor. Still pointing the gun into the dark room, he reached over and flicked the light switch next to the door. The room was instantly bathed in white light, and for a fraction of a second, Andrew had to narrow his eyes to avoid being blinded by the light.

As soon as the light came on, there was another moan from the far corner of the room. Andrew spotted a bed, and he realised that a man was lying there on his side and facing away from the door. He was huddled up partly under a small grey blanket, clearly trying to stay warm in the cool damp space, and Andrew noticed that the soles of his feet were purple and badly bruised, no doubt from torture beatings he had received by his captors. As he moved cautiously towards him, Andrew could see that the man was tall and had a big frame, but that his body was emaciated from a prolonged period of too little food.

Andrew's blood ran cold. He kneeled down next to the bed and placed a hand gently on the man's shoulder.

'Mate,' he said. 'I am here to get you out.'

The man stirred and began to turn over, producing an incoherent and barely audible mumble. He was clearly completely exhausted, and probably did not fully realise what was happening. As he turned over to face Andrew, he opened his eyes and looked up at his rescuer.

'Who are you?' he asked.

In that instant, Andrew's heart sank, and he knew that this was not Malone. However, he quickly forced himself to focus on the task at hand.

'I am with the SAS,' he said quickly. 'We've got to move. We don't have much time. Can you walk?'

'I think so,' said the man. 'What about the guards?'

'Don't worry about them,' said Andrew. 'They're busy getting acquainted with seventy-two virgins right now.'

It took the man a couple of seconds to work out the implications of what Andrew had said, but then he swallowed and nodded.

'What's your name?' asked Andrew. 'How did you end up here?'

'My name is Johannes Bauer,' replied the man, looking and sounding exhausted. 'I am an Austrian journalist. I was taken by the Taliban in Herat.'

'How long ago?' asked Andrew.

Bauer hesitated and looked perplexed for a moment, as if he either didn't understand the question or couldn't think of what the answer might be.

'I…' he said. 'I don't know. Many months.'

'Right,' said Andrew. 'We need to get you out of here and to the Austrian Embassy in Islamabad.'

Andrew then helped him out of the room that had been his whole world for God knew how long, up the stairs and past the three dead men and the unconscious Abdul Wasiq. Andrew deposited the freed prisoner on the lower step of the stairs leading to the first floor, where he sat almost immobile staring at the dead police officer lying in a pool of blood in front of him.

'Wait here,' said Andrew and went back into the living room.

He hurried over to Wasiq and yanked the still unconscious man to an upright position so that he was sitting on the floor and leaning against the radiator. Then he slapped him hard across the face several times.

'Hey!' he shouted. 'Wake up, you bastard!'

He had to shake him and slap him a few more times before Wasiq finally came to. As soon as he saw Andrew's face in front of him, he snarled.

'You'll get nothing from me,' he said, giving Andrew and evil look. 'You have no idea what or who you are dealing with.'

'Not yet,' said Andrew in a low and menacingly tone of voice. 'But you're going to tell me. Let's start with where Al Naji is keeping the weapons. Are they still in Pakistan?'

Wasiq just chuckled and kept looking at Andrew. Using as much force as he could muster, Andrew slammed the pistol grip into the bridge of Wasiq's nose. It instantly cracked and blood began pouring out of it.

'Where are the weapons?' repeated Andrew, more firmly this time.

'You're nothing but the lapdog of the Americans,' said Wasiq mockingly, his lips and teeth covered in blood from his nose. 'I pity you.'

Andrew sighed and reached down next to and behind Wasiq where he grabbed the man's little finger. He gripped it tightly and then bent it up and backwards until it snapped with an audible crack. Wasiq groaned loudly from the intense pain, but he was battling to remain in control of himself.

'Where are the damn weapons?' shouted Andrew angrily and punched him in the face with his fist. 'Where is Al Naji?'

When Wasiq did not reply, Andrew moved on to the index finger and snapped that too, at which point the pain was becoming almost unbearable for Wasiq.

'Fucking tell me!' shouted Andrew. 'Or I will break every bone in your body. And then I will dump you in a US black site where they will wait for them to heal, and then they will do it all over again for the rest of your miserable life.'

'You've lost,' sneered Wasiq through the sweat and blood smeared across his face, and then he spat blood into Andrew face. 'It's too late. There is nothing you can do now, except watch as your brothers and your masters die in agony.'

'What do you mean, "It's too late"?' roared Andrew.

Wasiq opened his mouth slightly, pushed his jaw over to one side so that his upper right canine tooth caught one of his lower front teeth. He grimaced and then forced his jaw back into place, at which point the front tooth cracked. He quickly closed his mouth and swallowed hard. Then he just stared contemptuously at Andrew as he waited for the SAS man to work out what had just happened.

'Fuck!' exclaimed Andrew, trying to open Wasiq's mouth.

Clenching his jaw hard, Al Naji's right-hand man would obviously rather die than reveal anything about his master or what had happened to the chemical weapons. As Andrew desperately tried to get Wasiq to spit out what he assumed was cyanide or some other fast-acting toxin, it struck him that if Wasiq had spilled the beans, then Al Naji would probably impose a fate on him that would be much worse than anything Andrew could come up with.

It was no use. Wasiq soon began to produce unpleasant visceral choking noises, and as his eyes began to bulge and his breathing became laboured, Andrew roared in frustration at having come this far only to be robbed of his prize in this way. Within less than a minute, Wasiq was dead.

Sitting over him and breathing heavily with his head hanging down on his chest, Andrew once again had to force himself to focus. He searched Wasiq's pockets but they were empty. Then he moved on to the senior officer, and when he pulled his wallet and ID from his trouser pocket, he could barely believe what he saw. The dead officer's name was Rahman Faizan. This was the chief of the Hayatabad Police Station that Qureshi had mentioned. Somehow, he had got himself involved in the business of taking and ransoming western hostages.

Deciding he was now fast running out of time, Andrew got to his feet and returned to a terrified-looking Bauer by the stairs.

'Let's go,' he said, reaching under Bauer's arm and pulling him to his feet. He was disconcertingly light. 'Let's get you to safety. Come with me.'

TWENTY-ONE

It was just after dawn as the man calling himself Al Naji, stood on the rooftop of his private residence inside the heavily guarded compound near the town of Nahrain in Afghanistan. He was wearing dark brown traditional Afghan *'Peraahan Tunbaan'* clothing, consisting of a loosely fitted top, and a trouser-like lower garment. He also wore a dark green cotton vest over the top, decorated with intricate gold embroidery on the front. On his head was his usual black turban, and in his belt sat a revolver in a leather holster. It was a short-barrelled M13 Colt "Aircrewman", which he had personally taken off a dead U.S. Army helicopter pilot after his MD-530 light recon helicopter had been brought down by small arms fire in the mountains in northern Afghanistan several years ago. The pilot had been dead by the time Al Naji and his men arrived at the crash site, but Al Naji had taken the outdated gun as a trophy. It was also a reminder of what happens to men who are stuck in the past, and who refuse to change when the world changes.

Looking down along the valley and across the fields towards the northwest, he could see the town in the distance. The sun seemed to be resting perfectly on the distant mountains to the east, and he could just make out the call to prayer making its way faintly from the minaret of the local mosque up to where he stood. Down there in the town, the locals would now be opening their stalls, shops and other businesses, and Nahrain would again become busy with activity. Simple people living simple lives. But not Al Naji. His goals were greater than anything any of those people could possibly imagine. Soon, the whole world would know his name, and understand what had brought him to this point.

This was usually a peaceful time for him, but today was different. A few hours earlier, he had received word from Abdul Wasiq that the heroin packaging facility in Peshawar had been attacked. According to Wasiq, all of the workers had fled, and there had been no survivors amongst the security team. At first, Al Naji thought it might have been a rival warlord who had hired local thugs to try to disrupt his business, but all of that changed when he had received an additional report from Wasiq. His right-hand man had gathered more information from a few of the workers and from locals in the area, and, incredibly, it appeared that there had only been one attacker in the facility. A single assailant had managed to wipe out the entire crew of fighters, and had then seemingly escaped without a scratch. The owner of a nearby petrol station had apparently observed a man dressed in black combat clothes arrive on foot at the station soon after the raid, and then get into a Toyota Hilux police car that was driven away by a uniformed officer. Wasiq was still trying to find out who had been driving it, but for that, he needed access to cameras hooked up to Peshawar's traffic monitoring network, and that would take time. He was supposed to have sent an update early in the morning, but had failed to do so. This was highly unusual.

Either way, the fact remained that his facility, which was the cornerstone of his heroin export business, and which he had also used to prepare the chemical weapons for shipment, had been compromised by what could only be a foreign special forces operator. And for some reason, parts of the local police force had been helping this individual. It was the only thing that could explain what had happened, and this was deeply concerning. It was extremely unlikely that foreign special forces soldiers would have hit a drugs facility inside Pakistan. It carried too much risk and not enough upside. He therefore had to assume that this was related to the chemical weapons, which meant that his entire project had somehow been compromised, and that western intelligence had got wind of what he was planning. But which special forces entity had it been? Was it the Americans or the British, and why was there only one operator involved? He thought of the text message he had read on Chris Saunders' phone, and felt a strange chill run through him.

He then stood immobile for several minutes, contemplating what Wasiq had reported back to him. He would need to get in touch with his assets in London to ensure that the plan was kept on track.

They might need to change the location or the schedule of the attack.

He walked down the stairs and into the office inside his residence, and then sat down at his desk. Almost immediately there was a knock on the door. It opened, and one of his deputies stuck his head inside the room.

'Emir,' said the man. 'I have the photo of the foreigner.'

Al Naji nodded and beckoned the man forward. He hurried over to Al Naji's desk and handed him an envelope. The Emir waved for the man to make himself scarce, and he duly did so without another word, closing the door quietly behind him as he left.

Al Naji took the envelope, opened it, and extracted an A5-sized black and white surveillance photo from the packaging facility in Peshawar. The photo was somewhat grainy and out of focus. In addition, it had been printed out on regular paper, making the end result lacking in detail and clarity. But despite its poor quality, it was still possible for Al Naji to see the attacker's face relatively clearly. He was a westerner, although wearing a dark beard. He was dressed in black special forces combat clothes and wearing a tactical vest, and in his hands was the unmistakable profile of the favoured weapon of the SAS – the MP5SD.

Al Naji examined the photo closely. The distance from the camera to the special forces operator had been around eight metres when the image was taken. He had his head down slightly and the submachine gun up and pushed into his shoulder ready to fire as he moved forward. Al Naji was unable to see all of his face clearly, but a disconcerting feeling began to rise throughout his entire body.

At that moment, an email arrived in his inbox via the satellite dish on the roof of the building, which for some reason had been out of order for the last day or so. Al Naji frowned. It was from Mikhail Tokarev. It was highly irregular for the Russian to communicate directly like this. Especially at this crucial time in the execution of their plan.

Al Naji immediately reached over to the laptop and opened the email. It contained a brief text describing a series of disconcerting events in Damascus, including the death of Major Zahir Obaid in his home in that city. There was also a readout from a Russian radar installation near the Syrian coast. It had picked up traces of a VIP aircraft that had been stolen from the Mazzeh Military Airport southwest of the capital. Apparently, there had been a problem with contacting Russian command in Syria, although eventually two Russian SU-34s had been scrambled from Latakia. However, they had been too late to intercept the aircraft before it entered international airspace and had landed safely at RAF Akrotiri in Cyprus. The pilot had escaped a fiery death by the skin of his teeth.

Tokarev also described how a Mukhabarat officer and one of his own men had been killed by a covert assailant inside his own nightclub Porok. Several years earlier, Al Naji had once visited the nightclub himself, but that was long before he had come up with the plan that he was now in the middle of carrying out. However, the most interesting part of the email was the attachment. It included two images taken by security cameras inside the nightclub, and they were both of excellent quality. The intruder had been wearing a white dishdasha complete with a keffiyeh headdress, but it was still possible to see a glimpse of the man's face. It was the same man from the pictures taken inside the facility in Peshawar. There was no doubt that he was on their trail, and that he was behind everything that had happened over the past week. Al Naji's hairs stood on end, and he suddenly felt flushed and deeply perturbed. A constricting and almost claustrophobic sensation began to spread throughout his body. It felt as if in just a few short moments he had gone from predator to prey.

In the final part of the email, the Russian ex-Wagner mercenary let Al Naji know that he was now personally on his way to Peshawar with a hit squad of former Wagner operatives, since the Pakistani city was the only logical place for the foreign agent to have gone. He would be arriving in just a few hours. And then Tokarev delivered the proverbial punchline. It was the name of the man he was coming to hunt down, and whose identity he had secured via his connections inside the Russian FSB. A name that, when he saw it, elicited emotions in Al Naji that he had not felt for a very long time.

He stared at the name in front of him for several seconds. Could this really be true? He flicked between the images from Porok and settled on the one that gave the best quality image of the intruder. Staring at it for a long time, a perplexed look and then a fleeting hint of recognition seemed to flash across his face. Then he lifted his gaze and stared straight ahead, bringing up his right hand to gently rub the bridge of his nose just where the scar cut across it next to his eyepatch. He then sighed with a hard, determined look on his face. It appeared as if a dark cloud had suddenly cast a heavy shadow over him, a grim expression making his scarred face look even more menacing than usual.

Al Naji grabbed the coin that was hanging on a leather strap around his neck. He squeezed it tight and felt the contours of its bent shape inside his fist. This had been Frank Malone's coin. But Frank was dead. He had died many years ago in a filthy shack inside an opium processing compound in northeastern Afghanistan. But Frank's companion on that day was still alive, and now, somehow, he was back. Andrew Sterling was back.

* * *

When Andrew woke up to the trill of birdsong outside his window, it was midmorning. He had spent the tail end of the night in the tiny guestroom of the house that Qureshi shared with his wife. He felt remarkably well rested, considering the previous night's events and the fact that he had only had about five hours of sleep. Before returning to Qureshi's house north of the city centre, they had taken Johannes Bauer to the United States Consulate near the centre of Peshawar. Neither Austria nor the United Kingdom had a physical presence in the city, so handing the emaciated former hostage to the Americans seemed like the most appropriate thing to do. There was simply no way the two of them would be able to arrange for safe and speedy passage for him all the way to the Austrian Embassy in Islamabad, and

Bauer was grateful to be delivered to the U.S. Consulate building on Soekarno Road, where he was escorted inside by two heavily armed U.S Marines.

On the way back to Qureshi's house, Andrew had been dismayed to discover that Wasiq's phone had been wiped entirely clean. Andrew cast his mind back to the night before and immediately understood what had happened. As he had advanced on Faizan, ultimately ending up having to take him down, Wasiq had been initiating a factory reset of his phone, which effectively restored it to the state it was in when it had first been purchased. All of its stored messages, phone numbers and images were gone and unrecoverable.

Andrew had sent a short message to Colonel Strickland back in London, informing him of the rescue and asking him to liaise with the Americans to ensure that Bauer was looked after and brought to Islamabad. He had also asked for the two of them to have a phone conversation as soon as possible.

After he awoke, Jinani cooked him a delicious late breakfast, and as he was finishing the last morsels, his phone pinged with a response from the colonel, asking if he was available for a chat. He excused himself and went into the sunny walled garden where Jinani had been growing vegetables, and where burgeoning flowerbeds gave off a sweet perfumed scent. He sat down on a wooden chair in a sunny spot near the back of the garden next to a rosebush. Then he hit Stricklands number on the speed dial.

'Strickland, Sir,' he said.

'Andrew,' said Strickland, clearly glad to hear from him. 'I received your message. Bauer has already been escorted to Islamabad. He will need a bit of TLC after that ordeal, I should imagine, but he's all right. Cracking job, Andrew. The PM has already had the Austrian Chancellor on the phone, gushing with praise.'

'Well, I couldn't just leave him there,' said Andrew with a faint smile. 'But I am glad to hear he's ok. I expect he'll be on the first available flight back to Vienna.'

Andrew proceeded to give Strickland a detailed debrief of everything that had happened since their last conversation. Abdul Wasiq's disconcerting last words about Andrew watching his "brothers and masters" dying in agony were met with a prolonged silence from Strickland.

'This really is extremely worrying,' he finally said, sounding deeply concerned by what he had just been told. 'We have to assume that Al Naji is preparing to carry out some sort of attack in the UK soon using the stolen chemical weapons. I will see what I can dig up on Crescent Logistics. Fiona had already identified that company as being of interest, but this clearly runs much deeper than simple art smuggling. This might be a major attack on the government.'

'Shit!' said Andrew suddenly. 'I think I might know what they are planning.'

'What?' asked Strickland.

'It is Remembrance Day the day after tomorrow,' he said. 'What if they are going to hit the annual ceremony at the Cenotaph in Whitehall? Everyone is going to be there. The Prime Minister, the Royals, the Cabinet, and hundreds of armed forces personnel. That has to be it!'

'Christ almighty,' breathed Strickland. 'I'm afraid you might be right.'

Andrew couldn't remember the last time he had heard the colonel swear.

'Just picture it,' said Andrew, whilst trying not to think of Fiona and her stated intention to attend the ceremony. 'If the weapons are deployed at that location when all the dignitaries are present laying wreaths, it will be like nothing we've ever seen before. It will be the effective decapitation of almost the entire UK power structure. Hundreds of people will be killed in the most horrific way imaginable. And it will be broadcast live to the entire world.'

There was again silence on the other end of the line for at least ten seconds before Strickland responded.

'Right,' he finally said, making an effort to remain level-headed. 'I will get straight onto GCHQ, MI5 and the other security services and ask that a broad effort is made to uncover any actual threats to the ceremony. We need to cast as wide a net as possible. However, I would obviously not have the authority to cancel the entire event, even if I thought an attack was guaranteed to happen. So far, at least, all we have is anecdotal evidence and speculation. There is nothing tangible that directly connects the chemical weapons to the Remembrance Day ceremony, but that doesn't mean it isn't going to happen. We have to mobilise every possible resource to try to prevent this, and we need to apprehend the people responsible.'

Andrew had never been much of a royalist, but he naturally felt an instinctive revulsion at the idea of the royal family and most of the government succumbing to the effects of a high-grade nerve agent on live TV.

The spectacle of it would be stomach-churning, as well as being an enormous PR-victory for the Taliban who would no doubt claim responsibility for the attack soon after the event.

'I think we should have McGregor and his unit on standby,' he said, referring to his old friend and one of the best and most experienced anti-terrorist units the SAS could muster. 'If Al Naji is really about to unleash these weapons in London, then there must be at least a handful of accomplices already there and ready to carry out the attack.'

'I will make sure that happens,' said Strickland. 'They will be on high alert and ready to deploy at a moment's notice. I bloody well hope we won't need them.'

'Better to have them and not need them, than to need them and not have them,' said Andrew.

'Precisely,' said Strickland. 'I will get onto that as soon as we are done.'

'And, Sir?' said Andrew. 'Please get in touch with Fiona and ask her to stay away from the ceremony at the Cenotaph. Just in case.'

'I will do that,' said Strickland. 'And there's something else that I think you should know. It is regarding Philip Penrose. I think it's fair to say there's been a development.'

'What has happened?' asked Andrew. 'Did you manage to get access to his phone records?'

'We did better than that,' said Strickland. 'All the calls in and out of the British High Commission in Islamabad are obviously recorded, and Penrose is too clever to use those. However, we also managed to pinpoint several calls made by unauthorised burner phones from inside the compound over the span of several months. Using some signals intelligence wizardry that is too advanced for me to understand, our people at MI6 managed to determine that those phones had been paid for with an account registered to a fictitious name that is ultimately linked to Penrose. It then turned out that the calls had been made to a Major Khan of the ISI in Islamabad.'

'Really?' asked Andrew. 'So, those two have been communicating with each other in the shadows?'

'It appears so,' replied Strickland. 'There's even evidence to suggest that Penrose has met up with Khan on multiple occasions in a house in the centre of the city, but without ever logging it in MI6's systems, which he is obviously required to do. So, something nefarious is clearly going on.'

'Sounds like he needs to be detained,' said Andrew. 'If he is in league with Khan, then, as crazy as it may sound, he might then be connected to Al Naji.'

'Well,' said Strickland. 'There's a slight problem with that.'

'What?' asked Andrew.

'Penrose has gone completely AWOL,' replied Strickland, sounding like he couldn't quite believe what he was saying.

'He's missing?' asked Andrew incredulously.

'Very much so,' replied Strickland. 'He cleaned out his office one evening and left. Hasn't been seen or heard from since. His apartment in Islamabad is deserted, and there is no digital trail of him anywhere that we have been able to find so far.'

'Crikey,' said Andrew. 'Well. At least we no longer need to speculate about which team he is playing for.

Can I suggest we do a deep dive on his financial interests? There's bound to be something there.'

'It's already underway,' replied Strickland. 'GCHQ are digging into it as we speak, but it could take some time. He a wily old bastard. He will have covered his tracks very well, I am sure.'

'If he has been working with Khan,' said Andrew, 'then it is almost certain that those two men who tried to kill me in Peshawar were ISI operatives. And I bet the men who killed Saunders were also sent by Khan. That means that Penrose is directly responsible for Saunders' murder.'

'It very much seems that way,' said Strickland, 'as sad as I am to admit it. It appears that Penrose went over to the dark side. But why? I can't for the life of me understand what could be the reason.'

Andrew thought back to his meeting with Penrose on his first day in Islamabad, and he could still hear his words as they were reclining on the sofas inside his office. *"It's all a game, old chap."*

'I didn't get the impression that Penrose needed the money,' said Andrew. 'But I don't think that was ever a reason for him to be in the intelligence business. Frankly, he seemed to consider it sport.'

'Well, that wouldn't be the first time that's happened,' said Strickland. 'Both ideology and a desire for excitement have been known to play a role in these sorts of instances in the past. Anyway, as you can imagine, this is a highly embarrassing thing to have happen, and the government is keen to keep it out of the press for as long as possible. But rest assured, there are obviously efforts underway to locate him and bring him in.'

'If I had to guess,' said Andrew. 'Penrose was probably playing as many sides as he thought he could get away with. And I wouldn't be surprised if it turned out that he has been the eyes and ears of Kahn and Al Naji in Islamabad. He might even have been getting a cut from the heroin trade out of Afghanistan. I am sure he has upkeep for a mansion or two to consider.'

'I have no doubt we will find out eventually,' said Strickland and cleared his throat.

'Anyway. Listen, Andrew,' he continued with an uncharacteristically hesitant tone of voice. 'There's one last thing that I need to tell you. I must say, I have been reluctant to relay this to you, but I think you deserve to know. And, uhm… you should probably sit down for this one.'

Andrew felt the hairs on the back of his neck stand on end. Was this about Fiona? Had something happened to her? Ever since he had asked her to look into Tokarev and Obaid, his concern for her safety had grown steadily. This was no longer just about art smuggling. This was now a matter of national security, and they were clearly dealing with people who had no qualms about murdering hundreds of people. They wouldn't think twice about killing someone like Fiona and dumping her in the Thames.

'I am sitting down,' he said tensely, steeling himself for what he was about to be told. 'Tell me.'

'It's to do with Chris Saunders,' said Strickland.

Andrew felt intense relief flooding through his body like a powerful drug.

'What about him?' he asked, various images of the MI6 spy flashing through his mind.

'We have had a chance to analyse the blood sample you retrieved from under his fingernails,' replied Strickland. 'We sequenced the DNA and ran it through all of our various databases looking for a match, and it came up with a name. Andrew, we're 99 percent sure that the blood under Chris Saunders' nails belonged to Frank Malone.'

Strickland's words hit Andrew like a hammer blow to the chest. He had to make an effort to take a breath and calm himself down. He sat completely frozen for several seconds, his own pulse throbbing in his carotid arteries as his heart pounded.

'I understand how this must make you feel,' said Strickland. 'I know that you two were close.'

'Like brothers,' Andrew managed to breathe. 'How is this possible? Are you sure about this?'

'They told me, 99 percent,' said Strickland, 'but I think that is just their way of saying that there is no remotely likely scenario where the sample could have come from anyone other than him.'

'Jesus,' muttered Andrew. 'How?'

His mind was racing back to the tiny courtyard and the stinking sewer in the Karkhano Market in northern Hayatabad. He closed his eyes and recalled the purple bruising on Saunders' neck. It couldn't possibly be the work of Frank Malone! Could it? His head was spinning. It was almost too much for him to process, and with his eyes still closed, he leaned back slowly and rested the back of his head against the garden wall behind him. The sun was on his face and the birds were chirping cheerfully, but inside he felt as cold as ice.

'I'd better get on with things here,' said Strickland. 'I am sorry to be the bearer of such troubling news, but as I said, I thought it was better if you knew.'

'Thank you,' said Andrew. 'I am not sure what to do with it, but thanks all the same.'

'I will be in touch if there are any developments,' said Strickland. 'You just get some rest and stay out of harm's way. You've already done the country a great service, but there is nothing more you can do from there. Rest assured that we will move heaven and earth to find and stop the attackers. I will speak to you soon.'

'All right,' sighed Andrew, opening his eyes again. 'Goodbye, Sir.'

Five minutes later, or was it twenty-five, Andrew was still sitting on the small wooden chair, having not moved a muscle and still reeling from what he had been told. For a man who had learned to master his physical and mental state, suppress his emotions and stay cool even under conditions of extreme stress and danger, he suddenly felt completely out of his depth.

If what Strickland had said was really true, then Frank Malone was back from the dead. Somehow, he had survived that day in northern Afghanistan twelve years ago. But he had never come back to the UK, and he had never let anyone know that he was still among the living. There was no other explanation than that he had chosen to stay in Afghanistan. But why? Did he not realise the toll his disappearance and presumed death would have on Andrew and the other guys from the Regiment? And what about his own family? It just didn't make sense. And what was he even doing in Peshawar? Could he be working for Al

Naji? That seemed completely insane. Frank had put his life on the line countless times to capture or kill warlords like him. Why would he even consider switching sides like this?

As exhausted and overwhelmed as Andrew suddenly was, he also felt a powerful compulsion to do something. Anything. On the one hand he was drawn back to London, partly to find Fiona and make sure she got out of the city, and partly because he knew that if there was going to be an attack, then his brothers in the Regiment would be in the thick of things, and that made him want to be there right next to them. On the other hand, he sensed intuitively that the solution to the mystery of Frank's reappearance was to be found here in Pakistan, or perhaps inside Afghanistan itself, and that made him want to stay here and see this through.

As he was contemplating his options, the door to the kitchen opened and Qureshi stepped out holding two cups of Kahwah green tea. Seeing the look of concern on Andrew's face, he approached without a word and sat down next to him and handed him a cup.

'Are you ok, my friend?' he asked, looking at Andrew empathetically.

Andrew shrugged, wringing his hands and pressing his lips together. He wasn't used to sharing his thoughts and emotions with very many people. But he knew that Qureshi had lost colleagues himself in the fight against the Taliban and their Pakistani enablers, so he decided to let him in on what was happening, minus the confidential parts.

'Anyway,' said Andrew after having shared his thoughts. 'The bottom line for you is that you and Jinani should pack your bags and get out of Peshawar. At least for a while. It is probably a matter of time before they find out that you have been helping me, but even if they don't, they are likely to come after me, which then puts you and Jinani at risk. I reckon I will soon have the entire corrupt contingent of the Hayatabad police department on my back. I can take care of myself, but I can't protect the two of you. Not in this city and not without support.'

'I understand,' said Qureshi and nodded sagely, 'But I am very sorry to tell you that I will not go. I refuse to back down now. I told you already, Andrew. This is my city, and these animals are choking the life out of it. I will not allow myself to run away. I would not be able to live with myself. So, I will stay here and help you with whatever you need.'

Andrew looked at Qureshi and was about to try to convince him that his sense of duty was admirable, but that ultimately his safety was more important. However, when he looked into the steely green eyes of the young police officer, he could see that there was no point in trying. His mind was made up, and there was nothing Andrew could say to dissuade him.

'All right,' he said after a few moments. 'I can see that you have made up your mind. But at least get Jinani out of the city.'

'Yes,' nodded Qureshi. 'I will talk to her and ask her to go to her mother's apartment in Lahore. It is plenty big enough for her to stay there for a few days or a few weeks. However long this will take. She will argue with me, I am sure. But she cannot stay.'

* * *

The building in the East London suburb of Barking was on the aptly named River Road, where all the properties on one side of the road backed onto a tributary river called the Roding that flowed south to join the Thames. It was located next to a self-storage depot and across from a mechanics yard where a dozen of the characteristic red London buses had been parked and readied for repairs and servicing. The unremarkable grey-painted building had originally been a 19th century factory constructed from redbrick, but it been many decades since anything had been manufactured inside it. For decades now it had mostly served as a storage unit for nearby businesses, most recently a timber merchant that had now gone out of business. After that, it had been acquired by an overseas property developer who had applied for planning permission to turn the entire building into high-end apartments overlooking the river. But even though planning permission had been granted, no work had yet been commenced, and the site looked rundown and derelict.

However, every once in a while, a truck would arrive and pull up in front of the large sliding door at the front of the building. The driver would then wait for the door to open, after which he would back the truck inside. Then the doors would close again. It was always the same truck that arrived, and every time it did so, it had come from the Cargo Terminal at Heathrow Airport. Sometimes it was carrying a shipment from Egypt, sometimes from Syria or Iraq, but today it was delivering a well-wrapped pallet with valuable ancient artefacts from Afghanistan that had been flown in from Peshawar in Pakistan.

Nadeem Yassin was waiting patiently as the pallet was unloaded inside the building. He kept a distance of a few metres as one of his two trusted collaborators used a forklift to extract it from the truck and place it on the concrete floor. In addition to the two men, one of whom also functioned as the driver of the truck, he had today brought in a third man, who was going to be vital to making sure that the plan was carried out successfully. Younger than the other two, and the son of two Middle Eastern immigrants, he was a chemistry Ph.D. student at a prestigious university in London, and he had spent the past several weeks readying the two explosive devices inside the factory building. He always arrived on foot, and he only ever entered the building using the small side-door away from the main road.

The devices were conventional explosive charges, made from a TNT clone that the young man had manufactured himself. The smaller of the two charges was powerful in its own right, but it was merely designed to induce panic and to herd the targets into the kill zone where the main device would then be detonated. That, in turn, would then ensure that the chemical agent would be dispersed over a large area and cause as many deaths as possible.

Anyone could kill a large number of targets with a conventional bomb. Such a bomb would have created fiery smoky havoc, but probably also ruined the camera equipment and the satellite dishes used to transmit the live feed to the broadcasters. However, the beauty of using a chemical agent like the one his uncle Zahir had managed to acquire and deliver to the Afghan warlord, was that it would leave all the electronics in the area still functioning, including CCTV, mobile phones and TV cameras, effectively ensuring that the event was live as well as recorded on dozens of phone cameras, even after the people holding them had died.

The chemical agent would also continue to disperse over an ever-expanding area for tens of minutes before it would eventually begin to dissipate. This would ensure the best possible exposure and subsequent dissemination of the footage from the attack, which was guaranteed to shock the country and the world. As a bonus, it would leave the UK without any effective leadership for days, possibly weeks, and it was highly likely to cause a sea change in public opinion about the constant meddling of the UK and its allies in countries where they had no business meddling, and where they should never have got themselves involved. Countries like Syria, Iraq, and Afghanistan.

Nadeem couldn't think of a better occasion than Remembrance Day for the attack to take place. The timing had not been his idea. In fact, nothing about the entire operation was, but he had appreciated the poignancy of it. In the act of remembering all the soldiers that the British Empire had lost whilst trying to dominate and subjugate the rest of the world for centuries, the Regent and the Prime Minister would perish in agonising fashion. And as a result of this devastating strike at the heart of the British establishment, the country would be revealed to be nothing but an impotent and hollow oppressor of weaker nations.

Several hours before the attack, Nadeem would take a flight to Paris where he would lay low in a safehouse provided by a sympathetic foreign government. After that, and as soon as the dust had settled, he would make his way to Lebanon and then back to Damascus. His time in London was coming to an end, and he was at peace with that. He had done his part, and he knew that one day he would be regarded as a hero of the downtrodden peoples of the Middle East.

After more than three hours, the pallet from Peshawar had been unwrapped, and its contents had been prepped for their onward journey. The two explosive devices were now also ready to be taken away. They were to be carried by a separate vehicle to their destinations, where, just a few hours before the attack, the smaller device would be placed in its intended concealed location by a member of the Metropolitan Police. Over the past several years, the officer had been cultivated as one of Al Naji's assets in the capital, and he had now become a fervent believer in the cause. The stage was almost set. Soon, everything would be different. Everything would change.

Twenty-Two

Late in the afternoon, Tahoor Qureshi took his pregnant wife Jinani to the Peshawar's Railway Station on Sunehri Masjid Road near the city centre, from where she would buy a ticket to Lahore. It was going to be a ten-hour journey to her mother's house, which would have been a long trip even if she wasn't carrying a child. But if she felt any reservations about it, she did not show them. She appeared calm and steadfast.

Andrew was sitting in the backseat of the grey Honda Civic, deliberately keeping quiet since he didn't want to impose himself on the last few minutes the couple would have together for days, possibly even weeks. When the time came for them to say goodbye inside the station, he could see that their parting was painful for them both, but also that they understood why it was the only sensible and safe path for them to take. As they embraced for the final time, there was a tenderness on display that again pulled his thoughts back towards London and Fiona.

Qureshi put a brave face on it for as long as Jinani was able to see him. However, as the two men exited the train station, Andrew could see that Qureshi was weighed down by her departure, so he offered to drive the car, and Qureshi accepted. After they drove off, it was several minutes before Qureshi finally spoke.

'At least now she will be safe,' he said, sounding like he was trying to convince himself that they had made the right decision.

Andrew glanced sympathetically at his companion, let go of the wheel with one hand and placed it on Qureshi's shoulder.

'You guys did the right thing,' he said. 'They both need to be kept out of harm's way.'

'I know,' said Qureshi, his forehead creased as he stared vacantly out of the windshield. Then he pointed ahead of them. 'Let's go and get some dinner. Turn right up here at the lights. I know a place that serves very good Nihari. It is a traditional beef stew. Slow cooked. Very tasty.'

'Sounds good,' said Andrew. 'I could do with a nice fortifying meal.'

Just as they were making the turn, there was a gentle trilling coming from inside the car. Qureshi instantly dug into his pocket and extracted his phone. At first, Andrew feared that it was Jinani calling him and that something had come up to scupper her plan to go to Lahore. However, Qureshi just glanced at it and quickly tapped it a couple of times to read a message that had just arrived. He frowned slightly as he put the phone back in his pocket, and readjusted himself in the seat with both hands now back on the wheel.

'A message from one of my informants,' he said. 'His name is Noor. He's a market trader in Karkhano. Says he needs to see me urgently.'

Andrew looked at him with a sceptical expression.

'Can we trust him?' he asked.

'You can't really trust anyone here,' said Qureshi and shrugged. 'But he has provided reliable information in the past. He helped me discover that Faizan was involved with the Taliban and the Haqqani seminary.'

'When and where does he want to meet?' asked Andrew.

'In about two hours, just after sunset at our usual spot,' said Qureshi. 'It is a scrapyard just north of Karkhano Market.'

'Any idea what this could be about?' asked Andrew.

'No,' said Qureshi. 'We never discuss those things over the phone. But if he says it is urgent, I will need to meet him. He might have information about Hayatabad Police Station. I am sure killing chief Faizan has stirred up a hornet's nest there.'

Andrew thought about the moment he had put two bullets into the man he had later discovered was the chief of police there. At that point, he had realised what danger that was ultimately putting Qureshi in, but they were in too deep to back out now.

'All right,' he said. 'I am going to come with you to provide backup.'

'Thank you,' said Qureshi. 'Let's go and have something to eat first. We have plenty of time.'

After a warm meal consisting of a bowl of Nihari stew served with Roti flatbread at the back of a small local eatery near Qureshi's home, the two men got back into the Honda Civic and drove west towards the meeting place. It was located on the other side of the road from where the Karkhano Market ended, and it was surrounded by a high fence built from rusty corrugated metal sheets. On the other side of the fence, Andrew could see a crane and the top of piles of car wrecks that were waiting to be stripped down or fed into the hydraulic car crusher and turned into cubes of compressed metal.

The sun had just set when they arrived, and the scrapyard lay quiet. Its workers had gone home for the day, but there was a single floodlight mounted on pole near the centre of the yard, which cast a cold white light across it as the sky gradually turned ever darker.

Andrew parked the Honda a few metres from the open gate and the two men got out. Everything was quiet, except for the distant noises of the main road on the other side of Karkhano Market. Qureshi had sent his informant, Noor, a message saying that he would be coming as requested and that he was bringing a friend for protection. There was a risk that this would spook the market trader, but Andrew refused to let Qureshi go alone. Both men were armed, Andrew with his suppressed Glock 19 strapped to him under the left arm, and Qureshi with his service pistol in the holster on his belt.

'You take the lead,' said Andrew, reaching inside his jacket and unfastening the leather strap on his shoulder holster. 'I'll be a couple of metres behind you. We don't want to scare the guy.'

'Ok,' said Qureshi. 'I think he will be fine. He is not easily frightened.'

As the two men passed through the open gate and into the scrapyard, the first thing that struck Andrew was just how many concealed positions there were inside it. Hard shadows created by the single floodlight near the centre of the yard were obvious hiding spots. There was a strong smell of engine oil leaking from rusting cars as they walked in, and now that the sun had gone down and the earth could breathe again, the rich scent of soil from the surrounding fields also hung in the air. Heaps of rusty stripped-down cars and parts were everywhere. They were placed in something that vaguely looked like it had some sort of system behind it, but that would need to be explained by the workers in order for it to make sense.

Everywhere he looked, there were things behind which it would be easy for a hostile shooter to hide, and given what had happened inside Karkhano Market just a few days earlier, Andrew began to feel a sixth sense telling him that this might turn ugly. What if more of Khan's ISI operators were here? What if they had set an ambush, and he and Qureshi had just walked into it like two mugs.

'I don't like this,' said Andrew in a hushed tone of voice, looking around the deserted scrapyard. 'Where is your man?'

It only took a few seconds before his question was answered and his suspicions were proven correct, although not in the way he had expected.

'Are you looking for this guy?' said a gruff voice in a heavy Russian accent.

From behind an old bus sitting on the ground with no wheels and all of the windows smashed, emerged a dishevelled-looking man with his arms tied behind his back and gagged with a cloth in his mouth. It was immediately clear that this was Noor, the market trader. Directly behind him and holding the trader tightly by the collar of his shirt, followed a short but well-built and stocky man wearing a green camouflaged outfit and holding what to Andrew looked like a Vityaz-SN, which is the standard all-black 9mm submachine gun issued to most branches of the Russian military. The man had dark short-cropped hair and a hard look on his face, and Andrew immediately recognised both his voice and his features. It was Mikhail Tokarev, and the muzzle of his submachine gun was resting on the back of the terrified Noor's neck. Andrew's right hand instinctively moved slowly up towards the pistol under his left arm. The distance to Tokarev was no more than fifteen metres. He could make that shot nine out of ten times.

'Everyone, just take it easy,' continued Tokarev in a tone of voice that betrayed total confidence with a large dose of arrogance.

As the Russian stepped out in the open with his hostage, four more men wearing full military gear and carrying various weapons emerged from nearby. This left Andrew and Qureshi standing inside a semi-circle of five men, all with serious firearms pointing at them. Andrew instantly knew that these were hardened Wagner mercenaries. How the hell had they tracked him here? No sooner had he thought of the question, than the answer popped into his head. It was Khan again. The ISI major had fed Tokarev Andrew's likely location, and they must have somehow worked out who one of Qureshi's informants were. From there, it was as simple as asking Qureshi to meet, knowing that Andrew would be sure to come with him.

Tokarev stopped and yanked at Noor's collar, making him stop. The market trader's legs were shaking, his eyes were wide with abject terror, and he was producing a weak whimpering noise as he breathed.

'Any sudden moves will mean that Noor here loses his head,' said Tokarev languidly, almost as if he was enjoying contemplating that particular outcome. 'And it will be very messy. Very bad.'

Andrew could hear the faint metallic clicks from the safeties on the four soldiers' weapons as they were being flicked to the Off position. At any moment, both he and Qureshi could be turned into mincemeat by the combined firepower of the Russian squad.

'Who are you?' asked Qureshi, sounding suspicious and remarkably calm. 'What do you want?'

'We are old friends of Andrew here,' smiled Tokarev, sounding almost reasonable. 'We would like to have a little talk with him. So, if you would be so kind as to stand aside and let him surrender to us, then both you and our friend Noor here can simply walk away.'

Fuck! thought Andrew, silently cursing himself for walking into this trap. His intuition had been trying to tell him that the message from Noor to Qureshi had been a bit too convenient, but he had simply not had the ability to imagine that Tokarev would turn up here in Peshawar with a handful of his men. And somehow, the Russian had managed to ID him, probably using connections within Russian intelligence back in Moscow.

As he stood there, attempting to control his breathing and feeling his heart pounding in his chest, his mind was racing as he assessed his options. A firefight was out of the question. He and Qureshi would both be cut down before they could even draw their weapons. Even if he managed to engage the mercenaries, he might be able to take down one or two of them, but then it would be lights out, and both Noor and Qureshi would end up dead as well.

He noticed that Qureshi had an angry look on his face, and he could tell from his body language that he was just about to say something that would probably not endear him to Tokarev, so he stepped forward.

'All right!' he shouted and raised his hands slowly above his head. 'It's me you want. Let these two men go.'

'No,' hissed Qureshi, turning his head to look at Andrew. 'I will not let you do this.'

'Don't argue with me,' said Andrew flatly. 'This has nothing to do with you.'

'Down on your knees,' said Tokarev, still with a firm grip on Noor, but now holding the Vityaz-SN with one hand and pointing it at Andrew. 'And tell your friend to step back and throw his weapon on the ground.'

'Do as he says,' said Andrew, looking intently at Qureshi as he took another step forward to draw level with the young police officer. He then slowly went down, first on one knee and then onto both with his hands raised.

Qureshi looked at him as if he had lost his mind, but he then reluctantly took two steps back and to the side, leaving the space between Andrew and Tokarev open. He also pulled his service pistol slowly from its holster and tossed it on the ground in front of him.

Keeping his eyes locked on Andrew, Tokarev turned his head slightly to one side and quickly issued an order in Russian. Immediately, and with the speed and efficiency of movement that hinted at bags of field experience, one of Tokarev's men advanced towards Andrew whilst still aiming his weapon at him. It was a Saiga-12 semi-automatic assault shotgun, with its characteristically long and a slightly curved box magazine containing around ten shotgun shells.

As soon as he was within a few feet of Andrew, the mercenary, who was particularly muscle-bound and sported a short beard and a bandolier of ammunition across his chest, quickly swung the shotgun around on its strap so that it hung vertical on his back, leaving his hands free. He grabbed hold of Andrew's left hand and began moving behind him whilst twisting it around in order to then secure the other hand and place them both in handcuffs behind his back. Fast and efficient. He had clearly done this sort of thing before.

At that moment, the terrified Noor must have realised that now that Tokarev had got what he came for, he himself was of no further use and would probably end up being killed. Whatever the reason, he suddenly lurched forward, wrestling himself free from Tokarev's grip and began to run for cover as fast as he could. Momentarily surprised by the sudden escape of the seemingly pacified market trader, Tokarev swung his assault rifle around, and instead of covering his colleague and Andrew, he raised the weapon and aimed at Noor. A quick burst of rapid gunfire rang out across the scrapyard, and five or six bullets smacked into Noor's back, causing spatters of blood to explode from his chest and sending him flying forward and crashing onto his front.

This was Andrew's only chance of turning the tables, and even before Noor had hit the ground, he was moving. The bearded mercenary that had been about to tie him up, as well as the three other soldiers, had now instinctively turned their heads towards the market trader as the shots rang out, and Andrew realised that he only had a couple of seconds to take the initiative.

Still kneeling, he quickly grabbed a firm hold of one of the mercenary's wrists and rose whilst twisting it around so that he ended up next to him and within reach of the shotgun. He grabbed hold of the weapon, which was still strapped to the man's back with the muzzle pointing downward, and then he yanked it partially off his back. In an instant, he had spun it around to jam the muzzle up into the mercenary's chest. With his right hand firmly on the grip, he placed his index finger on the trigger and squeezed.

The Saiga-12 produced a thunderous blast, and the impact of the shotgun shell's pellets, combined with the exhaust gases created by the explosion of the gunpowder inside the barrel, almost lifted the bearded mercenary off his feet as the small steel projectiles ripped up through his torso and exited through his spine, sending blood and bone shooting up into the air in a sickening red fountain above him.

Seeing their colleague be dispatched in such a gory fashion clearly shocked Tokarev and the remaining three mercenaries, because they froze for a few seconds as the man crumpled to the ground. This gave Andrew and Qureshi just enough time to scramble for cover behind a rusty car wreck. Qureshi leapt forward, grabbed his pistol off the ground and ran after Andrew, pointing his pistol in the general direction of their assailants and emptying the magazine. As the two men threw themselves behind the wreck, the Wagner mercenaries opened up with everything they had in a cacophony of shouting and gunfire from assault rifles and submachine guns.

As the bullets peppered the rusty car, Qureshi was fumbling to reload his pistol, and Andrew was taking a quick glance at the Saiga-12's magazine to try to gauge how many shots he had left.

'Are you hit?' he shouted, amid the deafening noise from the barrage of incoming fire.

'I don't think so,' replied Qureshi, for the first time sounding genuinely frightened since Andrew had met him.

'We need to get out of here ASAP,' shouted Andrew. 'I will lay down suppressing fire, and you run for the gate. I will follow you. Don't argue!'

Qureshi nodded, reloaded his pistol and gripped it with both hands. Tokarev was in cover behind a pile of scrap metal, but at least two of the remaining three mercenaries were moving, seemingly trying to flank Andrew and Qureshi.

'Ok,' he said. 'I am ready.'

'Go!' shouted Andrew as he got to his knees, raising the shotgun just high enough to aim over the bonnet of the wreck.

He immediately began releasing multiple rounds in quick succession, the semi-automatic shotgun feeding him shells as fast as he could aim and fire them, whilst Qureshi was sprinting for the gate some twenty metres away. Several bullets struck the ground and the rusting cars near him, but it was not obvious whether they had been aimed at him or at Andrew.

Andrew kept firing until a bullet smacked into the bonnet of the car and ricocheted so close to his head that he felt the wisp of compressed air as it flew past him. He ducked down into cover and turned around just in time to see Qureshi disappearing out of the gate in the direction of his car. If he had any sense, he would get in, start the engine and drive off as fast as he could, but somehow Andrew didn't think that was going to happen.

At that moment there was a short pause in the firing, possibly because the mercenaries needed to reload, but it was just long enough and quiet enough for Andrew to hear the sound of boots running on soft ground off to his left near the scrapyard's perimeter fence. Whoever was moving there was close. Andrew was being flanked.

Guessing he had as little as two or three shots left, he swung the shotgun around just in time to see a figure emerge from the shadows less than five metres away. He was a muscular and burly character with a red-tinted face that betrayed a lifestyle involving too much vodka, and he was wearing a plate carrier as body armour and full tactical gear. In his hands, he was carrying an SR-2 Veresk 9mm submachine gun, which is ideal for close quarters combat in confined spaces due to its small size and fast rate of fire.

The engagement could have gone either way. Had Andrew not reacted soon enough, the SR-2 would have taken just three seconds to spit out close to 50 rounds, which would have meant lights out for Andrew and a one-way ticket to a ditch nearby – if he was lucky. However, because he heard footsteps during the brief lull in the fighting, he was already aiming the shotgun in the mercenary's direction when the man emerged into the light from behind a tall heap of scrap metal. Within a fraction of a second, Andrew had brought the shotgun back up, pushed the stock firmly into his shoulder and aligned the barrel perfectly. When he pulled the trigger, the shotgun produced another loud boom, and in that instant the mercenary's head exploded in a gruesome cloud of blood, brains and fragments of skull. His momentum carried his headless body forward, and he fell and smacked heavily onto the ground like a carcass in a slaughterhouse.

Realising what had happened to their comrade, Tokarev and the two remaining mercenaries reengaged and began firing furiously at the location behind which Andrew was taking cover. Bullets slammed into the rusty bodywork of the car wreck with even more intensity than before, and Andrew realised that it was a question of time before a shot would either penetrate the rusty metal or ricochet into him after hitting the chassis or the engine block. He had to do something drastic.

Pulling a fragmentation grenade from his backpack, he pulled the pin and waited two seconds. Then he spun around and lobbed the grenade in a high arc over the rapidly disintegrating bonnet of the car. With only a four-second fuse, the grenade was still in the air when it detonated roughly five metres from Tokarev and his men, and around ten metres from Andrew's position.

The dry crack of the explosion roughly two metres above the ground was ear-splitting, and it sent metal fragments tearing through the air in all directions at supersonic speeds of almost 500 metres per second. A tiny fraction of a second later, hundreds of small sharp metal fragments peppered the immediate area with such force that many of them buried themselves deep into the ground and even into the bodywork of the rusting cars. Andrew heard a man cry out, but he was in no mood to hang around. He had created a short window for himself to withdraw, and now he had to move fast.

He got to his feet and bolted for the gate. The explosion had created a cloud of dust that was partially obscuring his retreat from the perspective of Tokarev and his two remaining men, and as Andrew ran, he was praying that he would have enough time to get out of the scrapyard before the mercenaries recovered and began reengaging.

As soon as he turned the corner at the gate, he saw that Qureshi's Honda Civic was about fifteen metres away. The headlights were off, but the engine was running, and inside it, Qureshi was gripping the steering wheel with a wild look on his face. He revved the engine and pulled forward whilst turning the wheel to present Andrew with the side of the vehicle. Then he leaned over and pushed the front passenger door open.

Andrew practically launched himself through the air and into the car, and as soon as he was inside, Qureshi floored the accelerator, making the wheels spin on the loose gravel and producing a big cloud of dust as the car fish-tailed slightly and accelerated hard away from the scrapyard towards the west along the dirt track that led further out of the city.

'Bloody hell!' shouted Andrew as he righted himself in his seat and turned around to see a huge cloud of fine dust whirling up behind the Honda. 'That was close. Thanks for waiting.'

'I could not leave you there,' said Qureshi through gritted teeth as he battled to keep the Honda on track. 'I was sure you would manage to get yourself out somehow.'

Andrew was about to thank Qureshi for having such faith in him, when the cloud of dust behind them suddenly lit up. Out of the scrapyard's gate had roared what appeared to be a Toyota Land Cruiser with four large floodlights mounted on top of the cabin. But that was not what caught Andrew's eye as he looked back at it through the dust clouds. Standing on the open cargo bed just behind the cabin was one of the mercenaries, and he was gripping onto a large machine gun with an almost two-metre-long barrel that was pointing forward over the cabin. It took Andrew only a fraction of a second to realise what he was looking at.

'Oh shit!' he yelled. 'We've got a problem.'

'What?' shouted Qureshi.

'They're on our tail,' replied Andrew, 'and they have a bloody 50 calibre machine gun mounted on their truck. A single one of those rounds will punch right through the engine block, or take your head clean off. Start swerving. Don't let them hit us.'

At that moment, the pursuing pickup truck had stabilised enough for the gunner to be able to aim and begin firing. The rate of fire of the American Browning M2 .50 calibre machine gun is relatively low at around 500 rounds per minute, but anyone finding themselves on the business end of this beast knows about it instantly. How on earth the Russian mercenaries had got their hands on one was a mystery that Andrew would have to ignore for now, although it probably involved both the Taliban and ISI Major Khan.

The loud and meaty staccato noise of the heavy machine gun began as it started pumping the tungsten laced projectiles out in the direction of the Honda up ahead. As the mercenary kept firing bursts of four or five rounds at a time, dozens of spent brass casings clattered onto the truck's cargo bed where he stood.

Qureshi immediately began veering off to one side of the road and then back again. The Honda's headlight lit up the road ahead, and as they raced further west, they emerged out into an area with very few buildings.

Suddenly a couple of rounds connected with the Honda. One smacked into the back and continued through the back seat and passed right between Andrew and Qureshi to slam into the dashboard, tearing through it and out the other side, just missing the engine and puncturing the bonnet at a shallow angle and continuing forward into the night. The second round burst through the rear window and then the windshield, shattering them both into thousands of pieces and ripping them free from their frames. Miraculously, none of the rounds hit Andrew or Qureshi, but they could both feel the rapid change in air pressure as the round passed between their head.

Somehow, amid the chaos of flying glass, Qureshi managed to hold on to the wheel and keep his foot on the accelerator, but it was clear that they were on borrowed time. Sooner or later, a round would either take out the car or end one of their lives in gory fashion. Up ahead on the right side of the road was an old one-storey mudbrick house.

'Take a right!' shouted Andrew 'We've got to put something between us and that gun.'

As they drew level with the house, Qureshi yanked the wheel hard to the right and the car drifted around the corner and behind the house. In that same moment, the gunner released another longer burst of fire that just missed the back of the Honda and instead tore into the mudbrick, sending fragments of brick and clouds of dust exploding out from its walls.

For the next ten or fifteen seconds, while the gunner did not have line of sight on them, Qureshi drove the car in a straight line and accelerated as fast as the car would allow. Being in a smaller and lighter vehicle than the Toyota Land Cruiser, this allowed them to open up more distance between them and their pursuers. They were now approaching the enormous abandoned site of the Nasir Bagh refugee camp, which had laid dormant for several decades. Most of the plots where tent cities had sprung up in the 1980s were now completely empty, but near the entrance to the site were a number of dilapidated buildings that had served as administrative centres for the United Nations during the operation of the camp. The buildings had been abandoned when the camp closed, and many of their roofs had collapsed inside the structures, but a few of them still had semi-intact walls and roofs.

'Over there!' shouted Andrew, pointing to the buildings.

Qureshi raced towards them, hoping to be able to get behind cover again, but that is when their luck finally ran out. As they were approaching the small collection of buildings, a fresh burst of 50 calibre fire began peppering the ground around them, producing small explosions of rock and dirt where they hit. One of the projectiles tore through the Honda's right rear wheel hub at 800 metres per second, causing a minor explosion from the near-instant conversion of its kinetic energy into heat. Immediately, Qureshi lost control of the vehicle, and was suddenly struggling to keep the car on the road as it swerved wildly from side to side with sparks flying out of the back where the rear axle was now grinding against the road. They were rapidly losing speed since the wrecked wheel hub now functioned as a brake, so Qureshi instinctively used what little control he still had over the car to swerve towards the abandoned buildings.

'Let's get out!' yelled Andrew. 'Take cover inside.'

Behind them the Land Cruiser was rapidly closing the distance, and as Andrew opened his door a 50 calibre bullet slammed into it and almost ripped it off its hinges. Andrew and Qureshi wasted no time and both sprinted for cover inside what appeared to be the main administration building. The interior was completely cleared out and there were no doors or windows in the entire structure. But there were walls, and that is all that mattered. They scrambled inside through the nearest doorway as the bullets from the 50 calibre machine gun pounded the brick walls, chewing them up and making them crumble. Andrew and Qureshi ran further inside and down what had previously been a wide office corridor towards the back of the building.

Soon, the firing stopped. It was clear that the gunner realised that his bullets would be unable to punch their way through multiple brick walls, and that Andrew and Qureshi had managed to get away from the threat of the heavy machine gun. At least for now.

Crouching next to a wall inside an office at the back of the building, Andrew and Qureshi heard Tokarev shouting orders in Russian, and then the distinct sound of two sets of heavy boots hitting the gravel where the Toyota had stopped just outside the building. Tokarev and his men were coming in with their personal weapons to finish the job, and they now had the upper hand. They carried superior weapons and they could employ their well-rehearsed tactics, working as a unit to hunt down their quarry. Andrew had two shots left in his shotgun and a full magazine in his Glock 19.

'How much ammo do you have?' he whispered to Qureshi.

'Twelve bullets,' replied Qureshi, his voice shaky. 'I think we are in trouble.'

'Not if we are clever about this,' said Andrew. 'I reckon the 50 Cal gunner is still up there providing cover while Tokarev and the third guy sweep this building. If you can hold off those two for a couple of minutes, I can circle around, take out the gunner and open up on Tokarev and the other guy from behind.'

'Sterling!' shouted Tokarev from the other end of the dilapidated building, anger and venom dripping off every word. 'You just killed two friends of mine. Now, I am going to kill you and your little lapdog.'

Andrew checked the shotgun and gave it to Qureshi. Then he handed him a flashbang.

'You have two shots in there,' he said. 'Make them count. Don't fire unless you know you're going to hit something. And this flashbang has a four-second fuse. Just pull this pin and throw it, and make sure you close your eyes and cover your ears. Are you with me?'

Qureshi nodded, but Andrew could see that he was frightened. However, there was no other way to get out of this situation. Andrew was out of grenades, and their pistols were no match for the assault rifles or the body armour carried by the Russian mercenaries. His MP5 was on the backseat of the Honda, and there had been no time to get it as they were escaping the car and scrambling to get into cover inside the building.

'All right,' said Andrew. 'Place yourself here on this corner where you can peek out and see along the corridor. As soon as you see them, toss the flashbang, and then use the shotgun and your pistol to hold them off. That should give me plenty of time.'

Andrew looked at Qureshi's face, and he could see that the young man was gathering up all his courage and composure as he stared directly ahead of himself and nodded.

'OK,' he finally said. 'I trust you. Let's do this.'

Andrew gave Qureshi a quick double-pat on the shoulder, and then he moved swiftly but quietly in a crouched position out of the back of the room towards the rear exit. Once outside, he immediately began moving around the back of the building and up along its side towards the front which was lit up by the four large floodlights mounted on the Toyota.

Moving as quietly as he could, he was gripping his Glock 19 in two hands in front of himself, ready to fire. As he neared the corner of the building, he slowed down and then stopped less than a metre from the corner. He could hear the sound of the Toyota's engine idling, and then there was a shout in Russian from the gunner. It sounded like a question. After a couple of seconds came a reply from the voice that he knew to be Tokarev's. It seemed as if every sentence spoken between the mercenaries included the expletive 'blyat', which literally means 'bitch', but is used ubiquitously and often to mean 'fuck' or 'shit'. Andrew had heard it used by Russians countless times before, and he had the feeling that Russian men thought it sounded manly to throw that word into virtually every single sentence.

After another quick exchange between the two men, there was a sudden loud bang and a brilliant white flash of light coming from inside the building. Qureshi had used his flashbang, and it instantly resulted in tense shouting followed by several shots being fired from assault rifles, which meant that Tokarev and his teammate had located Qureshi.

Andrew exploited the noise from the gunfight to peek out from behind the corner of the building. The Land Cruiser was parked about fifteen metres from the front of the building, its four powerful headlights bathing the crumbling structure in harsh white light. Through the glare, he could see the gunner standing on the cargo bed of the vehicle, one hand on the dual grip of the machine gun, and the other held up near his face as if he had been instinctively shielding his eyes from the intense flash of light inside the building. This was all the opportunity Andrew needed. He immediately brought up his pistol and fired two suppressed shots, one of which found its mark in the temple of the gunner. It punched through his skull and exited out the other side, at which point his legs gave way and he crumpled down onto the car's cargo bed among the spent shell casings.

Andrew sprinted to the Toyota and jumped up onto the cargo bed. Stepping over the dead gunner, he grabbed the dual handle of the 50 calibre machine gun and swung it towards the open doorway to the building's interior. Almost immediately there was more shouting and gunfire coming from inside. Both of the assault rifles were firing, but then there was the boom of the Saiga-12 shotgun followed by a chilling scream which did not sound like it was coming from either Qureshi or Tokarev. Another burst of assault rifle fire ensued, and then another shotgun blast rang out. Finally, there was one more long burst of assault rifle fire, mixed with a handful of pistol shots, and then everything went quiet. Andrew was about to jump back down and enter the building when he saw a shadow moving inside it. It looked like it was being cast by someone moving towards the front entrance of the building.

A couple of seconds later, Qureshi emerged holding the shotgun in one hand and his pistol in the other. He appeared to have a gunshot wound to his left shoulder with blood soaking his shirt, and he also seemed to be limping slightly as he made his way out of the building towards Andrew. However, his face carried an expression that was a mixture of surprise and elation, as if he couldn't quite believe that he had fought two trained killers and come out on top. His eyes were gleaming with pride.

'Andrew!' he shouted. 'I got them! I got them both.'

Qureshi was now halfway to the Toyota, but at that moment another figure emerged behind him from inside the building. It was Tokarev, and he was staggering and covered in blood and dirt as if he had been hit several times and had been knocked down, leaving Qureshi to believe that he had been killed. But Tokarev had been wearing Kevlar body armour and a plate carrier, and that combination had stopped most of Qureshi's bullets and probably knocked him to the floor where he would have played dead for several seconds.

'Get down!' Andrew yelled to Qureshi immediately upon seeing Tokarev emerge.

There was no way for Andrew to open fire since Qureshi was between him and Tokarev. Qureshi's facial expression changed in an instant, the exhilaration draining from it to be replaced with the horrifying realisation of what was happening. At that moment, looking severely impaired by the injuries he had sustained, Tokarev stumbled forward another step and brought up his Vityaz-SN whilst grimacing from the pain of his wounds. He aimed and then he fired.

'No!' shouted Andrew, as instant panic exploded through his body.

The Russian assault rifle produced a burst of fire, releasing five rounds which all slammed into Qureshi's back and punched out through his chest, spraying blood everywhere in front of the young police officer's mortally wounded body. With a stunned and strangely regretful expression on his face, Qureshi staggered forward, pushed by the force of the bullets, and then he stumbled and fell onto the ground where his body hit the dirt hard, sending a cloud of dry dust whirling up into the beams of the Toyota's floodlights.

Andrew's mind folded in on itself in unbridled rage, his vision constricting to a tunnel with only Tokarev at the end. Almost before Qureshi had hit the ground, he instinctively gripped the dual handle of the 50-calibre machine gun, depressed the two triggers and held them down. The heavy weapon instantly produced a sustained barrage of heavy metal projectiles that tore through the air and ripped into Tokarev's body, shredding it as he stood there, and tearing him limb from limb in a gory spray of blood, guts and bone fragments. What was left of his body was flung back into the building where it slid several metres across the dusty floor, smacked into a wall and came to a stop, like discarded meat in an abattoir.

Andrew vaulted over the side of the pickup truck and sprinted to Qureshi who was lying in a pool of his own blood.

'Tahoor!' he shouted, dropping onto the ground next to him, turning his fatally wounded comrade over and hauling him onto his lap while he supported his head with one hand. 'Tahoor. Stay with me, mate.'

Qureshi's green eyes seemed fixed on a point far above, but then for a few seconds he managed to focus on Andrew's face, and then he produced a faint smile.

'I am sorry,' he whispered as blood trickled out of his mouth. 'I let you down.'

'No, mate,' said Andrew, looking intently into the eyes of his friend. 'Don't be sorry. You did great.'

His words instantly felt completely empty and meaningless even as he spoke them, but he didn't know what else to say to this brave young man whose final moments of life were now unfolding.

'I should never have left you there,' said Andrew bitterly. 'It was my fault. I am sorry.'

'It's OK,' whispered Qureshi weakly. 'It was my choice to come.'

He swallowed hard, and Andrew could see that it caused him pain. Then he took another shallow breath before he spoke again, this time barely audible.

'Promise me you will take care of Jinani,' he said. 'And tell her to name our child *Amal*.'

'I promise,' said Andrew, wiping dirt and blood from Qureshi's forehead. 'I promise.'

And with that, Tahoor Qureshi let out his final breath, his green eyes glazing over and staring straight up at the stars in the night sky above.

Andrew closed his eyes and exhaled deeply, his head dropping and his chin resting on his chest. He felt wracked with guilt. It should never have come to this. He should never have allowed Qureshi to become so involved in his mission. The death of this young man was a loss to his country and its people, and it was a tragedy for his pregnant wife and their unborn child.

Amal, he thought, contemplating the fact that yet another Pakistani child would grow up without a father. He had heard the name before and knew that it was used both for boys and girls. It simply meant 'hope'.

TWENTY-THREE

It was just after closing time when the Metropolitan Police officer entered through the west entrance and made his way past the Font and under the Nave, carrying a large holdall in his right hand. He was wearing his usual uniform, and so the armed police by the entrance had barely looked at him as he walked in. As the last remaining visitors filed out of the enormous building, he walked purposefully under the huge dome to the High Altar.

It was the evening before Remembrance Day, and the venue had already been prepared for the ceremony the next day, with dozens of rows of chairs placed all along the Nave and stopping about twenty metres from the High Altar. In a few hours, those seats would be filled with 'the great and the good' of the nation. He checked the time on his wristwatch. He had about five minutes to complete the task and get out. Plenty of time. Looking around to make sure he was not being watched, he knelt behind the altar and unzipped the holdall. As he did so, his eyes caught the inscription on the altar.

> TO THE GLORY OF GOD AND IN MEMORY OF THE OVERSEAS MEMBERS OF THE COMMONWEALTH AND EMPIRE WHO GAVE THEIR LIVES IN WAR 1914-1918 R.I.P 1939-1945.

A scathing smile flashed across the man's face as he contemplated what his relatives in Karachi would have made of that inscription. Then he returned his attention to the holdall and reached inside to extract a long and heavy cylindrical object roughly a metre in length and slightly less than thirty centimetres in diameter. To the casual observer, it looked just like the large candles already sitting in the three huge golden candle holders on top of the High Altar. But this was no candle. This was the smaller of the two explosive devices that had been prepared the day before in the warehouse in East London.

Carefully holding the replica candle containing the device, the officer rose and performed another quick scan of his surroundings to reassure himself that he was not being watched. Then he adeptly grabbed the wax candle already in the candle holder with one hand, lifted it off the holder and placed it on the altar. Then he carefully placed the much heavier replica device in the candle holder and put the wax candle into the holdall. The replica was indistinguishable from the original.

He bent down and zipped up the holdall, and then he stood up and carried it back along the nave and under the dome towards the exit. As soon as he had left the building, he would send a message to Nadeem Yassin to tell him that the device was ready. By this time, he should already have received word that the main device had been placed and was ready for tomorrow. Yassin would then report back to the Emir.

As he exited, the police officer glanced furtively across the open space to the shopfronts on the other side of the road facing the enormous church. He felt his heart beat faster as the thrill of what was about to unfold coursed through his veins. A monumental event was about to take place here, and he felt a surge of righteousness and pride at the thought of it, and at the realisation that he had played a small but important part in making it happen. All he had to do now was to go home, and then wait until the morning to call in sick.

* * *

It was just before 11 p.m. by the time Andrew left the site of the former Nasir Bagh refugee camp. Before leaving, and in order to prevent wild animals desecrating it, he had placed Qureshi's body in a shallow grave that he had dug with a small steel shovel sitting in a rack behind the Toyota Land Cruiser's cabin. It had droplets of blood from the dead Russian gunner smeared across its handle, and Andrew had wiped it off against the mercenary's clothes before dumping his corpse inside the building near what little remained of Mikhail Tokarev. His intention was to somehow get a message to Qureshi's wife, but that would have to wait. She would still be on the train to Lahore, and even though it made him feel cowardly, he knew that it would be in no one's interest to contact her right now. If anything, it might put her at even more risk than she already was. He also wanted to make sure that the Gulbahar Police Station that Qureshi had been attached to was informed, but once again, this was not something he would be able to do immediately.

Sitting on a large rock about ten metres from the building and the Land Cruiser, Andrew looked up at the stars and inhaled the cool evening air after the exertion of burying Qureshi. Usually calm and unflappable, he had to admit to himself that he felt emotional turmoil inside himself. The loss of Qureshi had been bad enough in itself, but it had also once again dredged up the memories of Frank Malone, and the painfully open question as to where he was and what had happened to him. He instinctively knew that the key to solving that mystery was to find Al Naji, but the trail had once again gone cold. Tokarev might have known where to find him, but the only purpose the Russian mercenary would ever serve from now on was as food for the local fauna, large and small.

Andrew considered simply leaving and somehow making his way back to Islamabad from where he could return safely to the UK, but everything about that prospect felt wrong. Al Naji was still out there somewhere, and perhaps so was Frank. An eerie feeling began to spread throughout his body as his mind gradually closed in on a new thought. One that he did not want to entertain, but also one that he could no longer ignore. What if Al Naji and Frank Malone were one and the same?

At that moment, Andrew's mind suddenly lurched back in time to a conversation he had with Saunders soon after he had arrived at the British High Commission in Islamabad.

"That's how he got his nom de guerre, 'Al Naji'. It literally means 'The Survivor'."

Andrew's blood ran cold, and his head was spinning. It was almost unthinkable, but he had to force himself to consider the agonising possibility that somehow Malone had morphed into an Afghan warlord, giving himself a name befitting of his journey. Andrew shook his head. None of it made any sense. However, that did not mean that it couldn't be true.

But then another possibility began to form in his mind. Having worked so closely together as an SAS team, both he and Malone had been required to know most of each other's medical details, including their respective blood types. This was how Andrew knew that Malone's was the very rare AB Negative. Only about half a percent of all humans have that particular blood type. What if Al Naji was also AB Negative and had kept Malone prisoner for all these years to make sure he had a ready supply of blood available in case he was seriously wounded in battle? Or perhaps Al Naji suffered from one of the many congenital blood disorders that require regular blood transfusions. What if Al Naji had kept Malone chained to a wall in some dungeon in Afghanistan, simply for him to serve as a living blood bag? Andrew felt sick at the thought. However, at this point, nothing could be ruled out, and it just might explain why the blood analysis had come back with a match for Malone. Andrew sighed heavily. He didn't know what to believe anymore.

A few minutes later, he was about to get up and walk back to the Toyota, when his phone dinged with a lengthy message from Colonel Strickland. Andrew read it with increasing incredulity. Somehow, using Abdul Wasiq's unique phone ID, MI6 had been able to hack into the Pakistani mobile phone network and retrieve his location data and thereby trace his movements during the past several months. After discovering that Al Naji's deputy had travelled with his phone multiple times across the border at Torkham, they then repeated the exercise with the Afghan mobile network providers. What they had discovered was that when in transit, the phone was almost always powered down, leaving no location data at all. However, on occasion, it would be switched on inside Afghanistan, and a large number of those instances were at the exact same location. Satellite data had revealed it to be a compound located in a valley south-east of the town of Nahrain in the Baghlan Province of Afghanistan. Strickland had included the exact coordinates. It was assessed to be highly likely to be Al Naji's compound.

Mounting a raid using special forces assets currently located in the UK would never be signed off by the government, especially considering how tenuous the current evidence against Al Naji was, but Strickland had given Andrew a free hand to decide what to do. If he wanted to enter Afghanistan and attempt to track down the warlord, then he had Strickland's blessing. The colonel also relayed that Fiona's work on Crescent Logistics had proved invaluable, and that as a result, McGregor and his team were being deployed to an undisclosed location in London.

Andrew re-read the message and then turned off the phone and put it back in his pocket. It only took him a few minutes to make up his mind about what to do next. Locating the compound was by far his best chance of finding Al Naji and possibly obtaining information that could help avert the attack in London. On top of that, it would almost certainly give him the answer he was looking for regarding Frank Malone. However, it was also likely to be highly risky. The warlord's compound would undoubtedly have heavy security, so Andrew would need more fire power, and he knew just where to get it from.

He drove the Toyota Land Cruiser back to the edge of the Karkhano Market and parked it in a small alley between two ramshackle sheds built from wood beams and corrugated metal sheets. He got out and made his way through the warren of narrow streets to where he had spotted several gun shops on his previous visit. After locating one of them and managing to break into it unseen from the rear, he realised that, true to the market's reputation, the term 'gun shop' should be used loosely. The shop had every kind of firearm, explosive and any other weapon anyone could want or need. Almost all of it was Soviet equipment, some of it new and some of it looking like it belonged in a museum. However, it also had several types of NATO standard kit such as pistols and ammunition.

Andrew grabbed several boxes of 9mm Parabellum for his MP5SD, spare magazines for the Glock 19 and three fragmentation grenades. He also pulled what appeared to be a brand-new AK-47 off a rack on a wall, and shoved a couple of magazines of its Russian standard 7.62x39mm ammunition into his backpack. He hoped that he would not need to 'go loud', but as a backup, the AK-47 was not a bad option to have.

Sitting on a table in the corner of the shop was a stack of U.S. made M18 Claymore anti-personnel mines. These slightly curved and upright devices roughly the size and shape of a large book, each contained a powerful directional explosive charge and roughly 700 steel balls. With an effective range of up to 100 metres, they were ideal for ambushing groups of enemy soldiers, but could also inflict significant damage to vehicles and structures up close. He grabbed two of them, as well as two packs of demolition wire and an M57 clacker for remote detonation, and placed them all inside the backpack.

Finally, just as he was leaving, he spotted an RPG launcher on the wall. He yanked it from its hooks and bagged two rocket-propelled grenades for it. They were heavy and bulky, but he decided that since he didn't know exactly what he was up against, it was better to have them than not.

By midnight he was loading the weapons into the Toyota, and then he was ready. The last thing he did before setting off along the N-5 National Highway towards the west and the Torkham crossing, was to send a message to Fiona. Strickland should have been in touch with her already, but he wanted to make sure that she got his message to stay away from the Remembrance Day memorial ceremony which was now only hours away.

* * *

Al Naji was pacing slowly back and forth on the dark wide-beamed wooden floor of his private residence inside the compound in the hills south-east of Nahrain. It was sparsely decorated but positively palatial by Afghan standards. He had learned that getting items shipped in, whether it was via countries like Pakistan, the UAE or China, was relatively straight forward, as long as enough wheels were greased sufficiently along the way. In essence, despite being in Afghanistan, there was nothing he couldn't have, and he could have decorated his home any way he liked. But he preferred it simple and frugal-looking. It fitted better with the image of warlord and man-of-the-people that he had carefully cultivated for over a decade now, but it also helped him think. And despite his imposing physical presence, it was brains rather than brawn that had carried him to his current position.

He had just received word from Peshawar that Abdul Wasiq had been found dead, along with two of his most experienced fighters and the Hayatabad police chief. They had all been killed by some sort of special operations hit that seemed to have been carried out by a lone attacker, and Al Naji had no doubt who was responsible. It was Andrew Sterling, and by this time, Mikhail Tokarev should be in

Peshawar hunting him down and putting an end to him poking around once and for all. What Sterling probably did not realise was that the chemical agent had already arrived in London, and that there was nothing he would be able to do about it now.

Still, Al Naji felt a simmering unease at having discovered that the SAS soldier was now obviously on the trail of both himself and the weapons, which is why he had brought additional security forces to the compound. He also felt frustration at knowing that instead of being the hunter, he was now the hunted. This was a situation he had not allowed himself to be in for many years.

He walked with a slight limp into the modern-looking tiled bathroom, which was something that was virtually unheard of in this part of the country. Placing his large scarred hands on the washbasin, he lifted his gaze to look at himself in the mirror with his one good eye. As he watched his own reflection – the weathered skin, the beard, the large scar across his face and the black eye patch – images from his past flashed before his eyes.

He stared at himself for several long moments, trying to remember what he used to look like, but the image escaped him. He then reached up and closed his powerful hand around the £5 Millennium Crown talisman that had been on this entire journey with him. He shut his eyes and cast his mind back across the years to the moment he had sat tied to a chair inside a small shed in an opium compound in northern Afghanistan. It was like running a movie backwards across all the significant and unlikely events that had led him to this point.

Suddenly, he was back in that chair again. His face had been covered in dirt and grimy sweat as he sat there with his hands tied to the armrests. There was blood seeping from his right ear and from cuts he had sustained when the RPG had impacted and detonated just a couple of metres away. The right side of his face was partially scorched by the heat from the explosion.

It was pure instinct that had made him launch himself through the air and barge into Sterling to try to get them both out of the way of the blast, and they had both survived. But he had paid dearly. His lower left leg had suffered an open fracture, and he had broken his nose and sustained a deep gash across the bridge of his nose and the rest of his face from a piece of shrapnel. It had ultimately cost him his vision in his left eye, and transformed him into the one-eyed man he had been ever since. The blast had also knocked him unconscious, and when he finally came to, he was slumped forward, tied to the chair and looking down at his broken leg as his talisman dangled languidly in front of his face.

He drifted in and out of consciousness several times, until he came to again at the sound of the shed's door opening. He then heard what sounded like someone being dumped unceremoniously in a chair near him, and then the far-off baritone voice of the warlord who had been in charge of the opium production facility.

Despite the burst eardrum in his right ear and the faint ringing he still experienced after the blast, he thought he heard the muffled and strangely echoey sound of Sterling calling out to him.

'Frank!'

He felt like he was submerged in molasses, unable to see properly and barely able to hear anything. Everything felt distant and muted, and he was trying to break through it when suddenly a weapon was fired and he felt the sensation of being punched hard in the left side of the chest. Still tied to the chair, he felt himself lurch sideways and topple face first onto the dusty floor. The last thing he heard before passing out again was Sterling's muffled voice shouting the word 'No'. Then everything went black.

He had no idea how long it was before he came to again, but he was lying on the bed of a pickup truck being driven over rough ground through a ravine. As he slowly regained his senses, he had enough awareness to realise that he was lucky to still be alive, but also that he was so physically impaired that it probably wouldn't be long before he joined the ranks of the other KIAs of the British Army in Afghanistan. The left side of his chest and shoulder felt like a red-hot poker had been jammed into it, and his broken leg was a strange mixture of numbness and burning pain. He knew he had lost a lot of blood, and if he did not get some sort of medical attention soon, he would likely be dead within the hour.

As he lay there on the cargo bed of the pickup truck, he reached down into a small side pocket of his trousers and found what he was looking for – a small pouch with four auto-injectors. Two of them were morphine and the other two were epinephrine, also simply known as adrenaline. Using fingers that seemed hell-bent on disobeying his orders, he finally managed to extract a morphine injector, popped the cap off and slammed it into his upper left leg. The injector immediately delivered its contents into his thigh muscle, and soon a hot glowing sensation bloomed out from the leg and swept over his entire body like warm sun on a cold winter's day. After a few seconds, the debilitating pain he had felt before was reduced to mild discomfort. Then he popped the cap off one of the epinephrine injectors and jammed that into his right leg. The effect was less dramatic, but he soon felt his heart beat faster and stronger, and the fog of exhaustion begin to lift from his body and his mind. After another half a minute, he felt like he could have jumped off the pickup truck and jogged back to base, if it wasn't because his lower leg was broken and his foot was dangling disconcertingly whenever he moved it.

The pickup truck suddenly slowed down and then it came to a stop. He heard the driver's side door open, the sound of someone stepping out onto the rocky ground, and then footsteps moving slowly towards the back of the vehicle. He did the only thing he could think of and lay completely still, pretending to be dead, which is what he was sure the driver would think he already was.

The driver lowered the flap at the back of the cargo bed, reached in and grabbed hold of Malone's belt, and then began dragging what he thought was a dead body towards the edge of the cargo bed. It was obvious that he had been ordered to take the body somewhere isolated and dispose of it, and this ravine seemed to be his preferred choice. A dead body left out here would soon be consumed by scavengers, both the four-legged kind and the winged kind.

As the man began manhandling Malone off the cargo bed, the SAS soldier opened one eye just enough to see that he was carrying a pistol in a holster on his belt. Seeing his chance and using the element of surprise, Malone's right hand shot out and gripped the gun, yanked it from the holster, flicked the safety off and fired four shots into the man's body at close range. The man staggered off to one side clutching his stomach, and then he turned unsteadily and looked back at Malone with a shocked expression, dumfounded by what had just happened. The SAS soldier, still lying on his side on the edge of the cargo bed, then aimed the pistol at his head and pulled the trigger one more time. The bullet found its mark between the eyes of what Malone assumed was one of the warlord's fighters, and he collapsed heavily onto the ground. The shot reverberated through the ravine and off the rocky mountainsides that surrounded the area, but soon the echoes died down and all he could hear was the wind in the trees and the gentle sound of water in a small stream running down from the mountain above.

Malone rolled onto his back and breathed heavily. He did not have much time, and he needed to get as far away from there as quickly as possible. He slid off the cargo bed and hobbled around to the cabin where he got in behind the wheel. He managed to get the car into gear with his one good leg, and then he drove back out of the ravine and made his way to a T-junction where the dirt track led down into a valley on the left and up towards the mountains on the right. Deciding that the fighter who had been tasked with disposing of his supposedly dead body had almost certainly driven up from the valley, he turned right and began driving as fast as he felt was safe. The road snaked its way further up towards the mountains up ahead, and eventually began climbing up towards a ridge. After roughly another half an hour, he found himself on a relatively flat plain at high altitude. There was virtually no vegetation, and the road looked less and less well travelled and soon turned into a simple dirt track.

As time went by, he felt the effects of the injectors slowly waning. The pain in his chest and leg was now throbbing again, and the lucidness he had felt earlier was slowly but surely giving way to an oppressive tiredness that was rapidly closing in on him. He began to wonder whether all he had done was trade one humiliating death for another. Eventually, the dirt track snaked its way over another ridge and then down towards another valley. He had no idea where he was.

Suddenly the engine seemed to choke, and then it stopped. He looked at the fuel gauge. It was empty. He opened the door to try to walk back to the cargo bed to see if there was a spare petrol can there, but as he opened the door to exit the cabin, he stumbled and fell hard onto the ground. Then he passed out again.

The next time he woke up he was on a bed inside what appeared to be a small house. Next to him was a bearded man with a weathered face and kind eyes. Looking down at his body he realised that his wounds had been bandaged and that his leg was in a splint. His camouflage uniform had been replaced by traditional Afghan clothing, and his hands and lower arms seemed to have been washed.

As he attempted to sit up, sudden pain ripped through his chest, and his leg was screaming at him to stop moving. The bearded man propped him up against the wall behind him and called to his wife who arrived with a bowl of what looked like a meat stew and some bread. Malone wolfed it down. It was then that he understood that what the man was doing was to honour the ancient code of *Pashtunwali*, whereby it is incumbent on people to open their doors to travellers, virtually with no questions asked. Malone felt the sustenance re-invigorate him almost immediately, and he began engaging the man in conversation, thanking his lucky star that he had proven so naturally gifted with languages that learning to speak Pashto almost fluently had come more easily to him than anyone else in the Regiment.

It turned out that the man was a farmer, and that he had spotted Malone's vehicle up on the mountain that day. He had taken the unconscious man to his house down in the next valley, and together with his wife had tended to him and treated his wounds. Malone did what he could to express his gratitude, but then exhaustion overwhelmed him once again, and within minutes he was asleep.

Over the next several days he steadily improved thanks to the efforts of his hosts, until he was able to walk around with the help of a crutch that the farmer had made, and as soon as he could do that, he immediately began seeking out tasks to do and ways to make himself useful on the small farm. Within several weeks, he was able to put a bit of weight on his left leg again, and soon he found himself capable of contributing to the running of the farm in a meaningful way. It was then that the farmer had started referring to him as *Al Naji* – The Survivor.

It turned out that the farmer was growing poppy, since opium was significantly more profitable than anything else he could grow. Given Malone's whole reason for being in northern Afghanistan to begin with, he should have felt at least some reluctance to help the farmer produce the base compound for more refined drugs, but after having lived on the farm for several months and seen the reality of their daily lives, his perspective had changed dramatically. Out here in the arid mountains of northern Afghanistan, drugs had nothing to do with the abstract notion of substance abuse in some wealthy far-off country that might as well have been on an entirely different planet. It was simply about survival. Opium was a means to an end, and he couldn't blame the farmer for doing what was best for him and his wife.

Over the following months, Malone became completely fluent in Pashto. He took over many of the more physically demanding roles on the farm, but he never travelled with the farmer in his car down to the nearest town. He did not want to be noticed by anyone in the area, and even though he had now grown a long dark beard and only ever wore the Peraahan Tunbaan clothing that the farmer had bought for him, he did not want to risk people finding out that he was a westerner. It would also put the farmer and his wife in danger.

As it turned out, the danger would end up coming to them. One early and misty October morning, Malone was working in the field, tending to the poppy plants about a hundred metres from the house, when three shots rang out on the other side of it. He immediately dropped his tools and sprinted back to find the farmer and his wife bleeding out in front of the house, and a truck speeding away down the dirt track that led to the main road. He tried to save them, but their injuries were too severe. It would be many months before he discovered who had killed them and why.

He buried the two of them on a small hill not far from the house and decided not to do anything rash. Instead, he spent the next few days going over his options and trying to decide what to do. However, the days then just began rolling by, and soon he had settled into a new life running the poppy farm by himself. He even began venturing down into the small town a few kilometres away to trade and buy supplies, and no one there seemed to realise that he was not a local. His naturally muscular frame, the eye patch, the full black beard, the dramatic scar across his face and the black turban he had begun wearing, completed the image of a rough and weatherworn character that it was best to steer clear of. He also made sure that he always carried the farmer's aged Kalashnikov rifle over his shoulder. Some of the young men in the town were drawn to this imposing character, and soon several of them were working for him on the poppy farm. No one ever asked what had happened to the farmer and his wife.

The farm expanded, and he was able to hire more workers. Soon, he also decided that he needed to make sure he could protect what was becoming a sizeable opium operation. He took on a handful of young fighters who had come in from Pakistan's

Khyber Pakhtunkhwa province in search of fame and fortune. They were inexperienced and rash, but he put them through a rigorous training program that included weapons handling, hand-to-hand combat and small-scale tactics, and soon they were a proficient security force and an effective deterrent for the other much larger opium producers in the area. Little did his men realise that they had been trained by one of the world's top special forces operators. He also managed to procure more modern weapons than the ones they had brought with them from Pakistan.

Eventually, the opium production facility which had begun as a small farmstead began to attract the attention of the established local warlords. One day, one of them arrived unannounced with a small entourage of hardened-looking fighters in several pickup trucks. He jumped off the lead vehicle and stood imperiously with his feet apart and his hands placed on his hips announcing that the farm was now his, and that they had one day to leave or face the consequences. Malone and his fighters were heavily outnumbered, so he had instructed his men to lower their weapons, and he watched impassively as the warlord walked over to where the farmer and his wife had been shot dead. The man then urinated right on the spot where they had bled out, whilst looking mockingly at Malone. After that, he simply got back into the lead vehicle and drove off with his men down the dirt track, disappearing in a cloud of dust.

Malone was seething, but if he had tried to put up a fight, neither he nor his men would have been likely to survive. Instead, he called all of his fighters together in a room and laid out his plan. A preemptive strike to remove the threat entirely and elevate them all to a position of real power in the local area.

In the dead of night, he and his group of fighters carried out a textbook raid on the warlord's compound. Malone killed the two sentries that were meant to keep watch, and then he placed his men at strategic points just inside the compound's perimeter. He then entered the warlord's private quarters, beat him to a pulp and dragged him moaning and bleeding out into the central courtyard where he pushed him down onto his knees. As soon as the warlord's fighters began emerging piecemeal and bleary-eyed into the courtyard, Malone's men disarmed them one by one and forced them to kneel next to each other on the ground. Once they were all pacified, Malone walked up behind the warlord, jammed the barrel of his pistol against the back of his head and pulled the trigger. The shot rang out into the night, and the warlord fell forward like a heavy slab of meat onto the ground, a large pool of blood spreading out rapidly from his mangled face onto the ground.

There was a brief moment where things could have gone either way. Several of the warlord's men looked as if they were about to launch themselves into a suicidal charge against Malone's heavily armed fighters, but in that moment a short scrawny-looking man jumped up with his hands held high above his head. He was the warlord's deputy, and Malone would later discover that his name was Abdul Wasiq. He appealed to the men to remain calm and to realise that the battle was lost. The warlord they had been working for was dead, and he was not coming back, so there was no point in fighting. Wasiq then offered his own services to Malone and asked the other men to join him. To a man, they eventually all accepted.

As Malone stood there watching the scene unfold, an age-old phrase ran through his mind – *The King is dead. Long live the King.*

Wasiq, who would prove himself to be an extremely effective deputy, then prostrated himself in front of Malone's large bulky frame looming over him, pledging his allegiance and that of the other men. He then asked what they should call him.

Malone stood there silently for a moment, driving home the point that he was now their leader. Their new Emir. Finally, he spoke in Pashto in a calm gravelly voice.

'I am Al Naji.'

Twenty-Four

The SAS team moved quickly but quietly up towards the back of the old redbrick factory building in Barking in East London that was owned by Crescent Logistics. There were five people in the stack. McGregor was on point, followed by the explosives expert Dunn, recon specialist Logan, and finally the two men on fire support, Grant and Thompson. Across the road, lying on the roof of the bus repair terminal and covering the front of the building, was the team's sixth member, Wilks, with his Heckler & Kock PSG1 sniper rifle.

The breach team were all wearing black heavy body armour and helmets with integrated comms, and they were armed with MP5A3 collapsible stock submachine guns. They would be going in loud with a breaching charge, so there was no point in using weapons with suppressors.

As they filed up to the back door to the small factory building, McGregor raised his hand and made a clenched fist, at which point every one stopped dead in their tracks. He then signalled for Dunn to approach. The team's sapper moved up quickly to the door and began fixing the self-adhesive explosive charges to the doorframes. It only took a few seconds, after which he peeled off and re-joined the back of the stack behind Thompson.

'Charges set,' whispered McGregor into his mic in a broad Scottish accent. 'Wilks, any movement out there?'

'Negative, Boss,' came the calm reply from across the road. 'No movement.'

'Roger that,' replied McGregor. 'Dunn. Blow it.'

Almost instantly, the charges detonated with an ear-splitting crack. Amid a bright flash and sparks flying through the air, the metal door flew off its hinges and continued into the smoky space beyond. It had barely landed on the floor inside the factory building before the team swept in with all the speed and aggression required to overwhelm any would-be defenders on the inside.

With their weapons up they immediately fanned out to cover the entire interior of the building, but it quickly became apparent that the place was empty. There seemed to be no one there. They performed a quick sweep of the entire building but came up empty.

'Clear!' came the calls from all the members of the team one by one as they methodically checked the building in less than a minute.

'Wilks! Anything?' asked McGregor.

'Negative,' replied Wilks. 'Still nothing.'

McGregor lowered his weapon and walked back to stand near the centre of the empty space.

'Zero, this is Alpha One,' he said into his mic. 'There's nobody here. It's empty.'

'Alpha One,' came the reply from the operations centre at Hereford. 'This is Zero. Copy - No hostiles. Stand by for orders.'

'Hey, Boss!' called Dunn from near the back of the building. 'Have a look at this.'

McGregor walked over to a small area with tables and equipment that seemed to have been arranged around an old workbench.

'What have we got here?' he said.

'Looks like a bomb making operation,' said Dunn, pointing to the electrical equipment, metal cylinders and bits of wire lying on the workbench. 'Seems we were too late. If the chemical weapons were here, then they have already been moved.'

'Shit,' winced McGregor and re-activated his mic to talk to the operations centre again.

'Zero, this is Alpha One,' he said matter-of-factly. 'We may have a wee problem on our hands.'

* * *

It was coming up on 1.30 a.m. as Andrew entered the Pakistani side of what would eventually become the Khyber Valley further towards the northwest. The road was virtually deserted and he was able to make good time. With a full tank of fuel, he also felt confident that he would be able to make it to the compound in Nahrain before dawn, and if he was going to have any chance of getting inside undetected, he was likely going to need the darkness for cover.

Roughly three kilometres from the Torkham crossing, he peeled off the N-5 National Highway and proceeded along a small paved road. He did not want to try to cross into Afghanistan at the official crossing, and he needed to avoid going through the town of Nahrain on the way to the compound as well. There were bound to be lookouts there paid for by the local warlords, and the last thing he wanted was a welcome party of Taliban fighters.

He had studied the map of the surrounding area carefully before setting out, and he felt confident that this route would allow him to get close enough to the compound for him to be able to cover the last few kilometres on foot. The road initially led towards the east and then followed a river at the bottom of a wide valley, after which it gradually curved around to take him almost due north. It then continued through two small settlements consisting of mudbrick houses that appeared to be completely deserted at this time of night.

After another ten kilometres, the paved road stopped after a third settlement, and he then had to move on to a dirt track that began to climb steadily through the valley as it stretched up towards the southernmost mountains of the Hindu Kush. As he continued further up the rapidly narrowing valley, the dirt road began to curve left and right until it eventually presented him with precarious hairpin bends towards a saddle between two tall peaks. Once over the summit, the road snaked its way along a mountainside, and then it slowly began to climb again, at which point Andrew thanked his lucky star that the

Toyota had 4-wheel drive and wide tyres that gave it a relatively firm grip on the gravelly track.

Eventually the road levelled out at high altitude, and Andrew found himself on a dry plateau with no vegetation, which stretched for several kilometres ahead of him. Driving along the increasingly faint dirt track in the light from the full moon in what was now a clear sky overhead, and keeping an eye on his handheld GPS display, he felt as if he was travelling across a barren lunar landscape where no other human had ever been. Looking out across the vastness of the remote plateau and the multitude of impassable mountain ranges behind it to the north, he was in no doubt that there were countless places within his field of view where no human had ever set foot during the entire history of Homo Sapiens.

Andrew continued driving along in the dark for the next three hours or so, navigating several more valleys and mountain passes and making sure not to stress the vehicle or its tyres unnecessarily, since a mechanical breakdown out here would put him in serious trouble. With roughly ten kilometres to go, the dirt track followed the contours of the landscape and began to curve around to the west. However, he needed to continue north.

He now had to pull off the road as it curved west, and continue north across rough ground until he arrived at a point where the terrain rose up once again to a ridge high above. It was obvious that the Toyota would be unable to scale the mountainside, so he continued for as long as he could and exited the vehicle, strapping all the kit to his body and checking his various weapons and equipment. Happy with the way his loadout was secured, he then set off up the mountainside at a controlled pace, leaving the vehicle behind. It was now just after 4 a.m., and he estimated that he was roughly three kilometres from the compound, which was in the next valley on the other side of the ridge.

He was able to keep a decent pace and avoid accidents on the treacherous terrain, so he arrived near the compound about an hour later when the sky towards the east was beginning to turn from black to dark blue. Within the next hour or so, he would no longer be able to rely on the darkness to conceal him, so he couldn't loiter for too long. Coming over the ridge and looking down into the Nahrain valley on the other side, he could see the town out on the huge flat valley some five kilometres away. Behind it in the far distance were the snow-capped mountains of the central Hindu Kush range.

Directly below him was the compound. Distance, roughly two hundred metres. He lay down on his front and took his time to scope it out using his night-vision goggles and binoculars. He had already studied the satellite images that Strickland had sent him, so he had a decent sense of its size and layout, but he wanted to commit as many details to memory as possible before attempting to go in.

The compound was large, rectangular and about one hundred metres by one hundred metres in size. In each of the two corners closest to the road leading up to the compound from Nahrain, were tower-like structures on top of one-storey buildings. From his elevated position, he was able to see one sentry on top of each tower, and as he had expected, they were both facing the valley and occasionally bringing up binoculars to check the road that stretched all the way down to the town. Anyone approaching from that direction would be visible for several minutes before they could make it to the compound. Andrew also noted that the sentries appeared unnaturally bulky, which made him suspect that perhaps they were wearing suicide vests. That might seem extreme, but it was something he had seen first-hand several times in both Iraq and Afghanistan. The security detail of high-ranking Al-Qaeda leaders would often carry explosive vests, and if a special forces team tasked with taking down high-value targets got too close, they would simply clack themselves off and try to take as many coalition forces with them as they could. It begged the question: Was this standard operating procedure in this compound, or did they already know he was coming? Were they waiting for him? It was more than likely that Major Khan would have gathered all the intelligence on everything that had happened in Peshawar, and that this would have been fed through to Al Naji. Andrew considered the situation, but decided that it effectively made no difference to what he was about to do. He was going to get inside that compound one way or another, whether those fighters were wearing suicide vests or not.

Around the entire perimeter was what appeared to be a roughly two-metre-high mudbrick wall. On all four sides of it, all the vegetation such as small trees and bushes that otherwise dotted the area, had been cut down. This meant that for as long as there were sentries in the towers, it would be impossible to get close to the walls without being spotted. This was going to be a problem. If this had been a proper SAS operation, he would have had some kind of backup, probably even drone cover. But more importantly, he would have had a team with at least one sniper who could quickly have dispatched the two sentries. He would also have had an exfiltration plan. As it was, he was on his own, and he would have to do everything by himself.

Inside the perimeter walls were a number of buildings of various shapes and sizes, several of them with their lights on. A couple of them looked like the flat-roofed opium processing facilities he had seen before, others seemed to be accommodation of some kind, possibly barracks for Al Naji's fighters. From the looks of the barracks, the compound was likely to have a significant presence of fighters. Possibly as many as twenty or thirty.

At the very back of the compound nearest Andrew's position was a large single-storey structure that stood out because it appeared to have been constructed from concrete prefab units. It looked significantly more modern than the other buildings. It also had several antennae and a satellite dish on the roof. Andrew immediately knew that this would be Al Naji's private quarters. He also assumed that there would be several guards manning the front door, but because it was facing away from his location, he was unable to see the door itself. From his vantage point, he was able to see around eight people throughout the compound. However, because of the murky pre-dawn darkness, there could easily be many more that he could not see from where he was.

As far as he could tell, there was only one entrance to the compound, and that was through the tall metal gate between the two towers at the front. But going in that way was not an option. He had to create a new entryway, and in order to do that, he was going to need a distraction to minimise his chances of being spotted. However, before he could do any of those things, he needed to take down the two sentries.

Looking up at the sky, he reckoned that it would be less than an hour before the sun would come up over the mountainous horizon. He had to move out in order to take advantage of the final minutes of darkness, so he backed off the top of the ridge he had been lying on, and moved slowly and quietly down towards the compound. As he went, he made sure to keep as much of the terrain and vegetation between himself and the sentries on the towers as possible.

Roughly 50 metres from the rear perimeter wall, he arrived at a rocky outcropping that allowed him to once again lie prone with a perfect view of the entire compound. Offset slightly from the centre of the compound as he was, he estimated the distance to the two tower sentries to be around 80 and 100 metres respectively. This was not an easy shot, but it was within the effective firing range of a standard MP5. However, it was well beyond the recommended firing range of the MP5SD, which was only around 25 to 75 metres because of the lower bullet velocity.

Well. Here goes nothing, he thought to himself, and brought up the submachine gun, moving the fire selector to single shot mode.

He decided to attempt the most challenging shot first, and lined up on the tower sentry in the far corner. Andrew was a very competent long-distance shooter, but nowhere near the skill level of the dedicated snipers in the Regiment. However, he had probably fired more rounds with the MP5 in its various configurations than almost anyone currently in active service, so he felt confident that he would be able to make the shot.

He lined up the iron sights with the sentry and gradually began to relax and slow down his breathing, and with it, his own heart rate. Once he was down to around thirty beats per minute, he gently tilted his head slightly to the right and looked down the sights. The sentry was standing completely still, leaning against a support beam for the corrugated metal roof over his head. Smoking a cigarette, he was exhaling large puffs of smoke that languidly drifted off and dissipated in the cool morning air.

Keeping his eyes locked on the soldier through the sights of the MP5SD, and aiming slightly high to account for bullet drop as the projectile travelled the distance from the muzzle to the target, Andrew then moved his index finger from the trigger guard to the trigger. He exhaled slowly, inhaled again, and then exhaled half way and held his breath. Then he squeezed the trigger gently until the gun fired. He felt the familiar gentle recoil of the suppressed weapon as well as the click and the abrupt puff of the suppressor. The bullet covered the distance to the target in just over a third of a second and slammed into the side of the fighter's head. There was no audible sound as it impacted, but Andrew saw the man's legs give way and his body slump down onto the floor of the tower. Concerned that the other sentry might have heard something, Andrew took two deep breaths whilst shifting the iron sight to the second and slightly closer tower. Disconcertingly, what he saw there was the other sentry having risen to his feet from the chair he had been sitting in, and making his way to the side of his tower that was facing the other tower. The man already had his Kalashnikov assault rifle in his hands, and as he stopped and gazed over at where his colleague was supposed to have been, Andrew could have sworn that his body language was that of a man about to call out. There was no time to lose.

He quickly lined up the iron sight, held his breath and fired. The bullet smacked into the man's shoulder and spun him halfway around. The impact and the shock made him lose his grip on the assault rifle and it dropped onto the edge of the tower and went falling end over end towards the ground below. Before it impacted, Andrew had already fired two more shots, both of which connected with the man's torso. He looked like he was being punched once in the chest and once in the stomach, and then he fell forward and landed flat on his face. He didn't move after that.

Andrew lay completely still, half expecting to hear shouting. If someone had seen or heard the sentries being taken out, all hell would break loose. The integrated suppressor on the MP5SD would have choked off the muzzle flash, but if someone had spotted the second sentry's weapon falling to the ground inside the compound, then it would be crawling with fighters within a few moments. After about twenty seconds, there was still no sign of the alarm being raised, and Andrew realised that he was still holding his breath. He exhaled heavily and took another couple of deep breaths to re-oxygenate his blood. It looked like he had got away with it, but now more than ever he needed to speed things up and perform the wall breach before someone discovered the dead sentries or the AK-47 lying on the ground next to the nearest tower.

Still prone, he moved backwards off the rocky outcropping and then circled down through a bushy area along a ravine with a small stream that led past the compound on its eastern side at a distance of about fifty metres. Moving through the trees and bushes parallel to the wall and looking for a place to approach it, he suddenly spotted two fighters coming around the corner of the perimeter wall where the nearest tower was. He immediately knelt down behind a nearby bush and froze.

The two men were walking along calmly without talking. They were clearly just a regular perimeter patrol, and it was obvious that they had seen and heard nothing of the sentries being taken out. They were, however, coming almost straight towards Andrew, and would be passing him along a footpath at a distance of no more than ten metres. He considered staying quiet and simply letting them pass, but he decided that they were bound to come back again a few minutes later. On top of that, if it came to an open firefight inside the compound, these two men would represent two additional threats that would then need to be defeated.

Lying down and pressing himself into the dirt so as not to get spotted, Andrew listened to their footsteps on the dry gravel as they approached along the footpath, and as soon as he sensed that they had passed his position, he got to his feet and moved silently past a couple of bushes and out into the open near the footpath almost directly behind them. Distance – fifteen metres. He went down onto one knee, aimed and fired a three-round burst at the fighter on the left. Before the man was down, Andrew had let the second burst fly, and this too connected with its intended target. Within ten seconds of re-positioning, both fighters lay dead on the ground. He briefly considered dragging the bodies into cover, but it would make no difference now, since things were about to go loud.

Moving swiftly up close to the side of the mudbrick perimeter wall, he dragged his backpack off his shoulders and opened it to extract one of the two Claymore mines, which he positioned facing the wall at a distance of just thirty centimetres. Then he extracted the two rocket propelled grenades and placed them immediately in front of the directional charge. As soon as the Claymore detonated, it would instantly cause the RPGs to explode as well, creating a blast that ought to be more than sufficient to breach the wall. Finally, he grabbed several large and heavy rocks, and packed them in around the improvised breaching charge in order to contain as much of the blast's energy as possible, and direct it into the wall. The entire operation took less than a minute, and once he was happy, he then retraced his steps back through the bushes, unspooling a detonator cord as he went. He found himself a large boulder to hide behind, crouched down with the M57 clacker in his hand and took a deep breath. He was no demolitions expert, yet he felt confident that his plan would work. Only one way to find out.

Compressing the lever on the clacker all the way down, a small coil-sprung metal bar inside it eventually snapped back, inducing a 3-volt current to be generated inside a copper wire coil. At the speed of light, the current shot out of the clacker and along the detonation wire where it reached the Claymore mine which detonated its C4 explosive charge. An instant later, the explosion ripped through the two RPGs which then exploded, each with the force of roughly five hand grenades. The combined blast was deafening, and resulted in a huge flash and a bright orange fireball that tore through the mudbrick wall with such force that it sent hundreds of kilos of mudbrick flying into the compound and up into the air.

A fraction of a second after the initial blast, the pressure wave reached the boulder Andrew was hiding behind, and he could have sworn that the giant rock shifted slightly when it happened. Even as smoke, fire and dust were still roiling up from the epicentre of the explosion, and while debris was still raining down over the surrounding area, Andrew emerged from his cover and sprinted towards the huge cloud of dust where until a few seconds ago the wall had been. Inside the compound he could hear voices shouting frantically in Pashto, and he was sure that he heard Arabic as well.

As he reached the location where he had placed his wall-breaching IED, even he was surprised at how much damage it had done. It was only when he made his way through the three-metre wide opening that he realised that there must have been one or two fuel barrels sitting just on the other side of the wall. They had been torn open and ignited by the explosion and had then been launched about twenty metres inside the walled area where they had slammed against a building and erupted in a liquid flaming inferno that lit up most of the central part of the compound.

Immediately upon entering, Andrew turned left towards the nearest building where he took cover between it and a part of the perimeter wall that was still intact. The entire compound was in chaos. Fighters were running around seemingly aimlessly, some of them barking orders at each other but without much effect. Some were uselessly trying to put out the fire with buckets of water, and others were exiting their barracks clumsily and looking confused, their weapons engaged and ready for a fight.

Andrew exploited the general chaos to engage two fighters who had just emerged from a building. He fired two bursts with his submachine gun, and the two men crashed to the ground without ever realising what had hit them. He then immediately changed position and began making his way around the back of the building. However, what he did not see was that through the same door that the two fighters had come through, followed two huge German Shepherds who bolted out of the building, raced past their dead handlers and headed straight for the corner behind which Andrew had just disappeared.

Andrew was moving up towards the other rear corner of the building and getting ready to engage new targets, when he heard the sound of running feet on the ground behind him. They began as a soft but rapid patter but quickly increased in volume to the point where, by the time he realised what they were, they were closing disconcertingly fast and sounding like they were almost on him. He swung around and just managed to catch the lead dog with a three-round burst as it launched itself through the air in an attempt to get to his throat. At least two of the bullets caught the snarling beast's body with meaty thuds, and the third went in through its open mouth and tore through its skull. This turned the ferocious animal into a limp meat projectile weighing around thirty kilos, which then slammed square into Andrew's chest, knocked him over and left him splayed on the ground. He barely had time to get back on his feet before the second dog was on him. Whether it had any comprehension of what had happened to its companion and to its handlers, Andrew did not know, but it behaved as if it was in a murderous frenzy, growling and snarling aggressively and snapping violently at Andrew's face as if it knew that if only it could lock its powerful jaws with their razor-sharp teeth around his head or throat, then it would be able to defeat him quickly.

Andrew instinctively brought up his left arm and presented it to the wild-eyed canine in order to buy himself a few valuable seconds. The dog immediately locked its jaws around his lower arm, and it was all Andrew could do to not cry out in pain. The beast's teeth were cutting through his clothes, skin and deep into his muscles, and he felt such pressure from its vice-like grip that he thought his bones might snap. Initially fumbling during the mortal wrestling match, he was eventually able to reach his hunting knife. He yanked it out with his right hand, brought it out to the side and then rammed it into the dog's neck. He instantly felt a squirt of warm blood on his hand and some of it splattered onto his chest and face. But the crazed animal barely reacted. If anything, it re-doubled its attempt at ripping Andrew's throat open, perhaps in some deep instinctive realisation that now was a do or die moment, and that the only way to survive this was to kill.

Realising this, Andrew pulled the knife out and smashed it back in, but this time he aimed for the head which was moving around violently as the dog attempted to reach his throat. The knife entered through the soft tissue around the dog's ear, broke the skull and penetrated all the way into the animal's brain. In an instant, it was as if it had been a mechanical dog, and the power had been turned off. It collapsed heavily onto Andrew's body, produced a couple of quick spasms and then became completely limp.

Andrew shoved the dead attack dog aside and scrambled to his feet, concerned that the canine visitors might be followed by more human attackers. He grabbed his MP5 off the ground and tucked himself in next to the wall of the adjacent building. There he waited for about ten seconds, but no one else came. The shouting and general confusion was still ongoing throughout the compound. Fires were still burning violently, and it was obvious that no one had any idea who had caused the explosion or where the perpetrator was. Andrew realised that he had to attempt to exploit that state of affairs for as long as possible.

He continued back over to the corner of the building from where he was able to see the concrete prefab structure which he assumed belonged to the warlord. There was only one entry point, and that was a heavy steel door which was up three steps from the ground level.

There were no guards outside, so either they had already fanned out into the compound to help identify the threat, or they had done the opposite and hunkered down just inside in order to serve as a final bastion of defence in case the attacking force ever made it to the prefab building. What they did not know, and could probably not have imagined, was that they were under assault from just one man.

Andrew quickly leaned out a bit further to see if he could spot other fighters nearby, but the area immediately in front of the prefab building was empty. In all likelihood, everyone in the vicinity had moved closer to the point on the wall that had been blown up, naturally thinking that any threat to the compound was about to come through there.

'No time like the present,' said Andrew to himself with gritted teeth, and then he began swiftly moving forward towards the concrete building, knees slightly bent and at a pace that allowed him to keep the stock of his submachine pressed into his shoulder and pointing ahead, ready to engage any new threats.

When he was less than ten metres from the heavy steel door, it suddenly flew open and two fighters emerged. As soon as he saw them, Andrew expected them to come out and open up with heavy weapons such as belt-fed machine guns or even an RPG launcher. However, the two men were carrying AK-

74s, which are a lighter and smaller calibre weapon than the AK-47, and they were clearly unaware of the approaching threat. Already prepared to fire, Andrew kept moving forward and let loose a three-round burst that immediately cut down the man in front. The fighter behind him managed to bring up his assault rifle and fire several rounds in Andrew's general direction. However, the surprise and shock at seeing his companion drop to the ground immediately after exiting the building, caused him to release his rounds before aiming properly, and the bullets went wide. However, the rapid staccato bark of the AK-74 reverberated through the compound, and even as Andrew fired a second suppressed burst which smacked into the fighter's chest and sent him spinning and crumbling onto the ground, he knew that within a few seconds he would have all the remaining fighters in the compound converging on his position.

Without slowing down, and without wasting time looking behind himself, he proceeded past the dead fighters, up the three steps and into the building. Given that the outside was now rapidly becoming intractable, he needed to keep the level of aggression of his assault up and push into the building as fast as possible. Just inside was a hallway, and luckily there were no more fighters in sight. He quickly pushed the heavy steel door shut, and almost as soon as he slammed the bolts in place to lock it, he heard the metallic pinging sound of bullets smacking into the exterior. However, the door was clearly built for this scenario, and it was easily able to withstand small arms fire.

However, realising that the compound's fighters probably had a contingency plan for this scenario, he had to keep moving forward before the door was somehow either blown or pulled off its hinges from the outside. He pushed ahead through the hallway and into a short corridor with two doors on one side and a closed door at the end. He quickly cleared the two adjacent rooms and then pushed up to the closed door. He suddenly thought he heard voices on the other side, and then the unmistakable sound of the metal cover on a belt-fed machine gun being slammed down on the feed tray and the cocking lever being yanked back to ready the weapon to fire its first round.

Moving as fast as he could, Andrew threw himself to one side and pressed himself against the wall, and a split second later the corridor erupted in an almost debilitating chaos of splintered door and doorframe. An infernal hail of large-calibre bullets, many of them glowing tracer rounds, were tearing through wood and brickwork and slamming into the opposite wall. The roar of the machine gun, which to Andrew sounded like an American M60, was deafening. But like all machine guns, the M60 quickly runs dry and needs to be fed a new belt of ammunition.

As soon as the firing stopped and agitated voices shouted out in Arabic to load faster, Andrew reached up to detach a grenade from his tactical vest, pulled the pin and chucked it through the gaping smoking hole in the door. He took cover behind the wall next to the mangled doorframe as the occupants in the room realised what had happened and began panicking. A couple of seconds later there was a loud explosion and the noise of metal fragments slamming into the floor, the ceiling and the walls. He heard the sound of at least one body dropping heavily to the floor with a thud, but also of running feet retreating further into the building amid more shouting. Then there was silence again, except for the faint fizzing of some of the tracer rounds which were lodged inside the concrete wall, still burning the remainder of their pyrotechnic flare material.

Andrew quickly pressed the magazine release button on his MP5, let the near-empty mag drop to the floor and clicked a fresh one into the magazine well. Then he got up and kicked the shredded door open. Incredibly, a couple of the lights were still on inside the room, and he quickly moved up to the fighter that was lying on the floor to make sure he was dead. He looked like he had taken most of the blast, because his lower legs were missing and his body had been mangled by multiple metal fragments, one of which had travelled up through the side of his head. Wisps of smoke were still rising from his ripped clothes.

Advancing further through the room to the door at the other end, Andrew stopped next to the half-open doorway to the next room and listened. He was unable to hear any movement, and part of him was surprised that the defenders had retreated further into the building instead of trying to counter-attack immediately after the grenade had gone off. Were they trying to lure him into a kill zone further into the building? Without the interior floorplans that he and the Regiment were often able to study before a mission, he was left to guess and surmise what the layout was as he progressed into the structure. However, he intuitively sensed that he was about a third of the way towards the back where he reckoned Al Naji would be located, if he was even here at all. For all Andrew knew, the warlord could have left the compound many hours ago if Major Khan had warned him of a possible assault, or he could be in the process of escaping right now, possibly using secret underground tunnels. All Andrew could do was to press on. It was his only chance of uncovering the true nature of the attack that he was now convinced was about to take place in London in just a few short hours.

Steadying himself, he swung into the room on the other side of the doorway with his submachine gun raised but found it empty. Advancing quickly through it, he came to another corridor which he cautiously entered. Halfway along were two doors, one on either side, and both of them were open. As he pushed up towards them, his senses were working overtime to try to pick out the sound of movement close by, but his ears were still impaired from the noise of the M60 barrage and the grenade explosion a couple of minutes earlier.

As soon as he edged up to the door on the left to attempt to clear that space first, a pair of enormous hands reached out from the darkness, grabbed the barrel of his MP5 and almost yanked it from him. It was only because it was secured to his torso with a leather strap that he managed to hold on to it. Immediately thereafter, someone stepped out from the other doorway, wrapping a thick arm around his neck and squeezing so tightly that he couldn't breathe.

He immediately threw his entire body backwards as forcefully as he could, and he and his assailant barged into the wall behind them.

From the dark doorway in front of him emerged a tall bearded man who was so large that for a moment it looked like he would struggle to fit through the doorframe. Despite being strangled from behind, Andrew managed to bring up the MP5 to try to release a burst into the giant, but when he pulled the trigger, nothing happened. Somehow the huge man had managed, either by accident or through impressive cunning, to flick the fire selector to OFF. In an instant, the burly fighter was on him. He once again grabbed the submachine gun, and this time he yanked it so hard that the leather strap snapped and the weapon fell to the floor. He then slammed a fist into Andrew's stomach with such force that Andrew thought he might have ruptured some of his internal organs. He was instantly winded, and an immense pain bloomed out through his guts.

Despite everything, he managed to instinctively reach for his Glock 19 and pull it from its holster. He quickly brought it up and jammed it into the giant just under where he reckoned his heart was. Then he fired three times, which resulted in the man seeming to rise up onto his toes producing a strange grunt. Wide-eyed, the giant staggered backwards and fell heavily against the opposite wall in the corridor, where he crashed onto the floor, exhaled deeply and then remained still.

Andrew immediately brought the gun back down and fired again, this time into the foot of the fighter trying to strangle him. The man instantly let go with a loud cry of pain, at which point Andrew twisted free, took one step backwards and raised the gun again. Three more shots rang out, and the fighter slid down the wall behind him, leaving a bloody smear as he went, and staring blankly in front of himself.

Andrew reached up with his left hand to rub at his throat. The compression on it had been violent, and he quickly discovered that swallowing resulted in significant pain. But at least he was still alive. What he couldn't understand was why the giant had attempted to disarm him, instead of just shooting him.

He picked up his MP5, flicked the fire selector to full auto and advanced further along the dimly lit corridor to another doorway with a completely dark room beyond. He considered lobbing a grenade inside, but he had no idea what was there, and the last thing he needed now was to set off an ammunitions cache and die in an inferno of secondary explosions. Advancing slowly and using the faint light from the corridor, he moved through what appeared to be another abandoned room with sparse furniture, when suddenly something small seemed to fly towards him and hit the floor right in front of his feet.

He only just had time to register that it was a flashbang. Whoever had thrown it had timed it perfectly, because an instant later the whole world suddenly detonated in a deafening, brilliant white explosion of searing light and thunderous noise. He immediately lost both his vision and almost all of his hearing, except for a high-pithed ringing in his ears, and his legs nearly gave way under him as he felt a sudden urge to vomit.

With his eyes instinctively squeezed shut, and barely able to remain on his feet, he staggered backwards half a step. As he did so, he knew that in a couple of seconds, his entire body would be torn to shreds by a hail of projectiles fired from a handful of assault rifles built by the venerable JSC Kalashnikov Concern, known for decades under its Soviet name, the Izhevsk Machine-Building Plant. Not a bad way to go, really.

To his surprise, this did not happen. Instead, he sensed multiple people running towards him, disarming him and gripping his arms tightly, and then someone kicking his right leg hard and causing it to buckle and shoot searing pain up through his body to his brain. He was forced down towards the floor. Once on his knees and with his head pressed down onto his chest, he again waited – this time for the sensation of the muzzle of a gun being placed at the back of his head just moments before his brains would end up splattered all across the floor in front of him. Through the maelstrom of his sensory overload, he still managed to detect someone walking up to stand directly behind him. This was it. This was the end.

When the blunt instrument impacted on the back of his head, his vision exploded into a brilliant white starburst. All remaining sounds became muffled and slowly faded away, and then darkness enveloped him – as if he was falling down into an infinitely deep well from which he would never return.

TWENTY-FIVE

Andrew had had this dream before. He was back in Afghanistan, tied up inside the shed along with Frank Malone. His ears were still ringing from the RPG. His eyes were jammed shut and caked in dirt, sweat and coagulated blood. His body felt numb from having been flung violently through the air when the explosion had lifted him off his feet and sent him and Frank crashing onto the rocky ground. The white noise in his ears began to coalesce into faint, muffled distant-sounding voices speaking in Pashto. He felt several pairs of strong hands on him, grabbing his shoulders and shaking him whilst someone shouted at him. Icy cold water was thrown onto him, and then a hard stinging slap was delivered across his face.

He opened his eyes. This was no dream. Once again, he was sitting in a chair with his hands tied behind his back, but this time in a dark humid and musty-smelling room with no windows. His vision was blurred, but he could just about make out the contours and size of the space, and he concluded that it was a small room underground, possibly a basement under the warlord's prefab building. The only illumination came from a single white lightbulb hanging from the ceiling. In front of him was a man standing with his feet slightly apart and his hands placed just above his knees, as if he was leaning forward, inspecting his prisoner.

Andrew felt the man grab hold of his hair and then yank his head up and back as he shone a torch into his eyes. Despite being partially blinded by the light, Andrew was able to make out the man's face. He was probably in his late forties with dark leathery skin and an unkempt beard. A stocky character with a large scimitar of a nose, he regarded his prisoner with a cold stare laced with disdain. After a few seconds, he let go of Andrew's hair, grunted something unintelligible in Pashto, and then left the room through a door immediately behind Andrew's chair.

The man's footsteps seemed to recede up a flight of stairs on the other side of the door, and then the basement room fell silent. As he gradually regained more access to his sensory system, Andrew felt the restraints around his wrists cut into his skin, and he began to feel the dull pain in the back of his head more keenly. He had a slightly metallic taste in his mouth, and his heart was beating much faster than it should have.

After a few more minutes, during which Andrew methodically interrogated every limb of his body to ascertain if he had suffered any injuries, the door behind him opened again and he heard slow deliberate footsteps approaching him. A gruff voice spoke a couple of hurried words in Pashto, after which the door closed again. He sensed the speaker walk up behind his chair, stopping immediately behind him and then leaning down to place his head next to Andrew's right ear.

The man breathed calmly a couple of times, and Andrew could feel the warm air of his breath on his ear. Then a gravelly and strange, yet instantly familiar voice spoke. It was slow and deliberate with a distinct Geordie accent, and it was laced with a tinge of amusement.

'Hello, mucker.'

* * *

Andrew's hairs stood on end and a chill rippled down his spine. In an instant, his mind had gone from groggy and confused to turbo-charged and fully alert, racing to make sense of what he had just heard. It was like plunging back through a rewind of the events of the past 12 years of his life. Back to that moment in the shed in northern Afghanistan when the shot had rung out and his mate had toppled lifeless to the floor.

'Frank!' he exclaimed hoarsely as he turned his head to the side in an attempt to see the man next to him. 'Frank, is that you?'

'It me, all right,' came Frank Malone's voice, sounding both tense and angry.

'How?' said Andrew, the words catching in his throat and making him cough. 'How is this possible? What the hell happened to you?'

'I fucking LIVED!' spat Malone.

'But how did…' began Andrew.

'And you fucking left me there!' roared Malone. 'You fucking left me in this shithole. Left me for dead. A brother would have come back.'

Malone's words hit Andrew as if they were hard punches being delivered to his gut. He felt nauseous. You never leave a brother behind. His head was spinning. His worst fears had come true, yet his mind was writhing in an attempt to reject the undeniable reality of what was happening.

'But I saw you get killed,' he said, simultaneously feeling both deep distress and intense relief at seeing his old comrade again. 'You died. I saw it with my own eyes.'

'You saw me take a bloody bullet, that's all,' retorted Malone, now with condescension in his voice as he walked around to stand in front of Andrew, blocking out the light from the single lightbulb in the ceiling. 'You should have fucking known it would take a lot more than that to kill me.'

Andrew was stunned and opened his mouth to say something, but his brain was scrambled, and no words came out. Had he really left his mate to die? Could he have saved him? If he had gone back, would he then have found him alive? These were old questions that he had asked himself hundreds of times over the years. The answer to all of them was standing right in front of him now.

'What the hell happened to you, mate?' Andrew finally asked. 'How did you survive? How did you end up here?'

Malone straightened himself and walked over to a corner of the room with a slight limp. Here he grabbed a chair, which he then fragged across the dusty concrete floor and placed directly in front of Andrew. He then sat down, slightly bent forward with his elbows resting on his knees and his hands folded in front of himself. His large frame and broad shoulders were just as Andrew remembered them, and his talisman was dangling slowly back and forth on a leather strap around his neck.

'It's a long story, mucker,' he sighed, taking a long moment to get his thoughts straight in his head. Then he started to speak.

As he recounted the details of his decade-long transformational journey from being Frank Malone to being the warlord known as Al Naji, his demeanour drifted gradually ever more towards the former and away from the latter. Even his face seemed to change as he did so. Still, Andrew wondered whether at this point Malone knew who he really was anymore.

'You probably never understood this,' said Malone by the end of his tale, 'but I saw with my own eyes during my childhood that the only way to take out any gang is to take out the leader. There is no real hierarchy in a criminal gang, beyond the fact that the main guy in is charge. Sure, there are lieutenants and enforcers and so on, but ultimately there is the leader at the top, and everyone else is below him. Once he is gone, everyone else is just standing around looking at each other, waiting to see who steps up and claims the throne. All I had to do was kill the local warlord and then step up.'

Andrew leaned back into his chair and closed his eyes for a moment, suddenly feeling completely exhausted. He had been sitting with his head slumped in front of himself as Malone had described the events of the past twelve years of his life, barely able to take in the enormity of it all. Twelve years where he himself had been in active service with the SAS all over the world, doing what he loved to do. What Malone had once loved to do. Several of those operations had taken place right here in Afghanistan. And all that time his brother had been here. Alive, and busy building his own little empire in the mountains around Nahrain.

'Fuck,' breathed Andrew.

'Yeah,' replied Malone with a derisive chuckle.

Andrew looked up at him again, studying his scarred face as much as the silhouette from the light bulb would allow.

'What's with the beard and he garb?' he finally asked, attempting to lighten the mood.

Malone grinned, and for a brief moment there was a glimpse of the old Frank.

'We all do what we need to do to survive', he said dryly. 'Just like back in Grimsby. No one's gonna fucking give you anything, are they? So, you have to fit in and make the most of it. Turned out I am a bloody good warlord, and looking the part is half the secret.'

Then his demeanour suddenly seemed to harden again.

'The only thing I believed in back then was the brotherhood of the Regiment,' he continued bitterly. 'But you killed that off too. I trusted you, and you left me for dead.'

'I'm sorry,' whispered Andrew. 'If I had known…'

His last sentence hung in the air, weak and pathetic like the vacuous trope that it was. Several silent moments passed before Andrew spoke again.

'I know about Tokarev and Obaid,' he said. 'They're both dead.'

Malone nodded, once again seeming more like Frank than Al Naji.

'I know,' he said. 'I figured it was you. Tokarev sent me the intel from his club in Damascus. Nice little covert op you carried out there. I must admit that I was surprised to see your mug on the surveillance footage.'

'How the hell do you two even know each other?' asked Andrew. 'He's a bloody psychopath.'

'Abdul Wasiq,' replied Malone. 'He and Tokarev knew each other from years ago, so Wasiq was able to set up a route for my heroin via Syria, and Tokarev could supply me with all the Russian weapons I could ever need.'

'And Major Khan?' asked Andrew.

'He's just a puffed-up greedy little maggot running a desk in Islamabad,' replied Malone scornfully. 'But he has been useful. Especially in the beginning. Provided us with intel as well as money from the fucking CIA, would you believe. After all their failures, the Yanks still think they can buy influence here. Anyway, Khan was happy to funnel dollars our way, as long as he believed that I was on his team. In return, he used his ISI credentials to facilitate our heroin shipments out of Peshawar, no questions asked. Getting them into the UK was a lot easier than you might think. And Khan himself got a cut from us, as well as more rapid promotions from his superiors for supposedly being my handler. The whole bloody thing worked like a charm. Until you showed up.'

'Well, you know why I am here,' said Andrew evenly, now having regained much of his composure and fixing Malone with a hard look. 'The chemical weapons. What the hell is going on, Frank? What are you planning?'

Malone leaned back in his chair, and as the light from the light bulb in the ceiling caught more of his face, casting a hard shadow from his eyepatch down over his cheek, he seemed to again transform back into the violent warlord who had ruthlessly taken over this area of central Afghanistan over the past decade. He took a long moment during which he sat immovable like a statue, staring straight ahead with his one good eye. When he finally spoke, it was with a strained whisper and an ice-cold look on his face.

'Justice,' he said, baring his teeth slightly and sounding bitter and wrathful. 'Justice for myself and all the brothers that were left behind on countless battlefields all across the world.'

Andrew instantly knew where this was going. It was a line of thought that he himself had felt encroaching on his own thoughts more than once. It was an uncomfortable truth that was difficult to square with the pride and sense of purpose that he and his comrades in the Regiment felt when they were out there doing their jobs. And that truth was simple: Ultimately, they were all expendable. The suits in Downing Street who signed off on their covert operations did not care one bit if any of them came back home alive, as long as the mission was accomplished and the world never learned of what had really happened. There was a good reason why, to a man, all of the special forces operators that Andrew had ever known, at home and abroad, had all said the same thing. At the end of the day, the only thing they really fought for were their comrades. Not the King or the Queen, or even their country. Deep down, they all knew that such loyalty was misplaced, and that it would not be repaid. It was about the man next to you. It was about bringing everyone back alive.

Andrew felt a tight knot form in his stomach. The sense of failure felt like a crushing weight bearing down on his chest. He should have come back for him. Everything that had happened to Malone was his fault.

'As soon as I was listed as MIA,' said Malone. 'I might as well have been dead and buried. No one really gives a shit.

Andrew said nothing. There was no point in arguing.

'I also knew what would happen to me if one day I did return back home,' continued Malone scathingly. 'I would never return to active service. They'd stick a medal on me and then kick me out, and if I ended up living under a bridge, well, then that would just be too bad. Like thousands of other veterans of our nation's wars of empire, I would end up chewed up and spat out. Homeless and left to fend for myself, after everything I have given.'

He pointed to his eyepatch and then reached down and tapped his left leg.

'You know as well as I do that there is nowhere near enough support at home for people like me,' he continued. 'It's all right for people like you who were born with a fucking silver spoon in their mouths. But for someone like me, the only thing I would be able to look forward to would be homelessness and an early grave.'

Andrew felt like protesting, but he knew that there was more than a grain of truth to what Malone was saying. Too many veterans were simply discarded like spent cartridges halfway through their lives, and then left to try to find a new road ahead, often with nothing or very little in the way of formal training that could be applied to civilian life.

'On top of that,' continued Malone, once again pointing to his disfigured face. 'Can you imagine me returning like this to a celebrity-obsessed UK? I'd be an outcast. No chance I was going back to that,' he scoffed. 'But here in Afghanistan, people take one look at me, and then they realise that I am a true survivor. Someone you never ever mess with. Afghanistan is like the Wild West, and I realised that I would be much better off staying here. Especially after I set up shop here in Nahrain. In the end, it was an easy choice. I became fluent in Pashto, Dari and Arabic, so I could organise my local Taliban fighters as well as the Middle Eastern contingent of Al-Qaeda pretenders. This is the land of opportunity for a man who is not afraid of a fight. And the locals quickly learned that I am that man. Out here, brutality means respect, and respect means power.'

'Look,' said Andrew. 'I am sorry about what happened to you. But I have to ask you again. What are you planning with the chemical weapons?'

'I am going to clean house,' replied Malone disdainfully, seething anger building with every word.

'Take out the whole stinking lot of them. The incompetent corrupt government. The Lords. The useless top brass of the army. And the bloody royals. They really make me sick. The deference to them is a fucking travesty. For centuries these people have lorded over us, sent tens of thousands of us off to pointless wars, and tens of thousands of unwanted citizens off to the colonies, only to recruit them again when their position of power was under threat. And don't get me started on the bloody ruling classes, who for as long as anyone can remember have wilfully neglected and ignored the most deprived areas of our country, causing misery and death without a shred of remorse. They all fucking deserve to die. All of them. It will be a purge of the whole system. Like I said. It will be justice.'

Malone was now breathing heavily, and he had an angry snarl on his lips as he continued.

'The media will call it an atrocity. I call it a clean slate.'

There was a long pause

'Frank,' said Andrew, looking intently at his old friend. 'You can't do this, mate. Thousands of innocent people will die.'

Malone immediately produced a derisive scoff.

'There's no such thing,' he said. 'They're all part of the same machine. They all vote for the same toxic morally bankrupt arseholes year after year. Nothing ever changes, and for all the pomp and ceremony on Remembrance Day, no one really gives a shit if a few hundred soldiers come home in body bags every year. They are all complicit, and they need a wakeup call as much as anyone else.'

Remembrance Day, thought Andrew. *So, it really* is *happening in a few hours.*

'Frank!' shouted Andrew, trying to make him snap out of his tirade. 'You have to tell me what is about to happen. If you kill all those people, then what does that make you?'

Malone looked at him, momentarily appearing perplexed, as if he had never considered the question before. He seemed like he was about to reply, when the entire room shook briefly, causing dust to fall from the ceiling and making the light bulb sway slightly from side to side. It was accompanied by the dull but unmistakable sound of an explosion. Andrew would have said that it was a significant distance away, had it not been because they were underground. This had been very close by, and it would have been big. Malone jumped to his feet.

'Is this you?' he demanded of Andrew. 'Is the great SAS finally coming to rescue their man?'

'No,' said Andrew, shaking his head.

'Did you need to bring an army?' laughed Malone mockingly. 'Couldn't do it by yourself?'

'It's nothing to do with me,' insisted Andrew. 'I am here on my own. I swear.'

At that moment, the door behind Andrew flew open, and a voice spoke quickly in Pashto. Malone replied in the same tongue, and then he and the man had a brief exchange in tense tones. It ended with Malone barking a handful of orders in Pashto which Andrew struggled to get the gist of. Then the door closed again.

'What's going on?' asked Andrew hurriedly, looking up at Malone.

'Looks like the competition saw your little bonfire earlier,' said Malone. 'They seem to think this is an opportunity for them to take me out, so they have arrived in numbers. Heavily armed with a bunch of vehicles. Bloody upstarts.'

'You mean, other local heroin producers,' said Andrew.

'Heroin producers, warlords, Taliban,' shrugged Malone, reaching around to his back and pulling out a pistol which he immediately cocked. 'It's all the fucking same. They are here to kill me and take over my business.'

'Or it could be Major Khan who has decided that you are a liability,' said Andrew. 'He had no qualms about trying to take me out, and I bet he could get parts of the Taliban to come for you.'

'Whoever they are,' said Malone determinedly, 'they are going to get what's coming to them. I'll kill them all.'

Andrew felt a surge of adrenalin. He knew that the clock was ticking ever more loudly on the chemical weapons in London, and that he needed to find out how the attack was going to take place as soon as possible. But if either he or Malone did not manage to get out of the compound alive, then he would never find out or be able to relay it back to London.

'Frank. Let me help you,' he said urgently, looking straight at Malone. 'I mean it, mate. Untie me and let me bloody help you. I owe you that much.'

Malone seemed to hesitate for a moment, but then walked around to the back of Andrew's chair and cut his ropes with a knife. From above came the muffled sound of a few more explosions, and then the staccato sound of gunfire began to erupt. As far as Andrew could tell, there was both small arms and heavy machinegun fire.

'All right, mucker,' said Malone. 'I will give you a chance to redeem yourself. Follow me upstairs. I have a weapons cache there. That SD of yours is not going to cut it against these boys, but I will sort you out. It will be just like old times.'

As Andrew stood up and turned to face his old friend, he saw Frank Malone standing there wearing Al Naji's clothes. His face was badly scarred across the nose, and his eyepatch gave him a mean look, but he had the familiar wide grin on his face that once again took Andrew back twelve years to that fateful day.

'Thank you,' said Andrew, rubbing his wrists. 'Now, let's go give those bastards a fight.'

* * *

It was still dark in the streets of London as the small army of road sweepers trundled along past the eleven-metre-high Cenotaph sitting where Parliament Street meets Whitehall, their flashing orange lights strobing across the nearby buildings as they went.

Its name derived from Greek and meaning "open tomb", it has a sculpted stone tomb at its top and a laurel wreath on one of its faces. On its sides is written 'THE GLORIOUS DEAD' in capital letters. The monument was originally built as a temporary saluting point for a victory parade in 1919 after the First World War, but it was later replaced by a permanent monument made from limestone quarried on the Isle of Portland in Dorset, and intentionally designed to be austere and simple. It was unveiled by King George V on the 11th of November 1920, and has served as an annual focal point for Remembrance Day commemorations ever since.

It was a cold and blustery early morning, and it had been raining in the night so the road sweepers had to move slowly and deliberately in order to catch all the wet orange and yellow foliage that had fallen from the many lime trees lining the road on both sides. Four large white vans had already arrived with portable barriers which were to be placed along the pavement for several hundred metres in both directions. This would allow the ceremony to take place with the public held at what was considered a safe distance from the attending dignitaries. Another van had arrived packed full of wreaths which were going to be handed to the head of state, the Prime Minister and a whole host of other guests who would each have their turn to pay their respects to Great Britain's fallen soldiers.

TWENTY-SIX

Limping slightly, Malone led Andrew up the stairs and into a windowless room crammed full of weapons.

'Knock yourself out,' said Malone as he turned on the lights. 'Lots of kit here. Mostly Russian.'

On a wall virtually covered with submachine guns, Andrew spotted a Vityaz-SN submachine gun which he grabbed along with three 30-round magazines full of 9mm ammunition. He also picked up three hand grenades which he secured to his tactical vest. He then spotted the backpack that he had been wearing during his initial assault on the compound. It had been thrown in here and it still contained the remaining Claymore mine that he had brought from the gun shop in the Karkhano Market, so he shoved the magazines and the hand grenades inside and slung it over his shoulder. Malone grabbed a Russian RMB-93 pistol-gripped pump-action shotgun, loaded it full of 12-gauge shells and dumped a whole packet of additional ammunition into a pocket. He then picked up a GM-94 pump-action grenade launcher which was developed for the Russian special forces, and which fires grenades out to a maximum range of 300 metres. Finally, he also grabbed a small leather satchel with ten grenades for the launcher.

'Never leave home without it,' he grinned, slinging the GM-94 onto his back. 'Ready?'

'As ready as I will ever be,' replied Andrew.

Malone led the way through the rooms where Andrew had been in a firefight not very long ago. As they approached the front door, it became obvious that it was now open, and they could hear a cacophony of gunfire outside. They both advanced cautiously along the corridor towards the door, hugging the walls as they went. Andrew was immediately struck by the amount of daylight outside. It looked like it was now mid-morning. He quickly checked his wristwatch. It was 10:14 a.m. With Afghanistan being GMT+4:30, that meant that it would now be 5.44 a.m. in London. Remembrance Day was about to dawn in the capital.

Kneeling on either side of the door, they could look out and see a huge gunfight raging. Malone's fighters had taken up defensive positions inside the compound, but the attacking force was steadily coming through the front gate which appeared to have been blown off by the earlier explosion, most likely by a huge car bomb. Immediately in front of Malone's prefab building were several dead fighters lying face down in the dirt. They looked as if they had all been cut down by heavy machinegun fire as soon as they had exited the building.

As Andrew and Malone watched, some of the attackers lobbed hand grenades into the compound and two of them landed next to and slightly behind a group of Malone's fighters who had taken up a position behind a sandbagged pillbox with a heavy machinegun. The two grenades exploded almost simultaneously, and metal fragments ripped violently through the fighters and left them spinning and flailing where they stood, after which they all fell lifeless to the ground in a cloud of dust. Some of the fragments slammed into the prefab building right next to where Andrew and Malone were taking cover, and the two men instinctively pulled back behind the doorframe.

'Fuck this,' said Malone. 'There's a bloody army out there. Looks like everyone in the valley has joined in.'

As he spoke, another group of attackers poured in through the front gate and began laying down fire on Malone's remaining fighters.

'Seems like your boys are losing,' said Andrew urgently. 'We need an alternative exit.'

Just as he finished speaking, a spray of bullets impacted across the front of the prefab building, several of them zipping in through the front door and slamming into the walls of the corridor immediately above and behind them.

'Roger that,' said Malone and moved slightly to one side to allow him to close the door.

As soon as it had been shut and bolted, he rose to his feet and moved towards the rear of the building once again, his limp causing him to rock from side to side as he went.

'There's another exit at the back facing the perimeter wall,' he said as he hurried along. 'Follow me.'

He led them through a couple of storage rooms to a reinforced door similar to the front door. Grabbing its rusty bolts, he unlocked it and swung it open to reveal a narrow space between the building and the perimeter wall that was just wide enough for a person to walk along.

'We need to clear a path to where I blew a hole in the wall,' said Andrew. 'It's our only way out.'

'I know,' said Malone and yanked back at the shotgun's handguard to chamber a round. 'You lead. I'll cover.'

'Roger,' said Andrew. 'Let's move.'

* * *

Unaware of the SAS raid that had just taken place in East London a few hours earlier, Fiona was getting ready to leave the house in Hampstead. She had overslept because her phone battery had died, and when she plugged it in after waking up, it had refused to recharge and start up. Irritated at the inconvenience, she had then decided that maybe it would be a good opportunity to go without her phone for the next couple of days. She knew she spent too much time on social media and on 'doom scrolling', so perhaps this was not a bad thing. She could always check her emails later that afternoon when she came back to the house.

She hurriedly ate her breakfast and put on her coat and gloves. She wanted to make sure that she would be in plenty of time for the ceremony at the Cenotaph at 11 a.m. There would be two minutes of silence to mark the end of the First World War, and to mirror the guns on the battlefields of Europe finally falling silent on the 11th of November 1918 after more than four years of devastating war on the European continent and across much of the rest of the world.

Fiona had never attended the memorial ceremony before, but after visiting Frank Malone's grave with Andrew at the graveyard in Grimsby, she wanted to make sure that she did not miss this opportunity to honour the sacrifice of those that had given their lives for their country. She also thought of it as a way of showing her respect for the work Andrew and his colleagues at the SAS were doing and had been doing for decades. Both he and the rest of the Regiment had regularly put themselves at extreme risk for the greater good, without ever receiving any public recognition. This was her chance to demonstrate her appreciation for what they did.

* * *

The two SAS men made their way along the back wall of the prefab building, weapons in hand and ready to engage. When they reached the corner of the building, Andrew leaned out to attempt to spot a way back to the breach in the perimeter wall. Having initially blown up the main gate, the attacking force seemed to only just have realised that there was another way in, and a couple of them were now beginning to spill into the compound to engage the defenders from the flank.

'This place is going to be overrun in a couple of minutes,' said Andrew. 'We've got to get a move on.'

'Right behind you,' said Malone.

As the gunfight continued to rage, they proceeded along the perimeter wall towards one of the back corners of the compound. There was no cover, so they risked being spotted at any moment. Suddenly they heard the brief but sharp ping of projectiles striking the ground and the perimeter wall close by. One of the defenders had spotted them and opened fire from a distance of about fifty metres away where he had been taking cover behind a vehicle. He might have seen Andrew first and realised that he was an intruder, but he clearly did not recognise his boss, Al Naji, because he kept firing off short bursts, trying to cut them both down as they ran along the wall.

Andrew sped up to try to make it into cover behind a building as fast as he could, but not Malone. The big man stopped, crouched onto one knee whilst slinging the GM-94 grenade launcher off his shoulder. With bullets smacking into the perimeter wall behind him, he calmly but swiftly cracked the launcher open, inserted a grenade, closed it up again and took aim at his own fighter. A second later there was a hollow pop, and the launcher belched out a large bull-nosed grenade slightly smaller than a beer can. The grenade travelled in a shallow arc to the where the fighter was located, and there it slammed into the car he was sitting next to. It detonated less than a metre from him, producing a powerful explosion and a bright yellow fireball which instantly tore off the man's head and most of his torso, flinging what was left of his body about five metres away to land in a gory smoking heap on the ground. Malone then got up and ran with his characteristic limp to where Andrew was taking cover behind the next building.

'I never really liked the bastard anyway,' he said deadpan, as he stopped to reload the grenade launcher.

There were a hundred different things Andrew could have said in that moment, some of them attempts at black humour, but he decided against it. Things would only get even more dicey the longer they hung around inside the compound. They had to get out now.

'We need to get through the breach and grab one of their vehicles,' he shouted through the noise of the gun battle. 'It's the only way to get away from here.'

Malone nodded without a word, and then the two of them moved swiftly behind the building towards the gap in the perimeter wall. Just as they arrived there, three more attackers barged through the smoky gap with their AK-47s already up and firing at one of the compound's defensive positions where a handful of the remaining fighters were still holding out.

The two SAS soldiers never even needed to look at each other. After more than a decade, they both still instinctively knew what the other was about to do. Quickly going down on one knee into a combat crouch, Malone brought up his RMB-93 shotgun, and Andrew pressed the stock of the Vityaz-SN submachine gun into his shoulder whilst stopping his forward motion to steady his aim. They opened fire at exactly the same time, Andrew cutting down the man in front with a rapid three-round burst of 9mm fire, and Malone putting down the fighter at the rear with a blast of 12-gauge which delivered a devastating punch at such close range. Before the two men had even fallen to the ground, both SAS soldiers had shifted their aim to the remaining fighter and fired again. The combined impact of the submachine gun bullets and the shotgun blast almost lifted the third fighter off the ground as they knocked him over, spun him and flung him to one side to crash into the jagged edge of the breached mudbrick wall. Immediately, Andrew and Malone were back up and moving forward, advancing through the breach to emerge on the outside of the compound. Just as they moved clear, a Humvee in desert camo came barrelling around the corner from the front of the compound.

'That's our ride,' shouted Malone, lowering his shotgun. 'It's all yours. Don't hit the tyres.'

Andrew steadied himself and brought up the Vityaz-SN submachine gun again. As the American-made light tactical vehicle accelerated towards them, the driver either did not realise who they were or perhaps thought that he could mow them down. Whichever it was, he kept coming even as both soldiers raised their weapons.

The vehicle was now less than twenty metres away, but Andrew took the necessary time to breathe and aim, and then he released a three round burst which smacked into the toughed-glass windshield right where the driver sat. The bullets did not penetrate, but they instantly caused three large sets of spidery cracks that extended out from the three impact points. This clearly shook up the driver, because he immediately slammed on the brakes, and as all four wheels locked and began skidding, the Humvee started to swerve as he struggled for control.

The vehicle was now less than ten metres from the two SAS soldiers, and whilst Andrew adeptly moved out of the way of it, Malone moved himself to one side and forward so that when it finally came to a sliding stop on the lose gravel, he was standing right next to the driver's side door at a distance of less than two metres. Without a moment's hesitation, he took another step towards the car, brought up his shotgun to aim at the side window and fired. The shell created a small cloud of white pulverised glass fragments and dented the window, but it did not punch through. From inside the vehicle, they could now hear panicked shouting.

'Fucker wants to give up,' exclaimed Malone with a mix of surprise and amusement. 'Not on my watch.'

Still aiming the shotgun with his right hand, he grabbed the door handle with his left hand and yanked open the door to aim the weapon at the driver's face.

'Stop!' shouted Andrew. 'Don't kill him.'

'What?' exclaimed Malone incredulously. 'Fucker tried to run us over.'

'Just let him go,' said Andrew, coming up onto the other side of the vehicle. 'He is no longer in the fight. And besides, if you pull that trigger, you and I are going to have to sit inside a car that has been spraypainted with this man's brains.'

Malone grunted and looked at Andrew for a brief moment, considering what he had said. Then he shrugged and lowered the shotgun.

'You've gone soft, mucker,' he said with a chortle. Then he looked back at the terrified fighter inside the

Humvee. 'All right mate. It's your lucky day. Come out.'

Switching back into Pashto, Malone ordered the man out and barked at him to run up the ravine and away from the compound. The man whimpered and blathered a stream of unintelligible words as he exited the Humvee, and then he ran away as fast as he could with his hands raised above his head. Malone shook his head.

'Get in,' said Andrew. 'I'm driving.'

★ ★ ★

This was not how it was meant to go. He wasn't even supposed to be here now. Nadeem was on his way from his home in the West End to Malakbel Gallery & Auctions. The gallery was closed and the metal grilles had been lowered behind its large windows out to the street and St Paul's Cathedral. Everything was ready, but there had been a change of plan. One that meant that he had to stay in London and see it through.

He had never expected it to come to this, but after finding out what had happened to his uncle, he had found himself filled with a burning hatred for the British that he had only ever read about and seen in religious fanatics.

Zahir Obaid had been slaughtered like an animal by the edge of his own swimming pool in Damascus, and the man who had killed him was a British special forces soldier. Yet again, the insidious tendrils of the British state had inserted themselves into the Middle East, and soon after that, death had followed. Well, this time it was going to be different. This time, the tables would be turned, and the greed and decadence of London's super rich would serve as the vehicle for the delivery of his vengeance. He would not survive this day. He knew that now, and he had accepted it. But his life was a small price to pay for becoming a hero of his people. He was going to go to the gallery where in a few hours he was going to ensure that, by his hand, Britain would be brought to its knees.

* * *

Andrew got into the Humvee behind the wheel and waited for Malone to clamber into the passenger seat next to him. As soon as he was in, Andrew floored the accelerator to pick up as much speed as possible before they turned the corner of the compound and emerged into view of the heavily armed attackers near the front gate.

'Get ready,' he said to Malone who was loading more shells into the shotgun. 'This could get interesting.'

'We will be fine,' said Malone. 'Sounds like small arms fire only. Just as long as they don't shoot out the tyres.'

As Andrew turned the corner towards the front of the compound, they spotted a handful of parked Humvees that the attackers must have managed to acquire from an abandoned American military base. There was still sporadic gunfire, but by this point it seemed that most of the defenders had been eliminated. When the fighters by the vehicles spotted the Humvee with Andrew and Malone behind the damaged windshield coming towards them, they immediately recognised them as not being part of their force and opened fire with their assault rifles.

There was an instant and urgent-sounding metallic patter of bullets hitting the front of the vehicle, and several of the incoming rounds smacked into the already damaged windshield a short distance from Andrew and Malone's faces.

'I hope this damn ballistic glass can take more than one hit in the same spot,' shouted Andrew, wrestling with the wheel as the car threatened to fishtail on the gravelly surface every few seconds. 'I can barely see anything through it.'

'Just get us onto the road towards Nahrain,' said Malone. 'I have allies there who will back us up. I can guide you. Don't slow down.'

As they raced past the parked vehicles, more fighters joined in and sprayed their Humvee with bullets which came in and impacted the vehicle's exterior like horizontal lead rain. Within a few seconds, Andrew had steered the Humvee past the attackers and made it onto the narrow road that led down to the town. Another few bullets from assault rifles connected with the rear of the Humvee, but they either ricocheted off or were stopped by the vehicle's armour plating.

'We're clear,' he said. 'Tyres seem ok.'

Shortly after that, however, he spotted several bright headlights in the rear-view mirror.

'Shit,' he said and he pushed the speed of the vehicle as high as he dared along the slightly curving road through the valley. 'They're following us.'

As they proceeded around a long bend in the road, Malone suddenly pointed out of the windshield ahead of them.

'Roadblock!' he shouted.

Less than a hundred metres away, two pickup trucks were parked with their fronts facing each other, blocking the entire road as well as some of the verge on either side. Behind them were a handful of fighters who immediately upon spotting the Humvee took up firing positions behind their pickups and took aim.

'We need a Plan B, and sharpish,' shouted Andrew.

'Take that dirt road on the right,' shouted Malone just as the fighters at the roadblock opened up with their assault rifles. 'It goes up that small valley.'

Bullets smacked into the front of the Humvee, once again producing a metallic patter as they impacted. But the toughened windshield and the armour plating held up once again. However, it would be a question of time before one of the bullets managed to find its way into a tyre or the engine compartment to damage a critical component. As they reached the dirt road, Andrew yanked the wheel to the right, and soon they were heading along the rough road towards a ridge and a few low peaks a couple of kilometres up ahead.

'Bastards are everywhere,' said Andrew. 'How many damn enemies have you made in this valley?'

'Probably all of them,' grunted Malone with a sardonic chuckle.

Andrew shook his head but couldn't suppress a smile. This was the old Frank.

'Anyway,' said Malone as Andrew floored the accelerator and the two of them bounced around in their seats due to the uneven terrain. 'I've got good news and bad news.'

'Here we fucking go,' said Andrew with a grin. 'What's the good news?'

'There is an old ruined house up ahead,' replied Malone. 'It used to belong to a rival opium producer. We can set up a defensive position in there.'

'Used to?' said Andrew.

'Yeah,' said Malone, drawing out the word. 'I may have had something to do with his demise.'

'Jesus, Frank,' said Andrew, glancing sideway at the big man next to him. 'So, what's the bad news?'

'This road is a dead end,' replied Malone. 'In about one klick it ends in a ravine where the ruined house is. There's no other way out.'

'I guess we'll have to take up a position in the ruins as you said,' said Andrew. 'We've got a decent amount of ammo, so we should be able to take them if we have good cover.'

'Absolutely,' said Malone. 'And I will let you in on a little secret. Most of the locals can't shoot for shit, especially when someone is shooting back, so against the two of us they don't stand a chance.'

After a couple of minutes of fast driving, Andrew and Malone arrived at the ruined house, and 'ruin' was the right words to describe it. The footprint of the building had been of a respectable size, especially by Afghan standards, but the roof was gone and most of the walls had caved in. The ones that were left had all the brickwork exposed, and only a couple of them near what would have been the main entrance looked vaguely intact. The two men got out of the Humvee and approached the ruin with their weapons slung over their shoulders.

'I guess it hasn't fared too well since we evicted the owner,' said Malone, looking at the remains of the structure with a dubious expression. 'It was a few years ago now.'

'It will have to do,' said Andrew. 'I will rig up a Claymore by the side of the road. You set up inside. Let's hustle.'

'Roger that,' said Malone, and immediately the two soldiers set to work using what limited time they had to prepare for the arrival of their pursuers.

About a minute later they converged on the ruined building and took cover inside it, hearts pounding with the adrenaline of the situation, and weapons locked and loaded.

'Like Butch Cassidy and the Sundance Kid,' grinned Malone.

'With a better outcome, I hope,' said Andrew ruefully. 'Here they come now. Get ready.'

Just then, two pickup trucks came around the bend about one hundred metres away. They had two fighters inside their respective cabs, and two or three more on each cargo bed. They looked like the vehicles that had made up the roadblock a few minutes earlier. A couple of seconds later, two more vehicles followed. These were both Humvees, so they had a maximum capacity of four people each.

'Looks like around fifteen or twenty of them,' said Andrew.

'No problem,' said Malone, arranging himself so he was leaning with his grenade launcher on top of a broken piece of wall, whilst having almost all of his body behind cover.

'I'll blow the Claymore when the first Humvee passes it,' said Andrew. 'As soon as it blows, you try to take out one of the pickups.'

'Got it,' said Malone.

As the four vehicles approached with their engines roaring and clouds of dust rising up behind them, they sped up and showed no sign of suspecting a trap. They were now less than fifty metres from the ruined house. The two pickup trucks in front passed the Claymore mine, and as soon as the lead Humvee was right next to it, Andrew compressed the clacker and the mine exploded with a thunderous crack that sent hundreds of metal balls tearing into the side of the vehicle. Some of them would be stopped by the armour plating and the toughed glass in the windows, but enough of them would find a way through weak spots in the chassis and rip through the interior of the vehicle, shredding its occupants.

A split second later, Malone fired the grenade launcher and a fraction of a second later the front of the lead pickup truck exploded in a ball of flame that instantly ripped open its fuel tanks and ignited its contents. As the noise of the two explosions began rolling up the ravine, bouncing off the rockface and returning as echoes, the lead Humvee rolled to a stop, charred and smoking with its tyres blown out and the whole of its mangled side peppered by the metal balls travelling at supersonic speeds. The doors didn't open, which told Andrew and Malone that no one inside the vehicle had survived the blast.

The burning pickup truck at the front of the convoy kept rolling forward and to the left. It looked like some perverse roiling funeral pyre on wheels as it veered off the road into a ditch and toppled over on its side. As it keeled over, two of the men who had been standing on the cargo bed flung themselves screaming from the car and onto the ground. They were both ablaze with burning fuel. One of them did not get up, but the other attempted to run back along the road. Andrew took aim and put him out of his misery with a single shot through the top of his spine.

The two remaining vehicles swerved wildly through the carnage and came to a stop about twenty metres from the ruined house. Immediately, all their occupants disembarked in a hurry and began firing sustained bursts towards the house, forcing Andrew and Malone to duck down into cover behind the walls. Bullets peppered the already brittle and crumbling brickwork, chewing away at what remained of the house.

'I hope they run out of ammo soon,' shouted Malone with a grin. 'Or there won't be much of a house left.'

After about twenty seconds the firing subsided as the remaining fighters reloaded, but then there were two loud explosions just on the other side of the wall that the two SAS soldiers were hiding behind.

'Grenades,' shouted Andrew amid the pitter-patter of falling dust and debris surrounding them.

'No shit,' replied Malone. 'I'm not sitting here letting myself get blown up. Cover me.'

Malone got to his feet and ran across the open doorway where a door had once been hinged, in order to reposition to a more advantageous position that would allow him a better angle on their attackers. However, just as he pushed off against the wall behind him, one of the fighters opened up with an AK-47, and a bullet clipped Malone and travelled clean through his left thigh. Malone produced a grim roar but continued into cover behind the wall on the other side of the doorway.

'Damn it,' he shouted, more from frustration than from the pain of the gunshot wound. 'Fucking bastard.'

'Shit,' grimaced Andrew and looked over at Malone, instantly seeing blood beginning to soak through his trouser leg. 'Are you ok?'

'It went straight through,' wheezed Malone. 'It's going to leave a mark though.'

Andrew then pointed across at Malone's GM-94 grenade launcher. 'How many grenades have you got left?'

'Five,' replied Malone, wincing from the pain.

'All right,' said Andrew. 'I'll lay down suppressing fire, and you lob a couple of those bad boys their way. That should sort them out. They are all taking cover behind their vehicles like a bunch of amateurs.'

'Roger that,' said Malone, staggering to his feet behind the cover of one of the crumbled walls and reloading the GM-94.

'Ready?' asked Andrew.

'Ready,' replied Malone.

'Go!' said Andrew and jammed the stock of the Vityaz-SN into his shoulder, swinging it up and over the low wall in front of him and releasing multiple short bursts in the direction of the two remaining vehicles.

At the same time, Malone emerged in the doorway of the ruin, brought up the grenade launcher, aimed and pulled the trigger. There was a short metallic click, but the launcher did not fire. Momentarily surprised by the malfunctioning weapon, Malone stood there for a couple of seconds with an annoyed look on his face whilst Andrew continued to lay down suppressing fire.

'Fucking thing's jammed,' shouted Malone angrily. 'Cheap Russian junk. Never fucking works when you…'

At that moment, one of the fighters had mustered the courage to brave Andrew's submachine gun fire and released an extended and badly aimed burst from behind one of the vehicles. Most of the bullets went high or wide, but one of them punched into Malone's abdomen and made him stagger back half a step, as if he had been punched in the gut.

He instantly knew how serious this was. Without medical assistance, he would have only hours to live, and getting to a proper medical facility in time was simply not going to happen.

'Fuck,' grunted Malone as he scrambled for cover.

'Reloading! Get into cover,' shouted Andrew, who had not seen Malone get hit. 'Are you all right?'

'Yeah,' lied Malone as he knelt down and hugged the wall just as several new volleys of gunfire began peppering the old ruin. 'Launcher jammed. I don't think I can fix it. Last time I ever use that Russian crap.'

'Shit,' said Andrew, looking around the ruin as if hoping to spot some new way of extracting themselves from their dire situation. 'Any bright ideas?'

'Just one,' grimaced Malone, biting down hard on the pain in his stomach. 'Toss me your grenades.'

Andrew did as he asked, and his two remaining hand grenades rolled to a stop by Malone's feet. Malone picked one of them up and shoved it into the leather satchel that now contained the six remaining grenades for the GM-94. He then reached up and tore off his eyepatch and threw it on the ground. He pulled the pin on one of the hand grenades and let it drop inside the leather satchel. Then he looked over at Andrew.

'Get ready for some fireworks,' he grinned maniacally, and then he swiftly stepped out from behind his cover and through the doorway.

Almost immediately, the fighters opened up and bullets began slamming into the crumbling brickwork behind Malone. Somehow none of them hit him, and he was able to take a couple of quick steps away from the building. With his powerful right arm, he swung the satchel in a huge semi-circle around himself, as if he was in the middle of a bar fight delivering a massive roundhouse swing at someone else. Releasing the satchel just at the right time, it flew up and sailed in a perfect arc to the vehicles where it landed right in the middle of the group of fighters.

However, just as Malone had let go of the satchel, three rounds from an assault rifle burst found their mark. The first punched through his chest, tearing through the bottom of his left lung mere inches from his heart. Another slammed into his right shoulder, making his torso twist to the side. A third smacked into his left knee, kicking the leg out from under him and sending his leg flicking back and out to the side in an unnatural arc. Then his heavy bulk crashed face down onto the ground in a cloud of dust.

Exactly four seconds after its pin was pulled, and at the very instant the leather satchel landed on the ground, the cooked hand grenade inside it exploded, causing an almost instantaneous chain reaction that made the last hand grenade and the five remaining GM-94 grenades detonate as well. The combined blast almost fully enveloped the two remaining vehicles in an almost instantaneously expanding sphere of fire. It ripped through several of the fighters, tearing them limb from limb. A few seconds later, gore and body parts mixed dirt and rocks, as well as shredded metal, rubber and plastic from the vehicles, flew up into the air and started raining down over the surrounding area. There were clearly audible muffled thuds as the mutilated remains of the fighters impacted heavily onto the dusty ground. Both vehicles were on fire, and with ruptured fuel tanks there was plenty for the fire to consume. Within a few seconds, the whole area around them was a blazing inferno, and all of the attackers lay dead, mangled and burning in the voracious orange conflagration.

In front of the carnage lay Malone's body, riddled with bullets and bleeding badly. Andrew shot out from cover and rushed to Malone's side where he dropped himself onto the ground, brake-sliding in the dirt. He had seen Malone get hit at least twice, but he did not yet know how badly.

'Frank!' he shouted, as he turned the big man over onto his back and hauled him partially into a sitting position, supporting his head with his own leg. 'Mate. Are you ok?'

Malone was unconscious and bleeding badly, but without the eyepatch and the black turban that had been ripped off as he hit the ground, his face looked eerily peaceful. Despite the deep scar that ran across his nose and face, as well as the disfigured and scarred left eye socket, Andrew was able to increasingly look past that to see the old Frank. Andrew checked his pulse. It was weak but it was there, and his breathing seemed normal.

'Frank!' repeated Andrew. 'Wake up, mate. We need to leave. We have to exfil right now!'

The man lying in Andrew's arms suddenly opened his eyes, took one look at Andrew's face and then instantly tried to roll free and scrabble away. As he did so, he blurted out something unintelligible in Pashto. He was clearly confused and didn't appear to know where he was, or perhaps even who he was. Andrew had to use all his strength to prevent the big man from moving. Being this badly injured, any movement and agitation would increase his heart rate and cause the blood loss to speed up.

Malone stared up at Andrew again with a wild look on his face, studying it for a moment as if trying to work out who he was looking at. His body rigid and his breathing rapid, he once again mumbled something in Pashto whilst blinking several times, looking confused at the man above him.

'Mate,' said Andrew. 'It's me. Andy. It's your old mucker. We need to get you out of here.'

Slowly and gradually, Al Naji seemed to give way to Malone, as a hint of recognition swept across his face. He studied Andrew's face for another moment, and then his body seemed to relax and his breathing returned to normal.

'Andrew,' he said. 'Did I get them?'

'You did,' replied Andrew. 'Every last one.'

A grin began to spread across Malone's face, but it quickly morphed into a mask of agony as the intense pain from his multiple gunshot wounds began to make themselves felt.

'I think I could do with a shot of morphine,' he said. 'One of those bullets might have nicked me.'

'It's a bit worse than that, mate,' said Andrew whilst looking down over his friend's body, trying to establish the extent of his injuries, and feeling his blood run cold as he saw just how much blood had already soaked through Malone's clothes near his shoulder, chest, abdomen and leg.

Andrew didn't want to accept it, but he knew that Malone only had a small window to make it to a medical facility. Otherwise, he would surely die. But he also knew that the only way to stop the attack in London was to get Malone to talk.

'Frank,' he said intently. 'The attack in London. Tell me how to stop it.'

Malone didn't answer. Instead, he closed his eyes and shook his head weakly. Andrew instantly felt anger rising inside himself. He could not allow Malone to get away with this, and he could not allow him to die here before telling him how to stop the attack.

'Frank!' he shouted, causing the big man to open his eyes again. 'I know about the attack at the Cenotaph. Tell me how to stop it!'

There was a long pause where Malone's breathing became increasingly laboured, and Andrew thought he could hear the unnerving and visceral sound of a liquid gurgling somewhere inside Malone's lungs. He was about to allow his frustration to get the better of him and attempt to shake the information out of the dying ex-SAS soldier, when Malone spoke again.

'It's not the bloody Cenotaph,' wheezed Malone, speaking slowly with a pained expression on his face as he struggled to breathe. 'It's the commemoration service at St Paul's Cathedral. When all the so-called 'great and good' of the country are all sitting there like pious sheep. They will all be put down like animals, and there is nothing you can do to stop it now.'

A chill ran down Andrew's back. St Paul's Cathedral was a confined space where the chemical agent would be able to work to its maximum effect. And it would be packed full of people.

'Tell me how it will happen!' demanded Andrew.

Malone shook his head.

'I am sorry, mucker,' he said. 'I can't do that. They all deserve what they get. Every last one of them.'

'You're wrong!' shouted Andrew angrily. 'I agree that some of them are slithering parasites, but it won't just be them, mate. This year is different. There will be hundreds of injured servicemen at the service. Regiment guys too. Do you hear me? Our brothers!'

There was a brief twitch at the side of Malone's right eye, and he clenched his jaw. Even through the bearded scarred mask of the warlord, Andrew could sense the conflict inside his old friend.

'If you let this happen,' continued Andrew, 'you will be responsible for the death of more of our brothers than all of those people in that cathedral combined. Do you understand?'

Andrew's words caused a visible change in Malone's demeanour and face. Like a person suffering from multiple personality disorder, within the span of a few seconds he seemed to switch back and forth between Frank Malone and Al Naji several times. Did he even know who he really was anymore? Andrew's frustration kept building as he watched. The sun was approaching its zenith, and he could practically hear the seconds ticking away towards the point where the attack would be carried out. He was running out of time. And even if he got the information he needed and got on the radio right now to inform Strickland back in London, there might not be enough time to stop the memorial service and find the chemical weapons.

'Frank,' he said through gritted teeth. 'Don't let this happen, mate. Our lads never deserved this. And it's not just them. It's their families. Their children. They have already gone through so much. You might take out a few deserving bastards, but it won't change the system, and you will just create a lot more suffering. You can't do this to them. Please, mate. Tell me how to stop it.'

Malone clenched his jaw again and grimaced, or was it Al Naji doing so? Andrew watched the different emotions ebb and flow quickly across his friend's face, as Malone and Al Naji battled for control of Frank's soul. His one good eye moved frantically from side to side, and his face contorted and morphed rapidly through expressions of pain, frustration, guilt, defeat, anger, and then back again.

Like a schizophrenic on speed, he looked like a man whose very soul was being tortured. So enveloped by his new identity as Al Naji, and so consumed by his bitterness and hatred of the system that betrayed him had he become, that he had failed to realise the full consequences of his plan. Or perhaps he had just managed to suppress those thoughts up until now. But no longer.

His furious and painful internal struggle lasted for several more seconds. Finally, he suddenly inhaled and produced a drawn-out animalistic roar up into the sky, as if that could somehow rid him of his torment and frustration. Then his head slumped down, his chin resting on his heaving chest. The ex-SAS soldier-turned-warlord breathed heavily for a few seconds, and then he moved his head again to look up at Andrew. Despite him having just one eye and a heavily scarred face, Andrew could see that the man looking up at him was Frank Malone. He was covered in sweat and dirt, and he looked profoundly exhausted. His body was bruised and riddled with bullet wounds, and his soul was battered and anguished. Yet here he was. It was Frank. The old Frank, from before that fateful day twelve years ago.

'Malakbel,' he finally whispered, closing his eyes slowly. 'The weapons are inside Malakbel, across from the cathedral.'

As he spoke, it seemed as if a great weight of anger and bitterness lifted from him.

'Where?' asked Andrew.

'Inside a set of Afghan statues placed in the window,' replied Malone. 'The gallery was constructed so that when a massive explosive charge is blown at the back of the building, the blast will be forced through the windows out to the street. The statues will shatter against the metal grilles and the blast will envelop the whole area around St Pauls in a cloud of nerve gas. Nothing will survive.'

'Unless you tell me how to stop it,' pressed Andrew.

'Just find the explosives,' panted Malone. 'Disable the charges.'

'Thank you,' said Andrew, relief washing over him.

Malone then seemed to hesitate, taking several laboured and unpleasant-sounding gurgling breaths before speaking again.

'The Regiment guys at St Paul's,' he said. 'They were my brothers. They are still my brothers.'

Then he produced a sigh and exhaled deeply, as if purging himself of all the hatred and resentment he had built up over the years.

'You did the right thing,' said Andrew.

'Andrew Sterling,' chuckled Malone, immediately wincing from the pain in his chest, and coughing up a small amount of blood that dribbled over the edge of his lower lip. 'Always the bloody good guy.'

'I know,' replied Andrew, almost apologetically. 'I can't help it. It's my curse.'

Malone grinned, and with laboured breath and in obvious pain he lifted his right hand up and offered it to Andrew who gripped it tightly in a firm buddy handshake, and the two men looked at each other.

'I am glad you came back, mucker,' said Malone, speaking slowly and weakly. 'Even if this is the end of me. Not sure what I would have become if you hadn't turned up.'

'I am glad I found you,' said Andrew quietly. 'I wish I had done so twelve years ago. I am sorry, mate.'

'Water under the bridge now, mucker,' replied Malone, shaking his head weakly. 'I think I was meant to stay here. Meant to die here, probably. And I guess this country changed me more than I like to admit. Still… dying in this place next to a brother is not so bad. There are much worse ways to go.'

'There are,' said Andrew, almost overcome by the sense of impending loss.

'We gave them hell though, didn't we?' asked Malone and coughed again. 'Just like old times, eh?'

'Just like old times,' repeated Andrew, nodding and squeezing his friend's hand.

Malone winced again, and with his left hand he reached up to grip the medallion around his neck. He closed his big hand in a fist around it and yanked it hard away from himself, snapping the leather strap. Then he opened his hand again and showed it to Andrew.

'Take this,' he said in a barely audible voice. 'I want you to have it. Bring it back to Old Blighty. Seems it's no longer my lucky charm.'

Andrew wanted to protest, but he knew there was no point. When Malone's mind was made up, that was final. And he could hardly deny his old friend his dying wish.

'You should get out of here now,' whispered Malone, His powerful frame seeming to shrink in stature with every laboured breath. 'There'll be reinforcement coming soon. If you leave now, you can exfil safely over that ridge and make it back to Pakistan.'

'I can't leave you again,' said Andrew, mostly because he needed to hear himself say it, and not because he thought Malone would agree.

'You can and you will,' whispered Malone, looking up at him with his one good eye. 'I am not getting out of here and you know it. Just because I've carked it doesn't mean you have to.'

'Frank…' said Andrew.

'Don't argue with me mate,' interrupted Malone, sounding utterly drained and exhausted. 'Leave me here. You know I don't believe in any of that religious nonsense, but if there is a god, and if he still wants me, then I am sure he'll take me the way I am. No need for a fancy coffin or a priest. Just leave me.'

Andrew sighed, lowered his head onto his chest and closed his eyes. This was not his decision to make. The pain and frustration at losing Frank Malone all over again was tearing him up inside, but there was no way around it. Malone was slowly bleeding out, but there was a small chance that he could live if he received immediate medical attention. However, that was not going to happen now. He had made up his mind, and Andrew had to let him choose how this was going to end.

'All right, Frank,' he finally said.

'One last thing before you go,' whispered Malone slowly, his breathing shallow and his voice weak and papery. 'Promise me you'll remember me as I was. Not like this…'

'I will, mate,' replied Andrew, opening his eyes to look at Malone's face one last time as he felt the strength ebb away from the grip of his hand. 'I promise.'

And that was the end. Frank Malone was dead.

Twenty-Seven

It was 11:08 a.m. in London, and Colonel Strickland was in his office inside the SAS HQ building on Sheldrake Place. Six minutes had passed since the end of the annual two minutes of silence observed at the Cenotaph. And there had been no bomb. No attack.

He had been pacing the floor for the past hour at least, waiting for a call from Andrew, but no call had come. After everything Andrew had discovered in Syria and Pakistan, Strickland felt convinced that something terrible was about to happen right here in London. But at this point there was no actual evidence. It was all conjecture, and he was in no position to cancel the entire sequence of Remembrance Day events based purely on the speculation of one man, even if that man was Andrew Sterling. He had no proof, and no authority to do what he felt was needed. At least not yet. At this time, the dignitaries would be filing out from the cordoned off area around the Cenotaph in order to be transported to the memorial service inside St Paul's Cathedral.

Another frustrating fifteen minutes later, the phone on his desk finally rang. He rushed over and picked it up, remaining standing by the window on the other side of the desk.

'Sir,' said an urgent-sounding and partially garbled voice, which Strickland nevertheless immediately recognised as Andrew's. 'It's Sterling, Sir. The line is bad. Can you hear me?'

'I hear you,' replied Strickland. 'The ceremony is over. There had been no attack. Repeat. No attack at the Cenotaph. Where are you?'

'I am on a peak near the town of Nahrain in Afghanistan,' panted Andrew, sounding badly out of breath. 'It was the only way to get phone reception. Please listen carefully.'

Less than a minute later, Strickland hung up and then immediately dialled a number almost two hundred kilometres to the northwest. A few seconds later a phone rang at the headquarters of the 22 Special Air Service Regiment, formerly known as RAF Credenhill, now simply referred to as 'Hereford'. He had a brief conversation with the commanding officer, during which operational control of a small elite unit of experienced men who had worked for him before was conferred to him. Then he hung up and dialled a second number. It was picked up immediately, with a simple 'Yes' coming from the other end of the line.

'McGregor,' he said. 'This is Colonel Strickland.'

'Colonel, sir,' replied McGregor in his thick Scottish accent.

'I am about to send you a complete target package,' said Strickland. 'We are facing a possible attempt on the memorial service.'

'Understood, Sir,' said McGregor calmly, seemingly unperturbed by the call and what he and his team were about to do.

'I have just spoken to your CO at Hereford,' Strickland went on, 'and he has authorised you to hit the target from the rear entrance on Dean's Court. You must enter without drawing any attention to yourselves from the public, and then sweep the premises for explosive devices. We do not have any tangible evidence of a threat as of yet, other than the word of Andrew Sterling. But that counts for a lot in my book, so we need to make sure.'

'Roger,' said McGregor. 'Send over the package, and we will deal with it.'

'I gather that you are currently near the Cenotaph?' asked Strickland. 'Have you got transportation?'

'Ay, sir,' replied McGregor. 'We've been sitting inside a tin can on wheel for wee bit too long now. The lads will be happy to get out and stretch their legs.'

'Very well,' said Strickland. 'I will arrange for the Metropolitan Police to clear you a corridor along the river. You should be there in fifteen minutes.'

'On our way, sir.'

* * *

It had been a poignant moment when Big Ben had struck 11, and the huge crowd had fallen completely silent. Standing a stone's throw from the Cenotaph, it seemed as if the entire city of ten million people had stopped dead in their tracks – frozen in place for two minutes while each of them privately considered the sacrifices that so many of the country's armed forces had made, and paying their respects to those who never came home.

As she was leaving the ceremony and walking north along the pavement towards Trafalgar Square, Fiona spotted an unmarked dark grey van parked near the Cenotaph that suddenly pulled out onto Whitehall and raced around the corner onto Horse Guards Avenue towards Victoria Embankment and the river. The speed and urgency with which it travelled left Fiona with the sense that the apparent calm and order that she had just witnessed at the Cenotaph was often nothing more than a thin veneer belying the threats that constantly lurked in the shadows. Threats that Andrew and people like him had been fighting, often covertly and at great risk to themselves, for years and even decades.

She was happy that she had attended today's memorial ceremony, but what she really wanted now was to be back in the house with Andrew. She hoped he was ok, and that he would get in touch soon. She resolved to go straight home to recharge her phone.

★ ★ ★

Wearing black clothing and tactical gear, the heavily armed team of five SAS soldiers exited the van quickly but calmly. The van had pulled up off the road and onto the pavement in a position that would shield the team from public view as they stepped out. With

McGregor on point, and without a word, they filed into the narrow alley at the back of Malakbel Gallery & Auctions from Dean's Court and arranged themselves seamlessly in a stack by the backdoor. Using a heavy crowbar, McGregor quickly wrenched open the wooden door and swung it open. Using breaching charges would have been faster, but they could ill afford the noise that such an explosion would cause or the attention that it would attract.

⋆ ⋆ ⋆

On the other side of the building, facing St Paul's Cathedral, there was nothing to suggest that a heavily armed team of SAS soldiers were on an operation just a few tens of metres away. Across the street from Malakbel's large windows, dignitaries were arriving from the Cenotaph in a long procession of limousines. They quickly and efficiently offloaded their passengers onto St Paul's Churchyard immediately in front of the main entrance to the cathedral, and then drove off towards the east along Cannon Street.

There were hundreds of people watching their arrival, and once all the politicians and servicemen had been shepherded inside the cathedral, a small cortege of perfectly polished black vehicles adorned with the royal coat of arms pulled up. After a few seconds, the attending members of the Royal family stepped out to applause and cheers from the crowd. Moving across the churchyard, they walked up the steps to the cathedral entrance, disappeared inside, and then the huge oak double doors were closed behind them with a heavy clunk.

* * *

Rushing inside with their suppressed weapons up and ready to engage, the SAS team fanned out swiftly through the small rooms and offices at the back of the building. Calling out 'Clear' for every empty room, they quickly moved through a large and unusually heavy-looking door and found themselves inside the gallery itself. Its marble floor and soft lighting was at odds with the basic interiors of the back rooms, but it perfectly suited the many items on display. There were vases, statues, pottery and more, and each item was placed under a single ceiling-mounted spotlight that made them stand out individually in the elegant, dimly lit and moody space. Because it was a bright sunny day, and the gallery's interior was so dark, no one on the pavement outside was able to see in through the tinted windows. But the team could see out and observe the throngs of people assembled there.

'All empty, Boss,' said Logan, walking up to McGregor with his submachine gun slung onto his chest and the fire selector back to Off.

'All right,' replied McGregor. 'Building secured. We need to wait for the boffins from Porton Down to come and ferret out the chemical agent, if it's actually here. We can't be sure which of the statues it might be, so best we leave it alone until they get here. Meanwhile,' he said, turning to the team's explosives expert. 'Dunn, you're up. See if you can sniff out any explosives, there's a good lad.'

'Yes, Boss,' replied Dunn and began inspecting the gallery with a highly sensitive sniffer unit that could pick up even miniscule traces of a whole range of different types of explosives.

It was a prototype unit that had not yet found its way into the armed forces or police bomb squads. Only a select group of elite servicemen had been trained to use them, and there was no better day than today to put that into practice.

While the rest of the team performed a more detailed search of the premises looking for any clue to this being the location for an upcoming terrorist attack, however unlikely that might seem, Dunn systematically began scanning the entirety of the gallery. When he arrived at the back wall, the small sniffer unit suddenly shrieked. Not only that, but it kept producing a noise all along the entirety of the gallery's back wall, which was around five metres wide. When he placed the sniffer unit on the wall itself, the sound increased in strength, and regardless of whether he raised or lowered it, it kept showing more or less the same reading.

'Boss,' said Dunn incredulously, just as McGregor came over to have a look for himself. 'Either this unit is on the blink, or this entire wall is packed with explosives.'

'Wait one sec,' said McGregor and hurried over to the heavy door and the corridor that led to the back of the property.

He quickly walked to the first office which had a wall directly adjacent to the gallery space itself and stepped inside. He paced out the distance from the wall to the doorframe, and then stepped back out into the corridor and did the same for the distance between the door and the gallery's back wall.

'I think you might be on to something,' said McGregor. 'I don't think the sniffer is broken. There is either an extremely thick wall at the back of the gallery, or there is a significant cavity between *it* and the wood panels in the gallery.'

He stepped back a few metres, inspecting the whole back wall from the corridor to the far corner of the room.

'Bloody hell,' he said, sounding both impressed and disturbed. 'That's an enormous firecracker they've built here. Find the trigger system and disable it.'

'On it, Boss,' said Dunn and extracted a different device from his backpack.

It was about the size of a mobile phone, and it worked like a combination of a stud finder and a voltage detector, except it was much more sensitive. Within a couple of minutes, he was kneeling by the far corner where he turned his head to call McGregor over.

'Boss,' he said, tapping on the wood panel in front of him. 'I think I've found it. There is no regular electrical wiring in this area, but there are a whole bunch of low-voltage wires behind this panel right here. I am also picking up signals that indicate the presence of some sort of electronic control unit.'

'All right,' said McGregor. 'Let's break it open and disable it.'

Within seconds, Dunn had broken through the wood panels using McGregor's crowbar, exposing a small grey plastic case with several thin coloured wires sticking out of it.

'There she is,' said Dunn calmly, and reached in to flick the cover off the box. 'Let's get this done.'

The other team members had now also converged on Dunn's location in the gallery's back corner, so none of them saw the short elegantly dressed figure walking past the gallery's windows and stopping by its main entrance. The man punched a passcode into the keypad, and then the doors unlocked. Because of the noise and bustle from the street outside, the metallic snap of the locks disengaging was not loud enough for the SAS team to hear. Only when the doors were opened did they notice the sudden increase in street noise spilling into the gallery.

McGregor was the first to spin around and face the doors at the other end of the gallery. At that same moment, Nadeem Yassin spotted the heavily armed black-clad men that had been huddled down low at the back of the gallery. He instantly knew what they were, and that there was only one thing to do if the attack was going to have any chance of succeeding now. He quickly reached inside his pocket and extracted his phone, selected the newly installed control app and tapped a five-digit code to arm the explosive charge.

'Don't move!' shouted McGregor, advancing rapidly on Yassin with his MP5 submachine gun up and aiming at the small man.

Yassin froze with the phone screen upturned and his thumb hovering over a large blue button on the app, watching the terrifying sight of the armed special forces soldiers pointing their weapons at him.

'Don't fucking move, or I'll put a bullet in your head,' shouted McGregor in a commanding and intimidating voice, now less than fifteen metres away with Logan, Grant and Thompson immediately behind him, also with their weapons raised. 'Last chance!'

Yassin closed his eyes and tapped the button on the phone's screen. Nothing happened. He opened his eyes and immediately tapped again. Still nothing.

'Explosives disabled,' came Dunn's voice from the back of the gallery.

'It's all over,' said McGregor, now ten metres away. 'Put your hands up and get down on your knees.'

Yassin was about to comply when suddenly a rush of anger surged through him. He thought of his uncle. Of all that he had done for him, and of his humiliating death in Damascus at the hands of one of these special forces soldiers. He had come here today to make sure that the plan was brought to its ultimate completion, and he was not going to give up now. He also suddenly realised that there was no way these soldiers were going to fire, since there was a crowd of people immediately behind him out on the pavement just metres away. Shooting at him would almost certainly also result in the death of dozens of civilians, and they would not be prepared to do that.

He let go of the phone and immediately turned to his side to grab the nearest of the eight ancient Afghan statues on display in the window. Ripping it off its display stand, he spun around and launched himself at the door which swung open. At that moment there was the sound of suppressed weapons firing behind him, and of several bullets smacking into the metal frame of the door, as well as of glass shattering. Somehow, none of the bullets had hit his legs or ankles, which he was sure was what the team leader had intended, and within a few more seconds he was outside clutching the statue and barging into the people in the crowd in front of him. Using all of his strength he pushed through the mass of people and shot across the road to St Paul's churchyard.

'Fuck!' shouted McGregor, instantly launching into a sprint across the marble floor of the gallery and out through the door and onto the pavement.

The onlookers in the immediate vicinity could not have heard the shots, but they had clearly heard the glass shattering, and many of them had now turned around to see the small suited man bolt out of the gallery and charge headlong into the crowd.

As McGregor emerged in his full combat gear holding an MP5 submachine gun, the screaming started. As people scrambled and fell over in their panicked attempts to get away from the armed black-clad man, the crowd on either side of him rushed to the sides, creating a clear path ahead, like the Red Sea parting for Moses. Ahead of him was the short man running across St Paul's Churchyard towards the steps leading up to the cathedral's main entrance, still carrying the statue in his arms. When McGregor spotted him, he was perhaps fifteen metres away.

McGregor immediately began to give chase and sprinted after him, but he quickly realised that the slender man was surprisingly fast. There was no way he would be able to catch up with him before he reached the entrance to the cathedral. He unholstered his Glock 17 as he ran and yanked the slide back to chamber the first round just as he finished crossing the road to the square. There was no other option now. He had to take the shot. If he missed, the man would be inside the cathedral a few seconds later, and then all he would have to do was shatter the statue on the marble floor and everyone within a hundred metres would die a horrific death. But even if McGregor managed to make the shot, the glass spheres might still break. It was an almost impossible task.

Out of habit more than anything else, McGregor found himself falling back on the gallows humour that had seen him and his team through tough situations more than once in the past.

'No pressure, mate,' he said to himself as he stopped and forced himself to take a deep breath.

He quickly exhaled again, took in half a full breath, raised the pistol, aimed down the iron sight and fired a shot that he already knew would go down in Regiment history, for better or for worse.

The 9mm bullet covered the roughly twenty metres in a fraction of a second and slammed into the upper spine of Nadeem Yassin just as he was ascending the first steps to the cathedral entrance. It shattered several vertebrae and clipped his right lung, and then it punched out through his ribcage, spattering blood onto the statue he was still holding in both hands. The instant his spinal cord was severed, his legs gave way under him and he crashed onto the granite steps in front of him in an ungainly fashion, his face connecting with the sharp edge of one of the steps, breaking his nose and his right cheekbone and knocking him unconscious.

The ancient and brittle limestone statue had spun out of his hands, and it fell onto the steps next to him where it immediately cracked open and broke into several pieces. The sunlight instantly caught several of the now exposed glass spheres with their diabolical blue contents swirling inside them, lighting them up for McGregor to see.

By some miracle, none of the spheres had cracked when the statue smashed open on the granite steps, but as he watched, one of them came free of the remnants of the shattered statue and began rolling slowly towards the edge of the bottom step. Still at least ten metres away, there was nothing he could do except watch as the glass sphere made its way slowly to the edge of the step and then dropped off onto the century-old flagstone below. There was a clearly audible clonk as it happened, and McGregor involuntarily held his breath and froze as he looked on. Still intact, the sphere then rolled across the flagstone, continued into a small groove in the stone and came to a gentle stop, its mesmerising blue semi-transparent contents settling languidly inside it.

McGregor let out a long sigh of relief as his teammates arrived by his side, weapons pointing at the immobile figure splayed on the steps in front of them.

'Everything all right, Boss?' asked Logan.

'Just about,' replied McGregor. 'We need the lads from Porton Down here sharpish. I think they'll have a field day with this stuff. Me – I think I need a drink.'

EPILOGUE

The team of 'white hat' hackers hired by the anonymous client had been given an unusual but simple task. Working from a rented office space in a nondescript building in central London, they had signed a contract to dig up as much information as they could about a certain Philip Penrose, whether from private or public sources in the UK or elsewhere. The client had provided them with a few clues and starting points but had then left them to it, not least because their prying digital eyes might end up looking in secure servers owned by both enemies and official allies of the United Kingdom, and deniability in those instances was a valued commodity.

Of particular interest was Penrose's financial dealings, which, as it turned out, were significantly more extensive than his tax records would imply. The team soon discovered that through numerous offshore shell companies, he owned several expensive properties in London, which combined represented wealth that could not possibly be explained either by his family's wealth or by his current income. They also uncovered money transfers from a bank known to be a front for Pakistan's ISI to a shell company in Dubai, which had Penrose as its sole owner and beneficiary. Once the complete file on Penrose had been produced, it was sent in encrypted form to the client and then deleted permanently from all servers, never to appear again. The only place it remained was on a mobile phone.

* * *

The waves were lapping gently at the almost perfectly white sands of the beach, and the gentle breeze was rustling the fronds of the palm trees high above. Lying on a sunbed and watching the sunset over the distant watery horizon, Philip Penrose brought his cocktail up to his mouth and took a sip. Whoever conjured up this stuff back at the opulent villa about fifty metres behind him was a bloody magician.

Penrose had arrived at the private island in the Maldives several weeks earlier, and to his surprise, he was finding life here most agreeable, even if nothing much ever happened. But then that was the whole point of it. Having activated his exfiltration plan from Islamabad with the help of Major Khan, and after consolidating his financial holdings in a new vehicle in Macau, Penrose was ready for a new chapter in his life.

The Russian oligarch that Major Khan had put him in touch with had been adamant that his security and safety here on the island would be guaranteed, not just because the island was remote, but also because it had a permanent detachment of ex-Spetsnaz mercenaries guarding it, both on the island itself and off shore where boats were patrolling all day and most of the night. The only downside to their presence was that some of them got 'handsy' with the improbably beautiful Slovakian hostesses that tended to his every need at all hours of the day and night, and that irked him slightly. He found that he was not one for sharing. However, that was a small price to pay for decent security.

He had already consumed a large number of drinks that afternoon, and as he rose to go back to the opulent suite inside a small private garden, he was unsteady on his feet and staggering slightly, having to steady himself on the large linen parasol next to his sunbed. The hostess who had been standing behind him waiting for an opportunity to be of service, took a step forward to offer her assistance. Penrose held up a hand, palm facing the shapely young woman. He didn't need to be helped along like some geriatric old twat. That day would surely come, but not yet. He leered at her for a few seconds. Perhaps he would have her come to his suite later that evening. Or perhaps it was the turn of the long-legged blonde from the restaurant. Decisions, decisions.

When he finally made it back along the perfectly manicured footpath through the grounds to his private quarters, he pulled the large sliding glass door aside and entered the huge suite. It was a single large glass-fronted room with an enormous circular bed, a desk in the corner from where he could work and watch the beach outside, and a door at the back that led to a luxurious white marble ensuite bathroom.

He ambled slowly to the bathroom and relieved himself, and proceeded to the basin where he splashed some water on his face. He looked slightly podgy now, and not quite as gaunt as he had when he had spent every day of his life inside that damn office in Islamabad. He had also ended up mildly sunburnt today, so he would need one of the hostesses to come and apply ointment to his body later. Yes, the blonde would do nicely.

Stepping back out into the opulent suite that overlooked a wide stretch of gorgeous beach, he suddenly spotted something lying on the white satin sheets of the perfectly made bed. It was small and round and seemed to have a string attached to it. He walked over and picked it up. It was a £5 Millennium Crown on a leather strap. Penrose frowned as he picked it up and turned it over.

'What's this?' he mumbled, and at that moment, he sensed something out of the corner of his eye.

As if materialising out of thin air, there was suddenly a man wearing dark clothing standing immediately behind him. Penrose had not seen or heard him approach, so he spun around in shock and surprise.

'Evening, Penrose,' said Andrew, pointing his silenced Glock 19 at the ex-MI6 station chief.

'Sterling?' said Penrose flabbergasted. 'What the blazes are you doing here?'

'I think you know,' said Andrew frostily. 'You thought you could screw everyone over. You thought you could have Saunders killed and get away with it. And you and your chum Khan thought you could bump me off so you could carry on with your heroin smuggling business in peace. Well, you were wrong.'

Penrose's eyes darted to his desk and back to Andrew. He looked like he was about to say something but then didn't.

'That's right,' said Andrew calmly. 'Don't bother with the alarm. Your Spetsnaz boys are all dead. You get what you pay for, I guess.'

Penrose swallowed hard, and Andrew snatched Malone's talisman from his hands.

'What do you want,' he stammered. 'If it's money, I can…'

'Got it in one,' replied Andrew disdainfully. 'Walk over to the desk and sit down. Then access your accounts. We have plenty of time. And don't do anything stupid. I'll know.'

Penrose did as he asked, and within a few seconds, he had opened an app that allowed access to all of his main accounts in various private banks, mainly in Europe and the Americas.

'Not as much as I thought,' said Andrew with a tinge of mockery in his voice. 'I would have thought your little scheme would have been more lucrative.'

'That's all I have,' said Penrose nervously.

Andrew placed the gun at the back of Penrose's head and pulled back the hammer with a click.

'I swear!' blurted Penrose, taking his hands off the keyboard and holding them up into the air. 'That's all the money I have in the world.'

'Shit, Penrose,' said Andrew, sounding disgusted. 'Did you just wet yourself? Bloody hell. All right, listen, I believe you. Now transfer twenty million Pounds to this numbered account in Switzerland.'

Andrew placed a note with a twelve-digit number on it on the desk in front of Penrose. Across the top it read 'Hunziker & Cie - Banquiers Privés'.

Penrose typed in the account number, completed the two-factor authentication using his phone, and amid obvious hesitation finally clicked the transfer button to wire the money to the Swizz account. Then he sighed and closed his eyes.

'There,' he said. 'Happy now? You know, old chap. You're no better than me, coming here and stealing my money.'

'It was never your money, and you know it,' said Andrew icily. 'Now stand up and walk to the drinks cabinet.'

Penrose did as he had asked.

'Now, pour yourself a nice big glass of scotch,' said Andrew. 'Then drink it.'

Once again, Penrose did as Andrew had ordered, downing the drink in one long gulp, a small burp escaping his lips as he put the glass back down on a silver tray with a trembling hand.

'So,' he stammered, feeling slightly fortified by the small amount of Dutch courage. 'Come all this way to give me my comeuppance, have you? And decided to fleece me in the process, is that it?'

Andrew ignored the dig and raised the pistol so that it pointed straight at Penrose's forehead.

'Look,' blurted Penrose. 'I am sorry about Saunders. It was never supposed to happen like that.'

'I can tell you're all broken up about it,' said Andrew coldly.

'But,' attempted Penrose. 'That's just part of doing business. Nothing personal. I never…'

'Have you ever heard the name Tahoor Qureshi?' asked Andrew, now with cold venom in his voice. 'Think carefully before you answer.'

'I… I am not sure,' replied Penrose nervously, now devoid of any swagger as he seemed to search his memory for the man. 'It rings a bell, I think. Wasn't he…?'

At that moment, Penrose's eye widened and his mouth fell slightly open as he suddenly realised exactly who Andrew was talking about. Andrew noticed the recognition on his face and interrupted the now former head of MI6 in Islamabad.

'He was a good man,' said Andrew, his voice quiet and hard. 'Better than you could ever be. And because of you, an innocent child is going to grow up without a father.'

'I…' began Penrose.

The suppressed shot produced a small recoil in Andrew's hand, and a split second later, the 9mm bullet slammed into Penrose's forehead, ripped through his brain and exploded out of the back of his head, spraying the wall behind him with blood, bone fragments and brain matter.

* * *

Vicky Benton arrived in the office at her usual time and sat down at her desk. She switched on her computer and then went for a cup of coffee as it booted up. A couple of minutes later, and after a vacuous but pleasant chat with the new intern Pippa by the coffee machine, she sat down again and began going through the donations to the veterans charity from the past 24 hours that had been downloaded into a spreadsheet in front of her. They all needed to be tallied up, checked and then consolidated into a single figure that she could then include in the weekly report for senior management.

As she took the first sip of fresh coffee, her eyes scanned the columns of transfers, and then she frowned. Not because she couldn't discern the information presented in front of her, but because her brain was momentarily incapable of processing one of the figures halfway down the page. It could barely fit inside the cell.

She blinked twice and involuntarily leaned in slightly to study the pixels on her monitor. She swallowed once, and then the cup full of scorching hot coffee almost slipped out of her hand.

'Uh…Vanessa!' she called out in a high-pitched and unsteady voice, her eyes still locked onto the monitor, and hoping that her line manager was within earshot. 'Someone has just donated 18 million Pounds!'

⋆ ⋆ ⋆

Jinani Qureshi was nervous. Her baby daughter was cooing in the cot that had been gifted to her by a kindly neighbour. She had been struggling to afford basic items for her child and had been grateful to receive help from the other residents in the apartment block in Lahore a few minutes' walk from her mother's apartment. Taking care of her baby had been the easy part. A joy, even. But worrying about the future was something that never went away. Being a single mother was challenging in any country, but it was especially true in Pakistan, and especially if her child was a girl.

On the previous day, her bank manager had called and asked to see her, and he had offered to come to her apartment. Jinani had accepted but was filled with dread at what he might say and why he felt he needed to come and visit her at home. Was she late on her payments? Had one of them not gone through? Had she been defrauded somehow?

When the doorbell rang, she hurried out to open the door and invited the man inside. He did not seem perturbed, but then perhaps he was used to delivering bad news to people. Was he going to close her account? What would she do? Was her daughter going to be taken away from her?

Jinani felt herself tremble with fear as they sat down at the small kitchen table, and it was all she could do to keep it together. He opened his brown leather briefcase to extract a single sheet of paper, which he placed in front of her.

He drew her attention to a single line on the account statement printout that he had brought along by placing his index finger next to it. As he did so, he began to explain what she was looking at. However, as she looked down at the number written on the printout, his words dissolved into an unintelligible warble of distant sounds, and she felt her head beginning to spin. Five hundred million Pakistani Rupees. Almost two-and-half million Dollars.

In a daze, she then watched as his index finger travelled slowly out to the edge of the printout where a transfer reference had been listed. It included just a single word: 'Bahadur'. *Brave One.*

Jinani brought her hands up to cover her face, and then she burst into tears.

★ ★ ★

It was an unseasonably warm and sunny afternoon at Cleethorpes Cemetery in Grimsby when the dark metallic green Aston Martin pulled into a parking bay on the opposite side of the road by the main entrance. The engine purred for a few more seconds, and then it was turned off, the only remaining sound being that of the engine block ticking as it cooled after its three-hour run from London.

Andrew opened the door, stepped out and closed it quietly behind him. Then he crossed the road and entered the cemetery, walking along calmly whilst enjoying the fresh air, the late afternoon sun on his face and the chirping birds. He had been here enough times to walk the route to Frank Malone's tombstone with his eyes closed, but this time was different. Unlike during previous visits, he was no longer weighed down by guilt and unanswerable questions about 'what if'. He felt at peace, and when he arrived at the plot, he stood silently in front of it for a moment. Then he quietly spoke a few words and stepped closer to the tombstone.

A few meters away, a small robin was sitting in a tree. It watched as Andrew stepped back from the tombstone, turned and walked away. Then it flew down and sat on the tombstone, chirping and looking at the shiny object that had been left there. It was flat and round, and it had a strap running through a hole near its edge. The robin eyed it for a moment, hopped over next to it and attempted to peck it, but was quickly put off by how hard it was. Then it leapt into the air, flapped its wings and soared into the clear blue sky, leaving Frank Malone's talisman glinting in the sunshine.

NOTE FROM THE AUTHOR.

Thank you very much for reading this book. I really hope you enjoyed it. If you did, I would be very grateful if you would give it a star rating on Amazon and perhaps even write a review.

I am always trying to improve my writing, and the best way to do that is to receive feedback from my readers. Reviews really do help me a lot. They are an excellent way for me to understand the reader's experience, and they will also help me to write better books in the future.

Thank you.

Lex Faulkner

Printed in Great Britain
by Amazon

26471825R00324